THE SLAUGHTER

To the little group in Bilauk the rest of that day was forever stained with the tones of nightmare. The mors were reduced to quivering and moaning by the terror they had experienced, the endless screaming, the sound of axes hacking off heads. Only old Haloiko could tell them anything. The attackers were nothing that the old mot had ever seen before. But he knew them. He had heard them described at religious festivals all his life.

"They were men," he said. "Men like the men of old; they have come back."

As astounding as the burning of Bilauk had been, this information came as even more of a shock.

"But how can this be?" Nuza said, sounding stunned. "Man is dead, long ago."

"I'm telling you what I saw. They have huge noses and no fur! Just coarse beards and long, greasy hair. They carried spears and wore helmets. They had no fur on their legs. They were like mots but taller, uglier. They were men."

THE ANCIENT ENEMY

The First Book of Arna

Christopher Rowley

A ROC BOOK

ROC
Published by New American Library, a division of
Penguin Putnam Inc., 375 Hudson Street,
New York, New York 10014, U.S.A.
Penguin Books Ltd, 27 Wrights Lane,
London W8 5TZ, England
Penguin Books Australia Ltd, Ringwood,
Victoria, Australia
Penguin Books Canada Ltd, 10 Alcorn Avenue,
Toronto, Ontario, Canada M4V 3B2
Penguin Books (N.Z.) Ltd, 182–190 Wairau Road,
Auckland 10, New Zealand

Penguin Books Ltd, Registered Offices:
Harmondsworth, Middlesex, England

Published by Roc, an imprint of New American Library,
a division of Penguin Putnam Inc.

First Printing, February 2000
10 9 8 7 6 5 4 3 2 1

Cover art by Duane Myers

ROC REGISTERED TRADEMARK—MARCA REGISTRADA

Printed in the United States of America

PUBLISHER'S NOTE
This is a work of fiction. Names, characters, places, and incidents either are the
product of the author's imagination or are used fictitiously, and any resemblance
to actual persons, living or dead, business establishments, events, or locales is
entirely coincidental.

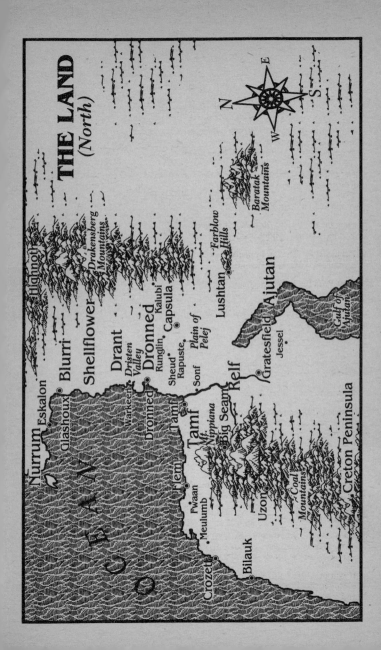

One day Simona realized that the old blind woman who scrubbed the pavements in their neighborhood was a human being. It happened in an instant. One moment the old scrubber was just another slave, a creature less important than Lad, her mother's pet dog. The next moment she was visibly human. Behind the huge black X that had been burned across it, the ruined face was like Granny's, except that it wasn't nearly as beautiful.

Simona was perhaps six, perhaps seven, and already she was reading well, and her written script improved with every week's tuition. She lived in the wonderful, whitewashed house at the head of the short street, West Court. She saw the scrubber from her window most days, but on this day she saw her as she never had before.

The old woman was tethered to her trough at night in a small shed at the end of the lane. There she slept on a narrow cloth pallet with her biggest brush for a pillow.

Simona wondered what a scrubber dreamed of. The world beyond her chain and little shed? Her former life? It was impossible to know. Little girls, no matter how intelligent, could not go up to the scrubber and ask her what her dreams were about. If you did that, then the "Hand" that mother spoke about, always with a finger to her lips, would come and take you away. You would never be seen again.

She tried to share her newfound knowledge with her parents. "The old scrubber is a woman, like Granny!", she blurted out that night. But they looked at her blankly. They accepted the existence of the different grades of slaves without question, as did everyone else. There were house slaves, like Minni the cook, and Dubbi the houseboy, and there were lower grades as well, such as poor creatures like the old scrubber. It was a fact of life.

Shasht was a great city, where gleaming marble thrust triumphant to the sky. But in its shadows existed an army of menial slaves who performed all the necessary tasks to keep it polished. They were virtually invisible to their betters.

For Simona, though, the world was never quite the same after that revelation. Some spark of compassion had been awakened in her heart. For a while she was fascinated by all the slaves of the lowest rank, the "animal-slaves." When she and her mother left the house in a covered carriage, she looked out the screened window and studied the prodigiously large young men chained to the shafts who pulled them along.

As the years passed, without ever discussing it with anyone, Simona came to understand that the scrubbers reinforced the authority of the lawgivers. If you disobeyed them, they could break you to the level of an animal, nothing more than a beast of burden.

She never forgot that.

PART ONE

Chapter 1

One fine day in the fifth moon of the year, Thru Gillo slipped away from his chores on the family polder. He was sixteen and in love, and he had more serious business in mind than weeding the waterbush beds. There was a warm breeze up from the south that ruffled the fur on his face and the side of his head, and he opened his good wool shirt to let the wind cool him.

"Where you go, Thru?" said Tucka dukka Tuckra, the leading chook rooster on the Gillo farm. "Where Thur go on such a fine sunny day?"

But Thru wouldn't answer, he just hummed and smiled and went on up the lane while the big bird watched him go with a wondering eye.

You could ignore a chook's questions, but you couldn't hope to fool a chook, not when your mission involved a matter of the heart.

"Thru got himself on the hook," Tucka of the Tuckra tribe said as he went back to the quest for earwigs nesting in the waterbush. The other chooks looked up, clucked, and went back to work.

Away from Warkeen Village, Thru hiked up the path to Cormorant Rock, his heart bursting with joy. He was in love with a sweet little mor named Iallia Tramine and was convinced she loved him back. Life had never seemed so wonderful.

Ahead loomed the sharp spike of Cormorant Rock, from the top of which one could see the islands of Alberr in the west.

As he went he mulled over what he would say to Iallia

when he saw her later that day. He planned to tell her what he had been thinking the last week or so, that he truly loved her and her alone and wished to wed her. They would be mot and mor, wed together by the words of the Book of the Holy Spirit, to have children and hold land, to work polder and make it grow.

At the Rocky Canyon just before the Rock he slipped down the shore trail and came out below on the sandpit where the stream ran out to the sea. Here the sea lilies grew up in dense patches every spring.

He kicked off his boots, stripped off his wool trousers and shirt, and stood there; lean, hard-fleshed, covered in soft grey fur except for the center of his face and forehead. He was grown now, a mot entering his prime. He and Iallia would make a fine couple.

He ran down the beach and dived in headfirst, enjoying the cold shock of immersion. He swam well, he always had, and was out on the lily beds in a few strong kicks. He swam down to the seabed and cut a half dozen long-stemmed seaflowers with his knife. Their iridescent green-and-blue heads would shine softly all through the night.

The old conger eel who lived in the wreck of a fishing boat close by saw the lithe young mot working on the bottom inshore and thought briefly about satisfying his perpetual hunger. But the eel also knew that mots carried sharp knives and were dangerous to approach. There were mackerel offshore, and when they chased the small fish inshore with the tide he would feed with greater safety.

Thru noticed the big conger at the limit of his vision offshore and dismissed the threat. The eel was fifteen feet long and as thick as his waist, but it knew better than to try a mot equipped with steel.

He pulled to the surface, flipped onto his back and lazily kicked in toward shore. He reached the shingle and laid out his sea lilies one by one. Their soft green colors were muted and cool in the daylight, but at night they would glow for Iallia. She always exclaimed at the sight of sea lilies, even more than for roses.

He dried himself by a vigorous shake and then some running up and down the strand before he donned his clothes and boots. He gathered up the lilies, now quite dry, and put them in his shoulder basket.

Iallia with her soft, dark fur, her flashing bright grey eyes, with that way of looking at him, so open and yet so concealed, would be waiting for him this afternoon. He'd given her his note at morning school the day before. She would know to be at the Game Tree by the fourth hour after the noon.

Thru wanted to lie with Iallia and make love. He wanted to lie with her every day forever and forever. And she wanted to lie with him, at least that's what she'd whispered the last time they'd snuggled.

That had been after the game with Snoyps Pond. Warkeen Village had won by sixteen runs at the old Game Tree. Thru had stroked a dozen runs himself. Iallia was just thrilled to be on his arm, snuggling with him in full view of her female friends.

Oh! The jealousy that would beat in the hearts of the prettiest mors in the village when they saw Iallia hugging with Thru Gillo!

They'd been snuggling since the festival at midwinter. At the big dance on Treevi pond, Iallia had danced close with him and afterward exchanged nuzzles and kisses during the walk home. Now it was early summer, and Iallia was always with Thru after a game.

From the beginning of the season in the third month, when the ground thawed out and dried, the younger folk of Warkeen played the great bat-and-ball game around the Game Tree. Thru Gillo had shown promise the previous year, playing for the junior team and scoring 280 runs in the season. This year he was the new star of the senior side and already a hero to all the youngsters in Drant.

Iallia's soft kisses and feminine wiles had him completely infatuated. He was sixteen, young for marriage, but like so many youngsters in his position he just knew that they would get by on love alone. He would borrow the gold to buy enough polder to get started. A quarter acre, perhaps a third, would be enough.

The thought of snuggling with soft, sexy Iallia brought on other thoughts, and he prayed to the Spirit for help in waiting until marriage before making love to Iallia. Sometimes being with her left him so aroused that he stayed awake half the night struggling not to think of her.

He looked up as he returned to the top of the canyon. The sun was over the zenith already. He turned south and moved along at a steady jog through the woods, startling a small herd of deer, who plunged away into the undergrowth. His father might have missed him in the polder, but Thru didn't care for once. He had his own life to sort out. At length he crossed Bear Hill, and there below him was Dristen Valley, with the green polder land snaking along the riverside. On that intensively farmed paddy depended the whole civilization of the Land.

He'd made good time on the return journey, and he stopped for a dip in the river to wash off the dust of the road before going into the village. He was still too early to expect Iallia to meet him at the Tree. But his heart was in such a state of expectancy and impatience that he simply couldn't wait any longer, and so he went down the lane, under the line of graceful old lime trees, and then directly to the Tramine house.

The Tramines were a big family, well placed with polder and fields. Their house was a long rambling affair, covered in yellow stucco and thickly thatched. At the rear was an extensive garden, which reflected the work of generations of Tramine females.

He knocked at the kitchen door and found Mousey, the family's youngest maiden aunt, at work rolling out noodles. Her big grey eyebrows shot up at the sight of him and when he asked where Iallia was she looked down and did not speak.

"Pray do not tell me that she is unwell," he said in sudden anxiety.

"Oh no, it is nothing like that," said Mousey, before she stopped, too embarrassed to continue. Mousey turned back to her noodles, the set of her shoulders suggesting that she would not speak to him again.

Puzzled, Thru slipped outside and took the limestone walk toward the rose garden. He knew that was Iallia's favorite spot.

To his surprise she wasn't there. The sundial was all alone in front of the bed of red roses trained up the trellis. Stymied, he paused and wondered what to do. And then he heard giggling from a secluded little nook beyond the old hedge. The giggling was a familiar sound. Iallia giggled just like that when she and Thru was snuggling.

Thru stepped forward at once, ducked around the hedge corner, and came to a halt so suddenly he almost toppled backward.

Iallia was there, but she was not alone. Pern Treevi was with her, his arms wrapped around her.

Pern Treevi was sixteen and the leader of a pack of younger mots from the wealthy end of the village. Pern had a special hatred for Thru Gillo, because Thru had always found a way to beat him in games. Pern and Thru had fought memorable battles in the schoolyard when they were younger.

As Thru watched Iallia and Pern kiss and snuggle he felt his senses whirl, his world shatter beneath him and fall away.

He stumbled back behind the hedge, still gripping the sea lilies in his hand. They had not seen him. His former infatuation, now fallen like ice from a winter sky, lay in ruins behind him.

More throaty giggles came from behind the hedge.

Closing his eyes against what he had seen, he ran back through the gardens and blundered into a small yard where Iallia's mother was handing out to the chooks. She looked up and understood at once what had happened. So did the chooks.

Her heart went out to him, a fine upstanding youngster, but at the same time her mother's heart was whispering that Pern Treevi was a much better catch for Iallia. The Treevis were the wealthiest family in Warkeen. They held a third of the village polder and were rich from selling grain and waterbush to the cities.

She stood there, watching him with her arms folded. The chooks understood the situation at once and were chuckling to each other about bent tail feathers and a young rooster who'd obviously been "dusted off."

But Thru didn't even notice her. The sea lilies he had held so tightly fell from his grip one by one, and he slipped out the gate like a ghost.

Chapter 2

Thru slid into a melancholy from which none of his friends could shake him. He became reclusive, taking long hikes up into the hills, living wild for a week at a time. He spent so much time up on Huwak Mountain that he became acquainted with the resident wolf pack, which he watched hunting elk on the high meadows and chasing rabbits in the valleys. He knew each individual and had names for all of them, from Uncle Grey down to Blackbird, the little female with the dark tip to her tail. Their primary den was up beyond the high meadows on a shelf of rock overlooking the deep valley of the Huw River, and he heard them howl most nights. Their howling was a kind of language, he realized, with different moods on different nights. When he returned from these trips into the wild he was always very quiet, seeming to fade into the woodwork at home.

Other times he would work absentmindedly in the polder. His weeding was obsessively good, but his planting had become haphazard, and his sister had to redo most of it. Planting waterbush took a particular swift hand movement to sink the stalk of the new plant into the surface of the polder to a depth of about an inch. It required a precise stroke every time, and it required concentration. Thru just didn't have that anymore, except for one place, on the game field.

Even as his parents grew worried about him, he turned to the game for a way out of his sorrow and humiliation.

Iallia no longer stood at his side after games, but that didn't matter. He closed his eyes to everything except the flight of the little white ball. His wrists moved without conscious thought, and his swing was perfect. During the stroke he floated in a quiet place that lasted for much longer than the split second in which he hammered the ball away toward the boundary.

His skill with the bat became the stuff of legends that summer. Against Juno Village he rapped out thirty-three runs and Warkeen won by ten. The Warkeen Village team won the championship of Drant County, and from that went on to reach the championship match for all Dronned. Their opponents were the great team fielded by the Laughing Fish, Dronned's most famous inn. Thru struck twenty-one runs in a tense and exacting match of skills, and Warkeen won by a single run.

The King of Dronned, Belit the Frugal, was watching from his customary place at the boundary. He handed over the Dronned trophy to Kels Geliver, the captain of the Warkeen team, and there was a long outburst of genuine applause from the crowd. The youngsters from Warkeen had played exceptionally well that day.

Afterward, the Warkeen players and friends and family were all dining at the Laughing Fish as guests of the innkeeper himself, but Thru slipped away from the celebrations. He didn't think he could make casual conversation. He just wanted to be alone.

He headed through the gate and into the city proper. Dronned was a city of grey-stone buildings, two or even three stories tall, roofed with slate and cut with long, narrow windows. The streets were cobbled and drained down the middle. Where important streets met there was usually a square, with a garden in the center. Thru slipped into one of these carefully tended gardens at the junction of Slope and Seam Streets near the river. He took a seat on a bench in a far corner and sat there thinking. Already the feelings of triumph from winning the championship of all Dronned had faded. Warkeen had played above themselves to win. Some of the catches they'd made had been amazing, and when they'd had to they'd come up with the runs. He'd struck twenty-one runs on his own, keeping them in the game; by rights he should be ecstatic. But instead, he just felt cold and empty. Without the game to fill up his thoughts he returned to a void, where all he could hear were Iallia's happy cries when she was snuggling that day with Pern.

Thru took a deep breath. He had to move on, he had to put it all behind him, but he was finding it very hard.

He was still there a few minutes later when some young mots and mors came running noisily up Seam Street and spilled into the little park. Thru was sitting tucked into one corner of the park. The newcomers gathered around the fountain in the middle, clearly in the midst of a wild revel.

Thru recognized some of them at once. There was Lem Frobin and Tugel Jixxe, who were both part of Pern's clique. Lem was waving a wineskin around, and they were both talking in loud voices. The mors were locals, Dronned mors with the fur on their heads tied up with rows of tiny ribbon bows of blue and red, a fashion of the moment in the town.

And there was Pern himself, with his arm around the waist of a young mor with very pale fur. She was unusually pretty, and clearly used to being paid attention to by males.

Thru watched as Pern snuggled openly with this young beauty. Then Lem Frobin offered the wineskin to Pern, who drank and then urged it on the young mor. They all laughed together and a little later Pern and the young mor went off into the bushes at the other end of the park.

Giggles soon erupted from their depths.

Sickened, Thru got up and left quietly, mulling it over as he walked up Slope Street. Pern didn't love Iallia the way Thru had. And, he realized with a dull sense of shock, Iallia probably didn't love Pern. What they both loved was the wealth that Pern possessed.

One day Thru would inherit a share of a polder and a part of a field. Like most young mots, he would have to earn his way through hard work and a little luck. If

Iallia wed him, it would be years before she would feel comfortably well-off.

Iallia was a practical-minded mor, and she was used to a certain level of comfort in her life. Pern Treevi would be well set up by his family with at least one polder, perhaps more, and access to all the extensive family commons.

And Thru Gillo? He was handsome and wonderful to watch on the game field, but he had hardly anything to his name in the way of polder. And as everyone knew, to have polder was to be wealthy, while to have a field was simply to survive, for only in polder could one grow waterbush.

Thru trudged back to the inn and climbed the stairs to his room, ignoring the merriment going on in the main hall below. The next day he returned to Warkeen and tried to put his heart into his work on the family farm. On the polder there was always weeding to do, so he became a fanatic of the weeds. His mother praised him for his efforts, but his father could tell that Thru's heart just wasn't in it. By endsummer Thru was taking off on long walks again. He'd finish his weeding early and take his bow and a small pack and set off for Cormorant Rock or some other promontory to clear his head of the dismay and pain that seemed to fill it when he was home in the village.

At the fest of the Summer Spirit when red Kemm rode above the horizon at night, his mother, bless her, tried to get him interested in the sweet, but plain, Xinne Batir. He was friendly and polite with Xinne, but the feeling for her just didn't grow. Xinne was dutiful, but quiet, and she didn't laugh often.

Snejet knew his real heart and told him so.

"You don't want Xinne. I can see that. You must tell Mother honestly. Stop playacting for her. Stop her matchmaking. You know she can't stop trying to help you."

Thru told Ual that same evening. Xinne stopped being

invited over for supper on feast days. Thru remained his silent, withdrawn self.

The chooks, who knew about affairs of the heart, having several every month, tried to help.

"That female don't return your love? Go find another female. There be plenty."

"Thank you, but you don't understand."

"Oh, but we do, we understand. Your heart got broken, and you just being slow about it mending."

"Yeah, that may be." But he didn't change.

The harvest came in quickly, and by the time the first leaves were falling everything on the polder was done for the season. Waterbush was cut, the pods harvested, and the rest of the plant set to soak in the seapond. The wheat and melons had already been harvested, while the nuts, apples, and root vegetables were still to come.

The main work of the farm went indoors as the nimble fingers of the entire family went to work on the harvested waterbush.

Waterbush was the source of many things. The shoots in the spring were abundant and highly edible. The early pods of summer and the ripe pods of autumn could both be eaten in different and tasty ways. Leaves mashed up with ripe pods and soaked in water produced bush curd, which could be dried and used right through the winter. But waterbush provided more than food. Fiber was stripped out of the soaked stems and run through a water mill. It was dried, spun into yarn, and woven into cloth, an occupation that would keep most of the older part of the population busy through the winter months. Finally, the juice extracted from the stems in the mill was then boiled down and fermented for the fizzy sap wine, a favorite drink for the snow festivals.

Seeing that his oldest son was just not recovering, Ware took him aside one evening after supper. They sat outside in the evening cool and sipped small mugs of cellar brew.

"Have you ever thought of going to Highnoth, my son?"

The mention of the northern lair of the Assenzi sent Thru's eyebrows shooting up and down.

"No, Father, but now that you mention it . . ."

"I think you may be the kind who would benefit from a visit with the old Assenzi. They have many things to teach us."

Thru nodded, liking the idea. Going up to the ruins of Highnoth for a year or two was a traditional remedy for young mots who became excessively restless or morose. Life among the Ancient Ones was famously austere, but always challenging.

It was agreed, therefore, and Ware wrote out a cover letter for the Assenzi that Thru was to hand them when he arrived at Highnoth.

Ual was heartbroken to see her eldest son go off alone into the wilderness. Highnoth lay two hundred miles north in the Valley of the Moon. There were roads all the way, and there were patrols against pyluk, but pyluk were crafty beasts, justly called the wood devils, and were the most feared enemy of the folk of the Land.

And yet, there were days when she wished he was gone, because having a silent depressed youth around the house was disturbing to the whole family. But no sooner would such a thought cross her mind than her maternal instincts were aroused once more and she would weep quietly until Ware came to her and took her in his arms and whispered in her ears to calm her.

Despite all the emotional confusion, Thru packed his kit, calmly, taking a few clothes, his winter cloak and gloves, his bow and a dozen shafts.

In addition, Ware pressed on him a staff, as tall as Thru and as thick as two thumbs, cut from a piece of ash and hardened by the fire. Ware had made it himself, with his usual skill with wood.

"I call this staff 'Strongwalker,' and I give it to you, my eldest and most dear son." Thru hefted Strongwalker in his hands. It was a good staff; light but strong.

"Thank you, Father."

Thru left the village before the first big storm of autumn rolled in off the ocean. Northward he took the narrow roads of the Land. Through Shellflower County and Canton Blurri he went. This part of the trip was on well-traveled roads, and he stayed in large roadside inns—sometimes in a room, sometimes bedded down in the common room, or even in the yard, depending on what was available.

After Glashoux in Blurri, by the Lake of Blue Swans, he took the less-traveled road to the northeast. Here the land was wilder. There were no cities beyond Glashoux, and the strip of cultivation was thin and soon left behind entirely. The road narrowed to a single lane, paved in only the wettest places.

Along the way he slept at small inns or in farmhouses, where the scattered mots were always glad to see a traveler and learn the latest news from the cities to the south. When he mentioned Highnoth to these folk they always nodded and whispered a prayer with a little awe in their faces.

At one small place he arrived on the Day of Sadness. There were three families living there, working the long narrow strip of polder they'd built in the valley bottom. They were a hardworking, narrow-faced folk, and they sat at the stone ring in a glum-looking clump and listened to the words of the Great Book, weeping with genuine emotion as they chanted from the "Song of the Broken Pig."

For the festival dinner they ate fried fish and pickled melon and washed it down with thin country beer. It was meager rations compared to the lavish table that Ual Gillow would set for all her relatives on the Day of Sadness, yet it filled their bellies and left them content. They sang the traditional songs of the season and asked Thru endless questions about the big towns and cities of the coast. He answered as best he could and later slept soundly on the guest pallet in the pantry.

These folk lived hard lives compared to the folk in lusher parts of the land, but still they were cheerful with what little they had. They praised the peace of lives carved out in the wilderness. He bid them farewell the next day and went on.

But the country now gave way to the foothills of the Drakensberg. The greater mountains glittered in the east. Thru went northeast to where the Valley of the Moon nestled among the feet of white-capped mountains.

The hills were afire with scarlet and yellow in the day, for the turning leaves were at their peak of beauty. At night he slept wrapped in his heavy cloak and got used to the hard ground. The stars gleamed down with chill fury. Great red Kemm was setting early in the evenings, and the nights were filled with many more stars.

The next night found him camped out on the shoulder of Mount Ulix. It was cold, so he made a small fire to heat water for tea to wash down the dried biscuit in his pack.

The tea brought a nice glow of warmth to his insides, and he huddled back inside his cloak with a blanket wrapped around his legs. The hillsides below shimmered beneath the light of the Moon. Once through the pass at Ulix he would be only another day's journey from Highnoth.

Then, from below, he heard the howl of wolves. The fur on the back of his neck rose instinctively. Something about the howls expressed a sense of warning. The wolves were telling the world to beware. The wolves knew he was in their territory, but they would not object to a traveling mot. Between mots and wolves there had always been respect. But wolves always howled when they detected pyluk in their range.

Thru took the warning seriously and put out his fire. He moved off well before dawn and took the short road to Pembri Village, a small place, inhabited by stonecutters. He had no intention of ending up in the bellies of the green-skinned lizard men.

Pembri lay up the Edejj Valley, which had been carved by repeated forays of the ice sheets and had high, steep walls. He hurried his pace. Pyluk hunted with the long spears, hardened in the fire and thrown with great force and accuracy. They were great runners as well, almost the match of mots in that regard. Thru had strung his bow and had his quiver on his hip, the arrows ready to hand, of which a good half dozen had steel points, just in case.

Dark clouds whirled overhead, and a stiff wind came out of the west. The road ran due north for a while straight up a narrow U-shaped valley. He made good time and came over the Stark Pike before noon.

Once again he heard the wolves, this time ahead of him, up on the higher parts of the pike. Again they broadcast a warning: Pyluk were nearby and probably aware of him.

He turned back at once, then climbed the steep gravel slope of a side canyon. It was narrow and twisty, and the walls were nearly vertical on either side. At the back of the space it simply came to an end on a pile of debris washed down by an intermittent waterfall high above.

He climbed. The rock was well bedded, with clear lines between layers. There were many handholds in the chert beds. He got halfway up and ran into a problematical layer of crumbly shale that did not offer handholds. The slope shifted away from the vertical, but the footing was treacherous. Every so often the shale would slide out from under him and a few pieces would go tumbling off the cliff and fall into the canyon below.

At one point he lost his footing and had to dig his fingers into the shale to hang on. Pieces of shale went wicketing down the slope. He was still sliding. If he went all the way down the shale, he'd go off the edge of the steeper cliff below. And then he got a foot into a slight gap and that gave him enough traction to halt the slide. He took a deep breath and started to move back up. A few minutes later he stepped up onto the top of the little cliff. He took a deep breath; it'd been close. He turned and looked down into the narrow canyon from which he'd climbed.

He felt his heart hammer in his chest for a moment. Three tall, green pyluk were standing there, great jaws

agape, long spears in hand. They looked up at him with
hungry eyes, then coughed and rapped their throwing
sticks on their spears, a chilling sound. Then they turned
and vanished back down the gully.

He had a good head start on them, but they would
find a way up in time. He would have to run the rest of
the way to be sure. Back above the pike he lifted his
own voice in loud cry, thanking the wolves for their
timely warning.

Then he ran.

When he arrived in Pembri Village, his news aroused
immediate alarm. Small gangs of pyluk were an occasional menace in the Edejj Valley. There were stone carts
coming up from Glashoux, and the drivers would be vulnerable to pyluk, who would spear an ox from concealment and then wait to collect it when the cart had freed
the dead ox and gone on with its remaining ox taking
up the slack. The pyluk would follow and spear the other
ox the next day. Then at night the lizard-skinned pyluk
would swarm the wagon and kill the mots. Oxen, mots,
brilbies, all would go into pyluk bellies.

The folk organized a patrol to set out the next day
and track down the pyluk and kill them, or at least chase
them out of the valley. That night they set a strong guard
on the village and howled to the distant wolf pack of the
Edejj to tell them that the presence of the pyluk had
been noted.

The village patrol spotted the pyluk trail the next day
and chased the three marauders all the way across the
valley and up the jambles stones in Soaring Creek. The
pyluk eventually escaped by climbing into the wild lands
of the higher Drakensberg.

Thru waited in the village for another day until the
patrol returned. Then he set out on the last section of
his trip, up the Edejj Valley to the watershed and down
into the Valley of the Moon. Highnoth lay at the northern end of the valley, where the great mountains of Basht
and Redapt faced each other.

Chapter 3

The mountain was wreathed in cold mists when Thru
arrived at Highnoth late in the morning. He was glad of
his cloak, for the damp seemed to go right down to his
bones. Like everyone else there, he would have to get
used to the cold and the damp.

Inside he was greeted first by a friendly mot named
Meu, a native of Dronned, who was to become a good
friend while they were at Highnoth. The Assenzi themselves were amazing little beings, smaller and thinner
than mots, looking almost like herons in their grey coats
and black cloaks. But it was their eyes, twice the size of
a mot's eye, that were the most striking thing about their
thin faces. They peered in at one with such intelligence
and understanding that it was a little frightening at times.
You never thought you could keep secrets from such
a being.

The place itself was nothing but ruins. Gigantic ruins,
of buildings so large as to be cities in themselves. Some
were nothing but hills of rubble covered in trees, but
others still partially stood, lurching up hundreds of feet
into the air. Great slabs of fallen wall material lay about
their feet, but the legs of these giant warriors of stone
still stood. And within them were areas that had been
kept habitable, for aeons, by the wit of the Assenzi and
the labor of their students.

Of all the Assenzi, Thru came to know Uzzieh Utnapishtim the best. Utnapishtim taught history, mathematics,
and astronomy. Thru enjoyed the first and the last and

struggled motfully with the mathematics. His efforts brought a twinkle to Utnapishtim's ancient eyes.

Then there was Master Graedon, the engineer. He was the Assenzi who maintained the physical plant, what was left of it, that kept them alive. Thru worked without complaint on many of the hardest jobs that winter, which earned him a place in Graedon's metallurgy class. There he was privileged to forge a sword for himself.

From Master Sassadzu he learned kyo and the art of weaving. Kyo included archery, and Thru became a very useful mot with his bow.

And from great Cutshamakim, the spiritual leader of the Assenzi, he learned that there were things that were unknowable, that just were.

He also learned how to adjust to a diet stripped down to its essentials. They weren't that far wrong in the Land when they said that the Assenzi lived on cold air and imagination. Gone were the hot pies and chowders from his mother's kitchen. Gone was the habit of dining in the manner of the Land. A bowl of porridge and sour butter became a luxurious dinner. And to wash down their twice-baked biscuit, there was usually nothing more than guezme tea or water. Thru got used to being hungry.

The kyo class met Master Sassadzu on an open gallery. At the slight sound of the command from the Master, they would spin on the spot, slant their upper bodies back with the smoothness of the cobra, and snap the foot out with the speed of the striking snake. The movement was fluid, the feet arriving in space in front of them with near unanimity. Sassadzu would watch, then let them return to rest. He would show them the motion again. His own slight form seemed to become almost a liquid as he sliced his foot through the arc of contact.

They summoned their sense of the Spirit, felt the strength rise through their waists and gather in their shoulders.

"Now!"

A bend, a smoother stroke, the foot seeming to flow out, unstoppable.

Cutshamakim's lessons were taken in his room usually, a veritable library in a warm part of the Red Brick tower. Sometimes they were taken outside though, where they practiced holding a handful of snow in their hands, watching it melt to water, and then drinking the water. The hand got so cold! The water tasted so delicious afterward.

"Why is it good sometimes to feel the cold?" asked Thru.

"Because it shows us that we are alive."

Utnapishtim's history class was another popular one. One day close to the end of the class, young Belloc, a Farblow Hills mot, raised his hand.

"Utnapishtim?" The Assenzi preferred not to be called Master by their pupils.

"What is it, Belloc?"

"I have heard it said that Man the Cruel came from a star beyond the constellation of the Calf."

"There is a school of opinion that believes this. There is no evidence either way."

Salish, from Sulmo, asked next. "You remember Man the Cruel, Utnapishtim?"

"I do."

"I sometimes think it cannot have been as bad as it says in the Book. Was it really like that?"

"Not all men were cruel, Salish."

"They teach us that there were good men, the men who raised us up."

"They raised you up, my fine young mot. That they did. The ancient men they raised you up."

"And before then there are no memories, and we did not know anything."

"Before then you were animals and had no need of long memories. The High Men remade you in their image. Just as they made us to watch over you."

"And we live in the Garden of Eden."

"That is one way to describe it."

"And we have always lived in it."

"No, young Salish. You have not been listening to

Master Acmonides. For a long time the world was frozen. There was ice a mile deep over the northland. The ice ground the mountains down. The ice filled the Valley of the Moon, and Highnoth was walled in by ice that towered over these walls."

"Did you live then, Utnapishtim?"

They were at it again, distracting old Utnapishtim and getting him off onto tales from the past. Which was much more fun than writing down the names of the local stars and also helped to prolong the class in a pleasant way, listening to the old Assenzi speak about the ancient world, gone forever beneath the ice.

"Oh yes, young Salish, old Utnapishtim lived then. Utnapishtim first came to life more than one hundred thousand years ago. The ice came four times and retreated each time. Now we think the period of the ice is over for a while."

But young Salish was still pondering something beyond the numbers.

"And when we were animals, we kept no memories. So we can never really know that time."

"Ah, you would not want to, young Salish. That was not a good time for animals. That was the time of Man the Cruel."

When the Assenzi spoke like this Thru always felt the familiar chill run down his spine.

"I am the broken pig." The words came unbidden to his mind, from the prayer for salvation. Several of them were mouthing them, just as they did on Spirit days.

The hanging cow that was torn and ripped.
The dying lamb that was born again.

In years to come, the dark days of deep winter would always bring up memories for Thru of wielding a hammer in the forge while the bellows roared and the coals put out so much heat it felt as if your fur might catch fire.

And on the anvil the bar of iron slowly became a sword blade, two and a half feet in length, an inch and a half across. Thru felt the force of the magic there, where metal changed its nature and in time became a shimmering piece of steel.

Then it was sharpened and polished to a mirrorlike glow.

On graduation night, Graedon presented each of them with a handle and a hilt. At last they wore the swords on their belts, sheathed in newly minted scabbards made of stiffened bush-withe bearing seven layers of lacquer.

"Thank you, Master Graedon, I will always treasure this moment."

Another time that winter, while it was snowing outside, the class sat in rows on the long, green carpet. The room was cold enough that their breath was clearly visible each time they exhaled. Yet they wore little in the way of clothing, with bare sandals on their feet.

"Open your hearts to the sky," said Cutshamakim, sitting on a pad of stone in front of them.

The wind soughed through the ruined latticework of the building above them. The snow was falling again. It was a dry powdery snow, and traces of it were already showing on the floor of the meditation chamber.

"When we breathe we put aside preconditions, we allow ourselves simply to be here. Feel the moment. Breathe in!"

The soft susurration of their breath echoed off the high ceiling.

They repeated the ancient syllables, ending on the great universal hum. Their eyes closed, their fingers forming the circle of wisdom.

In time and perfect accord they drew seven breaths through the left nostril and expelled them from the right. Then they reversed the procedure for the next seven breaths.

The regular soft sound, like a velvet-covered piston broke against the high ceiling, and mingled with the skitter of the falling snow.

Chapter 4

Winter passed and left Thru hardened against the cold. He had learned to enjoy the icy dip in the morning when they said their prayers at the shrine. He had come to accept the perpetual hunger and the hard physical labor. He had learned a great deal, and somewhere along the way he had regained a sense of peace. Even his broken heart had become less important, less relevant to him somehow. It was as if he had moved on from that person of the previous summer, so devastated and out of sorts. There was still a void in his center, there was something gone that would never be recovered, but he was no longer crippled by it.

Thru had left his thick jerkin in the cell and wore just a light shirt and a much-patched pair of trousers that were his most comfortable clothes, though he knew his sister and mother would have scolded him for wearing such shabby things.

In Master Sassadzu's gallery, Thru wove a decorative mat, working in waterbush-withe and colored grasses. By tradition carried down for thousands of years there were only a handful of acceptable patterns among weavers of the Land. He had chosen "Chooks and Beetles," a rich pattern with ocher-colored chooks chasing beetles in the center. Around them were shooks of corn in bright yellow and crossed scythes.

In a bold departure from the usual style he had outlined his chooks and beetles in black and given the big birds a jaunty, raffish air. He was quite pleased with the look of them, and was working a bright green grass onto the ground weave to fill out the background.

The chooks in the center of the mat were all done; they had a fine rakish appearance, feathers slightly askew, eyes big as onions as they hunted the leaping beetles.

The rows of corn shooks and scythes were nearing completion. Their bright yellow and red stood out sharply from the green background. He took up stained red grass and bent forward to work some in on the undersides of the scythes.

Master Sassadzu had complimented Thru on this mat, which he thought had shown signs of a great skill. Praise from Master Sassadzu was rare and was consequently treasured.

Thru worked in a corner where even in Snow Moon the sunlight warmed a patch of floor. He was cut off from view of the door by the curve of the gallery and several large looms but he sensed someone had entered the long gallery at the far end. Thru's right eyebrow rose quizzically. Master Sassadzu taught his intermediate kyo class at this hour. It would not be him, but it was definitely an Assenzi from the quietness of the tread.

A couple of seconds later he was surprised to see Utnapishtim come around the other looms and head in his direction.

"Greetings, young Thru Gillo."

"Greetings, Utnapishtim."

"That is a very vibrant mat you are weaving."

"Thank you, Utnapishtim."

"I like the rakish attitude of your chooks. You have changed the pattern a little from the traditional mode."

"Thank you, Utnapishtim. I like the old pattern very much, but I thought I'd try something new."

Utnapishtim's thin face broke open in a tiny smile.

"Young Thru Gillo, I have a requirement, and I wonder if you would like to fill it. I need two students to help me light the summer lamps in the temples of the

Farblow Hills. It will take a few weeks' travel. We will pass through Dronned to get there."

Thru was stunned at this honor, though just for a moment he wondered about going home so soon, if only to visit. Would it reopen old wounds? Then he dismissed the concern.

"I would be proud to be chosen to help you, Utnapishtim."

"Of course there will be some work involved."

Thru merely nodded. What else would anyone expect in Highnoth?

"The temples are very popular destinations for hikers in the summer months. So it's important that they have working lamps. But that means we must carry lamp oil to them. I need some strong young backs and a couple of donkeys to move the oil up into the hills and distribute it."

"I have not seen the Farblow Hills, but I have heard of their beauty. After this long winter I would love such an opportunity."

"We will head south in three days' time. I hope your weave will be finished by then."

"It will be, Utnapishtim, and I will take it as a gift for my mother."

Three weeks later, on the feast day of the Sea Spirit, Thru, Utnapishtim, and Meu of Deepford entered the kingdom of Dronned and glimpsed Cormorant Rock as a distant dark spike. Thru felt the excitement of homecoming after a long absence. He had not seen Warkeen for six months.

But as they came over the brow of the last hill, though, Thru's blood suddenly ran cold. The old line of lime trees along the lane by Tramine's field was gone, leaving just a row of stumps. Thrust up from the smooth slope of Tramine's field was a large new house, with two chimneys, lots of windows, and mots hard at work on the roof.

They passed the row of stumps and turned away down the lane leading into the village. Thru had loved those old trees; they had always been there, a line of shaggy titans, holding up one end of the field, or so it seemed to him.

The village itself seemed the same as ever. The rows of white-fronted houses, the dark thatch and the grey stone of walls and chimneys, it all made a pleasing picture to his eye after all those months spent in Highnoth's gloomy halls.

"Hail to thee, Thru Gillo." Lanky Moon Shapin came out the door of his house, and Thru paused to speak with him.

"Hail, Moon. How are things in the village?"

"Things are well enough. Are ye just now back from Highnoth, Thru?"

"Yes. See there's the Assenzi I'm with."

"You be careful around them old Assenzi. Spirit knows where you'll end up."

Thru had to chuckle. "That's all too true, Moon, but tell me what has happened to the lime trees along Tramine's field?"

"Oh, that's a shocking business." Moon's face wrinkled in anger. "That's young Pern Treevi's work. Built himself a new house, he has. He's too good to be living in Tramine house like any other Tramine has since I don't know when. So he built his own house and cut down the trees so he has a view to the sea."

Thru looked back up the hill to where the new chimney was visible through the trees and shook his head. The lovely lime trees were gone forever, and Iallia was probably living in the big new house with Pern.

"I thank you for your welcome, Moon. It is wonderful to be back home. I must go on and see my own people."

Thru went on, catching up with the Assenzi and Meu, who had gone on down the road into the village.

Outside the inn they halted and tied the donkey to the hitching post by the pump.

"We will take a meal here and spend the night. It looks as if there will be room."

Indeed, the Warkeen Inn seemed rather quiet.

"You go on to your family, young Thru," said Utnapishtim. "I can see you're itching to be off."

Thru came over the line of Polder Bank and saw the stone walls of Gillo house. It wasn't so grand, indeed the thatching was starting to look tatty, but it was home. A powerful wave of emotion rolled through his heart as he saw it once again.

He turned in at the gate and saw his mother at the door.

There came a scream from the kitchen, and she ran out and hugged him with all her strength. Father Ware looked out of his workshop, set his tools down, and joined them with his great hug. After a long moment, with tears streaming from their eyes, they stood back and Ual and Ware got another look at him.

Their son had changed in certain ways. He was more muscular and hardened, too. The sad, wounded look in his eyes was gone. Now they sparkled, as they had of old.

"Where are your eyebrows?" said Ual.

"Singed, while I made this sword."

Ware's bushy eyebrows rose dramatically at the sight of the sword and scabbard on his son's belt.

"And this is for you, Mother," he said, bringing the mat off his shoulders and untying the string and unrolling it on the stoop.

"You wove this, my darling Thru?" said Ual, running her hands over it, genuine awe in her voice.

"Master Sassadzu says I have an aptitude for the weaving."

"It's wonderful, it's beautiful, Thru." She hugged him close again. "Thank you so much. I will put it on the wall in the little parlor. It will go well there."

Ware took Thru's staff and gave it a once-over.

"Strongwalker has stood the test it seems."

"I have worn him down a little, but he is an excellent staff, Father."

"And your bow?"

"My old bow is creaking with every pull."

"It was my bow and before that my father's. The wood

is probably too old now. It is good to see you, son. I give thanks to the Spirit for bringing you back alive."

"Our son has grown strong, Ual!" Ware said with a happy roar, and hugged Thru again.

"He has grown up," she agreed with a happy smile.

"How long can you stay?" said Ware.

"Only one night, I'm afraid. We go south to take lamp oil up to the temples of Farblow."

"Only one night!" wailed Ual. "And I haven't seen my son for six months! Only one night!"

"I'm afraid so, Mother. I must go south with Utnapishtim tomorrow."

"It isn't right, I'm your mother!"

Ware smiled. "Then in that case I will have to finish the nocks on your new bow tonight."

"My new bow!"

"I've been working on it since you left. The wood is from that piece of Langler's yew that I laid up two summers back. You can take it with you tomorrow and leave that old veteran behind."

"Why thank you, Father, that's wonderful."

And then with a rush of feet and happy cries came Snejet and young Gil. They were covered in mud from planting waterbush on wet polder, but they wrapped themselves around him anyway.

"Thru, Thru, Thru," was all Snejet could say.

"Come inside," said Ual, tugging the whole mass up the step. "Your brother looks like he's half-starved."

"Actually, Mother, completely starved. The food at Highnoth is in limited supply."

"Come in then! I have dumplings all ready and bean broth a-brewing."

Dinner was a grand one that night in the Gillo house. Ual made her pie of meeks and sweet bewbies, and Ware brought over a big pitcher of ale from the inn.

Thru, of course, wanted to know everything that had happened in the village during his absence. Ual and Ware told him what they could, but everyone was too impatient for that to go on for long. Granma Biskin's

problems with her sick chooks was a subject of considerable complexity, after all.

"Your turn, Thru," said Snejet when a gap appeared.
"Tell us about Highnoth."

"Ah," he murmured. "Well, Highnoth is a very different kind of world, little Snej. For a start there's not much
to eat."

"You don't eat? How do you survive?"

"Well, we don't eat much, that's for sure, but somehow
we survive."

"What do you mean 'don't eat much'? What do they
feed you?" asked Ual with maternal concern.

"Porridge usually, bread and butter, pancakes, too, and
we get syrup sometimes, and fruits in season."

"What else?"

"Uh, cabbage. Plenty of cabbage."

"Yes?" They were staring at him as he spooned up
the juice from those sweet bewbies.

"Well, that's about it."

"That's all!"

He had to laugh.

"Well there's always guezme tea."

It was hard to convey to them how unimportant food
was in Highnoth. Along with leisure and a comfortable
bed, excessive food was, well, unnecessary. The young
mots were too busy, too wrapped up in the process of
active learning.

"We forged steel." He nodded to his pack across the
hall, beside which hung the sword in its scabbard. "My
sword came from Master Graedon's furnace."

Ware nodded soberly. "It is a great responsibility to
carry a sword, my son."

"That it is, Father. I am mindful of that."

"And what of the Spirit, have they neglected your life
with the Spirit?" said Ual.

"No, Mother, they have not. We have learned further
humility, further need for compassion. We pray with Cutshamakim on every feast day."

He broke off with a grin. "But we don't actually feast."

Later, under more questioning, he told them about his escape from the pyluk in the hills.

They listened with round eyes and open mouths.

"The pyluk would have eaten you if they'd caught you."

"Ah but they didn't, did they. The wolves warned me in good time."

"Did the pyluk come after you on your journey south?"

"No. This trip has been quick and free of trouble."

"It is the Assenzi then, I knew it," said Ual, holding up a finger. "The Assenzi are magical beings; the pyluk must fear them."

"Pyluk will eat Assenzi just like anything else, Mother. But the Assenzi can sense pyluk a long way away, that makes them safe. But it's my turn again to ask a question. What is going on on Tramine's field?"

"Oh, I was afraid you'd ask of that," said Ual. "I don't like to speak ill of the Tramines, but I think they were foolish to let Pern Treevi build that house."

"He inherited. Ful is dead?"

"Yes, Ful Tramine took the fever over the winter and passed up to the Spirit's hands."

"Pern inherited his portion, but he refused to live in the old house. He said Tramine house was already too crowded, and he wanted his own. He forced the family to give him half of that field. Then he cut down the old lime trees."

"The village is the poorer without those trees."

"Pern has a wicked heart, we've all seen it now."

"And Iallia, too," said Snejet angrily.

"Snejet!" her mother hushed her.

Thru appeared not to have noticed, but his eyes seemed to focus on the far horizon for a few moments. Then he shook it off.

"We planted all the polder this week," said Gil hurriedly.

"That is early; well-done."

"And it's been all the work of Snejet and Gil, too,"

said Ware. "I've been too busy with work in the shop, and your mother's been canning bewbies."

"Beautiful bewbies this year."

"It was a mild winter," said Ware with a nod.

"Well-done, you two." Thru raised his mug to his brother and sister. "Sounds like you've got the Highnoth spirit without having to go there."

Later, Thru went with Ware to the workshop. Ware lit the lamp and took down the bow he had carved so lovingly from yew.

Thru held up the gleaming bow. The nocks were of ramshorn. The string was of a fine linen and very strong.

Ware put a hand to his son's shoulder for a moment, felt the new muscle there.

"Before this winter I would have deemed this bow too strong for you, but now you are ready for it."

"Thank you, Father, for thinking me worthy of this gift."

The next morning Thru rose before anyone else. He did kyo in the yard, ate a piece of meek-and-bewbie pie for breakfast, and set off in the early light.

He found Utnapishtim and Meu waiting by the loaded donkey, and together they headed out of the village on the south road.

Chapter 5

From Dronned they went south, crossing the Cham and taking the old road across the fertile plain of Pelej to Ajutan. At the ancient town of Sarosh they turned east toward the Farblow Hills, Lushtan nearest, Gurs and Black beyond that.

Utnapishtim paused for a moment to contemplate the hills, purple in the afternoon light.

"Nine hills, my young friends, and nine temples, each at the top of one of the hills."

Thru and Meu had suspected as much. Uzzieh smiled at their weary expressions.

"We shall do one temple a day. Each one has its own distinct personality. We shall meditate at the end of the day. I hope that you will enjoy them as much as I always have."

"Why did they put them on top of the hills, Utnapishtim?" wondered Meu.

"It's quite simple; the views are wonderful. Folk lodge in Lushtan or White Deer and make day trips to the temples for the views and the contentment that comes with seeing them."

With this prospect before them they went on along the base of Lushtan Hill until they reached the little town of Lushtan itself. The river there formed a wide bottom that was perfect polder land, making Lushtan a rich town, famed for its high-quality cloth, woven from waterbush fiber.

Market Street was lined with rug merchants and emporia that sold both cloth and tailored clothing. There was a strong feeling of prosperity in the air.

The Assenzi knew Lushtan well. He took them down a side street to a stables run by an old mot retired from the clothing trade.

"Hail, Master Utnapishtim," said this individual, getting slowly to his feet.

"And hail to you, old Trumble, and how goes business?"

"Ah, I cannot complain. My donkeys see work enough. Folk are coming in record numbers this year. The festival of flowers will be spectacular."

"Then we are only just in time. I hope the oil is ready. I would like to set off for Lushtan Hill tomorrow."

"Aye, the weather promises to keep fine right now. And old Trumble has procured your oil, six jars of finest Ajutan lamp oil."

"And the donkeys?"

"I have three fat beasts who have been sitting around for a week without work. They will be loaded and ready in the morning."

"Excellent," said the Assenzi.

"Old Preeter has been up on Lushtan Hill since last moon. He sent word that all was ready for you."

"Excellent news, Trumble. And how is your wife?"

"Old Malerri has the shaking foot, Master Utnapishtim, but her eyes are still clear, and so is her mind."

"Has she tried valerian root for the shaking foot?"

"She has tried everything, Master Utnapishtim. It is just our age, I'm afraid. The aches and pains of growing old."

"Please convey to her my good wishes for her health. She should try the valerian root and soak the feet in warm water."

From Trumble's comfortable office they went on to the oldest inn, the Rose, which was a rambling hostelry of many rooms set out around a central yard.

Two rooms had been set aside for them, and they were shown upstairs at once. They had a good dinner in the inn's parlor, then went outside to watch a troupe of tumblers and jugglers called Nuza and Her Magnificents. Nuza herself was a fantastically supple and agile mor wearing a scarlet costume. She began the proceedings with a series of rolls and somersaults, ending in the arms of a big brilby who caught her and held her high. She finished with a flourish and a round of applause from the audience.

While the tumblers and jugglers took a break, the great swordsmot Toshak gave an exhibition of his skills. Thru watched in awe as Toshak leaped, whirled, and dodged while his sword ran like a ribbon of gleaming steel through the air around him.

Toshak offered his customary challenge at the end of his performance. Anyone who wished to have a bout with him would be welcome to try him in the morning at the town's Game Tree.

Thru chuckled to himself. He was working on the sword kyo, but so far Master Sassadzu had refrained from the slightest praise. Sword kyo was difficult; the standards were set very high. Failure was commonplace. Thru had yet to find the good form in sword kyo.

Now the jugglers worked the crowd, keeping a dozen balls whirling in the air above their heads. They finished to more applause, and then Nuza came out for a finale that involved her producing a series of fantastic leaps and somersaults into the arms of the big brilby.

A youngster came through the folk sitting out in the yard of the inn with a hat, seeking contributions for the troupe.

Thru and Meu tossed in a penny apiece, and Utnapishtim gave a shilling. The crowd was still applauding the performance, and the sound of coins chinking into the hat continued.

Nuza was a beauty, and with her grace and strength she completely captured Thru's attention. He and Meu chuckled together at how totally she had entranced them.

The troupe withdrew to more applause, and musicians took up their instruments to play the lilting music of the

Farblow Hills. Thru noticed that Uzzieh Utnapishtim was apparently very taken with the wild, skirling music and was beating his palm on his knee. There was a great deal he did not understand about the ancient Assenzi.

The next morning they loaded the donkeys, two jars of oil for each of the Lushtan animals, plus food and supplies for themselves on their own donkey, and set off up the narrow road to Lushtan Hill by the seventh hour.

It was a wildly beautiful morning, with occasional clouds scudding past above the verdant hills. The scent of the wild hedonias rose sweetly from their groves.

"Did you ever think you'd come this far?" said Meu, as they trudged up the stony little road behind the donkeys.

"I used to dream of traveling, but I never thought I'd come to the Farblows."

"I never thought about traveling. I thought I would just grow old in my village. Marry a village mor, celebrate the holidays with everyone else, and grow old working the polder."

"Well, you still can. You will return to your village won't you?"

"I will, but after seeing this beauty, my heart will never be still in my old village. I will need to travel again."

"Perhaps that is why they send us to Highnoth. So that there are some folk who do travel and don't settle down, keep the blood moving."

Meu chuckled at this absurdity.

On they went, and in time they grew tired and their step less lively, but the Assenzi never seemed to tire and where he went, so they were bound to go.

They came over the brow of the hill at last. The donkeys were getting very slow and stubborn, and the sun was slipping down the sky toward the far horizon. Off in the east the slopes of the Farblow Hills were glowing in the red afternoon light. The shadows between the hills were dark and purple.

Ahead, quite close by, they saw the temple, the top of the portico rising above the small trees on top of the hill.

"Hanging Falls Temple, my friends," said Uzzieh Utnapishtim. "A magical place. And remember what I told you of our friend Preeter."

"We remember, Utnapishtim."

With a full portico of a dozen pillars and a wide stoa, Hanging Falls was the largest of the Farblow temples. In the summer it had a full-time keeper, old Preeter, who pruned back the vines, swept the rooms, and set out bowls of water in the public rooms with a freshly cut vineflower floating in the center. He also undertook more serious tasks, like the ongoing rebuilding of the southwest corner of the chancel, which had become dilapidated in recent centuries.

The white-marble pillars glowed softly in the sun's light, but the rooms beyond were pools of darkness.

A cheerful voice suddenly called from round the back.

"Hold on, I'll be with you in a moment . . ."

There was the sound of movement in the vines. A few moments later a big fellow with the thick skin of a kob came shouldering through the tangles. As soon as he saw them a broad smile split his brown leathery face.

"Welcome to Hanging Falls."

"Dear old Preeter, how are you?"

"Utnapishtim! Is it really you? How good it is to see you again. You have not come down to the Farblows in years."

"I know, I know, Acmonides has done the Farblows for many years. I've had other duties, you see."

"Well, welcome back. As for myself I'm not in too bad shape, though I've been better, too. But the Spirit knows I have little to complain about. The work here goes well. Master Graedon will be most pleased with my progress. I have the new stone lintel in place, and I'm bracing it just now."

"Oh, excellent. The last time I was here you had only just begun replacing the stone."

"It has taken years longer than I expected, Utnapishtim. It was very hard to get the stone cut properly."

"My old friend, you have worked as hard as any of Graedon's folk."

"I thank ye, Master Utnapishtim, for I know those are kind words."

The Assenzi turned to the young mots.

"Here are Meu and Thru, a hardworking pair. They foolishly agreed to accompany me here and have now walked hundreds of miles as a result."

"Ha, hah, that's always the case with the Assenzi. Join them at your peril!"

Thru put his hand into the huge kob paw and prayed he got it back in one piece. The big hand that shook his was surprisingly gentle though.

The donkeys were unloaded, and a jar of oil was taken into the temple to fill the lamps, twelve of which were lit when darkness fell. Thereafter at each hour a lamp was extinguished until dawn, when the last three or four would be blown out together after a short prayer for the new day.

Thru walked the donkeys upstream a short ways to a place where they could drink while Meu moved the remaining jars of oil to the cache. Old Preeter moved around the rooms with his dipper filling the lamps, and the Assenzi sat in silent meditation in a corner of the stoa.

When the donkeys were watered and fed and the oil placed correctly in the cache the two young mots stood together on the steps. There was still time left in the day for them to climb the steps to the viewing platform at the rear of the temple. Utnapishtim was deep in meditation, and they did not want to disturb him.

"Let's look at these views then," said Thru with a nudge toward the stairs.

Purple-clawed shadows were cutting deeply into the glowing faces of the hills as the light turned ruddy with sunset. Hawks circled overhead, while in a far-off glen deer browsed before dusk. In the shadowy valley directly below, the first lamps were being lit in Lushtan town.

Thru absorbed the intense beauty of the scene. He loved this land, and blessed the Spirit for its existence.

He and Meu stayed out there until the sun was gone, lost beneath a riot of red-and-purple clouds in the uttermost west.

Preeter invited them to join him in his small quarters at the back of the temple. Outside he had a small terrace, and together they broke bread and sipped from a jug of fine suffio wine. After a meal of olives, cheese, and bread they accompanied the Assenzi to the stream, where they bathed by moonlight. Then they repaired to the meditation gallery. Utnapishtim read from the Book, the lesson from "Early Summer Month." They invoked the Spirit and drew it into themselves as they began the careful breathing of the meditation technique.

Later Thru stood above the chasm where the falls disappeared in a ghostlike curtain of mists and felt the Spirit rising in him. It was everywhere around him, moving in all of them, living in everything in some mysterious way. The world was interconnected, everything depended on everything else, and the Spirit governed all of it. This epiphany held him for several minutes, until the rising mists brought the heady scents of life and a wave of emotion so strong that his chest hurt for a moment. Briefly he gave thanks to the Spirit for the beauty of the world.

Chapter 6

The days in the Farblows proceeded with a satisfying rhythm. They rose with the temple bell, said prayers, and had breakfast before descending to town, where they fed the donkeys and loaded more oil. From Lushtan they worked north at first, provisioning Basking Ridge and Purple Stone Temples. Then it was the turn of the small hills of Bern and Capeter before they moved up to White Deer to take care of the eastern hills. These temples were both smaller and farther apart. To supply them they took only two donkeys and four jars of oil.

As they moved eastward the country became wilder. There were few farms and little good land for polder. Away in the northeast loomed the magnificent Drakensberg and due east were the Barataks, a range of mountains almost as impressive.

After Sunset Temple and Far Horizons they came to the very last, Rock Fall Temple on Hex Hill. It was a long hike but not terribly steep. Up they went on the narrow rocky trail and at last came to the square building, with no portico and only the simplest narthex and interior chamber. Seven stone steps lead up to the entrance, which was of plain stone.

After unloading the donkeys they stepped into the narthex, the entranceway to the main chamber, and immediately noticed a busy hum coming from the oil-storage chamber.

"That sounds like trouble," said Thru, pointing to the door.

Meu pulled the door open and immediately the hum

grew much louder. Thru started backing toward the temple entranceway. The Assenzi was outside, examining the facade of the temple for cracks. Meu scrambled back from the door to the storage cache. The hum continued to increase, and a few dark insects flew into the narthex.

Meu and Thru took to their heels.

"Wild bees!"

Accompanied by the donkey and the Assenzi, they ran across the clear space in front of the temple and took shelter in the trees.

"How are we going to get them out of there?" said Meu, after they'd got their breath back.

"There's a ventilation slit in the wall above the the storage chamber. That must be how they're getting in and out," said Thru, after a careful study of the temple walls.

"We'll have to smoke them out," said Meu. "Get some leaves burning and throw them in there."

"Is there anything in there that might catch fire? Like oil residues, perhaps?"

"Good question young Thru," said the Assenzi. "It won't help us to burn the temple down just to get rid of some bees."

"But we can't just leave them there. Nobody will be able to use the temple all summer."

"True. They must move. I will meditate upon the problem." The Assenzi went up into the narthex to study the situation, then he went out onto the western terrace.

After a while Thru went back to the narthex entrance. The bees had settled down a bit. He sidled in closer and nudged the door shut once more. There was a slight increase in the hum, but it soon died away. The bees preferred that door to be shut.

They could coexist with the bees for a while, but unless they wished to concede the oil-storage locker to the invading swarm, they would have to convince the insects to leave. Thru wasn't looking forward to that. Domesticated bees were used to the intrusions of the beekeeper, and they still reacted with a few stings. Wild bees were something else again and likely to put up a furious resistance.

"I've always been uneasy around bees. It runs in my family," muttered Thru. "My father stopped keeping them. He didn't have the knack of minding them. He got stung too often."

"Uneasy?" replied Meu. "How about terrified? My mother would not let my father keep bees even if he wanted to. She was petrified of them. I am, too. We always buy our honey."

"Well, we'll have to do something about them, terrified or not."

Thru and Meu filled the lamps. At dusk they lit a lamp on the western terrace. The sun had just finished setting in splendor in the west, outlining far-distant hills in gold as it sank from view.

They ate bread and olives with a little cheese and pickled vegetables, then laid themselves down to sleep on the gallery floor. The bees had not bothered them in the slightest—as long as they stayed away from the door to the oil-storage locker.

The Assenzi, however, sat on the floor near the oil locker and went into a meditative trance.

Thru awoke in the night and found the Assenzi was still there, still meditating.

He went back to sleep, and in the morning the Assenzi had moved to the eastern terrace and was watching the sunrise in tranquillity. Then, without ceremony he got up, entered the temple, and opened the door to the storage chamber.

Taken by surprise, the young acolytes watched with horror. There was a sudden loud roar from the bees and Thru and Meu put their hands to their mouths, expecting the worst. But the roar dwindled suddenly and died away to a gentle sort of hum after the slender old Assenzi entered the oil cache.

The bees remained quiet, and Thru and Meu exchanged a look of astonishment. No howls of pain erupted from the oil locker, and after a minute or so

Utnapishtim backed slowly out of the storage cache draped in a dark mantle of bees. The hive had swarmed out behind its queen, who had landed on his chest.

Wearing a shroud of bees while others flew around his head, the Assenzi walked slowly past the astonished Thru and Meu and out to the forest. There the queen left him with a sudden darting buzz and was immediately surrounded by the swarm, which lifted off with a roar of wings and departed through the trees.

Utnapishtim gave a slow shrug to his shoulders, as if adjusting bones as old as the mountains themselves, then he turned around and slowly walked back to the temple.

Thru and Meu stared at him wide-eyed. Then Meu got up and brought the Assenzi a cup of cool water from the cistern.

"Thank you, Meu, that was thirsty work."

"Are you all right, Utnapishtim?"

"Perfectly well, thank you. That nest was very cooperative. The bees are much beset in the wild, as you know. Honey will draw many predators. It leads them to prejudice against all creatures I'm afraid."

"Did they not sting you, Utnapishtim?" said Thru.

"No, young Thru, not one sting. I had given the nest to understand that its hive was in a dangerous place, and pledged my help in their relocation."

Thru and Meu exchanged a blank look. Given the nest to understand? He had spoken to the bees, and they had understood him? Assenzi magic, it was clear to both of them.

Still in awe at the Assenzi's calm handling of the bees the two young acolytes carried the jars of oil to the cache. The bees had left behind their hive, still filled with honeycomb, and they took the honey and ate it on their bread for breakfast. It was delicious.

Afterward they loaded the empty jars from the oil cache onto the donkeys and headed back down the trail to the valley below. The weather continued mild and sunny, although there were clouds far off in the east toward the Barataks.

The donkeys, overjoyed at being freed from the weight of filled oil jars, were eager to get down the mountain to the feed bag in the stables. They made good time.

But something was not right. A gradual mounting sense of unease afflicted Utnapishtim. Something was wrong, but he could not quite put a finger on it.

They came to the stone staircase, a place where the trail narrowed and doubled back on itself as it descended a steep slope and Utnapishtim stopped them with a wave of his hand, suddenly looking grim.

"My friends, I'm afraid we have enemies on this hill. I sense pyluk."

Thru and Meu stared at him for a moment while his words sank in.

"They will know we are here," said Thru, hurrying to the donkeys to pull his bow and quiver from the baggage. Meu retrieved his as well, an older bow that had been in his family for many years and in truth was in need of replacement.

Thru had twenty shafts, but only six of them had steel bodkins; the rest were hunting arrows with little flint broadheads meant for rabbits and pigeon. He strapped the quiver to his shoulder and slung his bow over the other one.

Utnapishtim had put himself into a meditative trance for a few moments as he allowed his consciousness to reach out to the surrounding hillside. He opened his eyes after a half minute.

"They are nearby, but I do not think they hunt us. We must move with caution, but with all possible speed. We need to get the word to White Deer so that a posse can be raised to hunt them down."

"Why would they risk coming so close to White Deer?" wondered Thru, who was not so sanguine about the situation.

"I have not heard of trouble from pyluk up here in many years," said Utnapishtim. "There must be war in the Barataks. Their hordes clash over the breeding sands every so often."

"This is a long way from the Barataks," said Meu, wonderingly.

They made haste down the trail, pressing the donkeys forward, which for once was not difficult. An hour passed in quick downward progress, and they came out on High Meadow, just a few miles from the first habitations of mots on the outskirts of White Deer.

Utnapishtim cast about himself once more and detected nothing. He remained uneasy, however. His ability to detect the lizard men was restricted. He knew they were on the mountain, but not exactly where. He hoped they had stayed behind on the high ground.

"They are far behind," he announced finally. "They must not have found our trail yet."

They relaxed just a little and continued on their way across the meadow, which was dotted with small copses of alder and spruce. Around the massive Gorn Crag, the path plunged downhill again with occasional openings onto narrow stream gorges. Some of these were bridged, others had to be crossed by stepping-stones. The donkeys were always recalcitrant about using the stones.

On the western side of the crag was a band of rock in which the immense spirals of ancient fossils stood out in rows. Thru had noticed them on the way up and been awed by their size and number.

"What are these things, Utnapishtim?" Thru asked, looking for something to take his mind off the pyluk.

"They are the shells of ancient squid, young Thru. Long ago they swam in the oceans in such abundance that their remains can be found all over the world, just like this."

"Squid don't have coiled shells."

"These were an ancient kind of squid. They long ago gave way to the shining little squid of today."

"And all this was at the bottom of the ocean?" said Meu with wonder in his voice.

"Yes, young Meu, all these rocks were formed from the seabed long ago. There is a great deal that we discern from the nature of the rocks. You shall study this, if you stay at Highnoth one more year."

Most of the small streams were dry, but the last one, the Exwem, was fed by a spring. The stream was low, but there was water enough for the donkeys to take a drink. This would be the last opportunity before they got back to White Deer, which was still a couple of hours farther on.

Thru took the opportunity to go off a short distance to relieve himself. The stream ran down the bottom of the rock strewn canyon between dense thickets of alder. He was soon completely alone. While he was there he watched an eagle in the distance, circling above the hill scanning the slopes below for rabbits. His father had told him how keen was the eagle's vision, and he chuckled at the thought that the eagle had probably seen him just as clearly as he had seen the eagle.

He hurried back and was working through the last stand of alders when he stopped with one foot still raised. A chill descended through him as he heard the harsh hisses and grunts of the pyluk tongue.

With his heart hammering in his chest he peered out through the stems of the alder. Four pyluk were pulling the gear off the donkeys, which were plainly terrified. But bucking and plunging did them no good. The pyluk had hold of their reins and were capable of holding them. Long spears were thrust into the ground nearby. There was no sign of the Assenzi, but Meu was visible, lying on the ground beyond the donkeys. He was not moving.

Another pyluk came into view from farther down the trail. He called to the four by the donkeys, who answered with hisses and guttural noises.

Thru stepped carefully back into the alders and crouched while he pulled his bow off his shoulder and nocked an arrow.

Five pyluk and six arrows with steel heads. It would be close work with little room for error. He wasn't even sure if a single arrow would be enough for pyluk. They were said to be hard to kill. He pulled the quiver around to rest on his hip and checked that his sword was loose in the scabbard. Then he moved forward again. He had to admit that he was afraid. One young mot against five grown pyluk was long odds. He took a deep breath, gathered himself, and looked out through the alder screen again. To his surprise the pyluk had gone off, taking the donkeys and Meu.

He followed along carefully behind them. There was no sign of any blood at the stream crossing. Nor was Utnapishtim's body visible. He checked for the slim, short tracks of the Assenzi but could not spot them in the churned dust left by donkeys and pyluk.

He could not tell if the Assenzi had gone ahead or gone back. There was no blood on the ground, so the pyluk had not speared either Meu or Utnapishtim, and Meu had not fired his bow, which had been discarded by the pyluk, who disdained the bow and arrow in favor of their long spears and throwing sticks.

The surprise must have been complete, he concluded. Somehow the Assenzi had failed to detect them in the twisted terrain of ridges and canyons.

Thru followed them back up the trail. He could not leave poor Meu in their hands. There was no time to go down to White Deer and rouse a posse. It was up to him.

Keeping a wary eye ahead and pausing frequently to scan the trail above for any sign of ambush, Thru stalked the pyluk. For the most part he kept to the sides of the trail, moving beneath the eaves of trees or in the shadow of rocks, but he needed to keep up a good speed so he had to use the trail.

Above the meadow, below the switchback, he sensed something was different. There was no birdsong from the slope above.

He moved off the bare rocky trail and into the heather. Scrambling up the slope he left fur and even some skin on the heather, but he kept going and climbed the slope above the trail. From the top he could survey the trail all the way to the crest.

He spotted them after a few moments, three pyluk

crouched below in ambush. They were spaced along the trail, hidden in the heather at a place where the trail turned up toward the switchback. The other pyluk were not to be seen, nor were the donkeys and Meu.

Thru considered shooting the three in ambush for a moment, but they were just a little too far for a good shot, and he could not afford to miss. Besides, they would warn the others up the trail, who might kill Meu, if he still lived, just to be sure of him before confronting Thru.

He crouched in the heather and watched until the pyluk stirred themselves from cover and loped up the trail in search of their fellows. They wouldn't want to miss the meat.

Thru climbed down to the trail again and followed with cautious steps while trying to think of a way to equalize the odds a bit. The pyluk were justly famous for their prowess with their long throwing spears.

The pyluk drove the donkeys back up to the top of the hill and halted just outside the temple. They were joined by two more members of their sept. Immediately all seven began the slavering ululations of the pyluk hunting call.

Thru heard the terrible sound as he approached the top of the trail, and tried to distinguish the number of voices making the ululations, in case all the pyluk were at their meat and they had left no sentry. It sounded as if all of them were calling, but he could not be certain. Caution kept him from charging ahead and attacking directly.

With great care he climbed up a steep rocky slope well away from the trailhead, then eased himself through the brush until he had a view of the temple precinct.

The pyluk had knocked one of the donkeys down and crushed its skull with a rock. They were tearing it open with their hands and teeth. The other donkey was raving on the end of its tether, bucking and braying as it saw its herd-mate devoured.

Meu was lying nearby faceup. Thru saw his friend's

chest rise and fall. Meu was alive! Thru took heart from that, but then he realized there were now seven pyluk and his hopes sank again.

The pyluk swarmed over the donkey with their usual avidity. They were smeared in blood and offal. One pulled its head out of the donkey's body cavity with a large piece of liver in its jaws. A gulp, a flash of bright sharp teeth, and it was gone.

The rib cage was disassembled between three others, who growled and snarled as the bones cracked and popped. Jaws ripped and tore at the meat while the remaining donkey continued to tug frantically at the tether that bound it to the hitching rail.

The dead donkey's legs were torn away with loud cracking and snapping. The pyluk ate quickly, as was their wont. Occasionally a long barking belch would be released, followed usually by grunts from the others and the sound of pyluk laughter.

Thru edged around the clearing, looking for the best possible spot from which to launch his attack. He had noticed a thick-boled ancient oak that was barely twelve feet high, but almost five feet thick. Behind that would be a good spot to shoot from.

He had also noticed that the pyluk spears had been set beside this tree. If he was stationed there he would be in command of their weapons. They would have to come at him to get them, and that should give him the chance to shoot them.

He reached the tree after a few minutes of careful movement. The donkey was little more now than a pile of bones. They had sucked out the brain and eaten the tongue, gobbled the eyes and gnawed down the ears. Five of the pyluk lay down where they'd eaten and began to drowse. Soon there were loud snores from their direction.

The two remaining, chosen as the watch by some process invisible to Thru, rummaged through the bones for a while, gnawing and sucking on them for any last scraps of the donkey. Soon they tired of this increasingly futile exercise, and turned their attention to Meu.

Thru already had his bow ready and an arrow nocked. He drew and took aim and was interrupted by a gentle tap on the shoulder. He almost released by accident, but looked back and found Utnapishtim there, a finger pressed to his lips in the universal signal for silence.

"Do not shoot," said the Assenzi in a tiny whisper. "Better to free Meu and make a run for it."

Thru's heart was still palpitating in his chest, but he slid back behind the tree where the Assenzi was waiting.

"Free Meu?"

"First, we must take their spears."

Thru nodded. He had considered that, but taking the spears without attracting notice had seemed impossible.

"How?"

The Assenzi waved a hand gently and closed his eyes.

Thru tried to still his heart. In the temple precinct, Meu gave a gasp and then a scream. The other pyluk shifted in their sleep and one of them growled something. The pyluk with Meu growled back. Meu was still sobbing and gasping.

Utnapishtim had gone into a trance state, with one slim hand held out in front of him and the other crossed upon his chest.

A sense of slow-rising tension had developed, as if a storm was gathering. Thru thought he heard odd little sounds, squeaks and cries as if mice were arguing in the undergrowth.

The cries from Meu had ceased. Did he still live? Thru peered around the trunk of the tree. The two pyluk that had been torturing him had nodded off. They were sitting with their backs to the temple, heads on their chests, snoring like the others.

Meu, abandoned once more, was now lying on his front, with his arms pulled behind his back. Thru glanced back at the Assenzi. Utnapishtim's eyes opened, and he gave Thru a nod.

Taking a deep breath Thru stepped out into plain view

and took hold of four of the spears. They were even heavier than he had expected, and he almost dropped them, recovering at the last moment. He moved them behind the oak and took them back to the edge of a cliff and tossed them down.

They fell into darkness far below.

Thru was already back at the tree. The pyluk still slept. He seized the other three spears and stepped around the tree, where he tripped on a root and almost fell over. He spun around, wobbled, and felt a small hand grip his shoulder and steady him at the critical moment.

He stood there, breathing hard; the Assenzi was looking back at him with wide-open eyes. Then Utnapishtim cracked a thin smile.

The pyluk continued to snore. Thru swallowed, took a breath, and carefully made his way to the cliff, where he threw the long spears away.

Back behind the old oak tree, the Assenzi was in meditation again.

Thru peered around the tree. The pyluk still slept, gorged on meat, with a little help from the magic of the Assenzi.

Utnapishtim's eyes opened once more.

"Now, young Thru, we must free the donkey, load poor Meu on its back, and get away down the trail. The pyluk will sleep for a while."

"Yes, Utnapishtim. Why not kill them while they sleep?"

"My spell is fragile; they would wake up before we could finish them."

Thru steadied his nerves, but kept his bow drawn, arrow ready as he stepped quietly across the plateau, slipped into the temple precinct, and approached the donkey.

The poor animal had exhausted itself. The rope was wet with foam, its jaw and front similarly soaked. It stood there trembling, eyes rolling a little as he approached.

Thru unstrung the arrow, put it in his quiver, and shipped the bow over his shoulder. He cut the rope with his knife and led the donkey past the pyluk. It wanted to bolt, but could not even raise a snort for some reason. More magic, he assumed.

Now they went past the two pyluk who were supposed to be on watch. Meu lay on the ground, wrists and ankles bound, breathing harshly.

Thru stopped the donkey and shook his friend to awareness.

Meu gasped at the touch. He opened his mouth and let his lips slip into a snarl as he struggled to contain any sound.

Thru waited. Meu got himself under control. "They broke my arm," Meu whispered.

Thru winced. "Have to get you on the donkey; can you stand?"

"Don't know. Think so. They didn't break my legs."

Thru cut Meu's bonds. Meu grunted a couple of times as Thru helped him sit up and get to his knees. Standing took another big effort, but at last he was up.

Thru held the donkey's head while Meu used his good arm to help pull himself across the donkey's back. He sobbed from the pain, but managed to get himself in position with one leg on either side. Thru led the donkey back past the two pyluk, out of the temple precinct, and onto the trail off the hilltop. None of the pyluk stirred.

Utnapishtim remained behind, his hand held out before him as if he were blessing the pyluk where they slept.

Chapter 7

Utnapishtim sent a prayer after the young mots and the donkey, urging them to their best speed. His spell would hold the pyluk for as long as he remained close by, and for a while afterward, but pyluk were astonishingly sensitive to the presence of prey and would notice its sudden absence and awaken, despite the enchantment under which they lay.

The sound of the donkey's hooves faded, and still he held the pyluk fast, though now there were some snorts and mutters from the sleepers.

It was a lonely moment for the ancient being, and one that brought up terrible memories from the long, long ago, when pyluk were far more common in the world, and they and their dread master, Karnemin the Great, were engaged in a war to conquer the Assenzi and expunge them from the world. In that time the Assenzi had developed their sensitivity to the presence of the lizard men. Utnapishtim cursed his own failings; he had sensed them, but had lost them again in those canyons and thus been taken by surprise.

More snorts from the sleepers. He pushed away the regrets and memories and concentrated on maintaining the spell. If he could build up a sufficient lead, then the youngsters would have a good chance of getting clean away. Time passed. High above, hawks circled in the calm air, oblivious to the terrible events on the hilltop below. Some crows flew past and settled in trees farther down the slope.

The moment of decision was come. The pyluk still

snored, but fretfully. The spell would hold them for a while longer, but not forever.

Carefully the Assenzi backed away, moving to the top of the trail, then turning and running as fast as his ancient legs could carry him. Sooner or later the pyluk would awake, and it would all become a question of speed. He consoled himself with the thought that at least the lizard men would not have their long spears.

As he ran, struggling for enough breath, he kept seeing the beauty of the land spread out in front of him and marveled at the terrible change that had come over his appreciation of the scene. Whereas before he had seen it as the essence of natural tranquillity under the midday sun, now it was but the backdrop to a nightmarish race against death. He also marveled at the fact that despite having lived a hundred thousand years, he was not yet ready to surrender his life. This was a question to be mulled over with Cutshamakim, if he survived.

He made the first turn on the trail and hurried down the stony track. It was imperative that he not turn his ankle there. It was going to be a close-run thing as it was, without any further difficulties.

The crows in the trees lifted up as he ran beneath them. They turned and flew up to the temple roof, where they settled with loud cries, harsh *caw-caw-caws* that rang out over the hillside. The Assenzi's heart sank.

The first bellow of rage ripped the air up above. Uzzieh Utnapishtim amazed himself by increasing his pace, bounding down the stony track like a skinny mountain goat.

The pyluk were awake, and they were angry! They turned for their spears and found them gone. Their rage became incandescent. Down the trail they bounded, determined to catch and rend the fugitives.

Far ahead Thru flew along with the donkey, trying to hold the terrified beast back. It seemed ready to launch itself straight off the cliffs rather than linger in the neighborhood of the pyluk. Several times Meu was almost thrown, and more than once he would have been tossed down a cliff but for Thru's quick hand.

Thru hauled on the rein, but the donkey was insensible to that kind of discomfort. Meu did his best by clamping his legs around the little donkey's chest, but even that had only limited effectiveness. The donkey had watched its stallmate killed and eaten right before its eyes. Come what might, this donkey was going home, to safety.

A plan formed itself in Thru's mind.

Just past the Exwem Stream where this had all started was the gorge of the Mile Out Stream. This was covered by a narrow rope bridge held up by two heavy ropes. If they could hold the pyluk off the bridge and cut the ropes, they could surely buy enough time to reach the village in the valley below.

They came out on the high meadow, still in the lead.

When he was halfway across he looked back and saw the Assenzi hurrying after him in a rapid shuffling run. Thru could not slow his pace—the pyluk were not too far behind, and the donkey knew it.

They had reached the point where the meadow narrowed and the cliffs drew in on either side when the screams of the pyluk sounded behind them.

"Have to get to Mile Out bridge and cut the ropes!" Thru bellowed back to Utnapishtim, who waved a hand to acknowledge his words.

They looked back, and saw that the pyluk were just starting across the meadow. They increased their own speed and raced toward the narrow cleft in the cliffs down which the trail proceeded.

At the edge of the meadow, beside the entrance to the trail, was a fallen tree. Thru took position behind it, drew his bow and nocked an arrow.

The pyluk came on with no attempt to shield themselves, berserk with anger.

The Assenzi went past and hurried after the donkey and Meu. It was up to Thru to slow the pyluk down.

Thru took careful aim. He recalled Master Sassadzu's kyo class of archery, and let himself flow into the arrow.

He made himself a tree to support the bow. It was a good bow, even a great one. His father had produced a masterpiece in this particular bow, and Thru prayed that he would not dishonor it.

The first arrow flew straight and true and sprouted from the throat of the leading pyluk, which gave a harsh shriek and fell to the ground, where it thrashed in the death throes.

With a wild series of leaps and hurdles the pyluk spread themselves out across the meadow, moving with the alarming rapidity of lizards in the hot sun.

Thru had brought up his second arrow and he aimed and released in the same moment, now in the full flow of archery kyo. The target jigged to the right, but too late and emitted a gasping scream as the arrow took it in the belly.

The rest of the pyluk had gone to ground, folding themselves into the terrain. Thru chewed his lip, considering the situation. Pyluk were the masters of stalking and concealment, able to hide in a fold of ground or a crack in the rocks. They were creeping up on him, he was certain, but he saw nothing. The tension grew as he cast his eyes this way and that. He whirled at a sudden movement and his arrow sank into the shoulder of the pyluk that was leaping toward him.

Thru ran. The wounded pyluk was still coming, as were the others and Thru was in a footrace for his life. He sprang down the trail, leaping from boulder to boulder where it was possible, and amazingly, he gained a little on the lizard men.

At the next bend he was able to turn and nock an arrow.

The pyluk dived for cover, but he shot a fourth, the arrow lodging in a leg so it could not keep up in the pursuit. That meant there were but three fully active pyluk left. And only two arrows with steel bodkins. All the rest were tipped with small flint heads designed for rabbits. They might wound pyluk, but would not stop them.

Thru edged backward. The pyluk would be moving closer; they were the absolute masters of movement while retaining cover.

After a few more backward steps he put up his bow and ran again.

He got to the next bend still ahead of them, and he turned and nocked an arrow. There was a flash of lizardskin and then nothing. No targets. He waited half a minute, then turned and ran again.

Thus went the deadly game down the trail, over the Exwem Stream crossing, and on to the Mile Out Stream gorge and the rope bridge. Thru rounded a curve and the donkey came into view, halfway over the rope bridge. The Assenzi was puffing along just behind.

Thru shouted a warning and saw the Assenzi's pace pick up. Thru pushed his weary legs into a sprint. Every second counted now.

Behind him the pyluk exploded around the corner. As they caught sight of the bridge they vented chilling shrieks. They hated all such works of civilization.

Rocks started flying past him; they were almost in range. One nicked his leg just above the knee, and he almost went down, but kept his feet somehow and staggered on. A rock the size of his fist skidded by, bouncing off the rocky trail.

Thru jammed to a stop, spun around, and drew his bow. A rock missed him by an inch or less, and then he had the arrow aimed, and the pyluk dived for cover.

There wasn't much cover to be had there in the narrow canyon. Thru got a shot at one and took it, but again only to wound in the shoulder. He held the position for a few moments, then started backtracking to the bridge, still holding bow and arrow ready.

A rock came hurtling toward him, and he had to skip aside. Another bounced in front of him and struck the bridge pole behind him with a loud thwak. He turned and ran onto the bridge.

The Assenzi and the donkey had crossed, and the slight figure of Utnapishtim could be seen wielding his sword on the left-side hawser. Thru increased his pace while a rock bounced along the bridge and struck him in the buttock, hard but not hard enough to knock him down.

The bridge was trembling, the left hawser was almost cut through. He reached the far side just as the left rope gave way and the bridge started to collapse. The pyluk screamed as they scrambled back at the other end.

Before they could even begin to get their courage up to try to cross again, the Assenzi laid his sword to the right-hand hawser, a stout four-inch-thick twist of bushrope.

Thru fired a few of his small stone-head arrows across the gorge to keep the stone throwers down while Utnapishtim sawed through the rope and sent the bridge falling into the gorge.

There were ways down into the gorge and up the other side, but they were very steep. The pyluk would be delayed, but Thru knew they would not give up after being tricked so.

Without more ado Thru and Utnapishtim turned away and hurried on down the trail. The steep slopes were behind them, and the trail passed through pine and redwood forest, enormous trees on either side.

Soon they caught up to the donkey, which had exhausted itself in the terrorized scramble down the hill. It was still trying to run, but with Meu's weight to carry it could only stumble along at a slow walk. When the donkey stopped altogether, Meu had to try walking. The dismount was an agony. Meu's arm throbbed savagely, but he kept from crying out. He was a little unsteady on his feet at first, but Utnapishtim and Thru helped hold him up and they set off again once they'd tied a strip ripped off Thru's shirt around Meu to hold his arm tight against his chest so it wouldn't move as he ran.

The donkey responded to its new freedom by running away down the trail for a hundred paces, then losing its breath and slowing to a crawl. When they caught up it sped off again.

Meu was consumed by the determination not to become pyluk meat. He kept putting one foot in front of the other despite the pain.

They crossed the Dupple Stream on a solid wood bridge, then passed down through a glade in the giant redwoods. Shafts of sunlight fell through gaps between the mighty trees, and far above was a strip of blue sky. The long glade came to an end in a thick stand of trees where the trail passed into semidarkness. Beyond that, after a mile or so came the beginnings of civilization. There was a small polder farm by the lake and a road into the village.

Thru looked back for any sign of the pursuit. The Assenzi halted and raised a hand, and both of them strained to detect a sound.

The woods behind them were noticeably quiet, however.

"They are not far behind now," said Utnapishtim.

"We will have to fight them, then."

"There, ahead, where the trail goes through those redwoods."

They let the donkey go on, Meu staggering along behind it, while they hid behind the trees one on either side of the trail.

Thru nocked his last steel-tipped arrow and kept watch on the trail behind them through a crack between the main trunk and a sapling. The Assenzi had drawn his sword. They waited.

The woods behind fell silent. The birds had sensed the pyluk. There was only the slightest breeze in the trees to break the hush.

Then he saw them, loping along, four strong, the pyluk with their deep chests, metallic green skin, and hot yellow eyes. Two of them bore shoulder wounds, streaks of dried blood down their sides, but still they sprang along, tails extended stiffly out behind. Pyluk were notoriously hard to kill.

They were just beyond effective bowshot, so Thru held off from shooting. Another ten yards and they would be in range. And then the pyluk abruptly disappeared, slipping into the shadows under the trees.

Thru and the Assenzi waited in their hiding place. It was as good as any ground for fighting from. Nothing seemed to move in front of them. Utnapishtim cast around himself for a trace of the lizard men. He could feel them, they were there, but he could not say where exactly.

Then suddenly a broken tree limb was hurled toward them from a patch of ferns to their right. Behind it came the pyluk, charging forward with death in their eyes.

Thru turned, aimed and released, and took one of the pyluk through the heart. His last steel bodkin was gone. He nocked a smaller arrow, aimed and released all in an instant. The nearest of the pyluk sprouted a shaft from its side and screamed horribly, but it kept coming, long talons at the ready.

Thru didn't have time for another arrow. He drew his sword just as the pyluk came up to the tree. It slashed at him with a heavy hand. He ducked underneath at the last moment, came up inside, and drove his sword into its belly. It gave a hiss of rage and shoved him away. The sword came free, and he bounced off the tree and fell back into the pyluk's grasp. It tore at his back and tried to bite his face, but he got an elbow up and blocked it while he ran his sword back into its belly. It went down on one knee, then collapsed. Blood ran from his arm, where the thing's jaws had closed on him.

To his right now the Assenzi's sword flashed and a pyluk spun away, disemboweled, blood flung wide as it rolled on the path. Thru saw no more because he was suddenly borne down by the one leaping from the left. He hit the ground with stunning force under the thing's heavy body. It slashed at him with its claws, raking him down the side of his face and chest. He heard himself scream as he struck upward with his left hand and connected with the point of the pyluk's lower jaw. The head snapped up and the intended bite for his throat never came. The other talons missed his face by a hairbreadth.

He got a leg up, hooked his ankle around the pyluk's throat, and pulled it away, then rolled, got his knees under him, and pushed himself up. The blood was running down his ruined cheek, but he could still see well enough, and his sword was in motion in time to meet the pyluk's next rush.

The blade went home in its deep chest, but the creature seemed to ignore it as it caught him around the shoulders with its long arms and snapped at his face with its jaws. The stench of its breath filled his nostrils, and the terrible glare of hate in its eyes almost undid him, but he ducked at the last moment and the jaws snapped down around the crown of his skull.

It was as if he'd put his head into a giant mousetrap. He saw stars, and fell to his knees. It would have ended there, but even as Thru looked up, he heard the pyluk's death scream and saw it spin away, one arm still flailing, while Utnapishtim stood over them, covered in blood, the small sword still in his frail hand.

The pyluk were dead. Thru struggled to get back on his feet but every part of him seemed to hurt. There was blood running from his face and the top of his head as well as his arm. His vision was blurry. It seemed Ual Gillo was right—her eldest son did have a hard head.

"Well-done," the Assenzi said. Thru nodded, but then everything started to spin around him, and he put out a hand to the tree to support himself. He leaned back against the tree and slowly slid down it to the ground.

When he came around a few minutes later, the Assenzi was crouched beside him.

"These pyluk are dead."

He nodded. Those steel heads had done the job. Ware's new bow had served him well in a stern test.

Thru shook his head and a clot of blood, partly dried, flew off his chin. Blood had soaked his shirt and matted the fur down his chest to his belly. His trousers were ruined, too.

He found his sword still in his hand, caked in pyluk blood.

"Sassadzu Rendilim will be happy to know what a good pupil you are, young Thru Gillo. First-class archery kyo you exhibited."

"My thanks for your compliment, Utnapishtim, but I should have done better."

"Perhaps one day you will, but by then I should think there will be legends told about this."

The Assenzi paused. "Do you think you can make it to the village?"

"I think so. Let me stand up for a moment."

Slowly Thru got to his feet. His head swam, but he could stand. The wounds on his face and chest were deep and needed attention, but he could walk.

He cleaned off the blade, sheathed it, then retrieved the bow and the steel points.

As they started forward, he could feel the left side of his face flapping in the wind. When he moved fresh blood welled up in the chest wounds.

Utnapishtim was unhurt, the blood on his robe was all from the pyluk. Flawless sword kyo had dealt with one pyluk, the other he had stabbed from behind.

They staggered out of the forest, made it to the farm of Yeezer Damb, where they found the donkey, and Meu with his arm in a sling. Damb put Thru and Meu on his donkey cart and carried the pair of them down to White Deer.

In White Deer Utnapishtim oversaw the cleaning and binding of their wounds. Pyluk bites could easily infect, so distilled white spirit was splashed on the wounds and stitches put in by a skilled seamstress, who winced at the sight of the left side of Thru's poor face. From the edge of his eyelid all the way to the bottom of the lower jaw he would bear a scar. Likewise, he would have scars on his chest, his arm, and the top of his head.

Later, when Meu's arm had been set and put in splints and their wounds cleaned, stitched, and treated with honey and disinfecting herbal rinses, they gave statements to the local royal agent, who wrote them up and sent them off under the Crown Seal to the capital of

Ajutan. Evidence was brought in by the posse from White Deer that had gone up the hill immediately and slaughtered the wounded pyluk where they were found. Eventually, after a search, seven long pyluk spears were brought in from the canyon.

No more pyluk were found, and the conclusion was reached that it had been a rogue band, driven by hunger. With a fair degree of awe, the agent sent off the report and filed his own copy.

Thru and Meu recuperated in White Deer for a few weeks, then they rode by donkey cart to Lushtan before they undertook the journey north to Dronned.

Chapter 8

In the great city of Shasht, it was the eve of the Summer Solstice festival. Simona was very excited because they were going to go to Lady Bezzad's garden party and those were always great fun. Simona had been wondering for days whether she would wear the orange gown she'd worn for the chorales or the green summer one that Mama had had made for her birthday. She was nineteen and she had to attract a man soon or it would be too late.

All those plans turned to dust when her papa walked in the door. She could tell the moment she saw him that something dreadful had happened. He stood in the entrance hall with a stricken look, his eyes puffy and red. He was not a strong man, she knew, but she had never seen him this upset before.

A magnificent purple envelope had been delivered to Filek Biswas's office in the hospital. Within lay a communication from the Imperial Court. The Imperial Seal was always a little intimidating to break. The great red *A* of Aeswiren III lay embossed in wax across the envelope and glittered with baleful power. Still, Filek had opened it with confidence. His work at the hospital had attracted the Emperor's favorable attention before.

He'd broken the seal and found orders from the Emperor's presumptive heir Nebbeggebben directing one Filek Biswas, to report to the Colony Fleet. He was being sent overseas. He blinked for a moment in horrified amazement, then he'd read it again with enormous care before slumping back in his chair.

When he got home he was still barely able to speak.

His wife, Chiknulba, could scarcely comprehend what he was saying the first time around, then she broke down into tears when it all sank in.

"I am commanded to leave the hospital. I am to take a position as second surgeon aboard the colony ship *Growler*. I am to take my family to the colony in the east."

At the name *Growler* Chiknulba had understood everything in a moment of dreadful clarity. Vli Shuzt had done this. Vli had had it in for Chiknulba since that dreadful party that had turned into a sordid orgy with slaveboys. Chiknulba had been brought up to despise that sort of thing, and Vli had not taken Chiknulba's obvious disgust very well.

Of course it was her, because Vli Shuzt was going on the colony expedition as well, something she was quite bitter about. Her husband was captain of the *Growler,* and she must go where he was sent.

But there was a great power attached to being captain of a departing colony ship. If necessary, the captain could request that anyone of social rank beneath that of the imperial purple join the expedition. Such persons, once they had been requested in writing under seal, could not refuse.

Of course, there were safety measures inhibiting this custom. If a captain reached too high above himself, he would be assassinated by the Hand of Aeswiren, which governed these matters in its own silent, implacable way.

Alas, Filek Biswas had no such protection.

"Old Klegg wept when I told him. He will now have to do his own work. It's been years since he ran the hospital. He was very gloomy when I left."

"What does he have to worry about?" cried Chiknulba. "He will still be here in the city. He will be able to order a cup of hot tea at any time of day or night. We will be at the ends of the world digging ditches. Trying to stay alive through the first winters."

"We will lose everything," he mumbled, staring blankly at the large comfortable rooms of his house.

"And you will be only a second surgeon?"

His eyes came back to hers.

"I will be under some drunken, worthless navy surgeon. Some oafish sot with a filthy surgery and a callous attitude toward the patients."

He would be a nothing.

"And what will we be?"

They would be women, slammed shut in the claustrophobic world of the women's deck of a ship, at sea for many months.

Lady Chiknulba took to her room, where she wept into her pillow all night, unconsolable.

In her own room Simona stood out on the balcony and felt the warm wind blow across her skin. There was a grand view across to the Temple Plaza. The city glowed in the rays of the setting sun; the first lights were being lit. Cooking fires sent up a reek from the residential neighborhoods. The upper classes were bathing and being dressed for dinner. On the great avenues the coaches would soon be in motion carrying wealthy patrons to the theaters. Tomorrow would be the solstice festival. Even the women of the upper classes would be out tomorrow, crowding at the viewing galleries around the temple.

A thousand hearts would be offered to the Great God, He Who Eats. Later the piñatas would be smashed in every household while wine was poured and musicians took up the wild, skirling tanburi music of ancient Shasht.

All this color and excitement would become no more than a memory. Once they'd embarked on the expedition they would never be allowed to return. They would have to rebuild their lives in the new world, wherever it was.

Her life with her tutors and her friends would be over. The leisured, intellectually stimulating life led by her mother and father would be replaced by a hard, plaincloth colonial existence, with lots of religious ceremonies to keep the faithful in line.

The sophisticated parties, the music, the poetry, all the arts of great Shasht, would be forgotten. They'd have nothing to read except what they could take with them. For music they'd have military bands thundering away, nothing delicate, nothing beautiful for its own sake.

And Shesh Zob?

Simona broke down at last and felt the tears running furiously. She would be torn forever from her beloved forest on their country estate. All her freedoms would be gone. The walls of purdah would close around her with an iron grip.

PART TWO

Chapter 9

Two years after the famous battle on Mount Hex, Thru Gillo returned to Warkeen Village from Highnoth. He had grown tall for a mot, at least five and a half feet, and though he had filled out a little, he remained slim and hard-fleshed, but his young face had a somewhat stern cast to it, disfigured by the pale scars down the left side. It could be a little off-putting until one became used to him. At least his eyebrows had grown back, though they were never as bushy as before.

Older folk marked him at once as the product of Highnoth. They recognized the inner strength behind his calm exterior.

Young chooks ran from the tall stranger with the scarred face while giving squawks of alarm.

"Hey, young chooks," cried their elders, "that's Thru the bat-mot, the striker of the white ball like no other. You'll see. He been to Highnoth, far far away, the place of the Ancient Ones. He has learned the secrets."

There were other graduates of Highnoth in the village. Old Penki Inors was one, usually to be found sitting outside the tavern, white-furred with age, hands resting on his walking stick.

"And how is Master Cutshamakim?" said Penki.

"He sends his blessing, old Penki. And I would add my own. It is good to see you still in good health."

"Glad to see you came back, young Thru Gillo. I heard all kinds of tales about you down in the Farblow Hills."

"Oh, you don't want to be listening to wild tales, old Penki."

"Not much else to do, now, young Thru Gillo. Unless you get back on the village team and liven them up. Shocking style of play they have right now. Very slack fielding. Haven't won in weeks."

There was also Derai Hux, who was a little younger than Ware Gillo, and the father of two daughters. Derai greeted him with the same calm smile and inquired as to Cutshamakim's health. Since Cutshamakim had been in perfect health for ten times ten thousand years, it was clearly no more than a matter of form.

In Cart Lane Thru found a gang of roosters out to welcome him home. At the front was Tucka, of course, and right behind him were Pok and Tikka Tonk and Chum and Ruddo, the noisiest males in chooktown.

"Back at last!"

"Yes, friends, I'm back in the village. Do you think people will accept it? Will they let me back?"

Wings flapped, and big chooks jumped on the spot and cackled.

"Everyone glad that Thru Gillo back in village."

"Especially the team. They need you."

"Need you bad."

"I hear that, and maybe I can help them, if I haven't lost the touch the Spirit gave me. And how are things in your house, Tucka?"

"Two new chicks hatched this year. Another egg on the way. We going to be busy chooks around here."

Pok dikka dikka Pokaduk, ruling rooster of the Pokaduk clan, pushed his way past Tucka.

"A new chick hatched this year. Pokaduk house is pretty noisy."

"Goodness, Pok, it already was. Hey, there, Tikka Tonk . . ."

"Hey, Thru Gillo, mot of the bat!"

Of course, not everyone in the village was as pleased to see him as the chooks. One evening in the town tavern he found himself only a few feet away from Pern Treevi. Pern was now locked in a dispute with the Gillo family over the seapond held by Ware. Pern looked at Thru, his lip curled, and he muttered something insulting.

Thru smiled, long used to Pern's dislike.

"Would you like to repeat that so I can hear it?"

Pern's sneer flattened and his eyes glared back at Thru, but he said nothing.

"Talking to yourself, were you?"

"Leave me alone, Gillo."

Thru was daring him to step closer, or even outside for a little knuckle play. Pern had lost in the old school-yard fights, and wasn't interested in trying that again. Pern turned away to where his friend Lem Frobin was standing. Frobin gave Thru a hard stare, Thru returned it with his habitual smile. Frobin and Treevi moved away.

Back in his home, he threw himself into the work of the farm. It was springtime, and there was planting to be done. Snejet soon remarked on the fact that Thru's planting was now perfect. All the waterbush for that spring was planted in a mere six days.

He rejoined the village team for bat and ball. Even the mot he displaced, Hemper Fravo, agreed to the move. Hemper would get back in, as soon as someone was injured. Meanwhile they had the hitting of Thru back in their arsenal, and Warkeen began beating the villages for miles around. Thru even set a few records, stroking in forty-eight runs in one match against the Barstool Runners, a well-known outfit from Yonsh.

Chooks hanging around the ball games called him Scars and cheered every time he connected and sent the small white ball hurtling away toward the distant boundary.

Ware noticed that Thru had become much more serious about archery practice, too. In the mornings, almost every day, he found his oldest son shooting at a target over two hundred paces away. Thru now carried a dozen steel points in his quiver, and all his arrows were fully fletched.

Ware Gillo was impressed. Suddenly he found himself wishing he had gone to Highnoth when he was young.

And yet, Ware had never felt the pull to do that when he was young. He had always wanted to farm, to improve his holdings.

The two hunted rabbits together one day. Ware rarely bothered to shoot since Thru was more accurate by far at the longer ranges. They took a brace and one extra. Old Aunt Paidi was alone now and needed help to make ends meet.

Ware made sure to take these moments slowly and to the full. For father and son would not have many more, something told him. His first son had grown up to be an unusually wise and gifted young mot. Soon, this most precious youth would move on to a wider world. Ware knew it in his heart. But he would have the memory of these times, when they were two mots together out hunting on the heath.

When they walked home, the evening light was bending golden gleams across the woods and fields. They discussed the major problem facing the family, Pern Treevi's claim against the seapond.

"Advocate Reems suggests that we will win. The deeds that Pern offers to back his claim are worthless. Only one of them refers to our seapond, and it does not confer inheritance rights. The deed that we have, from grandfather Thru, has full inheritance rights, with all names filled out and signed upon. Unshakable, says Reems."

"Sounds strong enough to me."

"It is strong, but there is one weakness. The Ugerbuds."

The Ugerbuds were the brilby clan that were also attached to that particular seapond. Every seapond had as partners in it a family or clan of brilbies. Brilbies were so big, so strong, and so good at swimming that they naturally undertook seapond work.

"We are still at odds with the Ugerbuds, I take it."

"Brilbies always cut a hard deal, but the Ugerbuds went too far. Half and half alike is the share. None of this percentages of whelk and percentages of mussel. I want no whelks in our pond."

"No whelks, of course. But brilbies always want to have whelk; they love the meat."

"And we get whelks going after the mussels and the clams. Still, it is a good seapond. We have farmed it for eighty years or more."

"How does Pern think he can win? Even Ugerbuds cannot dispossess you."

"But with their ancestral rights they can influence the judge and perhaps get him to offer us another seapond as compensation. But it would never be as good as ours, so we better not come up before a judge who likes brilbies more than usual."

"Pern must have had rights to a seapond, what happened to them?"

"Pern gave up his right to his own family seapond, when he swapped it all for the big field he set that house in."

"Seemed like a waste of a fine field to me."

"I heard that his pretty young wife wanted a fine house for her own. Wasn't content to bunk up in the old Treevi house."

"So Pern built a big house for Iallia?"

"Well, maybe. I tend to think Pern built it for himself. He gives himself airs does young Pern. He intends to buy a lot of polder, expand his waterbush production to make commercial quantities, and remake Warkeen Village into a thread-and-cloth town."

"There's not enough cloth on the market from the Braided Valley?"

"Not to mention Fauste and Mauste."

Thru thought again.

"But it is true that it can make a town powerfully prosperous. Lot of folk would come to live here. Work in the mills."

"All polder and no field. No beach, all seapond."

"Right, it would mean too many people. Warkeen is a village. So is Juno and Yonsh and every other place on the Dristen. Why should it grow to be a town?"

"Because Pern Treevi wants to be rich." Ware's disapproval was plain in his voice.

"That field does have a strong stream running beside it," said Thru.

"Comes out of the springs up on the hill above."

"So that'll run his mill, and he'd get folks from all around to come and live here?"

"I suppose. Have to build some houses. Be popular with the brilbies, see," said Ware.

"I do, and that's where we could have trouble with the Ugerbuds. Brilbies get a lot of work if Pern gets his way."

"But what they don't see is that Pern would also bring in more brilbies, too. They'd be attracted from poor parts of the coast. So there'd be a lot of competition for the Ugerbuds."

"So nobody would win but Pern Treevi. Doesn't sound like much of a plan to me."

Ware nodded. "Pern isn't the most popular mot in this village right now, that's for sure."

One day Thru turned a corner in the village and found himself face-to-face with Iallia. She was alone, carrying a basket of flowers, fresh cut from her mother's garden. It was the first time he had seen her so closely since before that terrible day.

"Hello, Thru," she said while she took in the changes in him.

Thru merely gave her a nod in reply. He had nothing to say to her.

"Thru Gillo, won't you speak to me? Stay a while."

"I think not."

"Don't you still love me, Thru?"

"No, Iallia, I do not."

Her brows rose at this. "You lie. You will always be mine. I know I held your heart in my hand."

"You did not want it. It no longer lies there. That is not the way of the Spirit."

"Bah, you were in Highnoth too long. You have lost

your balls. Don't you get hard at night thinking of snuggling with me like we used to?"

"No, I do not Iallia. You are Pern's now."

Something went cold in her eyes.

"Those old creatures up there took your Spirit. You are not worth breeding with."

She left him, anger evident in every movement.

He shrugged and went on. It no longer affected him. That callow young motling was no more.

Ual waited a good long while before she approached her son. "Will you wear waterweed this summer? Is there a mor that you desire?"

"Ah, no, Mother. I do not think I will do that this year."

"Why ever not? You are not too young to wed and start building your own family."

"I am not ready, that is why. It is too soon since I returned from Highnoth. I would be poor company for any female right now."

"All you have to do is listen to her, like any other mot. Let me suggest a pond for your waterweeds."

Thru knew her motives were pure enough. It was strange, especially to Thru himself, that he didn't want to attend waterweeding. It was a way of gathering together that brought on a different kind of intimacy. When lovemaking grew out of the waterweeds ceremonies and parties it grew on the strongest basis, for to be naked with each other was to be with the Spirit. Pretense and artifice were stripped away, and mot and mor responded to each other more naturally.

But he just didn't want to go this year. After Highnoth, where he had learned to control his sexual passions, he had achieved a sense of calm control. Underneath that he was a little frightened at releasing those emotions again. No doubt it was a result of being hurt so badly by Iallia's treachery. However, he had learned that delaying some things was not so bad an idea.

"The Meeders have many pretty mors your age that

are coming up. Might want to think about that, son of
mine.''

Ual would have been overjoyed to wed her son Thru
to a distant cousin in the Meeder clan, her own birth-
family.

Thru listened with one ear. He was thinking about
Dronned more and more. Master Sassadzu had spoken
highly of his weaves, and had even bought one of Thru's
"Chooks and Beetles" for the Highnoth weaving gallery
itself. That had encouraged Thru to consider the life of
a free weaver. In Dronned he would rent rooms to live
and work in, and sell his products in the open market at
festival times. That appealed to him more than the quiet
life of Warkeen.

Ware had warned him that the standards were high in
the Guild Crafts in Dronned.

"It may not be quite so easy to gain entry to the Guild
as you think.''

Thru was not to be deterred.

"If my work is good enough, surely that will be
enough?''

"Well, perhaps, but the guilds are exclusive. The city
is treacherous, my son.''

As summer wore on and time became more abundant,
Thru set up a loom and started weaving in earnest. He
produced a bold new pattern of large waterbush leaves,
entwined with lilies, greens upon a pale blue of washed
cornstalk. The waterbush leaves were worked in with
bush fiber, bush stem, and watercane split and peeled.
For the green leaves he used twisted marsh grass. The
result was a dramatic image, worked up to a high level
of definition. The mats were the sort that would be
placed in the best room and kept for years.

Once finished, the mats were wrapped in rough paper
and stored in Ware's carpentry shop, which had racks
and flats of many different kinds available. Thru was
working up mats that were two arms' widths wide and
three long, finishing each one in about five days, and he
estimated he would have perhaps nine or ten ready by

the time he set off to Dronned. That might earn him enough to get through the winter. He would find a room in a boardinghouse and a room in a work-house. He would need studio space to work. Eventually, perhaps, he would even expand and hire a youngster to prep the bush fiber and marsh grass for him.

So while Ual schemed to pair him with one of several young female cousins, Thru dreamed of a very different style of life in the city down the coast.

Chapter 10

It was a glorious day in midsummer and a considerable crowd had gathered at the ball field in Warkeen. Warkeen Village was playing a team put up by Meever's Tavern. The pretty young mors of the village gathered at the fence or took seats on the raised benches. Around them clustered young mots eager to make an impression. The older members of the crowd, mostly mots who'd played the game in their youth, were grouped behind protective netting close to the batting tree.

The tavern team had been boosted by the importation of a trio of high-quality throwers brought in with Pern Treevi's money. It was clear to anyone who knew the game that these young throwers were far too good for the village boys. Even when the Warkeen team got wood to the ball it usually flew off behind for no run and once or twice flew straight back and rapped off the red-painted tree trunk for a strike.

The Warkeen team, first to bat, was in danger of being routed. Kels Geliver was dismissed early for just eight runs when the score was twenty-one. It looked as if they might be all out for forty or less, and would certainly lose to Meever's.

Then Thru went in. He took up the bat and measured himself on the hitting crease. Behind him loomed the red zone, the target for the throwers. Ahead of him the throwers were waiting on the line, and beyond them the fielders were waiting.

Far beyond them was the line of white stakes marking the boundary to which he could hit, for a full 180 degrees in front of him. Every ball struck across the boundary line would be a run. Every ball that went past him and struck the red zone on the tree would add a strike. Every ball that he hit high and was caught was also a strike and every batter had four strikes.

The first ball came whizzing in. Thru judged it in the split second he saw it and swung.

Crack! came the sound of the perfectly struck ball, and it soared into the sky while fielders backed up and ran for the boundary.

There was a cheer from the crowd as the ball wafted safely across the boundary and into the trees.

Thru was on the scoreboard.

And in came the next.

Crack!

Thus it went and Thru moved in the kyo of the game. He watched, judged, and began the swing in the same moment. His motion was fluid and seemed effortless. The bat never felt heavy in his hands. Only occasionally was he forced to a defensive stroke, and those he always got down so that they bounced out into the field of play and did not offer up a catch.

He had passed ten before the first ball got past him and hit the red zone. He reached twenty-five before a catch put him halfway out. The third point was taken by a ball that clipped the top of the bat's blade and then slapped the red trunk on its way to the rear. By then he'd struck forty and was settled in and quite deadly.

The throwers were tiring. Thru had taken the starch out of them with an hour-long stand at the tree. As they tired, so they threw wide more often and Thru rested his arms and waited for the ball that would suit him best. When such a ball came he brought the bat around with the sweet swing that as often as not sent such a ball right out of the playing zone.

He struck up fifty after an hour and a half, and the throwers from Dronned were relieved by Pek Pilss, Rindo Yuster, and more familiar names from Meever's ranks. Unfortunately, they were not nearly as good as the pros up from Dronned, and Thru's bat continued to deal with them harshly.

He passed sixty and went on. Now the excitement in the crowd was swelling. Thru was hitting up a record number for a game played at this level. More folk were coming out of the village and even riding down from neighboring Juno, up the river, to see history in the making.

The Meever's throwers were in desperate straits. They ran to the line and hurled the small white balls at the tree, but Thru struck them back with graceful fury. Fielders ran hither and yon, wearing themselves to a frazzle. Thru played more defensive strokes as the time wore on, and he tired, but he avoided skying the ball and giving up that final out. Nor could the throwers get past him and strike the red zone.

And where a ball came wide, but was in his reach for a deflection shot, he would try his skill. Few fielders were stationed in reach of the near and farside parts of the field, and a well-deflected ball might easily bounce to the boundary before a fielder could run across from his more central position.

At seventy he paused for a large drink of water. The throwers were just as glad of the break. There was a hum of excitement in the crowd around the ball field.

He resumed and went on to seventy-seven, where he finally got under a ball and skyed it high, which allowed a catch by Pills.

Thru stepped out with Warkeen on ninety-eight runs. A solid enough score, but there were plenty of batters to come. It looked as if Warkeen could run up a comfortable 150 or so. A score that would be very hard for the Meever's Tavern team to approach.

Thru stood back behind the nets and the throng of the cognoscenti watching the batting tree. The congratulations poured in; he nodded and thanked folk and tried just to enjoy the moment. Seventy-seven runs in a single inning! It was a record, a tremendous record, far in advance of the old one, and the cheers and the sense of accomplishment were heady. It was almost like drinking one's first mug of ale after a long time without, and he felt a little giddy.

It was a good time to fall back on his training with Master Utnapishtim. The kyo of breath and relaxation, the way to the calm place.

He had found a unique fusion of the kyo and the swing of the bat, something to bless the Spirit for conferring upon him.

So he let the adulation wash around him, understanding that it was as much for the moment as it was for him.

And you had to wonder at the lot of them, getting this worked up about such a trivial pastime. Except that it pleased the eye of many on a warm afternoon in the lazy summer to watch young mots striking the small white ball for the distant boundary.

So much passion for such a simple thing!

Pern had been much in evidence behind the tree while Warkeen were tumbling badly in the early going. Iallia and her friends had taken a position on the raised bench behind the line.

As Thru struck his first fifteen Pern clung to his good humor. As Thru struck into the twenties before giving up a second strike, Pern became less amused. By the fortieth run, Pern was scowling and having notes taken of the quality of the throwing by the pros he'd hired up from Dronned.

Pern stayed for the fifty, but could not bring himself to join in the applause that was ringing around the small crowd. As the score continued building Pern scowled openly, groaned, and threw a fist into the sky. He departed at sixty-two, suddenly snapping and ordering up his flashy coach, pulled by a team of donkeys.

He left with harsh cracks of the whip over the heads of the animals. Before he left he had his hired tough, Ulghrum, pluck Iallia from her place on the high bench and put her in the coach, despite her protests.

The match was the crowning moment of the season for the village of Warkeen. The village team's best throwers were not as good as the mots from Dronned, but they were good enough to maintain the lead. That night the revelers kept it up way into the wee hours of morning. Thru enjoyed an ale or two himself, then retired and fell asleep, worn-out by the strong emotions of the day.

A few days later the lawsuit brought by Pern Treevi was heard by the traveling Circuit Judge sent out from the Royal Court in Dronned. The court sat in the constable's office, which was hot and crowded when all the Gillos, plus Pern Treevi and his team of legal advocates, were gathered inside.

The judge gaveled the session into order and began an examination of the papers. He searched through them, studied the deed, checked the seal for authenticity with a book of seals, and looked up.

"These papers as presented by Ware Gillo appear to be correct and in order."

Arguments were then presented by the legal advocates. These arguments were laced with airy verbiage and long, complex references to ancient laws governing the construction and maintenance of seaponds.

The judge listened patiently for several hours. When the Treevi lawyers had finally finished their presentation the judge referred to several notes. Then he called the lawyers forward and peppered them with questions.

"Where, in all this train of argument, do you make the case that Ware Gillo's deed to the seapond in question is without merit?"

The lawyers hemmed and hawed, one or two began long perorations, but the judge cut them short.

"Have you any evidence that invalidates this deed?" He raised the deed and showed it to them.

There was no such evidence.

After a short summation of the case the judge announced that he had found in favor of Ware Gillo. The seapond belonged to Ware Gillo, by clear title and deed.

Outside the constable's office Pern Treevi and his friends gathered in an angry group and raked the Gillos with hard stares. Ware and Thru brought up the rear of the Gillo family and returned the hard stares with smiles, ignoring the malice directed toward them.

There was a long, loud celebration at the Gillo house that night, and Thru found himself receiving the attention of several of the young mors who were present, as well as indulgent smiles from mothers and grandmothers. His own mother, meanwhile, watched him with an anxious eye.

He knew she was desperate to have him fall in love with a family mor and settle and live in the community, adding to her kin-group. Going off to Dronned opened up all sorts of other possibilities, none of which she liked to consider.

But Thru remained unmoved throughout it all. He was happy to talk, cheerful and open, and yet he did not call on the young mors afterward.

He finished the great "Chooks and Beetles" mat and laid it up with the others, then decided on a final hike up to Cormorant Rock, just to see the great view of the land once more before heading south to Dronned.

As he went northward on the trail he had the feeling that someone was following him. At a sudden turn in the trail where it hooked around a crag, he ran ahead and climbed to the ridgeline some two hundred feet above. He crouched immobile behind a tree and watched the trail below.

After a little while he saw Ulghrum, Pern's hired heavyweight, stealing along the trail. Ulghrum slowed when he realized that there was no sign ahead of Thru. He slipped off the trail and hid himself behind some bushes.

Thru thought about this and its implications. None were good. He doubled back behind Ulghrum and got into a position where he could watch. Ulghrum stealthily crept back to the trail and looked up and down, then he crossed it and began to climb the mossy soil under the trees. As Thru watched, Ulghrum carefully tracked up the ridgeline until he came on Thru's tracks near the top.

Ulghrum immediately hid himself.

Thru nocked an arrow and waited.

After several minutes had gone by he saw Ulghrum leave cover and start to move along the ridgeline, following Thru's trail. Ulghrum had drawn his own bow and nocked an arrow.

There was no doubt in Thru's mind that Ulghrum planned to kill him.

Still, he could not take the mot's life without breaking the law. It would be murder to kill Ulghrum. And there were no witnesses to a plea of self-defense.

Therefore, he released his arrow from hiding and at a long range. The arrow sank into the tree above Ulghrum's head, just where he'd wanted it. Ulghrum went to ground, but he did not know where Thru was, only the direction.

While he studied the ground desperately trying to spot Thru, Thru had already moved and was within easy bowshot.

"Set the bow down, very slowly," Thru called when he was ready. "Do it right now or you die."

Ulghrum stiffened, then laid down his bow.

"Keep your hands well up."

"Why are you threatening me, whoever you are? Are you a robber?"

"Why are you following me with a drawn bow, Ulghrum?"

"I'm just out hunting. There are rabbits up here."

"That's why you followed me?"

"I never saw your trail, stranger."

Thru laughed. "Make sure you stay off my trail, Ulghrum."

Thru watched until Ulghrum had retreated, leaving his bow behind. Then he took the bow and pitched it off the ridgeline down into a tangled mass of spine bush.

Thru went home and thought it all through very carefully. He was about to leave the village, and though he would come back, he was shifting away from the place of his birth. When he was gone there would be less opportunity for him to rub Pern the wrong way. Thru was sure that Pern's hate was directed at Thru himself, far more than at the other members of his family. Pern was pursuing lawsuits against two other Warkeen families over their seapond. There was no particular animus against Ware Gillo.

He decided to take no action other than telling his father, just in case Pern tried again with more success, and to be sure that the other families engaged in altercations with Pern could be warned. Ware understood, and agreed with Thru's conclusions.

"Pern hates you, young Thru. You outshine him, and he can't stand that. You will have nothing but trouble from him, that's plain as day. What if his thugs follow you to Dronned?"

"I will be hard to find I would think."

Ware laughed. "I don't think so, my son. Dronned's not that big a place, and when folk are determined they can find you. A little silver spread around always helps wag the tongues."

"But why would he bother when I will be so far away? It's thirty miles to Dronned. I'll be out of his hair and out of his mind. Besides, what's to be done? Should I waylay Pern and beat him senseless? That would only hasten his hate. Should I kill him? That would only make me outlaw. I would prefer to live with the Spirit."

Thru shrugged. "No. It is better I do nothing. Let him feel my contempt until I leave. He may even comfort himself by imagining that I have run away in fear of him. Let him assuage his pride with that thought and thereby end this whole thing."

Ware nodded agreement. His son spoke words of wisdom, but still he was not so sure that Pern Treevi's urge to revenge himself on Thru would end so quietly.

Two days later, Thru set out with a small donkey cart laden with his weaves and two packs stuffed with his possessions, everything from his clothing to his books.

In addition he had a number of samples of waterbush fiber from friends of the Gillos. These were to be shown to Merchant Yadrone in Dronned. Yadrone was a well-known figure in the Dristen Valley villages.

Altogether the little donkey had quite enough to carry as they moved away down the south road, quite a few of Thru's friends coming with him on the first few miles. Pern would not dare make a move against Thru on the trail with so many to witness. Afterward Thru waved them good-bye and went on to spend the night in the village of Sheen. The next day he went on down the coast road toward Dronned, amongst a constant traffic of carts and other travelers and stopped worrying about Pern Treevi's plots and machinations.

Chapter 11

When Thru arrived in Dronned, the grey walls were draped in bright tapestries in preparation for the upcoming midsummer festival. Atop the towers flew all the city's banners, dominated by the arms of the royal family—four black crows on a green flag. Also clearly visible was the long white pennon that marked the presence of an Assenzi in the city, in this case the very wise Melidofulo.

Dronned sprawled beyond its wall on the northern side, and Thru strode through a suburb of well-built wood-and-stone houses. Within the walls, the buildings were tall and narrow, built of stone and roofed in slate. The streets were paved, well drained, and clean. Travelers always remarked on how clean-smelling Dronned was.

And yet, the street life in the city was frantic by comparison with Warkeen Village. Traders and tradesmen were in constant motion. Dronned was an important center for several crafts and guilds, with weavers, ironworkers, and potters the most heavily represented. Shops and stalls lined the most important streets and were visited by large numbers of customers. There were mors by the hundreds, all out to buy supplies for villages in the surrounding region. While shoppers shopped, others relaxed in the beer gardens in all the important squares, where there were to be found troupes of musicians, jugglers, and mimes.

In the great market by the river, the permanent shops and emporia were all open and filled with early arrivals.

The festival brought in folk from far and wide, and they would also attend the market. Then the great space would blossom with dozens of stalls and stands set up by the fiber merchants. In the meantime the merchants got ready, laying in a provision of everything from ornamental tile to brightly colored house mats.

Thru stalked around the market once, peering in the windows at the goods within: fine silk from Mauste, rugs from the Farblow Hills, copper pans from Ajutan. He came across an office that listed lodgings available and realized quite quickly that rents in the Quarters, as the parts inside the walls were called, were too high for him. Rents in the northern suburb were lower, and so he turned back and tried along the leafy roads and lanes.

He passed the Laughing Fish Tavern and the old ball field where he'd played in that memorable championship game. But the memories of that day were mixed, and he shook his head and went on.

He was in luck, and soon found a nice room in a house on Garth Road. He had a view of the ball field and the distant royal park. The roofs of the palace were visible through the trees. Garth Road was lined with tenements, mostly three stories tall. In them lived many of the working folk of the city, most of them young and single.

The house had seven rented rooms, one of which happened to be empty when he called. The owner was a plump mor named Kussha, who lived in the building across the road. She was a cheerful sort, who pressed sweet cakes on him while they discussed his possible tenancy in her house. She was well used to young mots like Thru, come to the city to try their hands at the craft of one thing or another. She took a liking to him at once and showed him the room that she had free.

Thru liked the feel of the house, which was built on timbers of oak and foundations of stone. His small room at the back of the top floor didn't have much floor space, but he had a bed, a chair, and a small table on which to rest a lamp.

He paid Kussha some of his precious hoard of silver

for the room then she showed him her lock-up, a store-room in the cellar with a very stout door and a heavy iron lock. There he left his mats and his bow and the quiver with its dozen steel points.

In the room he hung his cloak on the hook on the back of the door. He put his few books under the bed, except for the Book of the Spirit, from which he read a few short pieces, seeking some kind of blessing for the room and his time in it. Then he meditated while sitting quietly on the cot, trying to let the great Spirit fill him with its wisdom. While in that quiet state he listened to the sounds of the empty house. A breeze rattled the shutters. Outside there came the clop of a donkey's hooves in the street. Later he put up the Spirit sign that Ual had given him on his tenth birthday, a small disc of polished wood with the words of the benediction carved into its rim. It hung on the wall from a hook, near the table with the jug and washbasin.

He washed and took a look at himself in the metal mirror on the wall. Level grey eyes looked back at him, and he noted the straight nose, the thin scars on the left side of his face, the eyebrows that weren't quite as bushy as everyone else's. He was the same Thru Gillo who had planted waterbush in the spring and hit seventy-seven runs in the game against Meever's. Only now he was living in the big city. Now he was just one of a thousand young mots seeking his place in the world outside the village and the agricultural life. Everything from here on would be up to him. He didn't have his father and mother to fall back on, nor his sister or brother to talk to if his spirits fell. He would have to make do with the company he found in this exciting place.

Kussha always served up a hot dinner at dusk. Her clientele dined in the manner of the Land, as the gourmets put it. She found that this was a great inducement to get her mostly male clientele back from the taverns and thereafter early to bed. This meant they rarely got drunk, and they usually paid their rent on time. Her cooking had long since made rooms in her house sought after. Thru had been lucky to find a space there.

At the evening meal that night, which was as good as anything he might have had in the finest restaurants, he met the other lodgers. The oldest tenant was Rogon, a plain-faced carpenter with a strong Dronned accent in his speech. Gulf and Ollo were both potters. Bluit was a day servant in a merchant's house in the South Quarter, and young Noop Minchant, from Yebesh out in the eastern hills, worked in a metal foundry in the River Quarter.

Noop and old Bluit remembered Thru. They'd been in the crowd at the championship match three summers before.

"I saw you play against the Laughing Fish," said Noop. "And you won the game. It was much against expectations around here."

"A fine stroke you have, young Thru Gillo," said old Bluit.

Kussha was most impressed when she heard that she had a young athlete in her house. She'd known in her heart that he was a good one. Sometimes she'd been disappointed in the past with young mots from the countryside trying to make a living in the town. Once in a while they skipped without paying the rent. But Thru she sensed was not that kind.

Over a plate of shrimp dumplings in oil sauce with beer and fresh-baked bread, Thru was drawn into the conversation.

"How you like Kussha's cooking " said Noop when he thought Kussha had left the house.

"Truth be told, I've never had dumplings like these, so light and yet so tasty."

"Wait 'til you taste her beanpod pie," said Ollo. "That is perfection."

"If you like beanpod pie," grumbled Gulf.

"What do you think the market will be like this year?" asked Thru, after a while, voicing the burning question in his own mind.

"Oh, it will be good," said Ollo. "All the portents are there. Large numbers of visitors are booked in."

Gulf shook his head. He and Ollo rarely agreed.

"I expect a more modest market this year. Last year's was too big. People will not come in the same numbers again."

"But the rites for the festival will be held in the royal park this year. That will be sure to bring folk in from the countryside."

"But that doesn't mean they'll be buying in Dronned market."

"Enough of them will be; there'll be money to be made."

"Good coin of the realm to rub together," said Rogon.

"Have you ever been to the summer rites in Dronned?" said Ollo.

Thru shook his head. "No."

"Then you have much to see. The rites are performed with a special intensity here in Dronned. With all the costumes and the dancing, it's far more of an event than it is anywhere else in the Land."

"Bah," grumbled Gulf. "It's all too much fuss and feathers. I like the village ceremony, with none of your acting and mumming, and a lot less singing those slow hymns."

"When was Gulf last seen going to any ceremonies?" said Noop with cheeky insouciance.

"Bah, it's all nonsense. I have weaving to do."

"Well, I'm looking forward to it," said Thru.

After a dessert of peach pie dressed with waterbush cream, Thru was completely converted to the cuisine of Kussha's house. Some of the others went up to their rooms, but Thru was too excited by being in Dronned to sleep just yet, despite a long day's traveling.

He sat out on the porch with Noop and old Bluit and shared a pitcher of ale. The moon was almost full, and it was a warm night. Bluit wanted to know if Thru planned to try out for the Laughing Fish, the top Dronned team.

"I don't know. I might be too busy." And in his heart Thru still played on the Warkeen Village team. He wasn't sure yet that he wanted to play for any other.

"The top teams will always help a player like you," Bluit suggested.

"It's different to play for money, don't you think?"

"Oh, of course, but if it's just a little help, what does it matter?"

"I'm here to sell my weaves. If I find the time to play, then I'll consider it. There are plenty of good teams in this city, I know that."

"Well, the Laughing Fish are already in the hunt for the championship of the city," Bluit said fervently, betraying his own active support.

Thru nodded politely, storing the information, but he remained determined on a career with the mats. The game worked on a plane above that of strictly material life. There was something about it that he didn't wish to trade for the gross gloss of gold.

In the next few days he explored Dronned with every waking moment. He felt the energy in the place awaken something in himself. Just having so many folk around one, with constant activity in the streets, was amazing.

His first order of business was to call on the Merchant Yadrone, for whom he carried some letters and the samples of fiber entrusted to his care by family friends. Yadrone's house was a tall, four-story building of stone in the North Quarter overlooking the New Bridge. Thru was welcomed in with enthusiasm by the housekeeper and ushered into a well-appointed parlor to wait. On the walls were various weave works, including an old version of "Chooks and Beetles" by the renowned Mesho.

Thru noted Mesho's meticulous use of scale, the sharp definition that he achieved with his mix of fibers. The chooks were so lifelike, so cleverly caught in their dance across the field, that it took one's breath away.

Thru wondered how his own work would stack up against it.

Yadrone appeared quite shortly and behind his portly

figure came the housekeeper with a tray bearing hot chocolate sweetened with sugar. While they sipped this delicious luxury from the tropics, Yadrone examined the fiber samples and barked notes to a scribe. Yadrone asked questions about Warkeen and inquired after Ware.

"I heard about that business with Pern Treevi and your family's seapond. Terrible foolishness."

Yadrone fingered the fibers and made mental calculations. Then he barked more notes to the scribe.

"Geluba's farm, I think you said, for this one." He held up a swatch of grey-green fiber.

"Yes, indeed."

"Good. Now listen to me, young Thru Gillo. You have to be careful in that weave market. There are plenty of skinners and blupers, and they'll cut your purse from under you if you let them. They're as bad as the cloth merchants."

"Thank you, sir, but my father gave me similar warnings. I promise that I will take them seriously."

"Good, see that you do. By the Spirit you need your wits about you in the market these days. Why just the other day . . ."

Thru listened, storing information as the merchant told stories of the market in recent years and contrasted it with earlier times. It was all fascinating to Thru, who knew he had a lot to learn.

"Pardon me, I'm a terrible host. Your cup is empty. Can I offer you more of this sinfully delicious chocolate?"

Thru was happy to accept. Chocolate was not unknown in his village, but it was a rarity, coming as it did from the tropical isles

He sipped and savored the rich intensity of flavor, so unlike any other flavor that he knew of.

After a while the merchant fell quiet after a particularly good story about cheats in the woven-mat business.

Thru tapped his cup.

"I know it comes from the tropics, but I don't understand how it gets here."

"Ah, the chocolate trade, a very romantic subject. It

is grown far to the south, on the isles of Berguba. The cocoa tree does very well there."

"How far is it?"

"The merchants speak of the sun standing due overhead, every day, which must mean they are in the equatorial regions of the world. It takes them two months to return, if the winds are favorable, and longer if they are not."

Thru mulled that over as he strolled along through the market after his visit to the Merchant Yadrone. As far as he felt he'd traveled in his own life, to Highnoth and to the Farblow Hills, his journeys were tiny compared to voyaging to the equatorial isles of Berguba.

It was a big world, and he felt the pressure of the opportunities that awaited him.

He took one of his mats with the bright leaf pattern on it around the bigger houses in the weave market. Merchant Ortenod liked the work and took consignment of a sample.

"If it sells, then I'll want more. Can you supply?"

"Oh yes, I have ten of this pattern."

"Excellent. Bring me another pair, and we will see. Understand that this is an exclusive for my shop. You may not sell them to anyone else in the market."

"I understand, but this exclusivity is only for this pattern. I have another mat, of a higher quality."

"Higher quality?"

"It is a new style of 'Chooks and Beetles.'"

"Indeed. So, you aspire to wall mats and the like."

"Master Sassadzu in Highnoth suggested I try the House Norvory."

"Ah, well then you're in good hands. Ueillim Norvory is a good mot to deal with for such high-end products. He has impeccable taste."

Thru hurried back to the house in Garth Road and picked up another couple of mats with his bold new leaf pattern. Back in the market, mats delivered, he took stock in a tavern on the corner. He had made his first placements. He had money in his pocket, and if his work sold, he'd have more money to come.

If he sold all of the mats he had he would realize two hundred silvers, about the same as two and a half gold crowns. That would be enough for him to live right through the winter at Kussha's house.

Thru went back to the house and took "Chooks and Beetles" out of Kussha's lock-up in the basement. He spread the mat out in the parlor and contemplated his work.

After Mesho it seemed crude in the finishing, lacking Mesho's incredible realness. He kept looking, though, and found that he still liked his own work. Mesho it was not, but the image on his mat was nicely rendered; his work had an interesting rake to it. The jaunty chooks looked quite crazy. The beetles were diagrammatical, faintly alarming in size. His work might appeal to someone who could not afford Mesho, someone who might enjoy the slightly eccentric cast he gave to the ancient pattern.

He rolled it up and put it away under his bed.

The next day he presented a note at the door of the merchant prince Uellim Grys Norvory three steps up from the level of the street and fronted by a small covered platform. The note was taken up by a very snooty little mor, who then closed the door on him.

"Wait here for a reply."

He waited standing on the solid steps of the merchant's rather grand house, "Chooks and Beetles" rolled up in its oilskin beside him.

The door opened and the young mor was back, with a slightly embarrassed look in her eyes. He followed behind her, frankly admiring her shapely little form all the way down a long hallway. She led him through a door into a large room, hung with mats and tapestries, then she left him with a smile and a nod.

There was another Mesho on the near wall, a strongly accented "Brilbies at the Gate." Behind the three brilbies of the classic pattern, the trees of the wood held dozens of birds.

And there on the end wall, in pride of place was a classic "Chooks and Beetles" by Oromi, the great artist of the weave in the 203rd century.

Just for a moment, Thru faltered and felt his self-confidence draining away. Who was he to be offering up a "Chooks and Beetles" here? Like he was some great artist. He was in the house of a baron, an important personage at the Royal Court, and he was just Thru Gillo, a complete unknown. Then he recalled Master Sassadzu's calm words of encouragement.

"Obstacles will appear, but you will sweep them away. Remain true to the simple message of the spirit, and your kyo will flourish." He had to hope that even if he wasn't as great as Oromi or Mesho, he might still be good enough.

The door opened a few moments later and in came the Grys Norvory, a well-fed mot of middle age wearing a white tunic and purple trousers. The Grys came right across the room and shook Thru's hands warmly.

"Welcome, ah, Thru Gillo. You have work you would like to show?"

"Yes, Grys Norvory."

"I am always looking for fresh weaving." Thru smiled and nodded, hoping that his work would be good enough.

"Good," said the Grys.

There was a twinkle in the aristocrat's eyes, and Thru immediately became wary. In this game Thru had only his work to play with, and the Grys had everything else.

"Now, you have something to show me I believe?"

"Ah, yes, Grys Norvory."

Thru unrolled his "Chooks and Beetles" and laid it out on the big table.

Ueillim Norvory cast an eye on the piece and nodded happily. The piece was charming, a wry twist on the ancient pattern. Fresh, but not unnaturally advanced.

"Mmmm. An interesting approach. You have talent,

young mot. 'Chooks and Beetles' is a favorite of my own, as you would expect seeing the Oromi on the wall, here."

"Yes, Grys Norvory, it is beautiful."

"Few of us can aspire to the status of Oromi, but some of us can at least make the attempt. Young Thru Gillo, I think you can certainly do that."

The Grys bent over the work and examined it with a magnifier.

"I think the piece will sell for twenty gold pieces, retail. I will mount it for the festival. If it sells, you will receive twelve."

Thru's heart jumped. Twelve gold pieces would keep him in luxury for a year and let him send coin back to Ware and Ual in the village, too.

While he thought about the offer, the Grys continued to wield the magnifying lens, going over the mat very carefully. He was checking Thru's stitching and knots, examining his technique for possible faults.

He turned it over and looked carefully, and then turned it back.

"This is good work. I am impressed, young mot. My gallery always draws a good crowd at festival. I'm confident we will find a buyer."

"Thank you, Grys Norvory. I will accept the offer."

"Good. I will have the papers drawn up at once."

The Grys rang for a secretary, then ordered some tea brought in. They drank tea and ate small butter biscuits to seal the deal.

After leaving the mansion, Thru walked along the main streets of the city with his head in the clouds. He had come to the city and found himself a good room to live in. He'd got a deal for selling his "Leaf" mats and he had a gallery accept his "Chooks and Beetles." If he sold a few "Leaf" mats, he would earn enough to make it through the winter. If he sold "Chooks and Beetles" he would be well set for a year or more.

It was time to turn his thoughts to finding a work space, perhaps in the Quarters. It would be nice to be in the center of things. He wandered that way and came upon a troupe of street jugglers and acrobats at work on the corner of Grand Street. A figure in a tight-fitting scarlet costume was tumbling and somersaulting. It was Nuza and Her Magnificents, the same group Thru had seen with Meu and Utnapishtim in the Farblow town of Lushtan. Flips and rolls, high jumps and somersaults, the scarlet figure continued down the pavement while her friends went by with drum and whistle, the signboard held high.

Thru watched for a while, enjoying the sight of the lithe figure bouncing and flying into the air. She ran, somersaulted, and flew into the arms of the big brilby, who caught her like she was no more than a kitten and set her down with a graceful flourish.

She bounced up with her hands high and bowed to the thin crowd along the pavement. There was more scattered applause. Her glance met his, and Thru felt something go through him that he never could explain. It was as if he knew her from a former life.

She grinned at him and went back into the air for another somersault down the block. The mot with the signboard gave Thru a peculiarly intense look.

Following the troupe came the barker, calling loudly from the street that Nuza and Her Magnificents would appear that evening, in the open space by the Laughing Fish Tavern. A full display was planned, with jugglers, clowns, and an exhibition of the craft of swordfighting by Toshak the Great.

Thru took the corner and went up Grand Street. That image of Nuza doing that backward somersault didn't go away. She had to be as supple as a snake, and probably just as strong. He had an odd urge to laugh out loud, which he suppressed; but he did find himself smiling. There had been a friendly message in her eyes, and he wanted to hear it from her lips.

He headed for the Guild Hall, where the craft industries in the city were regulated. He needed to register himself as a weaver working within Dronned. Only then could he be represented in the markets. Only then was he protected by the laws of the Guild and sure of having contracts with merchants enforced.

Under a complex roof of turrets and spires was a central hall with offices along the sides. Tables ran down the middle, where scribes and ordinary folk wrote with pen and ink.

At the first desk he explained to a narrow-faced mot with dark eyebrow tufts that he was new to the city and wished to set up a shop for weaving.

"Are you resident in the city?"

"Yes, now, I have a room near the royal park."

"Have you relatives who are already within the Guild?"

"No."

"Ah."

A message was scribbled on a scrap of paper.

"Take this to Desk Seven."

At Desk Seven he found a weary-looking mot of late middle age.

"You are nonnative to the city of Dronned, yes?" said this person.

"Yes."

"And you want to come to Dronned and take part in the craft of weaving?"

"Yes."

"Unfortunately the Guild of Weavers is full at the moment. Places rarely come open, and there is a waiting list."

"But I have already sold weaves here; surely I can join?"

"You have sold weaves? Here in the city?"

"Is it illegal? I'm sorry, I did not know."

"No. But it is outside Guild rules. We do not enforce such contracts."

"Can I not rent a room and just weave in it?"

"You cannot. As someone out to take work from the Guild membership, you cannot be allowed to rent work-rooms in the city of Dronned. If you do rent such rooms and work in them, you will be outside the Guild and therefore outside the protection of Guild Law."

"So if the merchants want to, they can refuse to pay me and I can do nothing?"

"Nothing within the law of the realm."

"Surely they will not be so harsh with me?"

"It depends on who you have dealings with. Some are like sharks, they'll take off your whole leg. Others are more subtle, but they bear watching, too."

Back outside the Guild Hall a little later Thru found himself standing on the wide plaza chewing his lip. He couldn't hope for a place in the Craft Guild of Weaving for two or three years. In that time no contracts he entered into would be legal. Anyone could cheat him.

His thought whirled to the Merchant Ortenod. Would he pay up for the mats that Thru had already delivered? He wouldn't have to, once he found out Thru's lack of status with the Guild. But he heartened himself with the memory of the merchant, who had seemed to be straightforward and honest. He had liked Thru's work.

But what if Thru had just been taken by a wise old trader who knew a pigeon when he saw one?

And then there was the "Chooks and Beetles." Even if the Grys Norvory kept his side of the deal, he would not be able to rent workrooms in the city.

Suddenly his enthusiasm for the city and his eagerness to try his mats in the market seemed foolish and ill–thought out. He should have checked here first. But he had been so keen to see if anyone would buy his work that he had put it off, and now he'd made himself vulnerable.

He could go back to Warkeen and work there, and bring his work to the fairs and the festival markets. But he would always be at the mercy of the merchants. And, somehow, such a move tasted of defeat.

Chapter 12

But before Thru could do anything about his weaving, the city shut down for the Rites of the Spirit for the summer festival, which were held in the royal park and drew a large crowd. Tiers of wooden seats had been set up, but all the best spots were taken long before Thru arrived. He wound up only getting the most distant glimpses of the mummers and the charms. But like everyone else, he was caught up in the huge emotions aroused by the singing of the great hymn that gave thanks for life to the Spirit.

Everyone left the rites that day with a fire in their hearts. It was a day of celebration and the markets were open and stands lined the road selling pickled melon and sweet beer. Others purveyed ears of grilled maize or crispy fried root.

Thru roamed around, enjoying the size of the crowd and the sense of occasion. He bought a bag of roasted chestnuts, ate some of them, and threw the rest to the squirrels that haunted the trees in the park. The squirrels always did well on festival days.

"Hail, Thru Gillo, how are you enjoying the day?"

"Hail, Noop, it's wonderful. This is very different from the village summer festival."

"Village festivals can be fun."

"I always thought so, but they're on a smaller scale."

"Have you thought about trying out for the Laughing Fish team yet?"

"Not really. Are they playing today?"

"No, not today; it would be disrespectful of the festival

to play today. They will play tomorrow, in the evening after work."

"Oh, of course." They took the rites very seriously in Dronned, it was plain. "Well, maybe I'll be able to watch."

"Won't you want to be out there swinging the bat?"

Thru grinned. "I don't know, not yet. I'm just enjoying the city too much."

"That reminds me, I'm thinking I'll stop in at the Laughing Fish for a draft on my way home. How about you, Thru Gillo?"

But Thru was staring over Noop's shoulder at a slender figure coming through the crowd.

"Excuse me, Noop, but there's someone I've got to speak to. I'll look in at the Laughing Fish, see if you're there later."

He moved to intercept her. When he was about ten feet away she looked up. And smiled.

"Hello." It sounded absurdly dramatic when he said it.

She had the street performer's confidence in public and knew all the lines. But he saw her eyes tighten a little when she saw him. There was something there.

"Well, hello to you," she said.

She remembered him! And his scarred face did not disturb her.

"What's your name?" she said. "I know you know mine."

"Thru."

"Thru who?"

"Thru Gillo. From Warkeen Village in the Dristen."

"The Thru Gillo, who holds the new record?"

She had heard of him? Slightly stunned, he nodded.

"Ah, yes."

"Why is it you seem so modest and nice when I would have expected a braggart?"

He shrugged.

"You aren't bashful, are you?"

"Well, I don't think so."

"That's good; bashful mots can be a trial. They have

a hard time speaking up." She grinned, enjoying his confusion.

"Sorry," he said, feeling oddly stupid and inept. "I just wanted to say, uh, hello. Your acrobatics were wonderful, I've never seen anything anywhere near that great."

"Well, thank you, Thru Gillo. That's very nice of you to say so."

For a long moment they stood there, smiling and looking around, unsure what to say.

"Well, I have to go." She nodded past him toward the city gate. "Guild Hall business."

"You have problems with the guilds, too?"

"Sure. We have to have a license, and it's renewed daily. Keeps us on our toes and makes sure we don't hurt any of the good citizenry of the town."

"Is it difficult to renew it?"

"Once in a while."

"May I walk with you?"

"You may. What's your problem with the guilds?"

"Oh, I want to be a weaver, but the Guild is full up and there's a waiting list."

"Well, you can't expect everything to just fall into your lap."

"I guess you're right about that." He tried to smile and almost succeeded.

"And it's the way the system works, you understand that, right?"

He looked up sharply.

"Ah, no."

"Well." She looked at him carefully, then went on. "The Assenzi keep our cities small deliberately. They control the sale of skilled products through the guilds, which are hard to get into. The cities don't grow. Folk stay in their villages. That's the way it was planned."

Thru was shocked by her words. He understood that the Assenzi had a plan for the Land, but he had never connected it to the Guild system. It seemed to go against reason. Why would they teach him the weaver's art if he was never to use it to make his living? Why would the

Assenzi, so kind and so gentle and so concerned with the lives of mots, set up such a heartbreaking system?

"But the crafts are set into guilds to keep quality high," he said. "Without the guilds, designs would be uncontrolled, the art would suffer."

"Quality can always be enforced by price. What does it matter if new designs are tried? How many copies of 'Brilbies at the Gate' do you want to see? Or 'Mots at Prayer'? How many 'Mots at Prayers' do you think we need? The Assenzi are very conservative about these things, perhaps too much so. Perhaps we need to grow, in order for our culture to expand, to achieve its potential. I sometimes think we're standing still, when we could be at a higher level."

She'd noticed his look of surprise. She was used to it. Whenever she spoke openly to somebody the first time, they usually had that look. She gave him a long look of her own and chewed her lip, suddenly certain of something.

"You ever been to Highnoth?" she said.

"Yes. For two years."

"Well, then you know them. The Assenzi keep alive our technical arts. They inspire young mots like yourself to go out and add their skill to the world. But they do many other things. They work to keep things from changing."

"You want to see more change?" he said, suddenly wondering about her. When he thought of change, he saw Pern Treevi's ungainly new house sitting in that field.

"I don't know. Sometimes I really question it all, and at other times I understand how beautiful our world is and how we must live to keep it that way."

"The Masters teach that stability is the way to the best kind of life, for everyone."

"The words of the Great Book are good. I don't question that. But there are so many rules."

"Not everyone obeys the rules."

"Another reason for the Assenzi to police our lives. They keep us on the straight and narrow track. But the most important thing is that our population must not outgrow our farmers' ability to feed it well. It keeps farmers from getting rich, but it also keeps people well fed and able to work."

"These all sound like good things to me."

"But they also make it hard for young mots to leave their villages. The crafts are partly hereditary. It gets hard for outsiders to break in."

"Yes, I see that."

"If they took you, they would take others, and the city would swell and the economy of the whole region would be distorted. Dronned might outproduce other places and cause prices to fall for craftwork. Some workers might be put out of the craft as a result. It happened once, in old Sulmo. The city got too big for its own region, larger than any city in the land. The Assenzi stopped it. The Assenzi are still not loved in Sulmo. Down there they call them wizards."

"How do you know so much?"

"I have read the histories, just like you mots from Highnoth."

"I see." He felt rebuked, but the blow was softened by the faint smile she gave him.

"And I've been all over the Land, all my life. My parents were troupers, too. My father was as strong as most brilbies. He used to bend iron bars. There were always some who would wager against him. He also worked with my mother, who was an acrobat."

He was awed a little by this thought. He'd been to the Farbelows and to Highnoth and that had seemed like a lot of wandering. Compared to Nuza's travels, though, it was obviously inconsequential.

"You have seen it all, then?"

"Well, not yet." She smiled. "I have never been to Highnoth or any of the northern realms. Dronned is as far north as we go. From here we head back toward Tamf and then help with the harvest and prepare to winter over. We only travel in the summer months.

"In the winter we live in my family's old house. It's

big, so there's room for everyone in the troupe if they want to stay. Sometimes they do, even Toshak."

"Does your father farm?"

"Oh, no, he has enough work to do around the house. He has a share of polder, but lets it all out to his family. He comes to harvest of course, and so do we. But we also buy a lot of food, which spreads our cash money around the village. It helps to keep trade flowing."

"Like good mats for their floors."

"Yes, like good mats. Tell me, did you bring mats with you to sell?"

"Yes."

"I would like to see your work."

Thru wondered if she would like it.

"I don't know if you'd like it. It's in the traditional patterns, well mostly."

"Oh, I like the old patterns. They're beautiful. I just wonder if maybe there could be some new ones."

New patterns? It was an outlandish idea. And yet . . .

"Well, I believe it will be shown in the gallery of the House Norvory."

"Oh, my! That is a very grand name."

The Guild Hall came in view as they rounded the curve of the street. On the steps to the front door they stopped. She pressed his hand.

"You should come to a meeting of the Questioners. There will be one in Dronned tomorrow."

"What are the Questioners?"

"It is a discussion group. We explore various subjects. We want to know more about the world than the Assenzi have told us."

He must have seem startled, because she went on.

"Don't you ever have questions about it all? Who were the High Ones and all that? Like the question of the Ur-world, you know that one?"

"No, not really."

"It is believed by some that this is not the Ur-world, the original Urth."

"It is Arna."

"But there was Urth before that."

Thru frowned. "I have heard about this legend, from the Assenzi, but they said there is no evidence for it. Master Acmonides taught us that Man the Cruel poisoned the land, the waters, the body, and the spirit. That Man dwindled because his own seed was poisoned and became infertile. Then the ice scoured the world clean and the High Men raised us up from the animals."

"But they never told us how they did that. We of the Questioners talk about that a lot. Was it by breeding technique? Or by some more subtle means?"

"Magic?"

"Great magic, in arts long forgotten in the world. It was then possible to cut the creatures into the right shape with the knife and mold them with the metals . . ."

"Well, I don't know. I was not taught such things."

"There. You see how soon you run out of answers, and you have been to Highnoth. Really, you should come to the next meeting of the Questioners."

"All right, I will." He was fascinated, by her and by all these dramatically strange thoughts she had introduced him to.

"Wonderful! The meeting is tomorrow, at the first hour in the afternoon, in the back room of Vesco's Tavern. It's just over the bridge, on the South Road."

She disappeared through the doors, while he tried to collect his thoughts. It was all simply too amazing. He was overwhelmed. He lurched off, feeling quite loose and disconnected. His original conception of her, as an acrobat with a beautiful body, had now been overlaid by this understanding of her as a very determined intelligence. Certainly she knew a lot.

And yet she was still the same lithe beauty who hurled herself around in double somersaults off the springboard before being caught by the brilby.

And, by the Spirit, she was a beauty. Almond eyes, short straight nose, and soft grey fur that grew longer on the back of her head. He wanted her like he had once wanted Iallia, but no mor since.

Thru had been a dutiful student. He had absorbed well the lessons of the Assenzi and viewed the world as they had taught him to. He had read the texts, and he had thought he understood something of the world and the stars above. But Nuza had suddenly challenged the orthodoxy he'd learned, and it was both stimulating and disconcerting at the same time.

Thru had learned from Cutshamakim that only Assenzi guidance could achieve the real stewardship of the world, which would outlast him and any memory of himself, too. Were the Assenzi wrong? Was there another way for the folk of the land to live? Could there be another way that would not result in a ruined land?

Though he did not want to give credence to what he had heard from Nuza, still it gnawed at him.

He would have to put it aside until the next day, when he'd hear more at this meeting of the Questioners. Perhaps they were all quite mad. Perhaps they weren't.

He went on up to the Market Square, where the crowds surged past stalls piled high with every kind of household item, from ax handles to bolts of fine cloth. Moving around the edge of the encampment, he came up on the House Norvory, a massive presence on the market square.

In the front was a long window, displaying the Merchandise of House Norvory: luxury rugs from Mauste, mats from Sulmo and Dronned, furniture from the craft shops of Dronned, and metal products from the forges of Dronned and other places.

The window had the largest panes of glass Thru had ever seen, as long as his leg and almost as wide!

He looked inside and saw his "Chooks and Beetles" prominently displayed. There was a "Brilbies at the Gate" and a couple of "Mots at Prayer" displayed as well.

The piece looked good enough to be there. It didn't look gauche or stupid. But he could not hope to weave mats for a living in Dronned anytime soon. He would have to go back to his father's house and pitch in the with family and weave art mats on the side.

Thru went on and passed by Merchant Ortenod's market stall, which was coverered in bright mats. Merchant Ortenod was bargaining with a customer over a plain wesker weave, with no colors. It was a modest purchase and soon completed. Another customer was already in line, and another was selecting his very own waterbush "Leaf" pattern.

Ortenod saw him and called him over.

"Your 'Leaf' pattern is turning out to be a popular one. Bring me more."

Thru spun about and hurried back to Garth Road and Kussha's lock-up. Within the hour he was back at Ortenod's stall with three more of his "Leaf" mats. He promised to check in the next day and see if any more were needed.

With more silver in his pocket than he'd ever had before, Thru stepped through the streets feeling a considerable sense of achievement. It was a heady thing, almost like a kind of drunkenness. And then his eye caught on the big gables of the Guild House, and the mood evaporated.

Again her face came into his thoughts. "That's the way they designed it . . ."

He shrugged inwardly. Maybe he'd give in and see if the Laughing Fish ownership would really pay him to hit the little white ball. He didn't like the thought, but he could possibly make enough to stay on in Dronned through the winter.

He wandered back out the north gate, strolled along past the royal park, and crossed the big road to pass by the Laughing Fish. Dinner would be served at Kussha's soon. He didn't want to miss that, no matter what.

And then his blood seemed to congeal in his veins. For a moment only he saw them, the Grys Norvory and Pern Treevi, walking across the front court of the Laughing Fish, and then they disappeared in through a door held open by Lem Frobin. Frobin followed them in, the door swung shut.

He stood there, irresolute for a moment. The Grys Norvory had many friends, no doubt. He was a powerful mot. But why would Pern Treevi, of all folk, be with him?

For a moment he wondered if he'd imagined it. Had he really seen them together? Or had it been a trick of the light? It had only been for a second or so, but it was definitely Lem Frobin. He knew the big bullheaded mot from way back. It had to have been them.

A great fear settled on his heart.

Chapter 13

In the morning, Thru found his morning routine of kyo and meditation more difficult than usual. He couldn't concentrate, and he chided himself. Why should it concern him anyway, who the Grys Norvory went with to the Laughing Fish? The Grys Norvory probably knew a great many people. If he had business with Pern Treevi, so what? It had nothing to do with Thru Gillo and his own problems with Treevi.

Most likely it was a pure coincidence.

But it was hard to get really comfortable in his meditation. His kyo movements were stiff and wooden. He stopped and exercised for a while, and meditated again with better success. Then he repeated the kyo and it went much better. When it was finished he was refreshed and looking forward to seeing Nuza at the meeting.

At the appointed hour he was in the back room of Veso's Tavern, a small establishment on the south side of the bridge, in a neighborhood of workshops and small warehouses. Exactly the sort of area that Thru had imagined he might search for a workspace of his own.

The room held about forty mots and mors sitting on benches and a few chairs in four rows facing a table with a chair behind it. He hadn't counted, but the audience was half female, he was sure. He looked around at the faces. Mostly these were light grey furred, like himself, suggesting that they came from the region around Dronned. The females did not tie off the fur on the back of their heads with colored bows, which was still a popular style. There was a consistently solemn tone.

There was no sign of Nuza. He wondered if he'd been had.

As the clocks struck the hour, a young mot stood up at the front and introduced himself as Heremi, a "traveler" toward truth, as he described it.

"The Questioners are not a group, not a movement," he said. "Most of you understand that. We merely seek to express the opinions and the doubts that we share. Some may disagree with these opinions, but they may not prevent the expression of them. They may instead express their own. I am in a sense the host of this meeting, but I am not an organizer."

He paused, looked down at a scrap of paper on the table.

"And now, we can move on to the first question."

A hand went up. It was a mor in the front row.

"My question is simple. Why is it that the limits on polder can never be challenged? Why can't we expand the area of polder? There is wetland that could be easily converted to polder, but it is held out of production."

Thru nodded. Here was a perennial question, asked in every village, every year.

Heremi turned to a stout mot at the other end of the front row. Thru was surprised when he recognized him.

"Master Yadrone, you customarily take such questions. Would you care to do the honors today?"

The figure of the merchant rose to his feet.

"I will be happy to answer. The official response is always the same. The balance of the land requires there to be room for all living things. Our area of polder is limited, to keep our populations limited. It is a restraint on our cultural development that we have always accepted.

"The Assenzi say that the life lived by the folk of the Land is a good life, with a natural balance to it and a quality of vividness that is the best kind of life. And it allows the other lives—those of the wild animals, the forests, and the bees—to keep their place in the world. It is good stewardship. If we allow more than fifteen percent of the Land to be converted to polder, then we will irrevocably alter the Land.

"Of course, it has been questioned before, many times, and it will be again. Essentially we hold our populations down to the present level. This is regarded as the maximum burden that we can impose on the Land and allow other lives to continue, as they must, for this to be the Land of the Spirit, which has lived in balance for twenty-four thousand years."

The Questioner got back on her feet, and Yadrone yielded the floor to her.

"Why can't we alter the Land a little? We leave too much wilderness. There are wolves howling on Huwak Mountain. Many mots are afraid to venture past the Dristen these days."

Heremi spoke up in response. "The wolves have not attacked the folk of the Land. Wolves are smart enough to know that we will not harm them if they do not harm us. Brown bears were not that smart, nor were the very big cats; they were too dangerous for our youngsters, and the chooks. So they were driven out of the parts of the Land we reserved for polder and field. But the wolves have never killed mot or mor, despite the fairy tales that are told."

"Wolves have taken chooks."

"Not often enough to be a real problem. Sometimes we have had to punish packs that took too many chooks. But it has not happened in Dronned in many years."

"Why can we not reduce the territory we allow for the wolves? It would leave more animals for our own hunters."

"If we kill the wolves, then the coyotes will increase in number. Maybe rabbits will increase, maybe antelope, maybe neither. As it stands now there is always plenty of game in the season for our hunters."

"We could harvest more," someone else suggested.

"In that question lies the root of our difference with the world of ancient Man."

There, it was out. The word. The name. That which

everyone tried to avoid outside the ceremonies of the Spirit.

"In the ancient world everything was exploited to the maximum possible. That was the world of Man. We have hardly anything left of that world, now. In the equatorial regions there are a few hulks of stone, but that is all. The metals long since rusted away except for a few things of gold that were found long ago.

"What we know of that world we know from the Assenzi and know in our bones."

Thru heard the words of the nursery rhyme go round his head: "We know in our bones, we know in our bones, that Man wants to eat us we know in our bones."

Just then, Nuza took a seat sit beside him on the bench.

"Sorry I'm late," she said.

He was just glad to see her.

They sat there quietly for an hour or so, as the meeting progressed. The questions asked were often ones that had obviously been asked before, at some other meeting. The folk filled the Land, and did so in peace, but they pressed against the limitations, as any intelligent people would.

Inequalities in the distribution of wealth, inevitable and almost necessary for economic success, created the circumstances of misery for many. Mots who lost their polder for one reason or another, sometimes through gambling, could be left in penury, surviving as wood scratchers, or poaching on the forest. Such personal disasters were often the roots of crime.

In time other questions were raised. One even questioned the existence of the Spirit! Thru was horrified, but kept his silence. Heremi handled the responses to questions, though he would confer with others for special advice at times. Heremi was gentle with all questioners, even the one who doubted the Spirit's very existence.

Afterward, Thru and Nuza walked over the bridge together.

"How do you feel about what you heard today?" She was looking at him with eyes full of curiosity.

"Interesting. I realized that my thinking has been mostly one-sided. I would like to know more."

"Yes, Thru, we must keep growing, and that means change. If we can't accept the changes in our lives, we become like clams, so walled off. Not much more interesting than clams either."

They arrived at the window of the House Norvory, which was filled with all the trade goods of the Land. Fine woolens, wine, cheese, waterproofs, shoes, hats, and mats.

There was a fine "Brilbies at the Gate" and an excellent "Mots at Prayer," but there, still in pride of place was Thru's "Chooks and Beetles."

It looked good, he had to admit. It looked strong and well executed. The "Mots at Prayer" that was being shown was of a high caliber, but it did not overwhelm his "Chooks."

He sent up a little prayer of thanks to the chook deities. All of them.

"I like it," she said. "I do." She gave his hand a squeeze. "The heavy styling of the chooks is interesting, and your beetles are weirdly cheerful. I would love to have it, myself."

Thru's heart soared.

"But look there." She pointed to a small tag that hung off one corner of the stand.

"It says it has sold. Already sold, Thru!"

"Sold?"

He stared down at the little scrap of paper that had been tied to the bottom of the mat. "Sold" it read in bright red letters.

"Sold!" he said in a whisper.

Then he had the money to stay over for the winter, and invest in a loom. Of course, he'd have trouble finding somewhere to put it!

"Well," he turned away from the window and looked across the market, the bright stalls and flags, with the

Old Bridge behind it. "I can always make another one, if you'd really like one."

They decided to celebrate with a visit to the beer garden by the Crown Gate Tavern. There they drank tall, chilled mugs of beer and talked for hours about their lives and their hopes. Nuza wanted to know how he came to be scarred, and he told her a little about the fight with the pyluk on Hex Hill. He wanted to know about her life as a traveling performer. As they talked, they felt their strong attraction grow even more.

"We saw you perform in Lushtan, just a few days before that fight with the pyluk."

"Then it must be fate," she said with a laugh. "I'm so glad you survived."

"The Spirit was watching over us that day, I'm convinced."

They sat so close their thighs were touching. Nuza gave him a very direct look.

"I learned that when I see something that touches me I should reach out and touch it myself. I feel like that about you, Thru Gillo."

Their hands met, not for the first time.

"I was in love once before," Thru said. "Her name was Iallia. She is wed now to my worst enemy."

Her eyes widened at his words.

"I'm sorry for the pain that must have caused you, but I'm glad you're still unwed." She grinned.

His eyes widened at the implications of that.

"I will set up a loom somewhere. I will weave another 'Chooks and Beetles' for you."

"I would like that very much." She leaned over and kissed him. He kissed her back, and they looked at each other like children on a dare.

"In the winter we knit," she said to change the subject.

"My father carves wood. He makes some great bows. He has the skill, they all say it."

"Well, so have you, Thru Gillo. That 'Chooks and Beetles' is so good, you deserve to be famous. But"— her face fell—"you still won't get into the Guild."

"Not this year."

"But if you can sell art pieces, then you may not need to be in their Guild."

"As long as the merchant keeps his side of the bargain."

They left the beer garden and wandered through the streets hand in hand. After a while they found themselves walking through the south gate. Beyond the city here was a narrow plain, and then a tall line of sand dunes that flanked a shingle beach. The water of the bay was sparkling.

They climbed the dune together, feeling very close, and found a hollow on the top where they lay down together.

Nuza talked about love, how it came into her life and how she had lost it.

"I was Toshak's lover for almost a year."

"Yes, Gem told me."

"Ah, Gem, don't tell him anything you want kept secret." She stroked Thru's face while he studied her eyes.

"I think there is something very special about you, Thru Gillo."

He took her in his arms and kissed her hard. She responded by pulling at the buttons on his shirt.

His body was lean and hard-muscled, as was hers. She admired it as she stroked the soft fur on his shoulders and back.

"More scars," she said as she looked at his chest.

"Same pyluk. We were lucky to survive."

They made love there, hidden in the dunes.

Chapter 14

He got back to Garth Road at dawn, in time for Kussha's breakfast. He ate quietly, absorbed in his own thoughts, while Noop and Bluit spoke excitedly about the game the night before. The Laughing Fish team had excelled, winning by twenty runs. Thru didn't pay much attention.

It was as if the world had suddenly changed directions. Nuza was like a giant breath of wind in his sails. She had reawakened his heart and amazed him with the intensity of her lovemaking. He surprised himself with his own almost savage response.

Still thinking, he set out for the city at the tenth hour. The market was bustling by then, and he made his way through dense crowds on the pavement. At the half hour he presented himself at the door of the House Norvory and requested an audience with the Grys.

He was expecting to be let in quickly, given the sale of "Chooks and Beetles," but instead he was made to wait on the doorstep for an hour. He began to wonder if the Grys intended to snub him, but eventually a door opened and an unsmiling servant emerged.

"Come in."

He followed the servant to a small waiting room behind a window curtained with lace and waited there for several minutes until the Grys entered, radiating a stern displeasure. Gone was the charm he had exhibited at their previous meeting.

"I consented to see you solely because I believe you should be informed by myself that our business connection has been severed."

"But why? What has happened?"

"I am afraid that you completely took me in."

"I did what?"

"You deceived me so smoothly, that I believed you were the weaver of that fine 'Chooks and Beetles.' "

"But, I am the weaver of that 'Chooks and Beetles.' "

The Grys's face grew thunderous.

"Enough!" he barked. "You are not. It was woven by Pern Treevi's wife Iallia. I have sold it, I got a good price, and the money is going to Pern Treevi."

It fell on Thru like a hammerblow.

"What?" he said, feeling faint for a moment.

"You heard me."

"But, you can't do that. I wove that mat! That is my work, not Iallia's."

"Nonsense. Your work I have seen. It is acceptable, but only for floor mats, not for 'Chooks and Beetles.' My friend Pern Treevi showed me the evidence. He bought it on a stall not a hundred feet from here!"

"Yes, that is my work, but that is not all my work. I also did the 'Chooks and Beetles.' "

"Nonsense. You are a jumped-up peasant! I've heard all about you, Thru Gillo!"

"From Pern Treevi?"

"My friend Pern told me about your family. A lot of claim grabbers. Jumped-up woods poachers!"

"You do not know my family, Grys Norvory. You do not know me! Yet you take the word of Pern Treevi, my sworn enemy, and refuse to listen to my own words."

"You are from an interloping clan that has stolen a seapond in your own village."

"This is completely unjust."

"I have heard it all from Pern. Now I must ask you to leave."

"I have witnesses that the 'Chooks and Beetles' is my own work." Thru felt his heart hammering in his chest.

"What witnesses? Your family? Your notorious kin with their chiseling ways and conniving, thieving habits?

There is nothing worse than a theft of a seapond, not for the House Norvory!"

"Others can be produced who have seen my work."

"But they cannot testify. You are not in the Dronned Guild, so you can just take your interloping ways and go back to your village and your thievish kith and kin."

"Grys, those are insulting words. To some they would constitute enough of an insult to draw a challenge. To me they are words of foolishness, of intemperate manners, the product of Pern Treevi's lies about me and my family. I will send you a copy of the legal writ produced for the trial held to adjudicate title to the seapond in question. Then I will demand your apology. If you refuse at that point, then it will be the sword."

"Get out!" snapped the Grys.

Thru stalked the streets for hours, angry beyond anything he had ever known. His work, his best work, his "Chooks and Beetles," had been stolen. Tricked out of him by the smooth-talking Grys Norvory, then sold on behalf of Pern Treevi. It was a sickening development.

After hours of wandering aimlessly, he found himself on top of the dunes just south of the city. Out beyond the bay the sun was setting and the golden light of evening had lit the dunes with a golden glow.

Life, which had seemed so wonderful at dawn, was suddenly filled with ashes and dust. The "Chooks and Beetles" was gone, and Thru was cut out of the deal, with no legal right to complain.

Somewhere inside of him there was a much younger Thru Gillo, who was close to tears. The theft was bad enough, but for Pern Treevi to profit in such a way was very hard to take.

And it was also pretty certain that Thru would be spending the winter back in Warkeen Village. He'd have to pitch in with the family work, and that would cut down on his time for weaving. Even if Merchant Ortenod honored his word and paid him in full for his "Leaf" pattern mats, it wouldn't be enough to set up a loom, rent a work space, and survive through the winter.

Suddenly he had a solution. He'd put the idea roughly aside before, but now he considered it more carefully. What about letting someone pay him to hit the ball! There were still a few games left in the season. What if he tried to make the Laughing Fish team? He might still make a few gold pieces and thereby be able to hang on in Dronned.

He came back from the despairing depths and pulled himself to his feet. He was still the Thru Gillo who had set the new all-time hitting record. That had to be worth something. He set his feet on the path down the dune toward the city walls. Mots and mors were at work in the vegetable gardens that lined the road, someone was singing a popular song, and others joined in on the verses. It helped to lift his spirits as he strode up to the south gate.

By the time he got to the Laughing Fish, the early-evening rush was on. Thru put his question to the second barkeeper and was referred to an office at the back.

"Thru Gillo, isn't it?" said the mot in the office. "I saw you hit very well that day. Took the championship away from us."

"I think we had our best game ever that day."

"And you want to know if we're interested in you as a paid player?" he guessed.

"Yes."

"Come with me over to the ball field, I'll introduce you to Rawli Perensa. He's the mot you want to talk to."

They crossed the street and entered the long narrow clubhouse that stood in front of the ball field. From the shelter of the long gallery the view of the field was excellent. There sat the worthies of the city who shared the passion for the bat and ball game.

The game that day was going well for the Laughing Fish, who were playing a village from up the valley. The village team were halfway out already and had scored only thirty runs. The Laughing Fish had the most prodigious young throwers, and they were taking a steady toll on the village batters.

In short order Thru was talking to Rawli Perensa, the owner of the Laughing Fish Tavern itself.

"So you'd like to play for the Laughing Fish?"

"Well, I don't like to play for money, but I need to earn some."

"I see." Rawli Perensa scratched his nose. "Well, we all remember what you did to us three summers back. Are you still a big mot with the bat?"

"Last time I checked."

"Then we'll try you. We'll pay two silver shillings for every run you score. How does that sound?"

Thru shook hands with Perensa on the deal.

As he left the clubhouse there was a sharp crack of bat on ball, along with scattered applause. The sounds made him feel stronger.

Chapter 15

Two days later Thru Gillo turned out to bat for the Laughing Fish Tavern. The opponents that day were the much-respected team for Crown Gate Tavern, and this domestic derby game always drew a large crowd. The clubhouse gallery and the open-air benches were full. There were even folk standing all the way around the perimeter of the field. It had much the same atmosphere as his last stand there in that memorable championship match.

Crown Gate had batted first and run up a score of 102. Thru had done his share of huffing and puffing in pursuit of well-struck balls. Crown Gate's leading hitter, Ledrun Paff, struck thirty-one runs on his own.

Harli, the opening batter for the Laughing Fish, was also a famously strong striker, running up eighteen before being caught out the fourth time. The rest of the batting order followed, and succumbed to the trio of hard hurlers that Crown Gate had deployed. Leading them was a youngster named Ormo, who had a tremendous throw and great accuracy. Thru was the last mot up to bat and he needed to score twenty-seven runs to win the game.

The lively little bat from Fivver's workshop that he'd selected swung lightly in his hands as he took the first few balls. Ormo did indeed have a powerful arm. His throws came in with a special zip that could overpower most batters. Thru deflected away the first couple of throws from Ormo, but missed the third and heard a sharp *whuck* as the ball struck the red pole behind him.

No runs and already one of his outs was gone. He took a deep breath, settled into the kyo mindfulness, and waited. The next ball he caught cleanly with a tremendous stroke and sent it away with that ringing *crack* that always thrilled the crowd. It landed far past the four-hundred-foot line, giving him his first run of the innings.

Ormo stepped back for a breather and another thrower took his place. The first ball was too high and wide and whizzed back into the netting behind Thru. The next ball was in reach, and Thru stepped out and met it with a crushing blow that sent it even farther than the first run.

His eye was in. His kyo with the bat was a near-flawless system of movement that even Master Sassadzu would have found acceptable. The bat crushed ball after ball in an inning that soon had great outbursts of applause coming from the crowd. Thru Gillo was at bat, and the Laughing Fish were gaining fast.

His second out came at sixteen, another venomous ball from Ormo that nicked the bat on its way to striking the red pole behind him. The next out came on the twenty, when he skyed a ball, and it was caught. He had one out remaining.

There were still seven runs to strike to win, six to force a tie. Ormo came up for the fourth time. The first ball was very fast and Thru's stroke was a fraction too slow and the ball flew high. The crowd went silent. Crown Gate fielders scrambled to get below it for the catch, but it went so high it started to drift toward the run line. The fielders ran on in pursuit, two of them ran into each other and a third was too far away when the ball came down and bounced over the run line.

The Laughing Fish crowd breathed a giant sigh of relief.

The next ball from Ormo was straight down the line, Thru knew from the moment he stepped into his swing there was no room for error and was rewarded with that fat *crack* that spoke wonders in terms of runs.

The ball flew away and soared over the run line, still going up.

The crowd roared. People were standing all along the clubhouse gallery shouting and waving their fists.

Another ball flew, this time too high and wide to bother with. More inaccurate balls followed. Ormo had lost his grip for the moment. He stepped out and another thrower came up to the line.

Thru concentrated, let the flow run through him. The ball seemed to float for that crucial moment and his body went into motion and the bat connected again and drove the ball straight out at a terrific speed, slowly rising as it went. The fielders didn't even move, they all just watched in awe as it flew into the distance. The crowd let loose another roar, but they too were awed and the noise subsided more quickly this time.

Five more runs followed, against throwers who were rapidly losing confidence. As the last one lofted into the air, a huge roar went up as the game was won. Thru turned around and raised his cap to the crowd, then walked back to the clubhouse with the rest of the team rising to applaud.

Thru Gillo had stepped up and delivered. His reputation was secure. And afterward Rawli Perensa handed him a fat purse, stuffed with fifty-four silver pieces.

"I must say, on behalf of the entire Laughing Fish bat and ball club, how glad we are to have you on the team. That was a great performance."

Thru took the purse with the thought that despite his earlier disinclinations, hitting the white ball for money was not such a bad way to earn some silver crowns.

Afterward he celebrated with Nuza. They drank a bottle of Ulschadein wine, the most expensive in the house, and dined at the Laughing Fish.

At some point in the proceedings he noticed Toshak in the room, giving him a hard look. The great swordfighter had been Nuza's lover until a few moons before and clearly still harbored strong feelings for her.

According to Nuza, Toshak had grown increasingly remote during their love affair. To her he would always be a great mot, head and shoulders above the rest, but she knew he could never give himself fully to another. She did not think that Great Toshak would ever be wed.

Thru did his best to ignore the hostility from Toshak. The other members of the troupe were pleasant company. Big Hob, the brilby who caught Nuza, was a cheerful fellow, who had been especially friendly.

While Nuza and Hob talked about her latest routine, Thru mused on the workings of fate. If he could keep on like this for the rest of the summer he'd earn enough to stay in Dronned for the winter at Kussha's place. He'd find a workroom outside the walls where he could weave a few high-end mats for next year's market.

He felt a grim chuckle go off inside him. Maybe he'd weave a mat for the Grys Norvory, a new take on "Mussels and Rakes," or "Brilbies at the Gate." Let him see that it was Thru's style in the "Chooks and Beetles" and nothing to do with Iallia Treevi. He had some ideas for "Mussels and Rakes" that were almost revolutionary, but right in line with what he'd done for "Chooks and Beetles."

Thru told himself that he hadn't completely failed in the market for mats. Merchant Ortenod had been very decent. When he heard the story about Thru Gillo's "Chooks and Beetles," Ortenod wrote a note to Thru explaining that he had given the affidavit of Thru's "Leaf" pattern mat to Pern Treevi quite innocently, with no ill will toward Thru. When Thru went to drop off the last three "Leaf" mats, Ortenod confessed that he'd been shocked by the Grys Norvory's behavior, but warned that no one would stand up against the Grys, who was very powerful in the Dronned guilds.

Ortenod had paid in full, as he'd promised. Thru, reassured, had left him the remaining three mats to sell at the next market, which would be held during the Harvest Moon.

Now, sipping ale in the Laughing Fish Tavern, he calculated that he had about two hundred shillings in his account. It was more than he'd ever had before, but by his calculations it was just enough to get him through the winter in Dronned. He just needed somewhere secure, where he could set up a couple of looms and start weaving. He'd also need some money for good materials. Golden grass and red tash were never cheap, and he already had an idea for using them heavily on his new "Mussels and Rakes." Next spring he would show the Grys Norvory how wrong he'd been.

Feeling satisfied that despite everything he was still progressing toward his goal, Thru treated himself to a dish of sweet bewbie pie to finish his meal.

Later he went back with Nuza to her lodgings for the night. The house owner had not objected, used as she was to Nuza's unusual ways. Not many mors of the Land were so free with themselves, and most preferred to be married young, but Nuza was an adult, and free to make love to whomever she wanted. Certainly there was no law to prohibit her from doing so. She was also free to bear the consequences in terms of difficulty in obtaining marriage back in her home village.

And for all the intensity of their new love, both knew that it was about to be interrupted. In a day or so Nuza would be gone, until the following year. Their communication would be a matter of letters until he could leave Dronned and go to visit her in Tamf, after the harvest was in.

Thru faced the thought of lonely weeks ahead with a new dread. It had been so long since he'd felt this happy . . . to be without her was going to be torture. He wished he could just travel with her and the troupe. But how could he do that if he was going to play for the Laughing Fish team?

As always since Highnoth, he woke at dawn and entered the morning kyo. Nuza was still asleep as he pulled on his boots and did up his jerkin. For a moment he studied the slim form under the covers. She was so beautiful in her sleep. He felt immensely fortunate to have found her.

He let himself out of the house and made his way through the empty streets to his own lodgings outside the wall on Garth Road. The city was absolutely silent, except for a cock crowing in the south ward.

He felt very blessed at that moment. That was something that he remembered clearly, later. Right before it happened, he'd been feeling wonderful.

He crossed the bridge, and started up Gate Street. A moment later he heard a step, then something hard and heavy struck him on the back of the neck and shoulder. He staggered, and everything went dim for a moment. A second blow drove him to the ground, but paradoxically the impact cleared his vision.

He rolled over and saw the dim shape of Pern's thug Ulghrum, wielding an ax handle. Instinctively he squirmed aside, and the ax handle hit the paving stone where his head had rested.

Ulghrum tried again and missed a second time, and then Thru rolled sideways and scrambled to his feet. Ulghrum was swinging, but Thru dodged out of the way, felt a wall at his back, and slipped to the side. The ax handle struck dust off the wall a moment later.

Thru pivoted and swung his right foot hard into Ulghrum's side, producing a gasp of pain. Ulghrum fell back a step. Suddenly another thug loomed out of the alley behind him, also holding an ax handle. This time Ulghrum had brought backup.

"Master Pern said your account needed to be closed," said Ulghrum with a sneer.

Thru was still shaking his head, trying to clear it, but not succeeding too well. He didn't think he could run, but he had to.

Ulghrum swung high at him, but he ducked the ax handle and staggered off down the street. The other one was coming. He was running out of time.

And then another figure suddenly came running up with a shout. There came the unmistakable sound of a sword being drawn.

"Hold or die," said a cold voice. It was Toshak.

The mot snarled and flailed at the swordsmot with the ax handle. Toshak dodged the blow with a liquid movement and brought the sword point up and under the mot's chin. A drop of blood ran down the fur on his throat.

"Drop it," snapped Toshak.

The ax handle bounced on the pavement.

"Back off both of you, or I'll be forced to spill more of your blood."

Ulghrum was already retreating, fading back up the alley. The other thug followed him at a clumsy run.

Thru sagged back against the wall of the nearest building. The back of his head was hurting.

"Thank you, they were going to kill me."

"I know. I was following them. They were watching our lodgings last night. You, of course, were too busy to have noticed them."

Thru said nothing.

"But I saw them, and I followed them to their lair. They slept in a cellar behind the House Norvory. I watched again at dawn, and they woke early and came out at once." The question in Toshak's voice was unavoidable.

"I have an enemy from my village. He is wealthy and ambitious, and my family thwarted him in court. I thought that I was safe from him here in Dronned."

"I detest this use of hired assassins. What is this mot's name?"

"Pern Treevi."

"I have heard the name before. A rake they say. Drinks too much, well-known among the gamers."

"As to that I don't know, but he hates me."

Thru found that his head had been laid open by one of Ulghrum's blows and that blood was seeping through his fur and pooling on the shoulder of his jacket. Toshak had noticed, too.

"I think you should get those wounds seen to."

"Where shall I go? I don't know the healers in Dronned."

"Try Nuza. She's the healer for the troupe, and damned good, too."

"Nuza? You'd encourage me to go to her?"

Toshak gave him a grim smile.

"After saving your life I want to be sure you survive. Nuza loves you, and anyone she loves becomes important to me. Go to her, she is very good at healing and sewing up cuts."

Thru groped for words.

"I thought you hated me."

"Hate? No, young Thru, I may be jealous, but I will not descend to hatred."

"I am very grateful for that. Once again, thank you."

Thru had some colorful bruising by the time of the next game for the Laughing Fish, but he still played. The game was held in Yupay Village, up the valley from Dronned. The Yupay team had beaten the Laughing Fish in three previous games that season.

Thru played well, making four catches and striking nineteen runs to help run up the Laughing Fish score to 112. Rawli Perensa and the others in the inner group of the club were delighted.

Nuza and the troupe had all come to Yupay to watch the game and support Thru. Afterward they traveled back to Dronned in a lighthearted group. Even Toshak was there, although he generally showed little interest in such outings.

Thru added thirty-eight shillings to his account with Kussha, who had a personal vault at the big Merchants Bank in the city. Keeping back a small purse, he went out with Nuza to visit the emporia and trade shops on the market square. He was feeling flush enough to be able to afford a few gifts for his family to take back for Harvest festival. At the House of Fanor he bought some cloth for his sister Snejet. For young Gil he bought a fine knife, sheathed with lacquered withe.

Nuza and the troupe stopped off at their lodging house while Thru went to the Laughing Fish clubhouse to see Gurb about a new bat. Old Gurb took care of the club's equipment. Thru found the main floor was empty, but he heard voices upstairs in the room where Rawli Perensa did the club's business. Gurb was in the big equipment room below, in the process of making up an order for new bats.

Thru wanted his new bat to be fractionally heavier than the one he'd been using. Gurb wrote some notes as he spoke about the bat he wanted, and then Thru's business was done. He headed up the stairs to the main gallery and the front door.

As he stepped into the exit hall he saw Pern Treevi standing with Rawli Perensa in the doorway. The surprise was complete. For a moment Thru struggled to draw a breath.

Rawli had spotted him and now waved him over with a big smile.

"Thru, I want you to meet our latest benefactor. He's from your home village I believe. He's going to join our club committee."

Pern had the most evil little smile on his face.

"I know him," said Thru quietly.

"Pern has a couple of good young throwers he's discovered in your valley. Gurb will give them a tryout in the morning."

The gloating in Pern's eyes was dreadful to behold.

"This is a great day for our village," said Pern in a tone just short of outright mockery. "Just think, Thru, you'll be hitting the ball for me."

Thru calmed himself by closing his eyes a moment and reaching for the peace of the kyo. Then he turned to Rawli Perensa.

"May I speak with you alone?"

"Well, yes, of course." Perensa's brow wrinkled. "I was just stepping over to the tavern for a spot of dinner. Are you sure you wouldn't like to accompany us?"

"Quite sure."

"You go ahead, Pern, I'll be along in just a moment. This won't take long, will it, Thru?"

"No."

Pern left them with a mocking smile.

Thru leaned on the wall with a sudden extreme sense of weariness.

"I cannot play for the Laughing Fish team anymore."

Perensa's jaw dropped.

"But why? I do not understand."

"Pern Treevi is my sworn enemy. I will not take up the bat for any team of which he is a part."

"This is a joke?"

"No. Pern has tried to kill me on two occasions." Thru pointed to the bandage on the back of his head. "His malicious lies turned the Grys Norvory against me and caused me to lose my best work."

"These are serious allegations. Do you have evidence against him?"

"I have a witness, someone who saved my life."

"Can this witness be produced?"

"Oh, yes. His name is Toshak; he accompanies Nuza's troupe. I'm sure you've seen him."

Shock spread over Rawli's plump features as the enormity of it all sank in. If Thru's charges were correct, then Pern had played a terrible trick on the Laughing Fish owner.

"This is terrible news. We have signed paper with Pern; there is no way we can go back on it. There are lots of gold pieces in play. And, on top of that, we have your contract. You cannot play for another team anywhere in Dronned."

Rawli's plump cheeks quivered with indignation. Thru sighed.

"I know. That's what I agreed to, for this season. Next season I can play for anyone I want to."

"Surely you will reconsider. Are you quite certain about these charges you have made?"

"All too sure."

"I have been made to look like a fool," Rawli said in disgust.

"Pern will not care about that."

With his dreams in tatters Thru left the Laughing Fish

and went back to his room at Kussha's. He sat there trying not to let himself be consumed with the rage he felt. What would Master Cutshamakim say about this? What would Uzzieh Utnapishtim tell him to do in these circumstances?

Every avenue had been sealed off by Pern's malice. And Pern's thugs would keep on trying to kill him until they succeeded. It was easy to feel doomed. But if Ulghrum could be brought to trial, then Pern's conspiracy might be unmasked. Of course, Thru was sure that Ulghrum would not be seen in Dronned again for a long time. Pern had other thugs at his disposal.

When Thru failed to appear at Veso's Tavern for dinner, Nuza grew anxious. She hurried out of the city gates and on to Garth Road and Kussha's house, finding Thru in his small attic room. His news shocked her. Pern Treevi's hatred knew no bounds. At the same time she felt a wild sense of hope.

"What this means, my love, is that you no longer have any reason to stay in Dronned. So you can come with us. Join the troupe." She was smiling, her eyes sparkling.

"I'm not that good at juggling, and I'm surely not good enough to be an acrobat."

"No, silly, you didn't learn those things young enough. But you can hit the ball."

"So?"

"So I have an idea."

Chapter 16

Thru was now a member of the Magnificents, who accepted him quite happily as one of their own.

"We're like a big family," said Gem, a tumbler and fiddler, who also kept stock of the troupe's store of gossip.

"If you ever need to know somebody's business, ask Gem," rumbled big Hob, the brilby.

"Oh, stop that. How will I ever gain his trust now?" said Gem in mock complaint.

At the head of the procession marched Toshak, the grim, grey one with the sword. Apart from saving Thru's life, Toshak hadn't spoken much to him. Behind Toshak came their wagon, with Serling and Nuza walking beside it.

Thru walked beside Gem while listening to the fiddler's tales of the life on the roads.

"Nuza's very pleased at having added you to the troupe," Gem said with a conspiratorial wink. "She has an idea that hitting the white ball for money will be a crowd pleaser, too. It will be something completely different for a carnival, that's for sure."

Thru got the feeling that Gem wasn't quite so sure. For all his flamboyance, he was a bit conservative at heart.

"Nuza is a great artist, you understand," said Gem, suddenly turning serious. "She's the best acrobat I've seen, and I've been around carnivals all my life."

"I've not seen that many, but certainly I've not seen one as graceful as she."

"And I owe her a lot, because when I met her I was,

well, very depressed. She helped me get back to tumbling and traveling."

"Is there anywhere you haven't been?"

"Oh yes, I've never been to Mauste. I spent a summer in Fauste, and that was hot enough to make me never want to go any farther south. But it was nice to see everyone walking around bare-chested, if you know what I mean."

Thru chuckled. Gem was an extroverted lover of his own sex, no doubt of that. There were some mots who held prejudices against such folk, but Thru wasn't one of them.

That evening they arrived in the village of Justero, twenty miles south of Dronned on the road to Sonf. They took rooms at the Oak Tree Tavern.

When the sun rose the next morning, Thru visited the famous Justero shrine of the Spirit. Set in an oak grove south of the village, the stone shrine was like a bowl cut in the gray stone fifty feet across. He sat in the bowl and heard the soft echo of his own breathing. Mindfulness was easy to achieve here, and he meditated for a while.

There was a shallow stone bath at the shrine, and Thru bathed in the cold water, conscious only of the feel of the water on his skin while he performed the ritual ablutions. Then he went up the steps into the stone building behind the meditation bowl.

In the cool, dark interior a single lamp burned. An elderly mot in a brown robe bowed to him from his seat in the narthex. Thru stood quietly for a few minutes, absorbing its peaceful essence. Three rows of seats carved from stone occupied one part. An altar for placing ritual sacrifices filled the far end. A gallery opened out into the west for sunset ceremonies.

He stood on the open stones of the gallery and did kyo. While he swept smoothly through the moves, the old brown robes watched him with complete fascination.

Later Thru strolled back to the village in a relaxed, confident mood. Despite all the reversals and losses he had suffered in Dronned, he still had the most important thing of all, Nuza's love.

After breakfast in the tavern's capacious kitchen, Thru took up his bat and walked the streets of the village behind the others while Hob shouted out his challenge.

"One throw for a shilling and win twenty shillings if you can hit the red."

That brought out a few interested parties. They told their friends.

"Win twenty shillings if you can hit the red?"

"You're on!"

Nuza performed on the village green with the other tumblers and jugglers. Toshak gave his usual display of skill with the sword, and then Thru went to the Game Tree and took his stance. Judging the contest was sturdy old Lemser, the captain of the Justero Village team.

There were quite a few young mots who thought themselves pretty good at throwing. They paid their shillings to Hob and stepped up to the line. The balls came whizzing in, hard, high, low, and wide. Thru eyed them, chose the ones that were on target, slid into his formidable batting kyo, and drove them back with one loud *crack* after another while a spellbound crowd watched a display of batting prowess the like of which they had never seen.

Several of the biggest young throwers were convinced they could still get past him. They kept on laying out shillings, and stepping to the line. But nothing got by him that might hit the red zone on the Tree.

When the last of the young throwers gave up after five attempts, Thru stepped away to applause. He was sixty shillings to the better. He gave twenty to Nuza for the troupe, and kept the rest.

"You see," said Nuza. "I told you it would work. You're famous, my love. Everyone's heard of Thru Gillo who hit seventy-seven runs in a single game."

"They didn't give up easily."

"Well, of course not. Twenty shillings is a goodly sum to win. And then there's the fame of being the one to throw out Thru Gillo at the Game Tree."

"And someone's going to get past me someday. Can't hit every ball."

"You were good today. I bet the Laughing Fish wish they had you on the field for them tonight." It would be the final game against Yupay Village that night, and sure enough the Laughing Fish would miss him in their batting order.

From Justero they went on to Rapuste, up the Slie River, then to Sonf and finally into Tamf. In Rapuste he struck forty-nine balls cleanly away before one got past him. Then he struck another eighteen before everyone was satisfied. He was left with forty-seven shillings. He gave Nuza fifteen and put most of the rest into the chest.

In Tamf he faced nearly a hundred balls and drove forty to the boundary, while only one got past him to nick the red pole. He took eighty shillings, paid twenty more into the coffers of the troupe, and now had more than three hundred to his account.

But summer was coming to a close. The vine leaves were already turning scarlet in the wine country of Tamf. The maples up north would be in their glory soon. It was time for Thru to get back to Warkeen Village, to help the family get in everything from the fields and the seapond. There was always a tremendous amount of physical labor required for the harvest, and no son of Ware Gillo would shirk it.

He took his purse from the troupe's chest in the form of three fat gold crowns and sixty small silver shillings and at the market in Tamf he bought a pair of fine chisels for Ware and several bolts of the finest Mauste silk. Thus equipped with presents for everyone, he bought a passage north to Warkeen aboard the fishing boat, *Conch,* skippered by Captain Olok, a weird-looking old mot; one-eyed, with almost white fur on his head and shoulders.

Olok was heading up to the Guni channel, where the mackerel would soon be leaping in their millions. For the consideration of a few shillings from Thru's purse,

Olok would be happy to put him ashore on the sand outside Warkeen.

On the stone jetty at Tamf harbor he and Nuza said farewell, with tears and kisses and many hugs, before he finally stepped aboard the *Conch*. It felt like he was tearing off a limb, but eventually he let go of her hand.

"I will come back after the frost. The fishing boats will be heading south then, back from the banks."

Nuza waved from the jetty. "Until then, my love. I will be in my family's old house awaiting your return."

The command to slip the ropes came down from Olok's place behind the tiller and the *Conch*, a forty-foot cog with a single mast, moved away from the jetty. The sail was run up and began to billow on a fresh breeze from the south.

He waved, but after a while there was only the distant line of the jetty to be seen, and then it was obscured by the northern headland.

Captain Olok had a reputation as a sea mystic and that night, after a meal of fish chowder, biscuit, and seabeer, he regaled Thru with tales of the sea.

He had actually seen mysterious beings like the Sea Mors, who swam in the ocean and sang to sailors to draw them onto the rocks.

"But why would they do that?"

"None can say, but 'tis thought they want to make love to them."

Thru shook his head at such a fantastic story.

The other members of the crew, Ushk and Duldli, were stolid types, well used to their captain's wild tales. They sipped their seabeer in silence and chewed seaweed every so often for the taste.

Thru spent his hours on watch alert to anything like the sound of Sea Mors wailing in the surf, but the *Conch* just kept sailing northward, driven by a steady wind out of the south all that first night. Once he thought he spied a light somewhere in toward the land on their right side, but it lasted only a moment. He heard nothing out of the ordinary.

After beating up the coast past distant Dronned, the *Conch* put into the estuary of the Dristen River. Soon they were passing seaponds to left and right and then while the *Conch* cast an anchor they let down the dinghy and Ushk rowed Thru ashore.

Thru gave him three shillings and stepped ashore onto the shingle of Warkeen beach. There was a definite bite in the air. Autumn had come to the Land.

"See you in a month's time, young Thru Gillo," said Ushk as he pushed off and rowed back through the waves toward the waiting fishing cog.

Thru turned about and walked up the beach to the lane.

Chapter 17

Harvest festival lasted four days in Warkeen Village, as it did all across the northern part of the Land, where winter bit more deeply than in the south. Fueled by the new season's beer, the usual dancing and singing filled the evenings in the village hall.

The Harvest festival was a traditional time for weddings in Warkeen Village, and that year there were four, including that of Snejet Gillo, who was wed to Oiv Melbist, a distant cousin of Snejet's mother. Oiv held some good polder and a full field on the north bank of the Dristen. He would move into the Gillo household, as was customary for newlywed sons-in-law, and remain for three summers.

The ceremony at the old oak tree had most of the village in attendance. Afterward trestle tables were laid out in the village hall and a tremendous dinner was served up. The pièce de résistance was Ual Gillo's grand sweet pudding served with custard sauce. Throughout the proceedings there were toasts from all the relatives and friends. By the time everything was eaten there were restless feet under the tables.

The fiddlers and drummers soon took up their instruments, and the dancing began.

Standing in the front row at the ceremony, Thru had felt a quiet pride in seeing that the cloth he'd bought Snejet in Dronned had been used to make her wedding cape. The vibrant yellow-and-blue stars stood out spectacularly against the white of her dress. As they sang the wedding song in unison, Thru noted that his sister looked radiantly happy. Thru knew that Oiv was well set with polder and field and that he had a reputation as a hard worker himself. Moreover, Ual was ecstatic about the marriage. Still, Thru might have wished for a bit more wit in his first brother-in-law. But Snej was very happy with him, and that was what counted.

Later, after the dancing had begun, Thru went up to young Oiv and embraced him. Oiv was darker and slighter in build, but Thru sensed he was strong and good of heart.

"You take care of my sister, Oiv. Don't let her work herself to death."

"I will try to stop her, but you know how head strong she is."

Snejet came up and embraced both of them.

"What do you think of him, Thru?"

Thru looked over at Oiv. "He seems a good one for you Snej. I think you two will be very happy."

"What about you, Thru? Will you be happy? I worry about my beloved brother wandering the face of the earth with no home."

Thru chuckled. "But I have more than one home now. I have a home with the troupe and with Nuza. And I still have a home here."

"You're living with an acrobat! Mother is seething, you know. All her plans have come to nothing."

"Oh I know. I'm a disappointment to her. But at Highnoth they told me that some mots are meant to leave their home villages and move around the Land. Mixes folk up, keeps our breed strong and true."

"Well, Oiv and I have a family. How about you and your lovely acrobat?"

"I think so. Nuza says she wants to settle down soon and have some children."

"And where will you live then?"

"Well, I don't know. Maybe in Tamf, maybe Dronned, maybe here in Warkeen."

Just then a squad of determined-looking chooks came up to present Snejet with a crown of flowers and the best wishes of all the chook clans in the village. Feathers were flying as the big birds jumped up and down and flapped their wings.

Eventually the bonfire was lit and the King of Sloth, a dummy tied to his throne, was brought out. Round and round the fire they marched, singing the harvest song, with the king riding on the shoulders of four mots. Then they pitched the king into the fire and everyone cheered as the straw mot burned and took the rule of sloth away from the village for another year.

More barrels of new ale were being broached. Foaming mugs were held high. The hops from the early part of the summer were dry, the new barley was in, and the strong ales of autumn were brewed once more, but as a consequence, Harvest festival also had a reputation for clownish behavior and fistfights.

Fistfights were discouraged, of course, although a few were inevitable. Clownish behavior on the other hand, was encouraged. After the hard labor of getting in the harvest, it was good for everyone to unwind. Masks and funny hats, often handed down for generations, were common at the evening revels.

The wild music was kicking up again, and the village threw itself back into the toe-to-heel, arm-in-arm, around-and-around kind of dancing that had always marked this night of celebration. The whole village was jumping, with the chooks crowing from the rooftops.

Thru took a breather after a while and got himself a fresh mug of ale. He slipped to the back of the crowd, where the benches were set up, and took a seat. Ware came and sat beside him. For a few moments they sat there together, sipping the ale and staring at the flames.

"We worked hard this year, didn't we, Father?"

"I was thankful that you came back, son."

"Oh, I wouldn't have let you down."

They sipped for a moment.

"So what will you do now, my son?"

"The repairs in the seapond need to be in place before the winter storms, but that will take only a few days with

Oiv and Gil both working. When that's done then I hope to get my passage back to Tamf. The mackerel boats will be passing soon. Captain Olok was going to look for me on his way back south."

"How long will you stay in Tamf?"

" 'Til spring. Then the troupe will take to the road, and I'll go with them."

Ware grimaced. "My son, this sounds like a vague, uncertain kind of life. You intend to wander forever?"

"Well, I can work through the winter on my weaves and sell them in the summer. You said yourself that I had earned good money on my expedition to Dronned. And I can earn money in the summer just by swinging a bat."

"Yes, my son, but only while you are young and have those quick wrists."

"Well, perhaps by the time I slow down I'll have gained entry to the Guild in Dronned. Then I can live in the town and weave full-time."

"Mmm, I suppose. You've set your course by an uncertain star, my son, but you have great talent. I don't doubt that somehow you'll do well."

"Thank you, Father, that means a lot to me, knowing that you understand. And while I'm young I'll be able to roam all over the Land, which is something I love to do. Nuza says we may even go to Mauste next summer."

Ware's eyebrows rose. "Mauste? As far as that? Well, I'll be blessed, that's a long way to go to juggle and bat the ball."

"But I will always come back to help with the harvest."

"You know we'll need you."

"Aye, Father, though you'll have Oiv and Snej too."

"Oh yes, and Oiv's a good worker. Of course he has his own land to work, and Snej will be a mother in no time, you mark my words. She'll have her hands full with youngsters, and that always cuts down a mor's time in the seapond."

"And Gil is grown now."

"Aye, Gil is a farmer in his bones. He will stay."

Gil was a sleepy-eyed young mot, with a gentle heart and a steady way about him, but little of the brilliance that had shown in the first son. Ware was still amazed by what his firstborn had grown up to become. Living with an acrobat in another realm! Earning money by hitting the white ball and weaving artistic mats. Such things were far away indeed from working good polder.

Together they looked over the festive scene. Mots and brilbies were dancing, the musicians were absorbed in their music, and the crowd was clapping along. A gang of chooks led by Tucka and Pok was bobbing about behind the musicians.

"I have not seen Pern Treevi throughout this festival," Thru commented.

"Oh, you don't see that one down here much anymore. He's got his mor locked up in her fancy house on that ruined field, and he stays in Dronned. He's a mischief maker, mark my words, and will come to a bad end."

Thru nodded, barely finishing his beer before he was pulled back into the dancing. Toward the end of the King-of-Dronned reel, Thru let go of his partner's hand and turned away to join the line of mots, idling to one side while the mors danced back and forth in the ancient pattern.

Suddenly he felt a hand on his arm. He looked down and found a child, her scalp done up with white ribbon bows.

"Please, Master Thru, this is for you." She pressed a small scrap of scroll into his hand, then disappeared into the crowd.

Puzzled, Thru stepped out himself and opened the scrap of paper under a lantern hanging from the eave of the village hall. Written in a hasty scrawl, he read,

"Come and see me, I have information that can save your life."

It was signed, "Iallia."

Stunned, he looked up. Past the crowd, over the low thatch roofs in the distance he saw a single light at Pern

Treevi's big house on the hillside. Was it a trick of some kind? Was Ulghrum waiting up there to kill him?

Trick or not, he was still impelled to find out. But first he went home and collected his bow and quiver of fine steel points. If it was Ulghrum up to his tricks, then he'd get more then he had bargained for. Thru climbed the road out of the village, which was alight from the bonfire and alive with the sound of the revels. Across the field to his right he could see lights at the main Treevi house, where some kind of party was in progress, Pern's big new house was dark by comparison. Cautiously he entered the front gate, and with an arrow nocked and ready, he scouted the house.

There was no sign of anyone around, but for that single light in an upstairs window.

At length he stepped up and rapped the door knocker three times, then stood back, ears straining. There came a sudden rush of steps and the bolts were pulled back and the door opened a crack.

"It is you. Oh thank the Spirit. Come in."

He did not move.

Iallia's eyes were red from crying, the fur on the side of her neck matted and wet.

"You sent me this message?" He held it up.

"Yes, but do come in. I don't want you to be seen here."

Her distress seemed genuine. He stepped in cautiously, his bow still partly drawn and ready.

"It's not a trick," she said. "Pern's not here. He's never here." Her voice turned harsh, and she went away into the house.

He followed her up the stairs to a small room with a desk, a wall of books at one end and a selection of fine-quality wall mats everywhere else. There was a grand "Wheatsheaves and Crossed Scythes" by Mesho on one wall. On the other was his own "Chooks and Beetles." It brought a weird kind of pang to his heart, like seeing a loved one laid out for a funeral.

"What do you want?" he said.

"Oh, Thru, I am so sorry for what I did to you. I know you'll never forgive me, but I have changed. I am not the selfish little mor who broke your heart."

"Neither of us is the same."

"I made the biggest mistake of my life when I wed Pern. I regret it every day. But I am here, pregnant, while he is in Dronned living a wild life. He's spending his family's wealth while everything here goes to wrack and ruin."

"So? I cannot help any of that. What did you want to warn me about?"

"He has planned to have you murdered on the beach. A message will be sent to you very soon. It will claim to be from a ship captain that you know well. It will advise you to come to the beach at Warkeen to be picked up from his ship. If you go to the beach, you will be killed, then taken out on a boat and fed to the fishes."

Thru felt a chill run through him. Pern had tracked him to Tamf, investigated enough to have found out about Thru's passage on the *Conch,* and deduced that he would be going back to Tamf on the fisherman's return sweep down the coast.

Worse, in a way, was that it was a clever ploy. That was worrying. Pern had learned from the failure of his earlier attempts at killing him.

"How do you know this?"

"Because Ulghrum tells me. Ulghrum thinks I desire him."

"And do you?"

"No. I love you, Thru."

He sighed, for a sweet vision of another life, a life that had gone forever. "Too late, Iallia. I love someone else, far from here."

"I know. I have heard all about you and this acrobat from Tamf. Pern enjoyed telling me every detail he could. Pern is very cruel, Thru."

"Why don't you leave him?"

"Because he swears he will kill my brother and sister

if I do. He is a killer. You have heard about Arin, haven't you?"

Thru nodded. Arin Huggles, who had been in a dispute with Pern over a seapond, had not been seen for days. Everyone in the village was worried for him.

"Arin was not the first. Nor the second." She saw the question in his eyes. "Not here, but in Dronned. Pern has killed mots who stood in the way of his dealings."

"Pern seems to think he can do anything without fear of retribution. Tell me, why haven't you gone to the constable?"

"Because I like the constable, and I don't want to get him killed. And then be killed myself. Pern thinks that he is above the rest of us and our petty rules."

"It will end with someone killing him. Not everyone will listen to the Spirit's voice."

For a moment he stared at the "Chooks and Beetles," where it hung in pride of place.

"It is lovely, Thru. You are an artist."

He turned to her.

"Then I am glad you have it, Iallia. You can appreciate it."

"Oh, Thru, Pern does, too. He has a very educated eye. He has three pieces by Mesho in this house. But he thinks your work is very good. One reason he wants to kill you. He is insanely jealous. When you broke the record in that game, something broke inside him. He was already bad, but after that he was evil."

Thru nodded to himself. That was when the attempts on his life had begun.

"If the result was to turn him into a murderer, then I wish I had never hit a run in my life."

Iallia sagged against him suddenly.

"Oh, Thru," she sobbed, "if you ever change your mind, come back and free me from this prison."

Thru patted her shoulders as if she was his sister, no more. It was gone, all that passion he'd once had for her. Burned out of him with grief first, then forgotten completely.

"You must leave him and return to your family. Others will court you, Iallia; you are very beautiful."

"But you would not come, would you?" Her softness pressed against him. She yearned to rekindle that fire that burned in him once. For a moment their eyes met.

"No, I would not."

He waited quietly for her to withdraw. She kept her eyes down.

"How will I know this messenger?"

"It will be someone from the village. An innocent party, given a message written by Ulghrum."

He nodded slowly. It was sneaky, and it might have worked.

"Thank you," he said. "I hope you can find your way out of this trap."

She was left only with a final glimpse as he slipped back out into the night.

His mother finally cornered him a couple of days later. She got him when he was immobilized by fatigue, sitting by the fire. He'd worked all day in the seapond, up to his waist in cold water rebuilding the pond's outer wall. Now, wrapped in a towel, he sat by the fire, drinking honeyed tea while Snej made some hot buttered biscuits.

Ual sat down across from him. From the stern set of her mouth he knew at once he was in for it.

"My son, you have not been straight with me. In fact, you've been avoiding me ever since you came home."

He stared back at her. She was perfectly correct.

"You're right."

"There, I knew it. A mother always knows."

"Mother," said Snejet, "don't start on him now."

"You be quiet, Miss Newlywed. I'm his mother. I didn't give birth in pain and blood and raise you from the cradle to have you run off and leave our village and wander the world like a vagabond."

"No, Mother, of course not. I understand."

"Then, when are you coming home for good? And when will you start to think about marriage? It is past time you were set to wed. You must come home and wear the waterweed next summer. I want to see my firstborn son produce grandchildren for me."

"Mother," said Snejet angrily, "you will have grandchildren soon enough."

"Yes, my dear, I know and I will treasure them. But this is my Thru, and I want him back."

"Mother," he said quietly, "I must find my own way. From an early age I was eager to roam. The Assenzi teach that it is natural."

"Let someone else's son be taken for this need. I want mine right here."

"I am sorry that this has hurt you, Mother. I will try and make you proud of me nonetheless."

"And who is this Nuza? Why are you snuggling and sexing with a mor that I have never met?"

"We met by accident, in the city."

The mention of the city was explanation enough to Ual, who had never been much interested in the wider world beyond her village. In that so-much-larger world anything might happen. The city had taken away her firstborn son.

"I must meet her. It is not seemly otherwise."

"Oh yes, you shall meet. Next summer we will come to Warkeen. Nuza has applied already for a permit to tour here in the early summer."

"Next summer! Well, at least I will see her. But I will not know her family."

"They are good people, Mother, but different from most that you know. They lived their earlier lives just as Nuza does, performing all over the Land."

"By the Spirit, vagabonds, just like you. But I never raised you to be a wanderer."

"It is not your fault, Mother. I was just born this way."

And with that Ual had to be satisfied, but she wasn't. Nor would she be. She would never accept this loss of her first son to some other village and some other mother's family.

Later, after supper, Thru sat with his younger brother

Gil out by the woodpile. They shared a pail of harvest ale, dipping their mugs as needed.

"We're gonna miss you in the village, Thru. There be trouble enough now."

Thru nodded. He wasn't the only mot in Warkeen Village who had stumbled onto Pern Treevi's bad side. There was a widespread fear of Treevi now.

"There's still no news of Arin?"

"None. He just disappeared. Went hunting for a rabbit up Buck Creek, and didn't come back."

"Was Ulghrum in the village then?"

"Ulghrum comes and goes. Sometimes he's here when Pern's here, sometimes on his own."

"He should be put on trial, but if there is no body found, then it would be hard to convict him. The constable would be loath to take it to trial."

Gil nodded. It was a disturbing likelihood.

Thru had another thought.

"Is there any possibility that there are pyluk up there, and that that's what happened to Arin?"

"There haven't been pyluk this side of Huwak Mountain in hundreds of years. We're too far from the Drakensberg ever to see them."

Thru sighed. "Remember, brother, do not let Father go hunting alone. Go with him and keep your eyes open."

Later, during the night, Thru lay awake for a while listening to the sounds of the house and the village at night. There were still grasshoppers *scritch-scratching* in the trees, but there was a definite coolness to the air. The first frost would not be long in coming.

Pern had become a very dangerous person, for he had seen that the laws that governed the Land were weakly enforced. His kind were a rarity in the Land. Hardly anyone ever broke the most important laws, like those against murder, violent theft, and sexual assault. Such crimes often resulted in village hangings, after judgment in a Royal Court, for the laws were strict in demanding adequate proof of any crimes. There had to be evidence, there had to be witnesses. For murder trials, there nearly always had to be a body.

Pern would try for Thru again. He wouldn't be stopped by failure. Perhaps Thru himself would be forced to abandon the way of the Spirit. Perhaps he would have to kill Pern, outside of the law.

The next morning there was a chill wind from the north. Whitecaps pounded onto the beach and the newly reinforced walls. That night there were fires going in every house in Warkeen, and the next morning there was frost on the ground.

Thru was with Ware in the workshop when the message came. He put down his adze and read the note, brought by young Iberto Clems.

It was exactly as foretold by Iallia. The note purported to come from Captain Olok and told him to be on the beach at dusk. The tide would turn soon after, and Olok would want to ride it out to deep water.

When the youngster had gone, tucking a couple of coppers into his purse, Thru showed the message to Ware.

Ware frowned.

"It is sooner than I had expected, but it is time the village dealt with this. We will settle this matter now."

In a few minutes they were joined by a couple of strapping Ugerbuds, who had long since grown to hate Pern Treevi for his lies, and some mots armed with staves, a couple with bows over their shoulders. It was quite a posse when they reached the beach and hid among the tall grass that grew on the fringes.

There was a boat on the beach.

Thru walked on, alone.

A figure suddenly stood up and drew his bow. Thru threw himself down, and the arrow meant for him whistled past harmlessly.

The posse charged from concealment. The figure in the boat gave a squawk and leaped out and started pushing the boat into the surf. But, before he could get far, the Ugerbuds caught up and overturned the boat.

They pulled Ulghrum out of the surf, stripped him of weapons, and thrust him into the center of the ring.

"You gave a message to Iberto Clems. You gave him a shilling, a silver shilling, to take the message to Thru Gillo."

"I deny it."

"Clems will testify to it, and we have the message. You intended to kill Thru Gillo. You are under arrest and will be taken to the constable."

Ulghrum wore a look of astonished rage as they hustled him up the lane.

At one point he managed to get close to Thru.

"That bitch will die," he hissed.

Thru bit back any response, not trusting himself in such proximity to Ulghrum.

The magistrate had opened the little courtroom, at the back of the village hall and was waiting when they brought Ulghrum in from the beach. The constable entered the charges. Ulghrum was invited to make a statement on his own behalf, which he refused to do without an advocate from Dronned.

A message was drafted at once and sent south to the capital city. The magistrate, Frey Wot, bound Ulghrum over to the custody of the constable, who put him in the single cell that served as a lockup in the village. It was really a meditation cell attached to the Fane of the Spirit, but it was fitted with a heavy oak door that could be bolted shut top and bottom from the outside.

Thru joined the constable in his office as charge papers were made out. Thru signed a statement that gave his part in the matter.

"Iallia Treevi may well be in danger now," Thru pointed out.

"She will go back to the Tramines. She cannot stay with Pern anymore."

"Unfortunately, she's pregnant."

"She can annul the marriage, on the basis of her fears. The child will then be raised a Tramine. Unless Pern can win custody, which I doubt. Pern has managed to tar himself with a lot of doubt and suspicion in a very short time. I wouldn't be surprised if the Assenzi took a look at him."

"If there's to be a trial, it will probably be held in Dronned, and you will be called to testify. Will I be able to contact you at your father's house?"

"No, I will leave an address. I will be in Tamf."

"I see." The constable pursed his lips, obviously not approving.

"In the spring I will be on the road, traveling with the troupe. I will send you an itinerary of our movements if you like."

"Mmmm, I expect the trial will be held sooner than that. Leave me an address in Tamf, and you'll be notified when a date's been decided on."

That night the taproom at the tavern was filled well past the normal hours as folk gathered to talk over the extraordinary events that had befallen the village. Pern Treevi was behind it all, that was certain, but Ulghrum had said nothing incriminating yet.

The tongues were wagging until the middle of the night, when the landlord finally shut up the saloon room and closed his door and put out the lights.

The folk made their way home, still talking.

In the morning the constable found that someone had come in the night and thrown back the bolts. Ulghrum was gone.

Within minutes the entire village was gathered down by the temple fane, and shortly a posse was sent out to search. It returned at nightfall after following tracks that seemed to peter out down the highway toward Dronned.

Over the next day or so several messages were sent to Dronned, and a guard was placed over Iallia Tramine, who had moved back into the Tramine house. Only a couple of servants remained in Pern Treevi's big house up on the hill.

Thru returned to the labors of autumn, working in the seapond, putting in a new drainage system for part of the family polder. Hard work, but useful, and at the end of each day there was measurable progress. Ware, Gil, and Thru all found themselves enjoying this time together. Even Ual was appeased to some extent.

Then one morning the weather-beaten visage of Ushk, crewmot of the *Conch,* appeared in the village, asking for Thru Gillo. There was intense suspicion at once of poor Ushk, who was on the verge of being arrested when Thru came running up, having been alerted as to what was happening.

The villagers apologized to old Ushk while Thru grabbed his pack and his bow. Then after a lengthy round of farewells, with tears from Ual, and more tears from Snejet, Thru set off with Ushk down the lane to the beach. On board the *Conch* he found the holds stuffed with dried fish and Captain Olok in a fine mood.

"We be tearing along with this fine wind. Be back in Tamf harbor tomorrow, I reckon."

Chapter 18

Once he'd reached Tamf, Thru had taken a room above a laundry on South Road, outside the walls and down near the bridge over the Tam. It was a spare space at first, but soon Thru acquired a few bits and pieces to make it home. First a bed and then some furniture, finally a loom and three long racks to hold fiber and weaves.

While he settled himself into his new lodgings he set to work on a "Leaf" mat, and presented it to Nuza's mother on his first visit to her house. It had been accepted, but coolly. Despite their own troubador pasts, both of them thought Nuza should retire from the life of the acrobat and marry a local farmer.

"It is much safer to live in a village," said Nuza's mother. "An acrobat gets one injury, and her career is threatened."

"She gets two, and it is over," said her father.

Nuza simply smiled and gave a Thru a wink whenever possible.

"Are you sure he's acceptable to the Dronned Guild?" said her father. "They are a very exclusive Guild up there, even more than our own in Tamf."

Nuza jumped in on that, of course. "The Dronned weavers have a high reputation, but Thru's work is better than theirs. Really, wait until you see some of his best. Do you like the 'Leaf' pattern?"

"It is different from the usual."

Nuza could tell that her mother did not approve of

Thru or of Nuza's making love to him. She sighed. She'd been afraid of this.

Thereafter their meetings had usually been here in his rough-and-ready room on the South Road. Around them the road echoed with the sounds of cobblers and blacksmiths at work, not to mention the bakery and the laundry below his own room. Despite Assenzi efforts, Tamf, like Dronned and most other cities of the Land, had grown beyond its old walls. Now most of the noisy and smelly industrial activities were carried out in suburban areas, while the city itself was largely residential.

Thru had come to like his big room, although he pined for Kussha's cooking. In Tamf, Thru was getting used to a diet of sweet tea, bread, and sugared rolls from the cookshops on the South Road.

He had started on a "Chooks and Beetles" for Nuza, and had made drawings of a "Mussels and Rakes" that was unlike any he had ever seen. His mussels were large and crudely drawn, and he would use dark green and black fiber for the dark areas and a hard, chalky white for the few areas of relief. Twelve pairs of mussels, each pair different from the rest in subtle ways, would run down the length of the mat, and to either side were the long rakes, crossed handles, dark iron tines at the bottom. For background he used a pale blue fiber made from cornstalk to suggest the sky and then shifted to a slate grey for the lower half, on which he wove a pattern in black to outline the stones of the seapond bottom. He was excited with the work, thinking about it even when he was away from the loom.

Nuza stirred beside him in the bed. She usually slept for an hour or so after they made love. The light was beginning to fade, and she would be expected back at her own house shortly. Her mother had become critical of any absences from the evening meal. Nuza was trying not to let the storm break while she kept the two halves of her life widely separated. Thru stroked the soft fur on the back of her head and ran his fingers down her neck.

She stretched luxuriantly under his touch, with the suppleness of a cat.

Thru hadn't pushed for more visits to the family house. Except for her visits he spent his time working, breaking only long enough to grab a quick bowl of chowder now and then. He had an urge to make every second count.

"Leaf" mats piled up on the rack. When he had six of them he switched to a new pattern, this time a dramatic reworking of "Bushpod" with bright green pods entwined with stems in yellow on a reddish background.

Nuza was convinced that he was on his way to acceptance as a significant artist. He was proposing the most radical shift in mat weave since the great Oromi. Behind his radical notions lay interesting design and solid competence in weaving technique.

She was awake by then, sitting up with the quilt around her breasts, her eyes blinking in the dim light of late afternoon.

"Did you sleep?" he asked.

"Yes, but I dreamed my mother was scolding me."

"Ah." He grinned. "You know, I can imagine how that must have felt." Nuza snuggled up against him.

"I really didn't expect her to be so difficult."

"Well, my mother gave me a good going-over before I got out of the village. She hates the thought that I might settle with someone outside of her own kin."

"That's the old village way of thought."

"I suppose I won't be invited to dinner on Midwinter fest."

"At the moment, no. But I think the troupe will hold their own dinner, at the vagabond's hall."

"And where will you be?"

"I will be at home. Mother will expect me to wait on her while she decorates the tree. It is a very solemn occasion in her family."

"Then I will loft a cup of mead in your direction before I sing with Hob and the rest of them. At least they seem like a cheerful crew."

"Everyone except Toshak. You'll find he's a quiet soul on that day. No one knows why."

"He never told you?"

"Toshak has many mysteries in his past. That is just a minor one."

She rose and dressed. She wore thick wool trousers and knee-high brown boots. Her blouse and tunic were of finest grey Mauste, and at her throat she wound a pale blue scarf of silk from Geld.

"When can you come again?"

"I'm not sure. Maybe the day after tomorrow. Mother has taken to trying to keep me busy with holiday preparations. She watches me like a hawk watches a rabbit."

"There's a meeting of the Questioners that day."

"Will you go?"

"Yes, especially if you do."

"It's at the house of the reverend elder, Mekel Hooser. You'll find it on River Road, close to the north gate."

Thru was holding her hands, looking into her eyes. "When I look at you, I think the Questioners must be wrong. There had to be a plan to make the world so fine and fair. It had to be guided by a beneficent spirit to bring me something so beautiful."

She smiled. "Flattery will take you far, my lover."

They spent the next few days together as much as possible until, at the last minute he decided to return to Warkeen for the festival. Nuza was going to be completely wrapped up in her own family's doings for the festival, and his own parents desperately wanted to see him at their table.

By great good fortune, the trade ship *Elmert* was in Tamf harbor and about to leave for the north. The wind was favorable and the *Elmert* made Dronned the next day. From there his luck continued, and a local fishing boat took him around to the estuary of the Dristen River. From the beach he walked up to the village and caught everyone by surprise. The joyful noise in the Gillo household brought inquisitive neighbors from all directions, and soon there was a party in progress.

The festival itself began the next day with the biggest feast of the year. In the morning there was a packed ceremony at the Fane of the Spirit and at noon an athletic contest. If the river had frozen in time, there would be skating and curling contests on the ice. Otherwise, there would be a footrace up the road to Meever's and back, the winner to become the feted Winter King.

This was one of the years of mild winter weather. The river had scarcely frozen at all, and so the race to Meever's was run. Thru was not the fleetest of mots, and though he was capable of running the distance, he doubted that he'd come in even in the first fifty. Instead he watched the runners start and then sat in Snejet's parlor and washed down a pie of honeyed bushpod with some mulled ale.

Snejet was obviously very happy in marriage. She wore tiny white-and-pink ribbons tied into the fur of her head and spoke happily about all that had happened in his absence.

"The harvest was very good. We sold Merchant Yadrone a fair ton of bushpod. Father was very pleased. He plans to put on fresh thatch for the whole house next year."

"And how has Gil been?"

"Gil has grown now that he's out of your shadow, brother. With his help and with Oiv, we've been able to free Ware from farm work so he can concentrate on carving. That's helped a lot, too."

Thru was cheered by all this news. But the inevitable question had to be asked.

"And Mother?"

"Oh, Thru, she grieves. When she thinks no one is listening she weeps. It's so sad to hear her, but she cannot be comforted."

Thru acknowledged that he had caused their mother hurt, but he refused to be talked into staying in Warkeen through the rest of the winter. His path was set, and it lay in Tamf.

"No one has come forward to claim the reward put on that villain Ulghrum."

"I didn't expect they would capture him. He's gone south. I expect he's in Fauste or maybe even Mauste."

"Funny you should say that, brother, because we heard that Pern has gone to Mauste. He has some plan for learning the secrets of making Mauste cloth. Everyone in the village hopes he stays there and never comes back."

"And Arin Huggles?"

"Has never been seen again."

"Ach, so I feared. A bad business that."

"Iallia isn't seen around much either. She stays in the Tramine house. I talk to the Tramine mors, and they say she's gone very cold and hardly has a kind word for anyone."

Snejet's gossippy tongue roved on. There was dame Eltha Bik's loss of memory, and Hinger Alford's incredible hive of bees, which had produced a record amount of honey that year.

"Hinger says they're amazing. He's had only one sting from them all season, too."

Then, at last, it was time to go downstairs for Ual's festival feast. Ware had already broached a keg of winter ale and the chooks were having a wild party in the yard. Chooks were notoriously light of head when it came to ale. Now the roosters were crowing and the hens were dancing while a foot drum thundered away to keep the beat.

Ual and Gil brought out platters of stuffed crabs with bushpod crêpes in honey. Then came a whole salmon baked on the hot coals and later a haunch of venison, roasted over a fire in the yard.

After the meal the family went down to the green in the center of the village.

Chooks, already well stuffed with bushpod and beans, were given more ale before they started their midwinter dance. It celebrated the role of the chook in the village economy, for chooks suppressed insect pests to such an extent that the village harvest was doubled from what it would have been without the big foolish fowls. After a while the jumping of the chooks infected even the oldest mots and mors, replete though they were, and they too got to their feet and started dancing.

When things were really bouncing there came a blast from the constable's trumpet and the Winter King was carried in by four stout mots and set on his throne. The Winter King this year was young Yerri Hipens, who'd won the race earlier in the day, coming in a good hundred yards ahead of the second mot. The Harvest Queen then crowned the Winter King, and ended her own reign. There was raucous applause and the Winter King sang his song and after a verse or two the musicians picked it up and amplified it and everyone returned to dancing.

So went the festival for Thru, a mixture of great meals and sentimental memories reawakened. Afterward he returned to Tamf in much the same way he'd come north, catching a ride on a fishing boat heading south to Dronned. The boat this time was *Dory Alma* under Captain Murflut. She was heading back to Dronned with a full hold of cod and halibut from the northern grounds. Murflut was happy to take a few more shillings from Thru to carry him around to the city.

That night, off Raker's Point, they drank seabeer together, and he told them how the festival had gone in Warkeen. They listened with sad expressions. For them it had been just another day of hard work. That was the lot of the fishermot: He must be at sea when the fish are there, not when festivals dictate.

"But though we didn't have much to feast on and nothing but seabeer to drink," said Captain Murflut with a grin, "we had a visit from the spirits."

"Oh?"

"We saw sails in the moonlight," said sailor Pukli. "Big as houses, tall as trees they were."

"They were stacked three deep. I never seen real sails like that." Murflut refilled their mugs.

"We all saw it," said Mitz, the remaining member of

the crew. "It was a vision sent to us all. It must mean something good, but I don't know what it could be."

Thru was excited by their news. These fishermots had been touched personally by the Spirit. The Questioners had to be wrong, the Spirit was real, and it not only listened passively to their meditations and prayers, it reached out actively to help them.

"Where did you see this?"

"We were out past the western banks, in the lee of Roam rocks. The sea shelf there is always good for cod in winter."

"Aye, we were setting lines at night when it happened. We were looking west when the sails appeared. They went from south to north, and we lost sight of 'em in sea mist."

"It were a misty night," said old Pukli. "Made me wonder if I was just imagining it. Trick of the moonlight or something."

"But we all seen it, so it had to be more than that."

"When you get home you have to tell the Assenzi. Go to the temple, talk to Melidofulo. He will guide you in interpreting your vision."

"Go to the Assenzi? I don't know," muttered Captain Murflut. "Not sure I like the idea of that."

"But why? The Assenzi will not harm you."

"I've heard tales of them things that could curl your fur."

"You shouldn't put your trust in tales. Ask the Assenzi anything, and they will respond. They are not evil mages or wizards or some such thing."

"Oh yes, and what do you know about Assenzi?" said Murflut.

"Or anything else for that matter," sniggered old Pukli.

"Well, about the Assenzi I learned a little when I was at Highnoth."

"Ah ha, you're a Highnoth youth. That explains it."

"But, by the Spirit," Thru had become passionate, "you should listen to me. Go to Melidofulo in Dronned.

The Assenzi can tell you much about matters of the Spirit."

Thus they argued for a while, until the conversation shifted back to the price their cod would fetch in the market.

Thru was not sure that he had converted any of them, but he hoped they would remember his words when they thought about this remarkable vision they'd had.

The next morning they made landfall in Dronned, and Thru bid them farewell. The weather had finally changed over to winter, and he was forced to stay in Dronned for several days while a winter storm battered the coast, leaving the season's first snow on the city streets.

Thru took a room at the Harbor Inn, which soon filled up as every boat in harbor stayed put. While the storm whipped snowflakes around the streets and alleys, Thru went about his rounds. He visited Merchant Ortenod and dropped by at Merchant Yadrone's house. The merchants welcomed him and treated him to sweet wine and biscuits and the blessing of the season.

Later he formally delivered a letter to the Grys Norvory. With it was sworn testimony from Iallia Treevi concerning the true ownership of the "Chooks and Beetles" mat. The Grys refused to meet him in person, which he had expected, so he simply left the letter and went his way.

He stopped in at Kussha's house and found Noop waiting for the evening meal. Together they joined Bluit down at the Laughing Fish over an ale or two before returning to a feast from Kussha's kitchen.

He learned that after he'd left them the Laughing Fish team had lost its last two games and finished well out of the running. Most of the club's members were convinced that Thru's batting would have changed that. Pern Treevi had not been popular around the clubhouse, and Rawli Perensa was said to be still outraged at the lies Treevi had told him. Treevi had last been heard of sailing south to Mauste, just as Snejet had reported.

The next day he stopped at the House of Norvory and

made an inquiry for the Grys's reply to his letter. After a wait of several minutes on the doorstep he was brusquely informed that his message had not been read and probably wouldn't be. Thru stormed off, biting his lip to keep from erupting with angry words. After walking blindly through the streets for several hours he made his way to Kussha's once more. There he took comfort in good company and later, from Kussha's magnificent evening meal.

Afterward he thought about the problem. He could not get justice in the Royal Courts because of his lack of standing in the Guild of Dronned. There was only one way he could force the Grys to give an accounting of his actions. It was very rarely used, but it was still legal and could be called on in an extreme situation, such as that which faced Thru Gillo.

The next day, the storm had abated and a fishing boat took him down the coast to Tamf. Before setting out he left another message for the Grys Norvory in which he protested about the lack of respect shown him and challenged the Grys to a duel come the summer, when he next returned to Dronned.

Chapter 19

4

That winter in Tamf was a time that Thru would always look back on as a period bathed in golden light. Between his affair with Nuza and his work, his life was immensely satisfying and full. Never had he felt so alive, so awake to every moment of the day. Despite the problems with Pern Treevi and the guilds in Dronned, it seemed that the future was his to shape.

Thru and Nuza read together and argued about the meaning of life and the words of the Great Book. They went to meetings of the Questioners, and Thru felt his thinking broadening with each visit.

"I believe we were made with a purpose in mind, and that purpose is that we fit within the world as it exists. The Spirit is real to me."

"There is no evidence that the Spirit exists."

"I can feel the Spirit inside me."

Nuza would smile, then sigh softly. "So do I."

They would laugh together.

"But some of the Questioners would deny it."

"I understand what they are saying, but I cannot agree with them."

Thru distrusted the idea that all was the result of chaotic chance. He clung steadfastly to the strength he felt from the Spirit.

He had come to understand that the Questioners came from many viewpoints and that some groups were larger than others. He knew that many folk who came to the meetings were like him, eager to learn, but certain in their hearts that the Spirit existed.

Meanwhile Nuza's mother had come to accept the affair. She had not issued an invitation to the house, but she had given up the constant assault on Nuza.

His room was always hot from the laundry below, so he would weave with the windows wide-open. He put up "Leaf" pattern mats for part of the day, then he would turn to another mat, either "Chooks and Beetles" or "Mussels and Rakes." There was also a new pattern for "Nets and Fishes," one of the oldest styles in existence, but he had to yet to start weaving that one.

"Mussels and Rakes," with its dramatic touches of high weft detail, was emerging as a masterpiece. His knotting was improving. Still not Mesho, but far above the average. Day by day the pattern became clearer, the shapes took on a lifelike quality, and the work grew strong. Nuza was thrilled with his progress.

The two lovers ate together, usually roast fish and bushpod bought out of the cookshop on the opposite corner. While they ate they talked of their plans for the summer. It promised to be a very busy time.

"Creton, that's where I want to be in the spring." Nuza was very definite. "Smaller places down there, like Bilauk, don't get a lot of attention from the troupes and actors. I think we'd get a good reception. We can work our way down as far as Cape Blue before the end of Early Summer Moon. Then we come back up on the inland route and pass through the mining towns in the mountains."

"I like that plan," said Thru, who in truth would be happy going in any direction. "Creton is said by all to be very beautiful country. But will we get to Dronned for the summer fest?"

"We'll take passage on a fishing boat. They'll be sailing up to Tamf and Dronned for the summer squid."

"You think folk will wager again on me in those places we visited last year?"

"Oh, yes. There will always be challengers for you. Toshak, well that's different. He's known as a product of the academy. You have to be very good with a sword to think about challenging him. But throwing the ball past seventy-seven-run Thru Gillo? Now *that* is something lots of young mots might dream of doing and telling their friends."

At Nuza's insistence they went twice a week to take lessons in swordfighting technique with Toshak. They met him on the dueling ground, a flat space just outside the city's western gate, where they drilled with foils and tried the wider-bladed weapons, too.

Nuza knew that Thru would challenge the Grys Norvory in the summer. There would be a duel with swords, and the Grys had been trained in his youth, as all young aristocrats were. Thru needed further training if he was to stand a chance.

Toshak's face, compressed by the intensity of the moment, was an image that became imprinted on Thru's mind. The eyes flared wide so the whites were showing, the ears back, the lips pulled taut from the battle cry.

Toshak had such speed in the advance and retreat and such incredible quickness in flicks and parries that Thru was left amazed. It was no wonder that hardly anyone ever took up Toshak's challenge. Certainly Thru was never able to take more than a point or two from him in a bout. Foil and epee, spadroon and short sword, they were all the same to Toshak.

At times it was like kyo with Master Sassadzu—the mantra of the pointed hand, direct and light, but unstoppable, the liquid movements that were impossible to counter. Toshak in flow was elemental.

"You have a steady arm; in time you will learn to use it." Toshak would give Thru no easy passage.

A few times they met with the rest of the troupe to discuss the next summer. One of the big issues they faced was the need for old Hob to retire soon. One more summer perhaps, that was all that Hob could give to catching Nuza. Beyond that they would need a new brilby, or a kob if one was to be found.

Nuza got very busy for a while working up new costumes for the summer. She liked to change them and not appear in the exact same catsuits and jumpers year after year. The previous year had been crimson and yellow, the next was to be more summery, more green and maybe even frilly. When she had settled on a design she worked together with her mother to cut and sew the cloth, using the best Mauste wool cloth and Gelden silks.

The months wore on. Mats mounted up. Finally "Chooks and Beetles" was finished. A glorious object, shimmering with bright color. Nuza took it home and showed it to her mother, Damora, who was stunned by the quality of the work. She saw, as had her daughter, that Thru was indeed gifted.

Damora, a potter, knew in her bones that something extraordinary was at work. The pattern was the age-old "Chooks and Beetles," but in Thru's hands it had taken on a fresh life. The rendering was superb, and the chooks had a jauntiness that was almost shocking. She took the "Chooks and Beetles" to show friends who she knew had an interest in the art of woven mats. All were impressed. Thru's reputation spread rapidly, and he received visits from a couple of the merchants of Tamf. By then neither Damora nor Cham was complaining any longer about their daughter's unconventional relationship with Thru Gillo.

Merchant Namp, the bearer of an ancient name in the world of Tamf guilds and politics, came to visit the workroom on South Road. The Grys Namp was a refined soul, and he found the smells on South Road very unpleasant. But when he looked on the work Namp saw at once that the youngster from the Dristen Valley had genuine talent.

"And this is the same work that Norvory of Dronned claimed had been stolen by you?"

"This is my fourth piece of this pattern. My mother always kept a 'Chooks and Beetles' mat in the parlor."

"It is an old, familiar pattern."

"Yes, but I felt it could be taken further."

And Merchant Namp agreed that he had done just that. He offered to buy it at once. Nuza turned him down immediately, and persuaded Thru to show the merchant the "Mussels and Rakes," which was now close to completion, too. Namp felt his eyes widen. It was powerful, original work, and it raised the art by a notch or two. This was work as good as any except that of Mesho and Oromi.

Soon there came a letter from Dronned, this time from Merchant Yadrone. He could take no mats himself, though he hastened to add that his wife had bought a "Leaf" pattern mat and hung it in the inner hall of the house. But traders in Tamf had spread the word that Thru Gillo had woven another "Chooks and Beetles" exactly like that which the Grys Norvory had seized. That Thru Gillo was showing signs of a prodigious talent, and Norvory had been terribly wrong. Norvory had withdrawn from the city to his country estate at Runglin.

Meanwhile, at the Dronned Weavers' Guild it had been suggested that the candidacy of one Thru Gillo be actively considered. Several members were reaching retirement age in the next year. Openings would be available.

Thru read this and felt a surge of triumph. He could succeed; despite everything, he could achieve his dream.

At last "Mussels and Rakes" was done. Thru agreed to let Merchant Namp display the piece in his window and conduct the auction, which would be held at the festival to mark the beginning of summer, the Flower festival of the fifth moon.

In the window "Mussels and Rakes" caught the eye with its boldness. The mussels were luminous in raised weft that gave them lifelike texture against the harsh angles of the rakes. The piece shimmered there and drew a small crowd on most days.

As winter drew on, so the late-winter festivals, of Shooting Stars, and Prince Frost, came upon them. On these festivals the Winter King was symbolically dunked in the village pond to get him to hurry up and get the winter over and done with. Music and dancing, raucous crowds in the streets until late, the festivals were a swirl of color against the dark of late winter.

During these days Thru and Nuza avoided the parties and taverns and withdrew to the room over the laundry and enjoyed long uninterrupted time together. Thru had never imagined himself being this happy. From the depths of rejection in Dronned the previous summer, he had soared somehow to success in almost every aspect of his life.

Chapter 20

That spring the troupe headed southwest into the Creton peninsula a hundred miles from Tamf. The land was lovely and green, with mists cloaking the moors. The grey seas lashed into foam at the feet of the startlingly white chalk cliffs. Small villages built of stone and wattle clustered in the valleys, and sheep grazed the hillsides. The weavers of the region worked in wool and specialized in a thick woolen cloth that was highly prized everywhere for outer coats and cloaks.

There were no large cities on the Creton, just villages scattered down the rocky coast and a few coal mining towns in the mountains, so few entertainers took the trouble to wander the flint-paved roads. Nuza's hunch paid off handsomely. The troupe was welcomed everywhere by small, but enthusiastic audiences wherever they stopped.

Thru found plenty of youngsters with powerful shoulders who thought they could get a ball past Seventy-seven-Run Gillo, and his purse soon had the weight of a good number of silver shillings. He'd also met a few throwers of the ball who were so good he'd recommended they try up at Tamf as professionals.

Even Toshak had found a number of challengers. He'd never visited these small places, and every village had at least one mot who reckoned himself an expert with the sword. Mostly they chose to fight with the light spadroon, the favorite blade of the Land because it was so economical in metal. Toshak preferred the flowing style that came with the foil, but he wielded the shorter, broader spadroon just as impeccably.

From Crozett they turned south on the coastal road for Bilauk. That night they camped outside a tiny hamlet called Shaffgums on the Bilauk headland. The folk were happy to see them and applauded the short demonstration that Nuza, Gem, and Hob put on. Then Serling juggled and Toshak performed the sword kyo and they were awed. A jug of fine ale and a pile of toasted pod puppies made of dried fish and flour was their reward.

A long, beautiful sunset ended the day while they built up the fire and made guezme tea. It was cool in the evening, and they pulled coats and blankets around themselves while they talked drowsily about Creton and their plans for the rest of the summer.

Thru was content, his legs were pleasantly tired, and he was looking forward to sleep and the next day's journey down to Bilauk on the bay. He lay back against the wheel of the caravan with Nuza at his side, holding his hand.

The next day dawned clear and bright. They breakfasted, broke camp, and bid farewell to the tiny population of Shaffgums before heading off across the headland and down toward Bilauk Bay. After about an hour they noticed a tall column of smoke rising ahead of them, somewhere down the bay toward Bilauk. The source was hidden from view by the central mass of the headland, which they were still climbing.

"Big fire somewhere," said Hob with a note of wonder.

The cloud of black smoke was awfully thick and roiling high.

"What can be burning?" asked Nuza.

"Something damned big," said Serling, watching the smoke roil up into the sky.

"Fire is just so awful." Gem's lip quivered. "We were burned out of the inn in Gratesfield when I was young. It was the worst night of my life."

"That is very big fire," said Hob, appraising the column of smoke once more.

"Could they be burning the fields of stubble?" Nuza suggested.

"Not in spring," said Thru, more familiar with the farmer's round than Nuza. "And besides that's black smoke, means wood is burning. Lots of wood."

"The forest, then?" said Nuza, still searching.

"Has it been that dry here?" said Serling. "It was normal enough in Tamf."

There had been steady rain for a week early in the month. It seemed impossible that Creton had been spared the downpour.

With rising concern, they hurried their steps up the winding road. A breeze from the sea began to take the smoke inland, and so the column became an ominous dark finger curving over the Land.

When they reached the top they gazed out across the broad waters below. The column of smoke was rising from Bilauk itself, far down the bay. That meant it was a bigger fire than anything they had imagined. Thick clouds of black smoke billowed up from the edge of the bay. The whole village was on fire.

And yet that was not the greatest cause for their consternation. Far more astonishing was the ship they saw in the middle of the bay, under sail and moving swiftly out into the open sea.

A mountain of white canvas rose up three tall masts, each of which boasted a long pennon, trailing off in the wind. Beneath the canvas was an exposed side of long dark wood that was ten or twenty times the size of the biggest cog ever built by the folk of the Land.

"It's the vision that I heard of aboard the *Dory Alma,*" said Thru. "Captain Murflut told me they'd seen a giant ship like this, a mountain of sails they called it. They saw it on the western banks—and now we see it here."

Toshak was examining the ship through a small brass spyglass that he kept in his pack.

"There are mots on that ship, I can just make them out. It is not a vision. It is real."

Nuza wrenched her eyes away from the great ship. "What is it doing here?"

"Are they raiders?" said Gem with a tremor in his voice. Raiders were known from the ancient legends, back in the days when the northern folk had sailed south and assaulted towns on the coasts. Outlaws in longships had once plundered the coasts, but this had all ended long ago, when the peace of the five Kings of the North was established.

"Come," said Toshak, pocketing his spyglass as the great ship disappeared past the southern headland. "We must hurry. The folk in Bilauk will need help."

"But what about the vision ship. What is it?"

"I know not, but it is real. The water breaks under its bows just as it would a ship one-tenth its size."

Shaking his head in amazement, Thru picked up his pace, and together they all began jogging along the road. Fortunately, it was mostly downhill.

As they got closer to the village the smell hit them. The fire was well and truly in control of poor Bilauk. The tightly packed houses of wood and stone, close set along the alleys around the harbor, were ablaze.

They reached the outskirts of the village. Flames were licking up from the town hall and the big fish warehouse. The smaller houses were already falling in flaming ruins. The smoke made them cough and gasp as they struggled down the streets.

Then they started to find bodies; a few mots and mors scattered through the town, usually with arrow and spear wounds, sometimes with smashed skulls. An old mor was huddled in the gutter outside her house, her neck almost completely severed by a savage blow. Her blood had run down the gutter and pooled lower down the street.

The doors to the houses were broken open, and smoke was rising from the windows.

Thru turned away in horror from an alley entrance, where five young mots had died after putting up a struggle. Blood was spattered all over the walls on either side, and great gouts of it had run in the gutters. The mots had been killed and their bodies mutilated: limbs hewn off, heads removed.

The horror of the scene made Gem sob openly. Thru felt his reason challenged. Why would anyone kill like this? Even pyluk would not kill so many. Once they had enough to fill their bellies, pyluk would have stopped to divvy up the meat.

Here and there, a few houses had escaped the general conflagration. A cluster of them lay at the end of one alley, protected by their stone walls and slate roofs. Still they had been devastated. Doors were broken open, shutters ripped off.

As they watched, a survivor stumbled from one of these houses, a middle-aged mor with her shift torn and stained with blood.

"What happened here?" said Nuza reaching out to the mor.

The mor could only stare back at them with eyes so big they seemed to stand out of her head. She spread her hands aimlessly and wept.

"All dead," was all she could say. "Dead, all dead. All dead."

Gem was trembling. "Who were they?"

The woman gave an inarticulate cry and darted back into the ruined house.

Toshak sprang forward and caught her at the last moment and pulled her out, weeping and screeching. Nuza leading the distraught mor by the hand, Toshak behind to prevent her running back, they headed for the harbor in the center of the village, where the jetty jutted forth in the middle of a broad paved area. This was where fish were landed, boats hauled up, and folk could stroll and look at the sea. If anyone else had survived, perhaps they would gather there.

There was an irregular heap at the point where the jetty joined the land. Gem drifted over toward it, then gave a scream and staggered back before falling to his knees and vomiting. The heap contained the heads of mots, mors, brilbies, chooks, and even donkeys. There was blood all over that part of the dock.

Nuza dropped down beside the hideous pile, and began to pray.

"Who do you pray for, Lady?" said Toshak.

"I pray for the souls of those who did this, for they are lost in darkness."

Thru saw the dead eyes of a dozen mots and mors staring back at him, and shuddered with horror and sorrow in equal part. A chill passed through him as if his very heart had suddenly been exposed to ice.

Who could have done this? Who were these enemies who would kill so wantonly?

"Where are the bodies?" said Serling suddenly. "All I see are their heads."

PART THREE

Chapter 21

Simona stirred and opened her eyes. She was still aboard the Imperial ship *Growler*. Still swinging in her hammock in the dark, crowded heat of the women's deck.

The stench, the noise, the vibrations of 450 women cooped up for ten months in the belly of the ship—by the pure skin of the Great God, Simona wished she were somewhere else. And, of course, being young and of little worth, she never got to use a porthole. Those were reserved for the grandmothers of the elite. They had their health as an excuse, and used it tenaciously.

Simona could feel the ship moving heavily through the water, a crisper thud with each wave. The *Growler* was under way and breaking through stiff seas. Something had happened: They had changed direction, or else a storm was coming up. The huge wooden members that held the decks together were creaking in a way that Simona had learned meant they were moving fast, usually with the wind coming from the west.

She wondered where they were going in such a hurry. For months they had simply patrolled up and down the ocean far off the coast of the New Land. Nothing but tantalizing stories and a few scraps of limp vegetation had come their way. Food was running low, even the fishing was poor.

Were they going to the New Land, finally, at long bloody last?

Oh let it be the New Land, at last! Let it be release from the women's deck. If she had known beforehand how long this confinement would last, she would have

begged her father to leave her behind. Marry her off to
Master Pilpio, anything, but save her from having to go
on this accursed voyage, packed in the ship like pigs in
a pen. Simona had never experienced anything so
degrading.

Mother, of course, was enduring it like a stoic, as she
always did, but Simona was heartily sick of it all. Months
and months of being cooped up in this huge harem! It
was horrible. And at night the men came in to enjoy the
rites of the rut. The cries of the women, the exulting
roars of the warriors, all of it made Simona feel ill.

At least back home a woman was mistress of her
house, her garden, and her kitchen. The man was the
master, of course, but he entered her domain when he
came into his house. She had some standing. Aboard the
ship she had nothing but her body and ten square feet
to rest it in.

On ship the women couldn't even cook the wretched
stuff they dared to call food. Endless pease porridge,
horrible old salt pork, some of it all gristle and bone,
biscuit of indifferent quality, it was monotonous and
bland. But all the cooking was done in the ship's galley,
where the work was reserved for men, indifferent cooks
who did little to improve the raw materials given them
by the Emperor.

The ship was beginning to dip its nose each time it
crested a swell, a sure indication that they were entering
heavier weather. Simona saw that Puty and Panala were
gone, their hammocks stowed on the hooks above. That
gave Simona an unusually large area of personal space.
She took advantage of it to perform some stretching ex-
ercises and finished with two dozen push-ups done in sets
of twelve. It was the only physical exercise available to
her, or anyone else on the women's deck, and she used
every opportunity. Simona had always been an outdoors
person. At home she had done her utmost to spend most
of her time at the family's country estate, Shesh Zob,
where purdah was a much gentler affair. The males on
the estate were eunuch and under the Law of Orbaz, so

she was free to ride her horses properly, and not sidesaddle as was required in company. She was free to run, to hunt in the forest with the bow, to swim in the lake and many other things that would earn her a death sentence were she to do them beyond the walls of her father's estate.

As she worked her muscles, she tried to ignore a screaming match going on across the passage in Kima Rezzigu's quarters. Kima was yelling abuse at her daughter, something that occurred several times a day.

Screaming, weeping, occasional bouts of laughter, these were the sounds she had lived with for almost a year in this hell on the waves. She turned her mind away from it all and went with the thud and slow quiver of the ship as they broke the waves. Where were they going in such a hurry? To the New Land with its virgin shores, its wealth of game and wood? Such wonderful tales she had heard about the New Land. There were endless verdant forests, uncut by man. There were fertile valley bottoms, already cultivated by the autocthonous animals. All that had to be done was to clear away the animals, remove their wretched huts, and build anew.

Of course there was no way to find out directly what was happening. She could not openly speak to the men of the crew. She would have to use the women's hierarchy.

She knew perfectly well that within a minute of the order being given the old crones that ruled the women's deck would have known of the decision and their destination. The crones ruled with a hard hand. The captain's wife was the worst; Vli Shuzt had ruled her family from within the confines of purdah since she was first wed.

So, Vli would know. And Vli would tell her cronies, one by one, parceling out the information to make sure they all felt the thrill of learning it. Eventually someone would tell Simona, too. If she asked the right person, the right way.

Her own mother, by her stupidity, had alienated Vli and caused tensions within the Gsekk clan itself. And so their family had been wrenched from their comfortable

life in Shasht and placed in this hell on water, with Chiknulba completely out of things with the rulership of the
women's deck. She was not even part of the hierarchy
that disseminated information.

Simona sighed unhappily. Alas, her mother was living
in a sort of mental fog these days. It was not from opium
or rum, either. It was self-generated, a way for Chiknulba
to slip away from the awful reality here, a filter that shut
out the noise and smell. Her response to the outer world
had grown erratic, halfhearted, and a bit chaotic.

Simona made up her mind. She would have to beg.

She finished wiping herself down and then went forward. Aunt Jemelm was her best chance of finding out.

"You got something for me?" said the mountainous
woman from her softly cushioned cell. Aunt Jemelm was
very well connected.

"I have nothing, Aunt. I'm skint. You know how it is.
None of the officers have been paid for months. Chiknulba will not exert herself, and Filek is afraid. He is
assistant surgeon, but he could be replaced."

"He would be surplus then."

"And without political friends on this ship. My poor
father is lost in this world of deception and treachery.
You know my position, Aunt Jemelm. I have nothing,
but I just want to know where we're going."

"Filek in bad position. He lose his position, he risk
losing his balls. Your mother is a Gsekk, they will be
very unhappy. There will be blood rites. Djinns and
demons will be summoned up. Sickness will spread. Oh,
old auntie, she knows. And you, red-mark girl, what do
you know? Why you want to know where going?"

"I'd just like to know, that's all."

Aunt Jemelm chuckled, her several chins wobbling.
"Oh, you need to know!" She laughed some more. "You
will owe me many sheep when we reach land."

"Their meat is yours. I have no sheep."

"We are going to meet the other ships. The *Anvil* has
signaled after returning from the coast. There is fresh
meat."

Meat? Simona salivated at the thought.

"Thank you, Aunt Jemelm."

"You owe me your sheep."

"Yes, Aunt Jemelm." Simona kissed Jemelm's ring and bowed out of her presence.

The light was brightening steadily as the day advanced. Belowdecks it never got brighter than gloom, but at least it was bright gloom in the middle of the day. She had groveled to her aunt and been rewarded, but her tally with Aunt Jemelm was already long. Someday she would have to pay.

Thus it was to live in purdah, belowdecks. Ever wondering what was happening beyond the door, past the guards and eunuchs. Always thinking about the outside, the free world, where men went to and fro, unconstrained, unshielded, in the sun and the wind.

In Shasht society, the shadow fell over women after their menses first broke. The doors closed around them, and they were locked away. Many women never again felt the sun or the wind on their bodies.

Simona positioned herself near the pump house. She saw Bera Fenida taking up her accustomed place as first in line. Bera would be getting breakfast for Vli herself.

There was a huge clatter above their heads then a gruff bellow from the guard, "Breakfast!" Simona hurried toward the door when it opened, but as always she was jostled and shoved out of the way as hundreds of hungry women scrambled for the trays.

The eldest did not stand in line. They allowed their most favored daughters to press to the front and fetch them a meal. Then the most favored daughters were allowed to go to the back of the line for their own meals. Nevertheless, there was intense competition to be among the most favored daughters.

Simona was not one of them, of course, and she waited patiently about two-thirds of the way down the line, as she usually did. It snaked forward, at less than a walking pace, but more than a crawl, and for some reason it was always unbearable. There was nothing to do but to pray to the Great God. *If He Who Eats can hear my message, let me eat, too.*

At last she reached the doors. Slaves were bringing in the trays, stacked six deep. That meant biscuit and cheese, not porridge. Porridge came in deep bowls and could only be stacked three deep. Good, the porridge had been getting thin lately as they came to the end of their supplies.

She took her tray and carried it back to her place between Puty and Panala. Puty was the pretty little seventeen-year-old daughter of an upstart family with a questionable relationship to the Gsekk. Puty had grown up in the country, she had virtually no education, and she was crude and knowledgeable about sex.

Panala was just a dolt. She was aboard because her father Beshup had been given the post of Keeper of the Small Purse. There was little patronage in it and much responsibility, which was why incompetents were always rewarded with such jobs.

It was humiliating, really, for Simona to be stuck down here with these two, but her mother had no standing with the elders and no leverage on place assignments. They weren't even able to sleep next to each other. Chiknulba was stuck down at the bilge end with two countrywomen who looked like they ate their own children. They spoke that way, too, and openly lusted for the men at the time of the rut every night.

"So what are you daydreaming about now, lady high-and-mighty?" Puty had a way of getting under your skin whenever she wanted to. Simona feared her sometimes. Puty could dig out your secrets, and then you were in her hands.

"Nothing at all," said Simona, hoping to glide by.

She started eating her biscuit and the hunk of ill-smelling salted cheese. There was a dab of lime paste, four biscuits, and the cheese on her tray. Washed down with tea, that would be all she would receive until midday. It wasn't much to keep hunger at bay. All the women were thin and gaunt in the face.

"You know where we're going, then?" Simona just sniffed. Let Puty beg for information like everyone else.

Panala had just realized that the ship was slapping along at a much faster pace. Somehow this basic fact had eluded her since sunrise. She dropped her cheese and had to scrape it with a nail to get the dust off.

"We're going somewhere?" she said in her usual tone of perpetual amazement.

"Yes, Panala, we are," said Puty with sarcasm dripping.

"Where are we going then?"

"You have to ask Miss high-and-mighty Simona Gsekk here about that. She knows, you can bet your virginity on it."

"Do you really know?" said Panala.

"Yes, of course," said Simona.

"Where are we going, then?"

"What do you have for me?"

Panala was as poor as Simona, that was the problem. And too stupid to think of anything beyond the obvious. She spread her hands helplessly.

Puty's patience was running out. She hated to have to beg from Simona.

"Come on, red-mark girl, tell us. Who do you think you are? You don't have any rank around here."

"Then find out from someone else," said Simona.

"Oh, come on."

"Give me half your biscuit, or ask someone else."

Puty shot her a venomous look, then broke off half of her last biscuit and gave it to her.

Simona nibbled it in front of her. She hated doing this, but it was the only way. It was what they were all reduced to in this hellhole.

"The *Anvil* has returned from the coast. We are going eastward to meet it. There is more."

"More?"

"The most important information."

"Then tell me. I gave you biscuit."

"You must give more if you want to know."

"I will give nothing."

"Then you will learn nothing."

Puty stared at her with bulging eyes.

Then she handed her the other half.

"There is fresh meat on the ship."

Puty started to cry. "Fresh meat! Oh by the Pure Skin of God what I would give for fresh meat now."

Panala was staring at her. "When will we get the meat?" was all she could think to ask.

Simona ignored her.

"Fucking red-mark, fucking strawberry girl," snarled Puty, hungry now, and angry. "How many times they show you? And you have no husband."

Simona stared back at Puty while a familiar dull sense of humiliation washed over her.

Eleven men had examined her naked body, but none had finally wed her, all because of the strawberry red mark on her left breast and on the side of her neck. A sure sign of witchery and poison in your own house. So it was believed in Shasht.

Eleven men with whom she had exchanged the brief glances allowed the woman when the man has finished examining her naked body during the setting of the bride price. Eleven men's faces, briefly glimpsed, and she kept the memories alive of each. Now she was almost twenty and past her prime. Now she was something to be married off to a lower caste man like Master Pilpio to solidify Filek Biswas's support in his home village.

Those eleven men had all wanted her, she had seen their lust clearly on their faces, but they had not bid for her. Too afraid of their own families to dare bring a strawberry-marked girl into the bloodline. One, tall Riban of the Knekt, had tried to buck the system, but he was overruled in the end by his grandmother, a particularly tyrannical crone.

All through her early years of life Simona had prayed daily for deliverance from the strawberry mark. She had prostrated herself on the steps before the altar to the Great God and begged for it to fade. They said that sometimes this did indeed happen, and the woman thus affected was often married thereafter.

The Great God had ignored her pleas. And here was Puty throwing it in her face again.

She sighed. There was nothing to do but endure it for now. Of course, she could hit Puty, but Puty would hit her back, and they would end up on the rack taking a whipping from Bera Fenida, who had a very strong arm. One reason she had found such favor with mighty Vli. Bera was justly feared on the women's deck.

Simona suppressed the anger, but told herself that someday she would give Puty a hiding. By the breath and balls of the Great God himself, she swore it.

Chapter 22

The roasting meat smelled heavenly. It had been so long since they'd had fresh meat that it was barely a memory. Chief Surgeon Zuik and his acolytes were grinning and elbowing each other as they waited in the line.

Filek Biswas, second surgeon on the *Growler,* stood there feeling only his usual dismal anxiety. Having to line up like children and then to formally beg the captain for meat made his soul cringe. But there was no way around it, not if he wanted to stay a man and free.

And so he stood in line behind the other officers of the ship, led by Jugdt the purser. The line snaked into the door of the galley and then out again to the high table, where Captain Shutz stood with knife and huge fork, ready to dish out the meat for the officers of the ship. Then, when they had been satisfied, meat would be given to the warriors, who were already coming up on deck, their eyes alight at the thought of a decent meal, the first in many months.

"Bushmeat, they're calling it. Fancy some monkey, do you?" sniggered Zuik to Third Surgeon Pesh and Assistant Surgeon Immok.

"I'll have anything, long as it's well roasted," said Immok.

"We had monkey before, at the islands."

"Tough, but good once you got used to it."

"Better be careful, Assistant Surgeon Immok, I think the chief's looking at you funny," commented a voice from further up the line, Assistant Purser Kudj.

"Old Zuik gets hungry, he gets to fingering that knife," said Trupp, the second purser.

"It's called the Surgeon's privilege," said Kudj.

Zuik and Pesh laughed heartily at this. Immok laughed, too, but less heartily. Filek merely stared in front of himself, appalled by their crudity.

There was a sudden hard nudge to his ribs. Zuik was glaring at him.

"Look lively, Biswas, don't let our surgery down. Stop looking at the deck like you're in some kind of pain. Relish and delight in the faces of the officers, that is what we want to show the captain! Relish and delight! We are taking meat from the captain. This is our most ancient rite."

Zuik exchanged a look with Pesh and Immok. Soon, soon, the look said, they would be rid of Biswas, the weak link in the chain, the weak-kneed fool who would soon be a eunuch, if Zuik had his way.

Filek groaned inwardly, but straightened himself and squared his shoulders.

"Certainly, Chief, relish and delight." Filek put a smile on his face and tried not to hear the jokes about men losing their balls from Immok and Pesh. Filek sometimes thought about suicide. He would have jumped overboard, he thought, but for his responsibility for Chiknulba and Simona. Their lives were hard enough, but without him they would face very bleak possibilities.

Filek wondered how it could have happened that he had lost his position in Shasht and wound up on this horrible ship, under the thumb of the detestable Zuik, heading into the unknown east. Depending on the will of Orbazt Subuus, the Great God, Filek might never again walk through the door into his lovely house on West Court.

Filek still could hardly believe it had happened, as if someday he would wake up in his old life and all of this, Zuik, Captain Shuzt, and even the *Growler* itself would have vanished like a bad dream.

Filek was tormented by the knowledge that his wife

and daughter were condemned to the hell below his feet. He loved his family with all his heart and had done his utmost to protect Chiknulba from the world.

Of course, Filek knew nothing of his wife's social blunder and would have had difficulty understanding it. He knew little of the world of rather wicked, wealthy women in Shasht city, and Chiknulba had never dreamed of telling him. The mystery, therefore, continued to haunt him. He had never made any request for military service, he had never asked to go to sea, he had no interest in such things. But he knew that an Imperial Command from the Emperor Aeswiren III's heir could not be ignored, and so he languished on this line for roasted meat, enduring the gibes and insults of Zuik and his assistants.

At last they were passing through the galley. Meat was searing on the grills and throwing up clouds of fat and steam. Great cauldrons were boiling with bones and offal, rendering them down for slave soup.

On great grills over a mass of hot coals the cooks were turning a multitude of joints and sides of various animals. Everything that had been available on the Land had been taken; beavers, donkeys, elk, deer, birds of several kinds, and lots of the monkeys. All were split and cleaned and set to sputter on the grill. The ground birds that had been nicknamed "chickens" were cleaned and spitted and roasted whole.

As the food cooked to a turn, the joints were handed up on platters to the High Table, where Captain Shuzt oversaw the distribution of the meat. Shuzt was that rare thing in the fleet, a fat man, stooped at the shoulders and clearly unfit for battle. Still, he held on to warrior status because of his connections to the upper nobility. Two assistants cut the joints, their knives a blur as they sliced and chopped. The officers approached from the left, the "inferior" side, and bowed over their empty plates toward Shuzt. Shuzt responded with the formal raising of his knife and fork, exchanged a few pleasantries with those men who were in his favor, then directed their plates to be loaded up with hot slices of meat, sauced liberally with thick gravy.

The meat he piled on the men's plates was not just for themselves, of course, but also meant for their women and dependents. On the women's deck they were waiting eagerly for it, and beneath them even the higher-status servants were expecting something, a few scraps at least.

The noble officers were done. Now the lesser officers came forward, cringing and holding out their plates. "I beg thee, my superior, for the good meat you have to give."

Shuzt would nod, and wave a hand to his assistants, who could judge with a nicety just how generous they should be. Some men left the table with plates groaning beneath the hot meat. Others were much more meagerly rewarded. Filek received a sufficiency, and no more.

In time all the officers had been dished out. The meat began to go onto the big trenchers that were taken out to the men. Every man aboard would get meat that day, excepting the castrated slaves, of course, who would simply get broth with their biscuit.

Filek took his plate of meat and headed down to the women's deck at once. Most men ate heartily before they went down to share with the women, and, some men even held to the ancient tradition and fed meat to their women by hand, as if they were animals. The women would beg, would kneel, and then be rewarded with a scrap of roasted meat.

Filek was not one of those men. He loved Chiknulba, and tried to behave as decently as possible when he was with his wife. In Filek Biswas's household the rules of purdah had been very much relaxed. In the city, Chiknulba had an all-female household staff and thus escaped many of the restraints of purdah.

His life had been set. He was second surgeon at the Mission Hospital. Old Klegg was number one, but had effectively retired. That had left Filek pretty much in charge. Mission was an old hospital set in a poor part of the city; there were many patients, but few were powerful.

In the hospital there were endless opportunities to advance the scientific basis of surgery. Filek had worked there for two decades, revolutionizing the use of anaesthetic and painkillers. This had not been done without incurring some cost, however, for he came up against the priests of Orbazt Subuus, who were against such improvements in surgery. The zealots denounced him as an enemy of the Great God. They demanded that he be given to the priests for trial. Such trials ended only one way, with the convict bound over the stone altar while the priests raised the knife high.

But Filek had a strong reputation among the Nuns of Pilki, and they had the ear of the Emperor. The zealots were whipped back into line by the Emperor's men, and Filek's work continued.

Fortunately for Filek and Chiknulba, they were not alone in their thinking about the world. An alternative society existed in the capital, alongside but hidden from the main one. At quiet gatherings and dinner parties these people drew together to read poetry, listen to music, and discuss the world openly with no reference to the Great God. With these friends the demands of purdah were largely forgotten. Women and men joined together in open social gatherings. As long as they avoided the scrutiny of the religious zealots, they could live a life that was enjoyable enough, behind the high walls of their gardens.

But that life had ended with the delivery of that order from Nebbeggebben, sending them to the expedition feet. And now, down belowdecks, Filek brought the meat to his women, and they sat together on a bench, knee to knee, and ate with relish.

On the upper deck, Rukkh of the Blitz Regiment took his place at table and set down his plate of meat. As a warrior of high status Rukkh sat among the demi-elite, his plate heavy-laden. He had not seen meat in many months and so he tucked in directly.

His companions, Forjal and Hukkit, took their seats and also got down to business. It was unusually quiet. Up and down the table the warriors of the *Growler* were far too intent on their meat to spare time for conversation.

Rukkh cared little for that. Of late there hadn't been much to talk about. It'd been ten months since they left Shasht. He was tired of Forjal's vapid dreams of the New Land, and if he had to hear another of Hukkit's stupid jokes, he'd scream.

So he ate and thought instead of the enticing girl with the strawberry mark.

Months earlier he had seen her for the first time. He had gone down to service old Maruga Okkada, who had requested a hard young body for the job. Captain Okkada had given Rukkh the chance to serve and he had grabbed at it. Maruga was older than his own mother, and less attractive, but to shine in Okkada's eyes was far more important than that.

On subsequent visits, usually to tup old Maruga, he had seen the girl a few times.

She was truly lovely. He wanted nothing more than to court her and then take her physically and ride her like the fierce mustang that he was sure she was.

He had investigated the girl carefully, as was the way of the wise warrior. Life had many pitfalls and hidden traps, and it was best to know where one was treading. The girl was a Gsekk, a powerful clan, on the mother's side, but clearly in some kind of disgrace to be quartered down there.

The father, Filek Biswas, was a good surgeon, a rarity in itself in modern Shasht. Maybe that was what had led to his being appointed to the ship. Poor fellow had probably never wanted to come. Biswas himself was of a minor house, the Ghuiter.

All of this made Rukkh think that he might yet apply to take the girl. He was of lowly stock, but hard in body and quick in mind. He would rise in the world. The girl was doomed to spinsterhood or worse because of that mark. No man in her social class would risk the taint of witchery in his own household.

The father and mother were under some kind of disfavor, so his proposal to them would not be as insulting as if they were back in Shasht. It might even be the best they could hope for. In the building of the New Land, social distinctions would be more flexible for a while. Rukkh was determined to seize the opportunity.

"Hello!" said Hukkit, banging the table beside his elbow. "Rukkh is having pussy dreams again," Hukkit said to Forjal.

"Hey, Rukkh, only pussy you get is grandmother pussy, and that's the way it's gonna be."

"You're just jealous. If you had the chance, you'd fuck the oldest grannies down there."

"You think you're going to climb in society by serving as stud? You're crazy, Rukkh."

"I know, I know. But I think it's more fun that way."

"Fun? What is that?" said Hukkit. "I don't recall when there was last any fun around here."

They all sighed. For months life had been grim indeed.

"Won't be long now; this meat is the first taste of the new world."

They returned to chewing and munching. Soon, everything would be different.

Chapter 23

To the little group in Bilauk, the rest of that day was forever stained with the tones of nightmare. Thru and the others could do little in the ruined village except to assist the handful of survivors they pulled from the burning houses: two mors and an elderly mot named Haloiko, who had lain under a pile of turnips in his cellar during the raid. The mors were reduced to quivering and moaning by the terror they had experienced, the endless screaming, the sound of axes hacking off heads. Only old Haloiko could tell them anything. The attackers were not mots, not pyluk certainly, they were nothing that the old mot had ever seen before. But he knew them. He had heard them described at religious festivals all his life.

"They were men," he said. "Men like the men of old; they have come back."

As astounding as the burning of Bilauk had been, this information came as even more of a shock.

"But, how can this be?" Nuza said, sounding stunned. "Man is dead, long ago."

Gem piped up with the first lines of the "Inheritance" prayer. *"For poison in the waters had become poison in their seed, And Man thinned with each generation until his light faded from the world."*

Nuza replied from the same prayer. *"And there came a time when no sound broke the stillness of the world except the play of the wind. Man was no more."*

Old Haloiko vehemently disagreed.

"I'm telling you what I saw. They have huge noses and no fur! Just coarse beards and long, greasy hair.

They carried spears and wore helmets. They had no fur on their legs. They were like mots but taller, uglier. They were men."

But the troupe members could not let themselves believe it.

"How did it happen? When did the attack come?" Thru asked.

"I was asleep. I woke, heard them killing in the street. I went down to the cellar and hid under the turnips. They searched the house, but they did not care about turnips. I watched them later. They had rounded up a lot of folk and they marched them down the street. I heard the screaming start later."

"You saw them."

"Oh, yes, I saw them. I watched them from the cellar; there's a gap in the plate over the sill. I been meaning to fix it for years. They carry round shields, they wear helmets. They are warriors, that much is plain. They took everyone down to the harbor and from what you say, they killed them all there."

"But why would they kill everyone like that? And where are the bodies?" Nuza wondered.

Toshak looked at them with eyes filled with ice. "They took the bodies with them, of course. They took them as meat."

The rest stood there frozen by his words. The shadowy nightmare of childhood dreams, Man the Cruel was upon them; the hooded figure, the face with the piercing eyes, the long nose, and the hungry white teeth, Man with the trap and the block, the long sharp knife and the heavy axe. Man the Cruel was alive, and had returned to slaughter the folk of Bilauk.

They turned their steps back to the road and retreated to Shaffgums. They did not speak amongst themselves along the way. They stared at the ground and occasionally looked out to the sea. Gem sobbed to himself. Nuza had tears running down her face. So, she found, did Toshak, which surprised her.

In Shaffgums the folk heard the tale with dumb-founded eyes.

"The killers, will they come back?" A young mot asked.

"We do not know. But they are very dangerous."

"You might want to consider coming with us," said Nuza. "We're going north to Crozett."

"I saw them," said old Haloiko, "I saw them, they were men."

The villagers' faces resonated with shock at this revelation.

"It cannot be."

"That's impossible."

"You know me, I'm Haloiko. Would I tell you these things if they hadn't happened?"

They stared at him, fear rising in their eyes.

"We must go to Crozett and send word to the north." It was their unspoken fear: What if raiders had attacked other places?

"From Crozett they will send pigeons to Tamf with the news. The King must learn of this as soon as possible. There must be some kind of response."

"We must learn to fight them," said Toshak implacably.

They stared at him, but Thru was shaking his head.

"We have forgotten how to make war."

"We will fight. If we have to, we will fight."

As they came over the brow of the hill they saw to the north another pillar of smoke, angling in across the land.

Nuza gave a sad groan at the sight. Thru felt his insides wrenched.

"Where are their ships?" said Toshak, striding forward with his spyglass in his hand.

He scanned the horizon, but saw nothing.

Hurves was a small place, tucked along one bank of the River Darnder. Polder stretched upstream, and small wooden jetties moored the handful of fishing boats. The houses were still sending up smoke although they had largely burned out by the time the troupe reached the paved place along the riverbank.

They found no survivors in Hurves, just a pile of heads: mots, chooks, and brilbies. The indiscriminate slaughter of everyone and every animal was terrifying.

They went on, searching. One of the mors from Bilauk started to talk, but what she said was gibberish, and after a while Nuza had to hold the mor in her arms and gentle her as she broke into wild screams and bouts of tears.

When at last she was calmed again, they went on up through the Rinon country, over the Slem Pike toward Harfield. They reached Harfield, a medium-sized place, about an hour before dusk.

The folk of Harfield, gathered in the taproom at the Swinging Door, would not believe them.

First off they thought it was all a sick joke.

"I see through you," said Mers Sachwan, the tavern owner. "You think to get a rise out of us, have us all running around like chooks scared silly by the wolves!"

The regulars at the bar were laughing along, secure in the impossibility of what the strangers were claiming.

"No, you have to listen to us. Listen to old Haloiko, he was there."

"It's true, they are men, and they killed everyone in Bilauk. In Hurves, too. They might come here tomorrow."

It then turned out that two fishing boats from Harfield had disappeared in the previous two days, though the weather had been fine, with little wind or rain.

Toshak shook his head grimly at the news.

"I'm calling for volunteers. We need to get as many mots as we can who can shoot. And we need to warn everyone, get them at least to prepare themselves to flee quickly as the need arises."

"Now you're panicmongering," said the tavern owner. "You better stop it before we call on Giffiam, he's the town constable here."

"You carry on like that, and you will end up in the lockup, just you see," added Mers Sachwan.

For a long moment they stared at each other. Toshak looked over to Nuza and Thru. Valuable time was being wasted.

Suddenly Thru drew his sword and brought it up under the throat of the plump old barkeep.

"Listen to Toshak, old mot. This is no stupid game. We need to talk to the constable all right, and he needs to understand what is happening. Otherwise, everyone in this village will die tomorrow, most likely, and there'll be nothing here but a pile of heads down by the jetty."

"You've gone mad."

"If I've gone mad, then I've gone mad along with quite a bit of company. Old Haloiko lived through it; he says they were men. They are like us, but larger. Isn't that the sign of Man? They are men, and they are coming here and they will kill you."

Mers was speechless. So were the others. This had gone way past a joke.

"You're serious," said Jebedel Muri.

"We are," said Toshak. "We have to organize some defense for the town and prepare everyone for instant flight."

The mots in the Swinging Door looked at the members of the troupe, plus old Haloiko and the mute mor.

"What about her?"

"She came from Bilauk, too."

"That's Denssi Orill," said Haloiko.

"She cannot make sense," said Nuza.

Denssi just stared at them all with wide, frightened eyes.

"They kill!" she said at last in a strangled voice.

Now Mers was backed up against the big barrel, with only one decision to make.

"We'd better call Giffiam, don't you think?"

A few minutes later, the constable had emerged from his smithy and was listening intently.

As with the mots of the tavern taproom, he had a hard time at first accepting any of their tale. The news brought by this Toshak, the famous swordsmot, seemed completely crazy, but the others all said it was true. And there was old Haloiko, who was from Bilauk, and who claimed to have seen men.

Men?

Giffiam decided that, as constable, he had to do something.

"Toshak, your fame has preceded you to Creton, but still you must realize that this news you bring us is hard to accept. But I will call the muster, and we will put this to the folk."

Giffiam turned to the door where his assistant lurked.

"Marsh, make a fire."

"Yes, Constable," said young Marsh.

Within a few minutes Marsh had assembled sticks and straw from the tavern's wood crib and got a blaze started.

Across from the Swinging Door Tavern stood a bakery and a dry goods store. In front of the bakery was a platform erected for the town crier, who broadcast any dramatic news from its eminence of two feet.

Dusk was falling as Giffiam mounted the town crier's stand and blew the ancient Constable's Trumpet. It had been years since the brass trumpet had been heard in the village, not since a posse had been called out to chase some bandits on the run from the coal towns. Four mots charged with highway robbery had eventually been caught and sentenced on that occasion, twenty years before.

Giffiam was a little rusty with the instrument, and his first efforts sounded more like a chook in terrible pain than anything else. But eventually he got his lips around it and the trumpet responded with a long clear peal. Heads popped out of doors up and down the narrow streets. They saw the glow of a fire in the village center and soon a crowd had gathered.

Giffiam got up and gave the warning, as he understood it.

The crowd became agitated as they heard the news of the massacres, and cries of astonishment and alarm rose up.

"What we gonna doo!" cried a chook sitting up on the low roof of the Swinging Door.

"That's a good question," said Giffiam. "For an answer, I'm going to hand over to Toshak of Sulmo, the famous sword-fighter, who brought this news today. He has some ideas."

Toshak got up and let them all take a look at him for a few moments. He gave off an aura of capable decisiveness. The sword and fighting knife in his belt were very obvious to them all.

"I saw the ruins of Bilauk and Hurves. The attackers left nothing but the heads of the folk behind. This is truth. We must prepare to fight to save the village. I think that the men come very early in the morning. Probably before dawn. They surprise the villages and catch everyone in their beds.

"So we must build barricades tonight. We must arm every mot who can fight, and prepare everyone else for flight in the morning. We will send the mors and children inland, to the coal towns."

"And if you're wrong about this, we're going to beat you black-and-blue tomorrow and send you on your way," said a mean-spirited brilby named Uank.

Voices shouted disagreement with Uank, who was not popular in Harfield.

"Don't listen to that idiot," said Giffiam. "But how can you be sure the raiders will come here tomorrow?"

"I cannot be absolutely certain. Perhaps they will not—but the consequences for you all if they do come and you are not prepared are too terrible to ignore."

They were staring at him, trying to make up their minds. Some were convinced, a few were openly unconvinced.

"Listen to me. They have attacked Bilauk and Hurve. You saw the smoke of Hurves, didn't you?"

A few nodded. Indeed, they had wondered about that column of distant smoke.

"All we found of the folk of those placecs was a pile

of heads and old Haloiko there. He saw them. Big noses, beards, and hair. They are men!"

The mots looked at each other in wonder and fear. What the hell was happening in the world? First two boats had gone missing, inexplicable in terms of the weather. And now these tales of villages burned, people slaughtered, and Man the Cruel coming back to do it. It was a terrifying thought, but still a few were not convinced.

Then old Haloiko got up and told them what he'd seen.

When he was done, Giffiam asked for a show of hands and found overwhelming support for building barricades and setting a defensive watch. All the mors and children would be ready to leave at a moment's notice. Chooks and donkeys would go, too.

"Everyone should get their bow, and their best points. I'd suggest sword and knife as well. If you have spears or shields, bring them. We will need all the best weapons in the village."

Mots scrambled in all directions.

Hob joined a gang of big brilbies and set to building the barricades. For raw material they brought out timber from the sawmill and some heavy farm carts which they turned on their sides. Other folk brought down anything that might be useful, old barrels and broken doors, window frames and wheels. Soon the streets leading into the village were blocked at the edges with big piles of wood, wheels, and motley stuff.

Meanwhile the mots who were good with the bow had gathered near the Swinging Door to hammer out a strategy. Toshak was the only one among them who had studied warfare. He emphasized the value of making their shooting count.

"Don't waste your steel points on long shots. Don't shoot until they are close enough for you to choose a soft spot. The second thing is how we make use of the available cover."

They made a tour of the three main barricades and

noted likely places for bowmots to shelter while still keeping a good field of fire.

An inventory of arrows and points was made and the handiest mots gathered in the smithy to fletch as many shafts as they could. Steel points were dug out of every keeping place.

Toshak examined the weapons available. There were a few war spears, ancient things unused in hundreds of years. The shafts were mostly worthless and had to be replaced. There were some hunting javelins, small versions of the long spear thrown by the pyluk, and even an old pyluk spear itself, taken from a lone marauder decades before. That, too, had long since gone punky and was useless.

There were more swords, many more. Usually the family blade, handed down for untold generations. They were made of good steel, with decorated handles and protective steel box for the hand, but most needed sharpening, and few mots had much knowledge of swordfighting.

Beyond that were long knives, which were pretty universal among the mots of the world, axes, of which they had seventy good ones, and a few with fractured handles.

The village turned out to work for its own defense. The smithy was running all night, the glow from his hearth visible in the darkness.

The constable sent out small parties of scouts to the nearest headland. They carried pinecones soaked in pitch that they could light to give warning.

Dawn came with nothing but the mournful croaking of a few chooks without sleep. The wind had died down, and the scene took on an absolute kind of peace and silence.

The village stood down, and went about its business.

Everyone was exhausted after a night of such tension, but the village life resumed its pace. Everyone had work to do. As they hurried about the polder and field, meeting in the lanes or back in the village they exchanged jokes and wry comments. "A wild sheep ride, that was!" was the general feeling.

"Sometimes I think we can be convinced of any fool thing that comes down the pike," said old Huhumpa, and there was quite a lot of agreement with him.

Toshak withdrew into himself. Thru and Nuza sat together in the taproom of the Swinging Door. They talked drowsily for a while and then slept there, heads back against the wall.

About noon there was another blast on the trumpet from Giffiam, and everyone rushed from the fields to the village to hear.

They found Giffiam, flanked by Toshak and Uls and Fel Diljer, who had hiked down to Hurves at first light and were just returned.

"It is true," said Fel Diljer. "The village of Hurves is burned to the ground. There is only a pile of heads on the wharf, no other trace of the folk. They killed the entire village."

"You're sure?" said someone in the crowd.

"I scouted all around the village. There's no one there."

The jokes were finished. Most folk did not return to the fields, but instead went to help improve the barricades.

Toshak had studied them, and had had them moved and rebuilt. All three were now situated between stone walls of sizable homes on either side. The houses were also barricaded and made fast against assault. The walls would tend to compact an attacking force and bunch them up so they would be more vulnerable to stones and arrows.

All that day a party of mors and children had worked at finding and bringing up good stones for slinging. They also had heavier rocks, hauled up by donkey cart and piled up ready to be used.

As the afternoon wore on, new scouting parties were sent out to relieve the first ones, who had returned with no reports of anything out of the ordinary.

But Hurves had indeed burned. A couple of the most recalcitrant mots who refused to believe even Fel Diljer had gone down there in person and returned to confirm that it was gone, village and villagers alike.

After that everyone worked with even more determination. A group of mors started cooking up a mess of clams and bushpod cakes. Mussels were raked up and set to boil. All the chooks in the village were sent inland, since they moved too slowly over distance to wait until an emergency.

At the end of the day of hard work the villagers ate and settled down for the night. A watch was put at every barricade and from the top of the dry goods store's roof, which had the best view out to sea in the village.

At midnight the moon rose, close to full in a sky with clouds blowing up from the south.

Soon afterward, there was a light flaring on the southern headland.

"A light!"

The village awoke.

Everyone stared off into the south, and waited.

Time passed, the wind picked up again so that small surf started beating on the beach.

Eventually they heard someone hallooing from the southern road. One of the lookouts from the south. He'd come to report that it'd been a mistake. They'd thought they'd seen something out at sea, perhaps a sail, but it would have been too big. Then they thought their eyes had been playing tricks on them. It had been way out, at the edge of visibility. But whatever it was had gone and not been seen again. They thought now that it was an illusion.

There was a collective sigh of relief. A fire was lit and water boiled to make guezme tea. Several mots retired to bed.

"Wake me if anything happens," they said to one and all.

Chapter 24

Five longboats moved silently in toward the land. Rukkh stilled his nerves with a pinch of war snuff and looked back over the dark water. There was always tension just before an attack, no matter who the enemy. The moon had frosted the edges of things and given the waves a silvery glint. He closed the little wooden snuff-egg and tucked it back inside his leather breastplate. The breeze brought them the scent of the land. The oarlocks were muffled in cloth, and the oarsmen knew their job. No sound betrayed their progress. Each boat carried twenty men, handpicked from the Blitz Regiment, the toughest of the tough.

Five other boats were heading in on the other side of the village. They would swing around on either side and then move in to trap the animals in a classic pincer attack.

The village was laid out like all the monkey places, packed tightly around a central core. There were a hundred or more small houses, set close against one another, as if they'd grown together over centuries. Rukkh wondered if the monkeys were afraid to build away from each other?

Small immaculately kept fields surrounded them, and offshore there were always wide arrays of circular ponds built of rock and shingle. It was amazing how much work they had put into it all, and yet left so much of the country quite empty. Beyond the villages and the small fields lay nothing but a tangled jungle of oak and pine, scouts reporting game animals by the hundreds on every hill.

Admiral Heuze had decided that the monkeys in this village must have learned of the destruction of the place just eight miles south. But, nonetheless, the monkeys had not fled their own village. Telescope observation from the top of the mast had shown that smoke still rose from the village chimneys. Either the monkeys were very stupid, or they were damnably self-confident.

Heuze had chosen the former. The stinking monkeys had no reason to be confident. They hadn't put up much of a fight anywhere yet, and eight ships had conducted successful raids along the coast.

Heuze expected some sort of resistance, however, even if weak and disorganized, and his men were prepared. Each twenty in the boats had five bowmen among them, and the warriors wore full leather armor. It was inconvenient but necessary, since the monkeys did possess bows and swords, though so far they had never used them very effectively. The priests claimed that the monkeys did not make these things and therefore had little idea of how to wield them. According to the priests the monkeys were pure abomination, inferior beings created by the Fallen Ones and intended to usurp the world from Man. The Great God himself called for their total extirpation.

The warriors had found little difficulty so far in carrying out the commands of the priests. So poor had been their resistance that no one had taken a monkey's head. The monkeys simply weren't worth the honor of having their heads shrunk for a warrior's personal shrine.

The war snuff had taken effect and banished any nervousness. Rukkh was confident enough about the upcoming action that his thoughts returned to the girl, Simona of Ghuiter.

She was the pretty one! Despite eating the same rations as everybody else, she retained her womanliness, her rounded hips and firm breasts, that spoke to him of good fertility. There was a fire in her eyes which spoke of passion in the bedroom.

Perhaps, if he could distinguish himself in some way, the girl's family would be mollified. He knew that her parents were bound to resist him at first. They were of noble blood, she more than he, but both were from landed families. His own bloodlines were poor and rural, of little account in the social world of Shasht.

But this was the new world, the New Land, and flexible conditions would exist for a while. If he proved himself worthy, he could rise into the nobility.

Someday soon, he swore to himself, he would take the girl, and they would found a mighty clan together on the New Land. He felt a surge of pride. He and his fellows were unstoppable. They were the warriors of Shasht. No one could defeat them, not since the days of the first emperor, Kadawak. Now they were in the reign of the twenty-third emperor, Aeswiren III, and Shasht stood triumphant over the entire world.

Except here on this distant shore, unknown to any except the priests. Where only the monkey folk stood to contest the law of the Great God, He Who Eats.

The boat ground ashore on the mud. The tide was out and they had a wide expanse of mudflats to cross. Toward the village, the flats were covered in the maze of walls that contained the seaponds. The walls were mostly about five feet tall and usually two or three wide, made of stone and cemented together by mollusc-growth mats. Between them wound torturous little pathways that had confused even the scouts. They would have to be avoided by the warriors.

The water was cold when he jumped out into the knee-deep foam. There was a breeze building off the sea now. He took his first step on the New Land.

"There's a light up there, damn it!" Captain Cauta was pointing to the headland up above them.

Piercing the gloom above and to the south was a single bright flare of yellow light. As they watched, it moved. Someone was waving it back and forth.

"They are signaling to the village?"

"What else?"

"I didn't think they were capable of such complicated thinking."

"We'd best hurry. Bowmen be prepared."

They moved out of the surf and across the flats, jogging at a steady pace. Above the mudflats was a bank of shingle, small loose stones the size of hens' eggs. They scramble up the bank in a roar of stones and emerged on top of a grassy open area along which ran a narrow road paved with rough flint cobbles.

Rukkh was mildly surprised by the road, which though only five feet wide ran ahead unbroken, paved with stone. He hadn't thought the monkeys would be capable of something like this. Then he thought that of course they must have inherited all these things from others. There must have been men here once, long ago.

Up ahead lay the village, the dark outline of the roofs and chimneys was visible in the moon's light. Despite the lateness of the hour smoke still rose from a few chimneys.

Hukkit was beside him, and behind them came Forjal.

"For the glory of the Great God!" said Forjal with the mad excitement of a berserker in his eyes. "Let's kill the fucking monkeys! Kill them all."

"For His glory!" echoed Hukkit.

"Silence in the ranks," hissed Sergeant Burok.

Rukkh said nothing, but his eyes glowed. He shifted and adjusted the strap that held his shield on his back, then took the spear in both hands.

They moved down the dark road as quickly as they dared. It was rough and uneven in places, but not as much as Rukkh had expected. It was as good as any road in his home village.

Ahead lay the monkey village, a cluster of deeper darknesses against the gloomy mass of the land beyond. Trees grew up close on both sides of the road, and there were stone walls, perhaps four feet high along the edge of the fields. The walls seemed extraordinarily precise in their layout.

They slowed a little.

The village ahead was quiet, but watchful. They could all sense it. The road ran into the village and became a narrow way between the walls of the houses. It did not look inviting. Unfortunately, there didn't seem any other way through the continuous wall of housing that stretched right down to the beach.

They would have to enter on the main road. A little tentatively, they pushed forward with a wary eye on the rooflines ahead. The monkeys had killed a couple of men with arrows during a raid by the *Batterer*. Ahead through the murk they saw that the road was barricaded.

Cauta halted them for a moment while he studied the situation and weighed the possibilities. He talked briefly with Sergeants Burok and Hugga.

"We're very close, and they've not shown any opposition at all."

They were indeed barely a hundred feet from the barricade between the grey-stone walls. But the barricade was only six feet high, easily climbed.

"Forward!" said Cauta crisply. They were the warriors of Shasht! Nothing could stand against their assault. They charged the barricade.

Rukkh took two steps, and with startling abruptness bright lights lit above their heads and dropped down toward them.

Pots of oil were smashing on the stones, and flames were blazing up. Someone fell over screaming, covered in fire. A hail of arrows and stones came flashing through the light. A stone hit Rukkh on the upper arm, another caught the crest of his helmet and bent his head sideways. Then he had his shield around and his spear in his right hand and was going forward again, with the war cry of Shasht on his hips.

Men were going up the barricade. Ulu in front of Rukkh. Big Ulu bellowed the war cry and suddenly there were monkeys standing up atop the barricade, with spears in their hands and bright steel swords.

"Kill!" bayed Ulu, and he plowed ahead. There was a flash of metal, Ulu gave a grunt and staggered back, dark blood spurting from his neck. Rukkh dodged Ulu's toppling body as he scrambled up. Something collapsed under his weight and he sank into the barricade. He put his hand out for support and came up with a handful of Ulu's intestines.

Then Hegg fell past him with a bubbling shriek as blood fountained from his neck. Magutta was going up, cursing steadily as he sought to keep his feet on the barricade.

There was steel clashing on steel and the constant roar of screams, clattering shields, and curses that made up any close-order combat. Someone deadly was atop the barricade though, for another man, Kunchovi, came sliding back, sliced across the belly.

Rukkh got out of the broken barrel, pushed past Kunchovi's still form, and surged up to the top of the barricade.

There were monkeys lined up all the way across, wielding swords, knives, and axes for the most part. One of them wielded his sword two-handed with ferocious skill, leaving dead men behind him wherever he stepped up.

Despite that, things were not so good for the monkeys. Forjal speared one through the exposed chest. Hukkit knocked another clean off his feet with a shield charge. A moment later Hukkit's spear sank into the fallen monkey's leg. It shrieked and writhed, like a serpent pinned to the ground. Rukkh's own spear flicked out and took its life.

Another monkey, this one with a shield of its own, was in front. Rukkh lunged overhand with his spear, keeping his shield up. His extended reach kept the monkey back while it diverted his spearpoint with its shield. Then it closed and they went shield to shield. Rukkh dropped his spear and drew his sword. They exchanged ringing blows, sword on sword, while slamming the other's shield.

Rukkh sensed he had an advantage. He dug in hard with the shield and pulled his opponent off-balance.

Then he swung in, from the hips with the sword. It should have worked. He had a glimpse of a frightened face, very much like that of a man, but with the huge eyebrows of a monkey. Then his sword caromed off the other's shield, and he was forced to clip off a sword thrust at his belly with the edge of his own shield. Before he could find his footing there was an overhand blow coming for his head. He got the shield up just in time and struck out with a foot, making solid contact. The monkey was driven back a few feet.

With a loud *thunk,* an arrow suddenly sprouted from his shield six inches from the edge. More arrows were slicing the air around him. He heard Hukkit give a shriek and turned his head in time to see his old friend go down over the broken barrel to sprawl on the cobbles.

Rukkh deflected the sword again and thrust back with his own. The monkey lost his footing on the barricade and Rukkh jerked his shield up and smacked his foe in the face with it. That knocked him over, and before he could recover, Rukkh drove his sword into the monkey's groin. It doubled up with a scream and he stabbed it again through the ribs.

Rukkh gave the war cry and smashed his heavy sandal into the monkey's head as it sprawled in death. He sheathed his sword and took up his spear.

More stones were flying by, one snicking off the very top of his helmet. He discovered that he was bleeding from a long cut that had gone through the armor into his thigh. A quick examination showed he could carry on. Other men thrust past him and over the barricade. The monkeys were either running for it or they were dying. Not even the skill of the one with the sword could staunch the breakthrough.

Mugutta was swinging his sword in the street beyond. Rukkh knocked another monkey flying with a smash of the shield. Its feet left the ground and his spear flicked into its back and pinned it to the ground. It screamed and squirmed as he trod on it and pulled out the spear and thrust it down again to finish it.

He roared the war cry. Heard echoes from other men's throats all around him. Shasht was victorious! As ever and always, in the name of the Great God Orbazt Subuus.

The monkeys were all running by then. Forjal was roaring out the glory of the Great God as he cut down monkeys from behind.

There were still arrows coming their way, though. Rukkh felt something strike solidly into his shield, and another shaft appeared quivering before his eyes. He snapped it off like the first. Another one clipped the side of the shield and spun away behind him. He was becoming a target. He darted to a dark opening for cover through a hanging hide door. He barged inside. Someone struck him with a cudgel and caught him on the shield shoulder. He went down on one knee, received another blow, then thrust out blindly into the dark. There was a squeal of pain; his spear had gone home somewhere.

Someone was on his back. He ducked his still-numb shoulder. The body on his back shifted, and he reached up and flipped it over and away.

His eyes had adjusted to the darkness. There was a young monkey with a knife. Another one was sitting in the corner of the small dimly lit space clutching his belly where the spear had gone home.

The young one lunged at him with the knife. He fended it off with his shield, caught it on the rebound, and slammed it into the wall. His spear came up and sank home through the creature's middle.

It gave a small cry, and as he withdrew it, collapsed with a cough that sent blood spattering over Rukkh's shield.

Rukkh looked about the small room, then tore open another hide door and looked into a larger space, lit by three oil lamps. On the floors and walls were brilliantly colored mats and rugs. Designs featuring unmistakable images, one of some insects patterned with what looked like chickens was very clear. Furniture of polished brown wood and walls painted creamy white completed the room. Hide doors led off in both directions to other rooms. A large green pot stood against one wall. Shelves filled with other pots and beakers lined another. It was a two-story dwelling; steps led up to the upper floor.

Rukkh was shocked. The priests had not mentioned anything of this finery. The monkeys appeared to live well.

Not for long, he thought with a grim chuckle. They made good meat. He turned and, dismissing the view from his mind, ducked back out to the narrow street.

The fighting had dispersed, although he could hear shouts, commands from Cauta, and the sound of something smashing not far away.

He hurried in that direction.

Mugutta was lying at a crossroads with an arrow sticking up from his right eye. Farther on there was a man sitting on the small stoop of a single-story house with his own spear thrust through him.

Rukkh heard someone coming down the nearest alley and positioned himself perfectly. The young monkey came hurtling by and he ran it through with a clean blow and dropped it to the ground. It writhed until he thrust down again to end it.

The remaining monkeys were running up the lanes, and the men from the other pincer were approaching.

"Glory to the Great God!" shouted Muka, the captain of the other force.

"He Who Eats blesses us!" replied Cauta.

The place was theirs.

Chapter 25

They ran from Harfield, heading inland, trying to keep from blind panic. Fear pounded in their hearts, terror ate at their souls.

They had fought Man, and they had lost. They had seen steel cutting flesh, spears running through mot chests, arrows sprouting suddenly from eyes and throats. They had tried everything, but despite all their planning and their courage they had not been able to keep the bigger, more experienced men from storming the barricades and taking their home.

In the process, dozens of mots had died and many more were wounded to one degree or another. Thru Gillo was one of them, cut on his thigh, cut on his face and the side of his head, bruised on the right side of the chest and all down his legs.

Thru had gone chest to chest with a man who'd snarled and spat at him and swung a heavy sword that Thru had parried, but only just. The man had a shield, and it made the fight unequal, and so Thru was forced to give ground. He parried another stroke, but the shield sent him stumbling back and exposed him to a killing thrust.

Toshak had saved him, whirling up the barricade with a sharp cry, his sword a flashing arc of steel that slit the man's belly under the edge of his armor.

Thru had taken the man's shield. It was strong but surprisingly light, a wooden frame wrapped in wicker and covered in leather. There were knobs of stone sunk into the leather every inch or so. Thru didn't know the finer points of wielding a shield, however, and the next man

almost knocked him off his feet when they clashed atop
the barricade and he hooked his shield inside Thru's and
jerked him forward.

After that the fighting became a blur. He remembered
scattered moments. A swordsman in front, trying a kick.
Thru instinctively dropped the edge of the shield down
on the man's shin and he backed off with a howl. A
spearman charging in, tripping on the barricade, and falling facefirst. A huge man using his shield to hurl a mot
right off the top of the barricade. The moment when in
the press of bodies Thru drove his own sword into a
man's belly. The shock of seeing the blade vanish, the
moment of killing another being, had stunned him for
a moment.

More men came up into the press at the top of the
barricade. The mot line could not hold them. They
broke, mots falling, others tumbling back off the barricade. Then Thru was in the street, off the barricade and
fighting with a man wearing a helmet topped by a red
crest. Another mot pressed in and the red crest was
forced to turn his attention to him. Thru hacked at the
man's side, his sword cut in above the hip.

The last glimpse he had of the red crest was of the
helmet, spinning on the cobblestones. By then he was
swinging furiously back at another swordsman several
houses farther down.

The fighting continued back through the village. Thru
saw Toshak kill another man, this time with a reverse
spin and a slicing stroke that cut the throat. Somewhere
in the fighting, Thru took a heavy blow in the ribs, although he couldn't say exactly when or how.

But over and above everything was the new knowledge. He had killed men and he had learned to fear
them.

They ran up the lane through the polder, across a field
and into the woods. He'd lost his bow, but he still had
his quiver and a few steel points. His sword arm felt
leaden, exhausted.

The moon reappeared from behind the clouds. The

smell of smoke grew suddenly much stronger. The village was burning. They came to Skanels crossing, where a rickety bridge spanned a fierce little stream. There they caught up with the mors and children, who had fled the village the moment the first light flared from the headland.

Thru waited anxiously by the rocks, looking back down the road. The men did not seem to be pursuing them, but Thru wanted to be sure.

Mors and children wept uncontrollably when they discovered that their husbands and fathers would not be coming. There were dozens of dead left behind.

A column of chooks had joined the main party, and the soft clucking of mother chooks to the chicks formed an undertone to the weeping of inconsolable children and wives.

Nuza joined him. She had been shepherding several old grannies, who had set out earlier and made it that far the previous day.

"Thru!" She wrapped her arms around him. There was fear in her eyes. "But you're hurt, there's blood all over . . ." Her voice dropped away as she saw the long cut on the side of his head.

"I'm all right, I'll survive."

"Oh, Thru, thank the Spirit!"

The feel of her body against him was a primal source of warmth. The chill in his heart subsided a little.

"Nuza, Nuza, Nuza." He rocked from side to side to comfort himself, or perhaps both of them. His side hurt.

"Are they coming?" she said to him.

"None that I can see."

"What happened? What were they like?"

He swallowed, wiped sweat, blood, and dirt from his face.

"They are terrible! Stronger and bigger than we, but we can kill them! Toshak was tremendous. He made them pay a price, and he saved my life, I know that."

Toshak had stayed back with a few mots to slow down the men if they came on in pursuit.

There were bright flames down by the shore, flickering beyond the dark mass of the forest. The refugees clung to each other, each shivering a little at the distant red light.

"They intend to kill us all," said Nuza in a toneless, quiet voice.

Thru heard her and could make no reply. It was true. He had seen the face of Man the Cruel, Man the wearer of the red crest, Man with the insane eyes filled with hatred as he came on with his sword and his spear.

"They broke our line. We couldn't stop them. They were too skilled for us."

It was exactly as they'd feared it might be.

"Where is Toshak?" she said after a moment.

Then Toshak arrived with six weary-looking mots who had bows over their shoulders. They'd come in from the side trail that led up more directly from the shore, but was steep in places and rocky in others.

Toshak was burdened with half a dozen belts over his shoulder, scabbards and swords on his back. He handed Thru a bow. With astonishment Thru saw that it was the bow Ware had carved for him.

"We can't afford to be without your skill with that bow, Thru Gillo."

"Thank you, Toshak."

"They aren't following now. They grew nervous after we ambushed their scouts."

"That's a mercy," said Nuza. "The old ones will be slowing down soon. They did well yesterday, but this is all a bit hard on them."

"They must still go on. Compared to the other villages they killed only a few of us. They will not be happy about that."

"We head for Uzon, that's the closest coal town. From there we can send a message to Tamf."

"It will take the children at least three days to reach Uzon. And we have little food to give them."

"The coast road is too dangerous, who knows how many of these attacks there will be?"

"Yes," Nuza conceded that point. "Uzon it will have to be. I pray that messages have been sent to Tamf to report this calamity. Without aid, we will surely all die."

Chapter 26

The *Growler* moved gently with the sea. On the women's deck it was stifling and hot; Simona wore no more than a shift. Puty and Panala lolled in their hammocks, unable to so much as move.

Simona couldn't stand hanging there listening to them gossip about the love affairs that were thought to be going on between various girls. There was a certain amount of homosexuality on the deck, and in these conditions it had grown considerably.

Instead, Simona prowled on the outer aisle. Sometimes one of the older women would leave a porthole for a while to sleep. Then came occasional opportunities for someone like Simona to grab a few moments of precious air and light before she'd be pulled away by the rightful owner of second place on the line.

There was a sour mood aboard the *Growler*. The haul from the raid had been very disappointing. There had barely been enough meat to feed the ship and none to give to other ships, from whom the *Growler* had taken plenty from previous raids. The *Growler*'s captain and crew lost status within the fleet. The warriors aboard the ship faced humiliation when next they met their fellows.

Captain Shuzt had been testy and upset. His last visit to the women's deck had been marked by a screaming bout with his wife that ended in blows and the captain storming out in a fury.

The whole women's deck had its ration cut the next day by a biscuit. This did nothing but focus more resentment upon Vli Shuzt. The women's deck was a hungry deck and had been for many months.

In all the general misery, Simona had one slender shaft of hope. Twice more she had seen Rukkh. He sought her out whenever he was sent down to the women's deck. When he found her he simply looked at her with smoldering eyes. She could feel his desire, exciting her on a most primal level. At the same time she knew that he was from a peasant background. He might be illiterate, certainly uneducated compared to her.

For some odd reason, that did not matter. It was something just to be looked at like that, just to be desired. Her spirit had sagged under the weight of eleven rejections. She knew deep down somewhere that she was not worthless, but when everyone else thought she was it began to rub off. Especially when living in such close proximity with so many other haughty women. "Redmark girl" had been permanently scarred on her psyche on this voyage in hell.

Indeed, many of the women were wondering why Simona had not been sold down to the whores' deck. She was the unproductive daughter of a questionable marriage by an unstable Gsekk female. That was virtually the profile of the higher-class whores: unlucky younger daughters who could not be wed, or whose fathers died young. They did not understand why Filek, himself under pressure, did not sell the girl and use the proceeds to ingratiate himself with the priests. Filek, however, was not that kind of father. He loved his daughter as much as he loved his wife, and he had promised them that he would always protect them from that sort of horror. Chiknulba swore to protect her, too, but Simona knew her mother was weak, and would not be able to stop other Gsekks from casting Simona out if they could. Filek was her lifeline, until she married. Then she would be safe within the confines of matrimony.

She had to marry beneath herself, it was all there was left. And here was this Rukkh, who came to stare at her every opportunity and exhibit his need for her.

Alas, Filek had not been receptive to her wishes.

"He is nothing but a peasant."

"I know, Father, but we are going into the New Land. Property in the old world is meaningless here."

"Do not say that, my darling. All status and hierarchy depend on our name from the old world. Without it we would be submerged in the common ruck!"

Simona could hear the enormous fear and the loathing in her father's voice. She sympathized. If she could have had her wishes, she would have gone back to her old life at once. But such wishes were worse than useless.

"Father, we must also be flexible. If I am not wed, I will be vulnerable. Unless you can protect me, I will be sold as a whore."

"Ah, my sweet Simona, do not say such horrible things. You will be wed, my dearest, but to a fine man of good blood. This peasant soldier is scarcely a citizen of Shasht at all."

"Nor are we, Daddy. We are citizens of the new world."

"Hush, you must never say such things. That could easily be taken the wrong way and construed as treason against the Emperor."

Simona put a hand to her mouth.

"Oh! I meant no such thing." She looked around anxiously; no one appeared to be listening to them. She hadn't been loud. No one was loud on the women's deck, unless she wanted her business spread far and wide on the gossip circuit.

Filek looked her in the eye.

"Now, no more on this subject. I do not wish to discuss it."

"Yes, Father." Simona knew when to give in.

Later Filek and Chiknulba coupled behind a sheet in the common lust bunk for that section. Several other couples had already used it, and it stank. Chiknulba wept afterward in his arms, with her head cradled in the hollow of his shoulder, her stoicism shattered at last.

"Oh, Filek, I am so degraded by this awful business.

Sometimes I just wish I were dead." She kept her voice to a tiny whisper. There were often listeners lurking outside the lust bunk, hoping to catch embarrassing revelations.

"I know," he whispered back. "Remember, it is scarcely any better on the upper decks. I am constantly insulted and threatened by Zuik and his cronies. You cannot imagine how galling it is to be humiliated by a creature like Third Surgeon Pesh."

"Oh, Filek, Filek, when will it end? When will we be free from this living hell?"

"Shuzt has it in for me, dear. You must get back in Vli Shuzt's good graces."

"Oh I wish I could, believe me. I would grovel to her if it would help. But it won't. Vli enjoys this sort of thing. I am her current victim. When I am destroyed she will move on to the next."

"Listen, dear. Shuzt is against me, and Surgeon Zuik constantly threatens to take my balls. You understand what I'm saying? They intend to strip me of my position and take advantage of the rules aboard ship to have me castrated and sent down to the slave deck."

Chiknulba could no longer breathe.

"No, nooooo, without you we would be doomed. Vli would sell Simona down to the whores at once."

"They have not had an opportunity to move against me yet, but their time is running out. Once we land we will come under army rules and their power over me will be gone. Zuik will try something soon, and I have to be ready for it."

Chiknulba was curling up into a fetal ball, and Filek, who was not so strong himself, gave out a sob and hugged Chiknulba tightly. They remained that way for a long minute or so of silent communion. Then somebody rudely pulled away the sheet.

"Hey!" snapped Filek. "Would you mind closing that?"

"Sorry, Master Assistant Surgeon." It was one of the men he'd patched up recently. The sheet was restored.

"Someday soon, my darling," he reassured his wife. "Someday all this will be behind us. We will have a place to do good surgery. We will have a house and land and we will live as once we did. I promise you that we will. But first I have to survive the next few days. Once we have landed then everything changes."

Chapter 27

The following day was a terribly tense one for Filek Biswas. The *Growler* had rejoined the main fleet. All forty vessels were gathering at the mouth of a wide bay that had been selected for the initial landing in force.

About an hour after breakfast Filek happened to pass by the medical lockers and found Pesh there. Something about the lock on his own locker caught his eye. He examined it. The metal had been attacked with a saw.

He exchanged a look with Pesh. Pesh said nothing.

"Leave my locker alone, Pesh, or I will put the matter before the priests. Let the Great God determine my innocence."

"Haven't touched your locker, Assistant Surgeon."

"Well someone has. And if I find them doing it, then I'm going to the priests."

"Don't be blaming me to the priests, Assistant Surgeon. He Who Eats knows I've done nothing wrong."

Filek examined the contents of his locker. His bandages and thread were in order. His needles and knives wrapped and put away in their pigeonhole. Bottles of spirits of alcohol were ready. Everything was in order for immediate surgery.

He relocked the door and examined the hasp of the lock. The metal had been cut, but not very far. He'd been lucky in deciding to stop by the lockers. Zuik and his henchmen were getting desperate. Landfall was a day away.

Filek realized that he would have to guard his locker constantly. Zuik would try and use something like the loss of imperial goods from his locker as a pretext for putting Filek out of his position. It wouldn't take much.

All that day the game went on, with Filek attending to his duties in the surgical saloon, then leaping down the passage to his locker to ward off Pesh, Immok, or Zuik himself. Twice he found Zuik in the locker room looking shifty-eyed. Both times Zuik left quickly without even going into his own locker.

Filek was a sensitive man, used to the ways of civilization. This barbaric treatment was deeply upsetting, but no crime had been committed against him, and so he could not go to the priests.

Nightfall came and Filek left only to secure his ration. He ate in the surgery by lanternlight. Twice Pesh looked in. Once Immok came in and went to his own locker. Captain Shuzt walked by at one point and gave Filek a pursed-lip sort of smile. It was the kind of look you might give a pig about to be slaughtered.

During the long hours of the night Filek fought off sleep, afraid that the moment he nodded off they would attack. He stayed awake, a long knife in his hand, ready to defend himself.

Several times he heard soft sounds and detected Zuik creeping up to the door. Each time Zuik looked in he found Filek awake. Zuik tiptoed away in disgust.

The following morning, with land sighted from the leading ship, there came a signal from the flagship for the *Growler.* Admiral Heuze wanted to interview Assistant Surgeon Filek Biswas. He was to attend upon the admiral at his earliest convenience.

Filek groaned. He would be off the *Growler* all day. His locker would be emptied, and he would be put up on charges. They would be packing him down into the slaves' deck before nightfall.

Filek sent a gloomy message to Chiknulba, then packed his knives and needles. At least he wouldn't be cut for the loss of those precious tools.

A boat was lowered, and eight men rowed Filek across

to the flagship. He was hoisted aboard on the sailor's lift and taken to the admiral's quarters.

He found the admiral reclining in a hip bath.

"Come in, ur, Biswas, that's the name, correct?"

"Assistant Surgeon Filek Biswas, Your Excellency."

"Ah, yes, and until this expedition you worked at the city hospital of Shasht."

"Yes, sir."

"And became famous for surgery without pain. Very successful surgery they said."

"Thank you, sir."

"But the priests didn't like it. They think we're supposed to feel pain, even in surgery."

"Yes, sir." This was dangerous territory. Filek was inclined to say as little as possible.

"Priests nipped that one in the bud. Most people still scream their guts out when they have to undergo an operation."

"Not my patients, sir. I have almost perfected the art of drugging them into a state of stupefaction."

"Then that is what I want you to do." The admiral heaved a blackened, stinking foot out of the tub. "My foot must come off. It has rotted."

Filek frowned in concern. The foot was gangrenous. The leg was going. Time was of the essence if the man was to have any chance at all of surviving.

"I'm afraid, Admiral, that the leg below the knee must go, and right away. Anything else, and you'll be dead in a day or so."

Admiral Heuze groaned.

"You're certain of this? It all started with a cut on my big toe."

Filek sighed. If it had been cleaned properly at the beginning, it would never have reached this condition.

"Certain. We must hurry. In fact, we should operate at once. I will need a quantity of opium, some spirits of alcohol, which you will drink at once. We must clean the leg with spirits of alcohol as well."

A pint of spirits and thirty drops of opium tincture

later, the admiral was strapped down on the table completely insensible to the world.

Filek was a stickler for absolute cleanliness during and after an operation. He dipped his instruments in spirits of alcohol many times and washed all surfaces with spirits as well. He had learned that this kind of cleanliness was rewarded with the survival of more patients. The admiral's own ship surgeon was not invited to attend. The admiral had placed all his trust in Filek. Of course, if the admiral didn't live, then Filek would almost certainly face interrogation at the hands of the priests.

Somehow he pushed all of that out of his mind as he took up the familiar instruments and began to work.

The foot was a mess, but the rot had not yet moved above the knee. He severed the leg, put his own specially made spring clamps on the blood vessels, and sewed them up. This technique had made a great improvement on the survival of patients, compared to the older one of cauterizing the stump with boiling pitch. The shock of that last maneuver took a good ten percent of them, though it did help to cut down on postoperative infections.

The leg was off in a few minutes. The sewing took longer, but the opium he'd dosed the admiral with was keeping the poor man unconscious, or he'd have been shrieking and shaking in the straps.

As he finished up, he cleaned everything again with spirits of alcohol. After years of careful experimentation Filek had theorized that microscopic life, which he called dikla, or small seed, lived everywhere and could grow easily on open flesh. He imagined tiny forests of this life covering wounds. Causing the rot. It was like mushrooms, he thought, the way the fungi attack a tree.

Filek had removed a great many arms and legs in his career, many of them from poor people with gangrene from some filthy little cut that hadn't been cleaned at all. Sometimes they came after trying poultices of this and that, but in the city they lacked the herbal knowledge of the countryside and access to fresh herbs. Nearly always the limb had to come off if they were to have any chance of survival. Over the years the survival rate had slowly crept up, but when he began to operate in clean conditions things had improved enormously. When he used spirits of alcohol on every surface and instrument, they improved far more. The final piece of the puzzle had come when he'd started to use massive quantities of opium and stiff quantities of alcohol to completely anaesthetize the patient. This increased the time he could spend actually operating and in turn allowed better sewing and repair work.

The admiral was placed in his bunk, and Filek sat beside him all day and through the following night. The pulse was steady. The man was in good health for the most part, but reverses could occur at any time with this kind of condition. Filek was aware that the admiral's survival and his own were now closely entwined.

A series of priests came in to examine the admiral, followed by Sub-Admiral Geppugo, who questioned Filek closely for a few minutes. Filek had the sense that Geppugo was praying mightily for Heuze's demise.

Jarls, the admiral's secretary, came in every half hour or so to check. In the thin, neurotic-looking Jarls, Filek saw his own reflection—the same gaunt face, the same nervousness in the eyes. Here was another meritocrat, serving the powerful but having no security. Jarls would carefully scrutinize the admiral's sleeping face, looking for any hint of a change. Then he would turn and nod to Filek before leaving. Jarl's fate also depended entirely on Heuze's survival.

Filek dozed on and off through the night and finally slept for two hours straight just before dawn. He awoke to find the ship was no longer in motion. There was a steady drum of feet as hundreds of men moved around the ship preparing equipment. It had started. The expedition was about to land in the new world.

Filek checked the admiral and found his pulse nice and steady. The breathing was regular. The wound was clean-smelling. He applied spirits with a liberal swab, just to be certain, but it all looked good.

Outside, the waters of the bay were dotted with boats heading inshore toward the forested land.

Landfall, at last.

The problem for Filek was that before he could reach that land, so tantalizingly close at hand, he would have to return to the *Growler,* and then his enemies would have him. They would have looted his locker and brought spurious charges against him. Shutz would have given them the go-ahead, and the priests would be waiting for him with the shears in their hands.

Meanwhile, the admiral was alive, and so far the amputation had produced no crisis. If the wound stayed clean, the admiral would survive. That meant ensuring that the leg's dressings were changed regularly and that spirits were used to disinfect everything, constantly.

He knew the regular ship's surgeons, who were waiting outside, thirsting for the chance to displace him, would kill the admiral in no time with their methods.

So Filek sat tight. As long as he was on the flagship he was safe. Slaves brought the foods he suggested, pap and sausage. He tasted it gingerly, to make sure that no one tried to poison the admiral. That look in Sub-Admiral Geppugo's eyes haunted him. When it passed his test, he set it aside to wait for the patient to wake up.

The admiral finally awoke quite late in the day. He was thirsty as hell, but in no immediate agony. The loss of the leg brought on the grieving, of course. For a while he sobbed to himself quietly. Filek had seen this sad reaction many times before, and he knew the man would get over it. They always did.

Filek waited for the right moment, then suggested food. The admiral took some gruel and some beer. Filek spooned a blend of ground herbs and dried berries into the gruel along with salt. In the beer he placed a squirt of lime juice and honey.

The admiral slept again afterward. Filek watched the boats coming and going among the ships. The fleet was anchored in line, the ships within hailing distance, about a mile offshore.

Smoke drifted up all afternoon from the monkey places at the head of the bay. This time, so he'd heard, they'd found a whole city of them. It was hard to conceive of the monkeys being able to build a city, but it was certainly an unusually large nest of them, anyway. There had been some fierce fighting, but the monkeys had been overcome as usual and the place taken. Columns had been sent out to capture the fleeing females and young, and a great haul of meat had been sent out to the ships.

The looting had been terrific. All kinds of monkey-made goods had been brought back. There were things of metal some useful, like knives, and some mysterious. There were also many fine weavings and carvings. A market had already sprung up for the craftworks, though the priests were said to be furious.

But there was also plenty of work for the ship surgeons. Hundreds of wounded men had returned. Mostly the wounds were arrow punctures, some with stone heads. Filek soon understood that the monkeys had fought back harder here than at any other place. The drums of mourning were already beginning to throb on the warrior deck.

The admiral awoke that evening, while Filek was in the ship's surgery removing a crushed foot. He hurried the work, then cleaned up and raced to the admiral's cabin.

The priests were already there. Red tops kept him away from the admiral. A yellow top was talking into the admiral's ear. Jarls was standing in the corner, rubbing his hands together with anxiety.

Then the admiral saw Filek and waved.

"Ah, my surgeon. Come here, Biswas, you did the trick. I am alive, alive!"

The priests all turned to glare at Filek.

The admiral gave a little shriek and then a whistle. "Damn me, but it hurts to move it."

"You must try not to for a few days. I will dose you with opium again, though not as heavily. It will keep the worst pain away."

"That's what I want to hear. Damned good work, Biswas. Dine with me. I feel as if I haven't eaten properly in a week."

Filek was happy to join the admiral, who dismissed the priests. Jarls followed them with a rare smile on his thin face.

Slaves brought in trenchers of sizzling meat. Filek insisted that the admiral also eat a salad of greens and bitter herbs. He complained but ate it anyway.

Later, he sipped a goblet of wine and belched contentedly.

"The monkey was excellent. What did you think, Biswas?"

"Oh, very good, sir."

"Tender and with a nice sweet taste. The cooks did well, I think."

Another gulp of wine.

"Good work, Biswas. You shall be rewarded."

"Thank you, Admiral."

They were interrupted by a messenger from the Imperial Scion, Nebbeggebben. Admiral Heuze read it and dictated a reply to Jarls, who hurried out to send it off.

"So Biswas, what can I do for you? A promotion, perhaps?"

"Well, sir, I have enemies . . ."

Admiral Heuze listened attentively as Filek told him about Captain Shuzt and Surgeon Zuik.

"I see. You will remain on my ship, and your women will be brought over at once. Biswas, I think you may be very useful to me."

And so, special orders went across to the *Growler* for a purdah boat to bring over the Lady Chiknulba and the Lady Simona, along with Filek's things, to the *Anvil*.

Chapter 28

For three days and nights the ragged column of fugitives struggled inland toward the coal towns. Mount Nippiana grew steadily larger to their eyes until it loomed over them. On the second day the rooster chooks were sent out as scouts to find shelter when dark clouds billowed up from the south.

Chooks came back with word of a cave set behind an overhanging ledge of rock before the rain came down. Huddled together under the rock, they rode out the storm.

At one point when lightning was crackling down on the hills and the rain was falling very hard, someone said loudly that the storm had been sent by the Spirit of the Land, who was angered by the return of Man the Cruel. There would be war between the two, and Man would be destroyed once again.

Some of the older folk agreed with this idea, while old Haloiko, the survivor of Bilauk, gave a hoarse laugh and reminded everyone that the Spirit was exactly that, spirit, and thus not involved intimately in the workings of the material world. The subsequent discussion of the Spirit and its doctrines helped to take everyone's mind off their misery for a little while.

One thing about which there was no argument was that Toshak was their leader. Life had been peaceful for a long, long time in the Land. With his training at the Academy of Sulmo, he knew what little there was to know about war. They needed him.

The most immediate need was food, however. Nuza

and the chooks had been out investigating from the moment the rain stopped.

"We gathered some wild corn, some crab apples, and some berries. But it will hardly feed the small children, let alone the rest of us," Nuza reported. "The chooks have found a few insects, but they too are growing weak from hunger."

"We have to get some food," said Renacles, the miller of Harfield, who had been helping the elderly folk. "Many of the old ones are reaching the end of their strength."

"How far is it to Uzon?" Toshak turned to Sand, the scout.

"Another day at least. It depends on how fast the old ones can walk tomorrow."

"How are they getting by?" Toshak turned back to Nuza and Renacles.

"They did very well today," said Renacles. "But without something to eat, they will be much reduced in strength tomorrow."

"We need food, then."

"There's a small village about ten miles farther on," said Renacles. "A small party will go and food can be sent back."

"Flour, milk, bushpod, anything they have, the need is very great."

Soon afterward a small group was dispatched down river to the village. It began to rain again soon afterward, and for a while the rain grew heavy. Thunder boomed in the distance.

They huddled about the smoky fires and slept pressed together for warmth. There was little talking. Their lives had been shattered, and they now lived in a new world filled with pain and suffering that they had never dreamed might come to them.

Worse was the feeling that their own legitimacy as a people, their right to exist, was challenged. For Man was the Ruler of the World; so it had been since the beginning. So it was said in the Book. They were merely the inheritors who came after the fall of Man. This had never mattered before, because they believed they were alone in the world. But now they were faced with the awful truth; Man lived, and meant to reclaim the world.

For many the initial stunning surprise of the raids had given way to a burning desire for revenge. Thru, for instance, was eager to fight again. He felt he'd learned a few things, just by surviving the battle at Harfield. Man the Cruel was not invulnerable. He could be killed just like any other living being.

For others, a terrible sense of despair had set in. Man the Ruler was returned, and he would crush them beneath his steel-shod shoes. Their own existence would vanish as if it had been no more than mist.

The storms finally passed after a long interlude when lightning flashed and flickered on Mount Nippiana and thunder boomed through the valleys. Beneath the overhang, the fugitives clutched one another for warmth and tried to find some kind of shelter from their thoughts. Several of the smaller chook chicks died in the night.

Scouts were sent out again at first light. Toshak was still anxious about a pursuit. If the men realized how slowly the column was moving, they might yet mount the effort to try and capture them. Those soldiers that had attacked Harfield would be easily capable of overhauling them.

There was nothing to eat, and nothing to do but get everyone on their feet and moving, slowly, wearily down the narrow track beside the river. Hungry bellies rumbled everywhere. Children wailed and were hushed by desperate mothers.

The scouts, however, brought word that no pursuit was visible. It looked as if the men had burned the village and then left.

The column struggled on. Some of the elderly lay down and declared they couldn't go on. Some more of the little chicks were dead. A baby mot was dying, too, and its mother's wails were heartrending to hear.

And then Toshak's prayers were answered. There were

shouts from up ahead. A caravan of donkey carts was coming out of the woods. In the carts were sacks of wheat and bushpod, with dry wood and cauldrons on others.

The exhausted fugitives raised a cheer and hurried forward. Fires were built, water was brought from the river, and within half an hour cauldrons of wheat and bushpod mush were being dished out while chooks ate cracked wheat directly from the ground.

Being this hungry was something that few of the folk had ever known. In their comfortable lives within the Land they only knew hunger, if at all, in late winter after a poor harvest the previous year. The skillful husbandry of the Land's resources enabled them to exploit the plentiful wild areas when drought or hail affected the crops.

Now they ate with a peculiar intensity, sweeping up handfuls of mush from the cauldrons so as not to waste a bite.

That night in the village of Essifields, after most were bedded down, several young mots gathered at Toshak's fire. They'd reached the point where the urge for revenge had overcome the fear.

"Teach us, Toshak! Teach us how to fight."

Those who had seen Toshak whirling through the fighting knew they could stand against these men. The men were slower than mots. They were heavier, they were stronger perhaps, but they were slower. In that fact lay the folk's salvation. None of them might match Toshak with the blade in his hands, but they could all improve until they could kill men!

Toshak returned their enthusiasm as if from a mirror. He spoke with passion in his voice as he explained some of the most basic principles of war.

Never attack unless you have superior numbers.
Never be brought to battle on bad ground.
Keep the initiative if at all possible.

And most important, perhaps of all.

He who runs away lives to fight again another day.

Thru watched Toshak and felt his understanding of things grow large. The moment trembled with great potential. This was a beginning, a spark of the fire that would blaze up across the Land.

The mots and brilbies, kobs and chooks would not let themselves be slaughtered like sheep. They would fight. Before they went under Man's cruel knife, they would send many of their enemies to the dark halls of eternity.

Chapter 29

The news of the catastrophe came to them while they were travelling through the coal country. They had left the folk of Harfield behind in Uzon and made their way up the valley through Big Seam and Little Seam to the town of Gabik. A runner came panting into the town just before dark.

He was in tears, soaked in mud.

"Tamf is burned! Monsters that some call men have destroyed the city. Many, many folk are dead."

Nuza sagged to the ground keening in agony. Kneeling there in the street she wept and could not be comforted. They spent a harrowing night in Gabik and left at first light and hurried northward. By noon they were on the main Creton–Tamf road and soon came upon crowds of refugees from the north.

Among the fugitives the troupe found friends, but no word of Nuza's family. They went on northward.

Again and again they were warned not to go near Tamf. Man was there, and he would kill them. They ignored the warnings and pushed up on Amble Pike, coming to the edge of the wide vale of Tamf. The land was empty. The villages were silent. No smoke rose from their chimneys. There was a strange kind of tension in the air. They saw occasional parties of chooks, hurrying south, and that was all.

When they came over Amble Rise the bay was visible ahead, stretched out wide and blue. In the bay were the ships, clearly visible, even at this distance of many miles.

"There are so many. I count thirty, thirty-five."

"There are forty," said Toshak, who was examining the fleet with his beautiful little telescope.

"They are so enormous, I don't understand why," muttered Thru.

"They had to be. They've come a very long way," said Toshak.

"How do you know?"

"Because we've never been troubled by them before. If we had, we'd have never forgotten it. So they must live somewhere so far away that even with ships like these they have never come this far."

"Then they aren't planning on going home."

"They are here to invade the Land and take it from us."

Toshak had voiced their common fear, growing steadily for days. Not just a raid—invasion. Unending.

"And for us?" said Gem. "What do they plan for us? We live here already."

"Extermination. They will destroy us completely."

The chill wind ran through them all, a wind off a mountain of empty skulls.

"The Assenzi, we must warn them! They will help us."

"I imagine they have already been warned," said Toshak, practically. "But what will they do?"

Finally, they came within sight of the town. The walls still stood, but that was all. Blackened ruins jutted up from the charred central area. Farther out the buildings were being demolished by men seeking to reuse wooden beams.

"Look!" said Gem, pointing down the shore to the west.

Large sheds were rising there, crude, boxy structures, of three and four stories in height.

"What are those?" said Hob in simple wonder.

"Those must be for the men. They have landed. They intend to stay," Nuza said in a sick voice.

"There is no one here. Let us head east," said Toshak.

"Get down," whispered Gem, pointing to a patrol of six men that had come into view far down the road.

They crouched low and moved off into the trees, retreating a ways into the undergrowth. The patrol moved up and went past, marching at an easy pace, carrying spears, with shields slung on their backs.

They waited until the patrol was gone before slipping across the road and turning east toward Sonf. The hamlets along the road were empty. Some had been looted and partially burned. By the end of the day they reached Sonf itself, and were out of the area touched by the raiders.

Nowhere had they seen a mot, a chook, a brilby, or anything else but a few wild birds. The whole world had come shuddering to a halt and every eye was wide-open while the ears listened with exaggerated care. Every living thing knew the feel of Man in its bones.

It was too dark to cross the River Songbird that night. They bedded down in West Sonf, and kept a careful watch throughout the night. In the morning the river was at low tide, and they walked across on the stepping-stones.

Now they began to see a few mot scouts, carrying bows and full quivers. They reported that King Rolf had retreated to Sonf, and was organizing his army there. This was the first news of any organized resistance, and they were further encouraged by the knowledge that mots from all over Tamf, Pelej, and Creton had flooded to the muster of the King's banner.

As they hurried east, Nuza asked everyone they met for news of the refugees. She heard all kinds of wild tales, mostly spun from exaggerated fears, but learned nothing of the fate of her parents and family. She found it hard to sleep at night, not knowing if they still lived. Thru's efforts at comforting her were not completely successful, either.

Gradually they pieced together the events leading to the destruction of Tamf. The city had received warnings from Creton. Preparations had been made. The battle for the walls had been fierce and by no means one-sided. Many men had been killed or wounded, but they were skilled in the manner of such assaults and soon found a way to stretch the defenders and then mount the walls at two separate places. Once they were inside, panic and lack of discipline had undone the defenders.

All over Sonf parties of mors, children, and the elderly were setting out, heading inland to Ajutan. With them went the flocks of chooks and all the domestic animals. Anything they left would be slaughtered at once if Man came. Many folk promised not to stop until they reached Lushtan in the Farblows.

Word of the horror at Tamf and down in Creton had spread right across the Land now, and the folk everywhere were in motion. It was as if an anthill had been kicked over. Man had come to kill them.

One terrible image that stayed in the mind was that of the slow-moving columns of refugees that had been captured after the fall of Tamf. They had set out too late and swift-marching forces of men had caught them up. Terrible scenes had taken place as the men beat the folk into submission, then drove them with the whip back to Tamf.

The next day the troupe reached Sonf. The central part of the village was filled with a crowd of mots and brilbies, most carrying weapons. Rumors abounded, most of them wild exaggerations of the casualties incurred in Creton and Tamf.

Toshak waded through the crowds and sent in a message from the door of the inn, which had become the King's headquarters.

His presence was welcomed, as was that of the others. King Rolf of Tamf was eager to hear about Creton and to meet the famous swordsmot Toshak.

The King had been twice wounded in the fighting inside the city and was lying on a cot along the wall. He struggled to sit up to greet them. His advisors fussed until he shooed them back.

"Speak, Toshak. You are a graduate of Sulmo; you know more of these matters of war than do I."

Toshak gave an oral report of the events in Bilauk and

Harfield, then the King asked questions of Nuza and Thru, and absorbed their news with pursed lips. It filled in the picture he had already received from the first warnings. Coastal places had been hit, the folk either slaughtered completely as at Bilauk or fled inland.

"Great Toshak, your fame precedes you, but your words do not help the pain in our heart. Terrible slaughters have occurred in Creton. My folk cry out for justice and retribution. We are massing here, I have more than a thousand mots already, but we have few ideas. When we tried to keep the men from climbing our wall, they tricked us with a diversion and got onto the wall in two separate places."

"They are well trained, Your Majesty. Veterans of many wars I'd say."

The King put his hand to his chin, as if for reassurance. King Rolf was the fourteenth king of that name in Tamf and had no more expected this war than any of his predecessors. It had been a long time since there had even been serious trouble with bandits in Tamf or Sonf.

"How should I proceed? What do you suggest?"

"We have much to learn, Your Majesty. And we do not have much time to learn it in."

The King sighed, heavily. "You believe they have come to invade the Land?"

"They have come to annihilate us."

The King stared back at him for a moment. This terrifying realization haunted them all. They were fighting for their very survival.

"Great Toshak, I can see that you have been thinking about this matter. And I am glad, for I can see only the prospect of taking the mots of this muster and going to Tamf and fighting these men."

"No, Your Majesty. I would suggest that you take your men to Dronned and join forces with King Belit. We shall need the largest army we can muster. And we shall have to train that army. It is pointless attacking the men until our mots can perform a few battlefield maneuvers. That takes time to learn."

The King shook his head a moment, not liking these words.

"We have to fight them. If we do not, they will take the Land."

"Yes, Your Majesty, we must fight them, but we must fight wisely, and carefully. They will defeat us otherwise and destroy us forever. We are not ready to meet them like the ram, horns on horns. They will cut us down for meat. We must fight them as the smoke fights the ram, filling their lungs and choking them. We take away their air, they will lose the will to fight."

King Rolf had been on the walls of Tamf and had fought his way through the city afterward to escape. He understood the truth in Toshak's words.

"We will be like pyluk, skulking in the forests."

"Even that, if we have to. All that counts is that we build our army and prepare. We must fight again, and we must win."

Chapter 30

Everything was so much better, and so much worse. Simona leaned against the rail of the luxurious women's gallery that extended off the stern of the flagship. Protected from male eyes by a heavy awning, the women could stand in the open and take deep breaths of the fresh sea air.

After being cooped up in the fetid conditions of the *Growler*'s women's deck, it was a fantastic luxury. Just another example of how their lives had been improved by leaving the *Growler*.

Even more importantly, Simona and Chiknulba were sheltered beneath the wings of Juguba Heuze, the admiral's wife. Juguba came from humble stock. Her position depended on the survival of her husband, and Filek Biswas had saved his life. As a result, Filek's womenfolk were to receive the best treatment from everyone aboard *Anvil*'s women's deck.

Juguba went so far as to speak to some Gsekk matriarchs and ensure that Chiknulba was treated with full and proper respect by these haughty ladies.

Now Chiknulba and her pathetic unwed daughter shared a small cabin and enjoyed gallery privileges. They stood in the first quadrant in the daily lines for meals. They were even allowed to dip water from the big brass bucket delivered to Juguba Heuze every morning.

Juguba ruled the women's deck with a firm hand, however, and at least once a week her niece, Amrusa, handed out a whipping to some poor sister who had broken the rules and been convicted. Petty thefts, reported insults, and curse calling against Juguba were the usual crimes. Everyone realized that they needed Juguba's affections and behaved accordingly. Chiknulba had sensed that Juguba enjoyed receiving worship and indulged her whenever possible.

Simona hated to see her mother become a groveler, but she also understood why poor Chiknulba would do it. They remained aboard the *Anvil* only as long as they enjoyed the favor of Juguba Heuze. Without that favor they'd be going back to the nightmarish, poverty-stricken existence of the *Growler.*

There was no other choice until they could get off the ships, and even then it would be years before they had the chance to live as they once had, in reasonable comfort with access to the open air. Until then, Chiknulba would trim her sails to the prevailing winds. She'd learned her lesson from Vli Shuzt. If bowing and scraping was what it took, then Chiknulba of the Gsekk would be happy to do it.

But for all the luxury Simona wanted nothing more than to be sent back to the *Growler,* where Rukkh could come and look upon her. Where he could promise her marriage in his eyes.

Simona had realized that Rukkh might be the last chance she would get of reaching the safety of legal marriage. Single women were not considered part of Shasht society. Dire things happened to them.

Also at work, as she herself sometimes reflected on bitterly, was her need to have a man, any man, almost. She wanted to feel more than just this empty longing for fulfillment on a physical level. No amount of prayer made this desire go away.

Rukkh was her way out, but now she would not see Rukkh, unless he came to her after the landing. And that might not be possible, since he would be under military orders.

Later, when things were sorted out in the new colony and Filek's improved status confirmed, it would be impossible for her to be shown to Rukkh. They would go on showing her to men of her own class, who would look on her and yet turn away because of the strawberry mark.

Simona felt a familiar choking despair rising up. She looked out over the rail and into the blue waters. The land was visible, just a mile away. A green blur of slopes, a distant set of hills, but it might as well have been a thousand miles distant, for she could not reach it. It would remain there, verdant, inviting, cloaked in mists that spoke of the freshness of morning, and always out of reach.

It would be months before the first purdah building was completed and women could be safely moved ashore. Simona could hardly wait for that day, and yet she dreaded it, too, because it would sever her line to Rukkh.

Oh, she thought, *to be back home in Shasht and in my old life.* Simona thought she'd give anything for that. To be able to ride up at Shesh Zob. To walk in the woods, to swim in the lake, to live completely free of restraint.

She turned away. It was not wise to stay too long on the gallery, or someone would comment upon it to Juguba.

While his wife and daughter were enjoying an enormous increase in the quality of their lives, Filek Biswas, too, had found himself elevated in the world. He continued to tend Admiral Heuze, whose stump healed quickly.

Thanks to the admiral's explicit orders, the *Anvil*'s ship's surgeon and his staff were still kept at arm's length. The admiral had appointed Filek as his personal surgeon, and in his position he was quite capable of making that appointment.

The priests had accepted Filek's move and had made no protest. Heuze was a good ship commander, and his squadron had performed well throughout the mission. Heuze also had good relations with Nebbeggebben, the

Imperial Scion. So Heuze was indulged by the yellow tops. The surgeon, Biswas, would be watched carefully and his dossier expanded. Someday they would take him, but not yet.

At first the admiral had simply been grateful for Filek's medical skill.

"No pain!" he said over and over. "Didn't feel a damned thing."

Then, over the next few days, the admiral grew fond of talking with Biswas while Filek kept the stump clean and dressed. Admiral Heuze had found, as he might have expected, that Filek Biswas was a very cultured man, attuned to the life of the great city. In other words, someone to talk to.

Heuze himself had grown up in the city in a good family and recalled that wonderful social round. Being at sea a lot removed him from the glamorous scene, but he remained a devotee of the great arts: the chorales, the orchestras, and the theaters. He tried to attend such events whenever he was lucky enough to be posted to the city.

Regrettably, the admiral had to admit, he got to the theater relatively rarely now. In recent times the pressure to feed the shipyards in Shasht had kept him working the Bekwana route. He'd spent far too much time in those frigid waters, fetching the very materials they'd built this damned great fleet from.

And so, that afternoon, as his daughter gloomed alone several decks farther down, Filek sat down to dine with the admiral, alone in the grand cabin. Filek had sensed the admiral's hunger for the world of culture and had been able to tease it along a bit with stories of great performances he had seen at the theater or participated in at the chorales.

On this occasion he could see that the admiral was especially excited about something. Then the servants brought in platters of hot moogah and steamed pudding bread.

"Biswas, you're a man with an interest in the artistic

side of things. I have something to show you, just as soon
as we've cleared our plates. Damned fine moogah tonight, don't you think?"

Ship's moogah was a stir of onions and meat scraps
flavored with hot peppers and served over the steamed
bread pudding. The result was very filling.

"Excellent, Admiral."

Filek spooned up the heavy stuff, thick with fat. It was
a welcome change from the biscuit and rancid cheese
that was all they'd been eating a few weeks before.

"Here, have some of this grog." The admiral poured
a generous dollop into Filek's mug. He took a sip. It was
sweetened and mixed strong, the way the admiral liked
it, and Filek felt light-headed almost at once. Filek had
never been a man for strong spirits.

"Ah, very good," he said, setting the mug down
carefully.

They ate steadily while the admiral discoursed on the
situation ashore, where things were going more slowly
than they should have.

"And if something isn't done to speed up those buildings, then I think Master Muis will be losing some prize
possessions between his legs and going down to the slave
quarters." He laughed.

Filek nodded and smiled and shivered inside. Muis was
the builder in charge of erecting the sheds for the camp.
In the old world he'd been the architect of the new Imperial City buildings in Shasht. Somewhere he'd fallen afoul
of the highest authority, for now he risked his manhood
for some stinking sheds built from scavenged beams on
this wild, though beautiful shore.

The admiral concluded his thoughts on the situation
ashore and took a pull on his grog.

"So, that's my scuttlebutt. What's yours, Biswas.
What's been going on in the surgery? Or the rest of the
damned ship for that matter. Jarls won't tell me a thing.
Can't wait until I can finally get up and move around
again. Been lying around in here for far too long."

"In the surgery we've had fewer operations. We seem to have sewn up everyone who survived the fight."

"Indeed, that's good news."

"Far higher casualties than I was expecting."

"Yes, well let us say that high command is thinking furiously about that. The damned, fornicating monkeys put up quite a fight for the little city."

"It is a city isn't it?"

"By all accounts. I've yet to go ashore myself, either."

"I wasn't expecting a city."

"Heh, don't tell anyone this, but nor were the priests."

Filek chuckled, but carefully. This was a dangerous area for someone in his position. For all he knew, Heuze was a creature of the priests, and they were using him to test Filek Biswas for rebellious taint. But the admiral plowed on into the priest-infested waters.

"All that stuff about the monkeys not having a culture, you can forget it. They have culture, and it must be quite an interesting one."

Filek's eyebrows rose at this. The admiral was certainly stepping over certain lines. If the priests were listening, they could put him to the questions at once.

"How could you be so sure? These places they inhabited might have been built by higher beings, men like ourselves. The monkeys have merely taken them over as shelters."

"So the priests have been saying. But they put up a helluva fight, and we took a lot of casualties. Lots of arrowheads in our men, is that right?"

"Lots."

"Which means the damned monkeys are bright enough to use a bow, and presumably smart enough to make one. You see, they must have culture of some sort."

"Well, I will let the priests make that determination. 'Tis the business only of the Great God." Filek hoped that would be enough to see him to safety, if the conversation was being eavesdropped by a red top hidden in the walls.

"Oh yes, He Who Eats will take care of us all, but

these monkeys are more than the priests thought they were, that I can guarantee you.''

Filek shrugged.

''Take a look at this.'' The admiral took up a roll tied at both ends. He loosed the bows, and unrolled a very finely made mat. Filek was struck by the immediate beauty of the design, limned in very strong line and executed in bold colors. Large chickens with a wild sense of glee about them were dancing alongside oversize beetles on background of green wheat. It was all made of straw and similar fibers, but it was stunning work, and Filek sat back and stared at the admiral with his mouth open.

''This is work of the monkeys?''

''It came from the city, along with lots of other stuff like it. This is a really good one, what do you think?''

''It's beautiful. It's incredible, I've never seen work so fine.''

''What do you think they'd fetch back in Shasht?''

Filek's eyes boggled. Among the cognoscenti, work like this would fetch fabulous sums. ''Hundreds of gold pieces, at the least.''

''Heh, heh, I'm going to bet that quite a lot of these things are going to find their way back to Shasht, despite the priests' best efforts.''

Filek stiffened.

The admiral had noticed.

''Calm your nerves, Biswas. No red top can get close up here without my knowing about it.''

Filek shifted uncomfortably. ''This is amazing work. And you say there is more?''

''Oh yes, there are lots and lots of mats like this, plus carpets and tapestry work that is just as good. There are wood carvings, too, very realistic work, as good as any you'll see in Shasht.''

''This is amazing. Such artistic heights in such humble creatures.''

''Heh, heh, might make it hard to stamp them out completely, eh?''

Filek swallowed hard. This mat with these delightfully

wicked-looking chickens was the work of creatures that he and the admiral were cheerfully eating.

After a moment, he began to feel distinctly queasy. He made it to the rail, but only just in time.

Chapter 31

When the first round of meetings and talks finally ended, Thru and Nuza fell asleep on a corner of the floor of the taproom of the Sonf tavern. Their sleep was haunted by terrible dreams in which piles of heads appeared again and again. In those piles they saw the faces of friends, parents, brothers. They awoke many times, and clutched each other in the dark for comfort.

When the dawn's light finally broke over the Land, they pulled themselves to their feet. It was a grey morning, with clouds covering the sky.

Nuza looked out the window while Thru admired her. Her beauty never failed to cheer him. The smooth workings of her muscles, her amazing natural grace.

"There are carts all over the street," she said. "Everyone's packing to leave."

She turned back to him; their eyes met and they nodded, each understanding the situation. Sonf was probably going to be attacked that day.

"Better find out what's been happening," said Thru, pulling up his trousers.

They had hot tea and a biscuit in the taproom and learned that in the night scouts had reported that a large column of men had set out from Tamf the previous evening and were camped on the road to Sonf. Everyone was leaving at once while the King organized his small force into some kind of pattern. Harassing parties went out to find the flanks of the advancing party of men.

Carts and donkeys were already rumbling out of Sonf onto the roads heading east. The folk of Sonf were determined not to be caught like those from Tamf. The stories and rumors were terrifying.

Hob found them while they were still finishing their tea.

"I have messages for both of you."

For Thru there was a brief note from Toshak, who wanted Thru to accompany him immediately on the trip to Dronned. Most of the Tamf mots were going that way.

Nuza received a small scroll sealed with her family's ringseal. Her hands were trembling as she broke it and unrolled the scroll.

Then she lifted her head up with a sob. Thru's heart sank for a moment.

"They live, oh thanks to the Spirit, they live. They are in Lushtan, in the Farblows."

"Thank the Spirit."

Thru wrapped her in his arms, overjoyed at this news.

And then the chill thought ran through him. He and Nuza were about to be torn apart. The Farblows lay in the opposite direction from Dronned. Nuza's face crumpled as she understood. Her joy evaporated so instantly that he thought his heart would break.

"Oh, my love, to be without you will be hard, I don't know how we'll manage."

Thru felt a crushing stab of fear. This could be the last time he ever saw her, and the light would go out of his life. But he could not refuse to go with Toshak.

Nuza's family, it turned out, had been very quick to abandon Tamf when the ships entered the bay. Her father, Cham, had had a powerful premonition of disaster, and had the whole family and all the animals on the road within the hour. They headed south and east, chooks and all, for Lushtan, where Cham had relatives. His wariness had saved their lives, for they were well ahead of the enemy columns that set out after Tamf had fallen.

The troupe was splitting up. Also going south were Gem and Serling, while Hob was going north with Thru and Toshak. Saying farewell was terribly hard. Letting go of Nuza was dreadful. He felt as if he were drowning while he waved to her until she was a tiny dot down the road. Then he turned back with leaden steps to the tavern to wait for Toshak to finish a final round of meetings.

He sat there in the taproom and stared blankly at the wall. There were some youngsters who had heard that he was Seventy-seven-Run Thru Gillo and wanted desperately to speak with him, but when they saw him with his face like stone and his vacant eyes they passed on and said nothing.

Would he ever see his Nuza again? Ever kiss those lips and stroke that soft fur? If he lost her and survived, if they defeated the invasion, then he would be left to live alone, and he didn't think he could stand that. It would be worse than death in some ways.

Toshak appeared at last, free from meetings, with his hat on his head and his pack and bow on his back. He was eager to be off at once. Thru picked up his own things and joined him. Hob appeared with a donkey carrying panniers of food and water.

"Nuza has gone to Lushtan, to join her family. Gem and Serling went with her." Toshak's face fell. "Ah, Nuza, I will miss her. Gem and Serling, too. Our happy family has been torn apart."

He stood there for a moment, then with a decisive snap of his bushy eyebrows Toshak shrugged it all aside.

"We have to face the future, my friends. There is much to do and little time available. Dronned by morning, think you can do it?"

"That's thirty-three miles, a pretty good hike," said Thru, stretching his legs carefully.

Hob chuckled. "These donkeys not going to be too happy, but we can keep them moving."

"The moon will be full tonight. We'll be able to see the track."

"We will do our best, then."

They marched until the sun set, whereupon they ate bread and rested. When the moon rose they set off again and walked on trails over the moors of Sheud.

As they walked Toshak spoke of the things the folk

of the Land would need to learn. The arts of war had become foreign to them.

"This enemy is very strong, very mighty. There is no possibility of compromise with them. It is us or them; one of us must fail. They have trained long and hard as well and have experience in war. We have a long way to go to catch up."

"We outnumber them," said Thru. "There are just those forty ships."

"In a way that is an advantage to them, because our population is vulnerable and has to be guarded."

"Our folk can retreat inland."

"Only so far, and then they come to the mountains."

Big Hob grunted at this. "So we fight with our backs to the wall. That makes us better, because we cannot afford to lose."

Toshak allowed that there was truth to this.

"Also in our favor is that we know the Land well. Ours will be a war of ambushes. His numbers are limited. We must make them more so, a constant attrition of his strength has to be a priority."

Thru nodded, the outline was becoming clear.

"Our people are going to get very familiar with hunger," said Toshak grimly.

"Without bushpod and use of the seapond it will be impossible to prepare thread and cloth," Thru added thoughtfully.

"Our folk will have to raise more sheep and use wool."

"And we will lose the fishing."

"That is true. What lies ahead of us will be hard, very hard, but we have no alternative."

The hours went by in a moonlit dream while their legs kept them moving, ignoring fatigue and sore feet. Somewhere along the way the first light of dawn cracked the far horizon.

Soon they came up the south road, with the coastal dunes on their left and the city walls ahead. They entered by the south gate and made their way through the city to the Guild House. Toshak left messages there for several important citizens of Dronned. Then they went on to the Laughing Fish, where they took breakfast and hot tea.

Sitting in the Laughing Fish Tavern brought on a host of memories for Thru, and he found himself contrasting the difference in the times.

Dronned had received full warning. The city's own folk had fled, while mots from all over the Land had gathered for the King's muster.

Toshak was finishing his mug of hot tea when a message was brought to him. He showed Thru and Hob the royal seal before he broke it, all three heartened to know that King Belit was awake to the need for haste.

Before this, Thru had only viewed the exterior wall of the royal palace of Dronned. Now he was welcomed through the huge black double doors and ushered down a very large passageway by a brilby wearing the royal colors. More doors opened, and they entered a large room carpeted in green, with a great tapestry depicting the founding of Dronned covering the walls. At the far end on a dais sat the throne under a banner bearing the four black crows of Dronned. The King, however, was sitting at a table in the corner poring over maps of the border regions between Dronned, Sonf, and Tamf. Still in his night robe and slippers, King Belit sipped a cup of guezme tea. On a bench nearby sat an Assenzi, dressed in black. Thru guessed that this was Melidofulo, the resident Assenzi of Dronned.

The King was apprised of Toshak's arrival by a young secretary. The King whirled around and raised his arms in welcome.

"Ah, very good. Welcome back to Dronned, noble Toshak."

Toshak stepped forward and bowed, then handed the King a message.

"From King Rolf, Your Majesty."

King Belit nodded with a frown.

"Thank you for coming so quickly." The King broke the seal and scanned the message, then handed it to the secretary.

"I will reply. Bring quill and scroll."

Belit turned back to Toshak and the others.

"And let me welcome your companions, Hob there, the fellow who catches Nuza the acrobat. I've marveled at your catches many a time."

Hob bowed, obviously pleased to have been recognized. The King turned to Thru.

"And you are Seventy-seven-Run Thru Gillo. I saw you play for your village team some years ago, defeating the Laughing Fish for the championship. You were good with the bat that day."

"Your Majesty, you are very kind. That was a grand day, and I will always treasure it."

"Yes, indeed, such glory comes to few of us." He sighed and laid a hand on Thru's shoulder. "But these days are very different and we have a war to win. Unfortunately we have never fought a war before. If it was a ball game, then I would have far more confidence, especially with Seventy-seven-Run Thru Gillo in our ranks."

The King turned back to Toshak. "Yes, my friends, I understand well what we will have to do. But Melidofulo is not so sure."

They all turned to the Assenzi, who rose from his bench and approached them. As he came Thru felt a wave of calmness go through him. Those eyes, so huge, so wise, they must hold some answer to this madness.

"You come from Tamf?" he said after a little nod to each of them.

"Tamf has been destroyed. What's left is being dismantled by the men."

"Ah, the men," said Melidofulo, ignoring Toshak's news of Tamf. "Can we be sure that these creatures are really men?"

They exchanged a look. Indeed, what evidence did they possess, other than old Haloiko's firmly voiced opinion? There had been no communication with the raiders, that was for sure.

"We can only go by what they looked like," said Toshak. "They conform to everything we have been taught.

They have long hair, and long fur on their faces. They are not mots or brilbies and certainly not kobs."

"You have seen them yourselves?"

"Yes, we fought them at the barricade and in the streets."

"Ah," Melidofulo looked down, his jaws moved angrily. "You admit there has been fighting?"

"Oh yes, Melidofulo, fighting and much slaughter. First, at Bilauk, on the Creton coast, we found the entire population dead. Their bodies gone, their heads piled on the jetty."

Melidofulo looked at them, and for a moment Thru saw blank confusion in that face. The Assenzi was unable to accept their words.

"Have any of these creatures been killed?"

"Oh yes, we have killed them. They bleed and die just as we do."

Melidofulo's small mouth pursed in distaste. "Three days ago a bird brought a message from King Rolf claiming that Tamf was under attack. I found it hard to believe."

Toshak's eyes took on a glint. His voice was husky with emotion. "Tamf has been burned to the ground."

King Belit spoke up quickly to head off a clash. "I ordered the Muster of the Land at once. So far we have more than fifteen hundred names on the roll, and more are coming in all the time."

"A thousand mots from Tamf will be following us today and tomorrow."

"Excellent. Our only problem will be feeding everyone."

"Your Majesty, has a message been sent to Sulmo?"

"Indeed, it was sent yesterday, but it will take time to get there."

Melidofulo still studied them with pursed lips. Thru could tell that the ancient being had not fully accepted their story.

"What do you advise, Toshak?" said the King.

"We must raise an army and train it to fight in a disciplined manner."

"You seem very sure of this," said the Assenzi doubtfully.

"Master Melidofulo, you do not seem to understand. We have witnessed the beginnings of a great invasion of the Land. They are men, and they are here to destroy us."

Chapter 32

"Halloo!" Thru's voice echoed in the empty lanes of Warkeen Village. A raven flapped off the roof of the tavern with a melancholy caw. Thru watched it fly off inland, still cawing. The village seemed quite deserted. For the first time since leaving Dronned he wondered if he'd undertaken a fool's errand coming up to the village. But there'd been nothing for him to do in the city. Toshak was always busy with the organization of the new army, and Thru had been left pretty much to his own devices after the initial meeting with King Belit and his advisors. So he'd decided to make a quick visit to Warkeen, just to assure himself that all was well. Now he found the place completely empty.

He made his way through the familiar streets to his own house, but there was no smoke in the chimney there, either.

He knew that at the first word of the danger the females and young would have been sent inland, along with the elderly, but he hadn't expected to find the whole place totally deserted. For a few minutes he wondered if he was entering one of those nightmares he'd had so often. Soon he'd come around a corner, and there would be the pile of heads.

He found the door locked and the windows shuttered and barred. Without much hope he called "Halloooo!" a few times, while he climbed the fence into the backyard. Here, he found evidence of recent visits, for the yard had been swept recently.

Hopes renewed, he tried the back door and found it

bolted top and bottom. So Ware had gone out the front door and locked it. The back windows were all shuttered, too. He went back to the lane and headed toward the tavern.

"Halloooo!" he called once more, and this time was rewarded with a faint "Hellooo!" back.

He saw a figure in the distance and started to run. Halfway there he saw it was Ware, and he ran harder. When they met they almost knocked each other down. They embraced for a few moments. Ware had tears of joy on his cheeks.

"My son, you live, you live!"

"Father . . ."

"So much to say," said Ware happily as he put a hand to his son's face. "Thanks be to the Spirit that you are brought back to us."

Still blinking back the tears, they stumbled over to the steps of the tavern, where they sat down and haltingly asked and answered many questions. Ware had the key to the tavern, which was being used by the small group of men who had stayed in the town. So after a while they went inside.

"Everyone and everything has gone inland, my son. They're building a wall around Meever's, would you believe? I'm only here with the weed squad. We weed the polder for a few days every week. Most of the younger mots have gone to Dronned for the King's muster."

"The whole Land is rising, Father."

They made tea, and Ware fixed some bushpod-flour biscuits, which they ate with butter and curds. Thru worked up the fire and got it good and hot. At least one chimney in the village was still warm.

As they worked they talked, and Thru was pleased to hear that Snejet was well, and waiting for her baby's arrival. They were all up at Juno Village, except for Gil, who'd set off for Dronned and the muster.

"Everyone's up there, even Aunt Paidi. The chooks, too, of course, although some of them have been slipping back down here to go over the fields."

"How is it with the folk of Juno?"

"Well, it's crowded, and there are disagreements, but everyone knows why it has to be that way for now. Until these attackers are defeated, we have to keep away from the coast."

The biscuits were great. Thru realized his stomach was growling with hunger. He tucked in with a will. He ate so heartily that Ware worked up another batch.

"The word came first from Dronned, and many didn't believe. You know how folk are: They don't care to be moved out of their ways too much. And this all sounded completely outlandish. Then a fishing boat put in and said they'd been chased by a huge ship. Then two of our own boats didn't return, on a clear day with little wind. Then we heard about Tamf."

Thru dipped biscuits in hot butter and ate.

"Did the fishing boats come back later?"

"No. We had the funeral and said the rites for them on the beach."

Thru shivered, ate silently for a while, then told Ware some of what he'd seen on the coast of Creton. The piles of heads on the jetties, the stench of smoke overhanging the Land.

"We fought them at Harfield, but they were too strong for us. We have to learn discipline, Toshak says."

Ware's eyes dropped to the floor, and he rubbed his hands together anxiously, fretful. There was absolutely no doubt now.

"It is Man, truly Man?"

"None other, Father. They are exactly like the description in the hymns. 'Man of the beard, brown beard, red blood, they carry the shield, they wield the sword!' They kill us for food, Father. They kill every chook, every donkey, every animal they can find. All they leave behind are the heads."

Ware put his head in his hands for a moment and composed himself. The future seemed stark and terrifying.

"May the Spirit help us to defeat them."

Chapter 33

The bell was tolling again. Simona dimly heard the splash as the body, wound in a sheet and weighted with rocks, was tossed over the side. Another bell was tolling farther off elsewhere in the fleet.

The *Anvil* moved sluggishly, her sails slack.

Simona was soaked, clammy, suddenly cold under nothing but a single sheet. She struggled to move. Her mouth was so dry, so hot.

Her eyes opened, for the first time in days she could see.

Filek was sitting beside her on a chair pulled up against the door of the little cabin. There was a jar of water and a ladle beside him.

At the sight of it her thirst became overpowering.

"Father," she croaked.

His snores stopped.

"Father."

His eyes popped open.

"My daughter speaks!"

The water was so cool, so wonderful, she thought she had never tasted anything better in her entire life.

"Will I live, Father?"

"Yes, daughter of my heart, you will live. Just about everyone who has recovered by the sixth day has lived."

"Mother?"

Filek's mouth tightened, and Simona felt her heart melting inside. Chiknulba had died of the plague. In this she had not been alone, not by a long shot. On every ship the fever had taken them, without pattern or discrimination. In the end one in three had gone, and many survivors were never the same again.

It had begun in the work crews ashore, and spread to the ships all at once. For two weeks it had raged until virtually everyone had come down with it. The disease had a remarkably simple, but virulent set of symptoms. First and foremost the fever, rising higher and higher until the victims often went into a coma before death. Then there was the bloody flux and violent coughing that afflicted a small percentage.

"Did the admiral live?" she said.

"Yes. His wife died."

"Juguba? Oh, no."

"Don't worry," Filek squeezed her hand. "Our position is much stronger now. The admiral is the commander of the whole fleet."

Her eyes widened. In which case Filek would have risen, too.

"And what of the Scion?"

"He will never walk without crutches."

So Nebbeggebben had survived, but only just.

"And how are you, Daddy?" She tried to squeeze him back, but was barely able to.

"I am still here. Count me among the lucky ones who were resistant to this fever. Losing my Chikki has been the worst thing. I am lost without her, my darling, I feel so alone, now."

"You aren't alone, Daddy. I am here."

He smiled at her, held her in his arms, and rocked her back and forth, just as he had when she was a little girl.

"That's right, my darling daughter is still here."

"It'll be all right now, Daddy, won't it?"

"Of course. We will mourn her, we will always mourn her, but we will live on. And yet I wish sometime that I had gone and she was still here."

Filek's eyes squeezed shut; his body shook with sobs.

"Ah, my lovely little wife, I miss you!"

"Daddy, where did the plague come from?"

"I think it came from the monkeys. Probably something that is endemic to them, like the itchypox is to us. Perhaps we will give them that and wipe them out."

She lay back with her head swimming. Mother was dead! *Oh Mother, Mother, Mother,* her cries echoed within her, and her tears ran freely.

Chapter 34

After three days in Juno Village with his family, Thru returned to Dronned, despite their protests. He knew that soon Toshak would have work for him to do, and he could not shrug that call aside.

On his return to Dronned, he found the city bustling. There were camps set up in the fields on either side of the road leading into the city, and Thru saw groups of mots armed with newly made spears and shields practicing the arts of war. Even to Thru's untutored eye they seemed crude and unskilled, especially when he recalled the fluid movements of the men with their spears and shields.

The folk had much to learn, but they would do it. He felt his determination harden inside him.

At the Laughing Fish Tavern he found that there were no rooms available, but his personal belongings had been stowed safely away. The city was jammed with the several thousand mots and brilbies that had now flocked to the Royal Muster.

A very welcome letter was waiting for him from Nuza. She had received his last letter just before writing her own. She offered prayers that his family was as well as hers. All went well in Lushtan, but they were all working very hard on the new emergency farms. The town was crowded, but folk were making do, coming together in order to resist, and such a spirit had built up that she knew they would overcome.

Thru had felt something just like that in Juno. Everyone understood now that Tamf had been burned and huge slaughters made of the folk of Creton. Mots every-where spoke of taking the sword to the enemy.

Thru took a scrub down in the Laughing Fish pump room, then found another message waiting for him, this time a scrap of paper folded and sealed with the Royal Seal in red wax.

He was welcomed back, and asked to come at once to a meeting in the palace of the army command.

Army? Toshak clearly hadn't wasted any time.

Thru grabbed a drink and some bread and ate on the run. The meeting was well along by the time he entered the small room behind the throne room that served as the King's private office and changing room.

The big throne room was buzzing with a crowd of courtiers and functionaries, all waiting on word from the small room behind the throne. Thru had to work his way through the throng, many of whom stared at him with aristocratic disfavor as he pressed on.

At length he reached the door, and the guards let him pass in.

Around a table he found the King, Toshak, and Meli-dofulo. Sitting on benches along the wall were several mots and Hob. A scribe worked at a lectern, hurriedly scribbling messages on command, which were then passed out the door.

Toshak looked as if he hadn't slept in days. His eye-brow tufts were drooping.

Then Thru realized that one of the figures seated along the wall was the Grys Norvory! He stiffened as he saw again the face of he who had stolen his "Chooks and Beetles." Then he pulled himself away. Toshak was sig-naling to him to approach the table.

"Thru Gillo is back," he announced.

Thru went up to the head of the table. King Belit stamped his seal onto another message. A runner took it at once.

"Hello, Thru Gillo, welcome back. You have been chosen to be one of the first new regimental colonels of the Army for the Defense of the Land. How do you plead to that?"

Thru bowed. "I will accept, Your Majesty, and endeavor to do the best that I can in such a position."

"Good, you will join the others, then." The King nodded to the three rows of mots and brilbies sitting on the benches. Thru realized that the infant army officer corps was being assembled there.

"How are our subjects in the Dristen Valley?"

"They are well, Your Majesty. The coastal villages have emptied, everyone has gone inland. Villages are building walls and defensive works. They ask for more weapons. You hear that from everyone. And they're training with what they have."

"Yes, yes, that is what I hear from all quarters. Well, we are working to increase our capacity to smelt iron and work steel. That was the first thing we heard from Highnoth! Make more steel at once. Toshak has been pressing forward with that for several days."

As Thru took a seat he recognized another face.

"Meu!" he said in surprise, seeing his friend from Highnoth.

"Thru, I was wondering if you'd see me."

The King was listening while Toshak and the Grys Norvory huddled with him, talking about some problem. Thru wondered what it would be like working with the Grys Norvory, considering the history between them.

"Good to see you again, Meu. How long have you been here?" he said, taking a seat beside his friend.

Meu shrugged. "I came in a few days back. There was a raid at Deepford, but just one ship, and we beat it off."

There was a rap of the gavel. The King called for quiet.

"Toshak wishes to recapitulate what we have decided. Listen carefully, and then we will come to objections and considerations."

Toshak had three long pieces of paper in his hand from which he began to read a few quotes.

"Training is proceeding well. We have passed two thousand of the first arrivals through the early training period. We are now working with the second two thousand. We have established six regiments so far, and we may start a seventh soon."

Toshak paused and looked them over.

"The chain of command is clear. His Majesty is commander in chief, I am second-in-command, but will be acting commander. That is the pattern through the rest of the army. Hereditary commanders, such as the Grys Norvory and the Kark of Duglee, will be accompanied by our newly appointed colonels. We will expect close cooperation. Disputes will be passed up the chain to my staff when possible. If we work together, we can minimize disputes."

Thru exchanged a look with the Grys Norvory. *Please, not that,* he prayed.

"Regiments will be composed of seven companies of one hundred apiece. Each company will be commanded by a lieutenant. Captains will command two companies apiece. Companies will consist of five squads, each of twenty mots. These will be lead by sergeants, assisted by corporals."

Toshak looked them over again.

"Your assignments will be given out at the end of the meeting. We are in the process of organizing the central staff. It will take time for that to settle out. At any time anyone may be redirected into a new role. We all have to be as flexible as possible and prepared to work harder than we've ever worked before."

Thru was realizing what a huge undertaking lay in front of him. Seven hundred country mots, armed with a motley bunch of spears and swords. They had to be trained very quickly to fight men as more than just a suicidal mob.

May the Spirit protect us!

"Now," said Toshak, setting down the paper, "we have some strange, possibly wonderful news from the scouts around Tamf. The men there seem to have fallen sick. There has been little activity for days. Nor have any boats put in from the ships. We think they may be suffering from a widespread pestilence."

"Great news," said Melidofulo. "Perhaps we need not turn our Land into an armed camp after all."

Toshak chewed his lip.

"That would be wonderful, but I expect they will still come against us. No plague will kill all of them. And there might still be other fleets of them to come. We must prepare ourselves, or we will be wiped out sooner or later."

Most of them agreed, though Melidofulo looked scornful still.

"What we need," continued Toshak, "is prisoners. We need to learn their language. We need to understand who they are, where they come from, and how many there are in their host."

They nodded.

"So I plan a raid on their sheds. We will try and capture as many of them as we can, so we can interrogate them."

Chapter 35

Thru Gillo and ninety-seven other mots crouched in the damp woods outside Tamf. It was cold in the hour before dawn, and they were all shivering slightly, scared but determined.

The early glimmerings of dawn were visible on the eastern horizon. A short birdcall came from their front, where the trees thinned toward Tamf.

Thru nodded to Meu and the other second officers.

"It's time." The officers dispersed quietly through the woods. Now the other mots rose up and began to move forward.

Soon more small birds were calling, swelling toward the full chorus of dawn. Through the woods below passed a line of mots.

Shortly, they emerged on the edge of a field, across from which stood the log palisade that the men had erected around their settlement. Beyond the dark line of the wall humped up the rude shapes of the large buildings they'd thrown together. The whole thing had been done hastily, and the work was shoddy. Their wall was irregular in height, in places ten feet, in others only eight or nine.

At the edge of the woods the assault party halted to pick up the ladders that had been hidden there the day before. Four mots carried each twelve-foot ladder.

Now they were in the open, running across a field used for pasturing ponies and donkeys. They covered the ground quickly. Thru had his bow in one hand, arrow ready in the other. He was slightly in front of the line, and like the other good shooters he was scanning the top of the wall ahead.

They were aiming for a section of the wall that was no more than nine feet high. As far as the scouts could tell there was hardly anyone on the walls at this time. The men had grown lax in keeping watch in the last few days.

Thru waited for the first shout from the wall; they were close now. He could see how the wall had been built of a mixture of roof beams, some charred, some not. The light was getting stronger every second though; still there was no one on the section of the wall ahead.

The buildings were ugly things, like huge barns. Whole sections of buildings from Tamf, spared the fire, had been torn down and reused. Twelve barns built from the ruins of lovely Tamf. They aroused hate in the hearts of the ninety-eight mots and brilbies legging it toward the wall.

Toshak had picked Thru to command this vital mission, and sent him south with the best-trained company in the army. The ladders went up against the wall. As much as they tried to be silent, this still brought some noise. Still no howl came from above. Thru and Meu exchanged an exultant fist in the air. This was better than they had dared to hope.

The first mots scrambled up and signaled that the wall was not occupied. They were joined by a couple of big brilbies, and then more mots with bows. Then Thru was climbing the ladder himself. It was solidly set and seemed to take but a moment to climb, and then he swung a leg over and dropped onto the platform behind the wall. No men were in sight.

Mots were moving quickly along the wall, a couple descending onto the ground inside. The nearest of the big buildings was about a hundred feet from the wall and now he could see smaller structures of only a single story. Most were grouped around the gate.

More mots and brilbies were coming over the wall, heading down into the Man-Place. And now, at last, there came an astonished shout from the direction of the gate.

Thru's mouth had gone dry. He felt his pulse quicken. There would be men to fight.

A door opened in the tower, and men came stumbling out onto the platform behind the wall. They were met by a flurry of arrows and fell back in a hurry, but not before a couple had gone toppling off the platform. The door closed again.

Men on the top of the gate had begun firing back, and their shouts had brought answering shouts inside the giant barns.

Thru dared to hope that Toshak was right. The place was virtually defenseless. He dropped down inside the wall and started for the nearest of the big barns, whose door had been carelessly left wide-open.

The ground had been churned to mud by heavy traffic, but for now there wasn't a soul abroad in the muddy streets. More shouts and noise in general was coming from the far end of the settlement. Thru peered inside the door. There was a sour smell from the interior, as if something had died there.

A bugle was blowing. Now a drum was going.

A large room filled with tables occupied much of the ground floor. It was empty.

"Colonel, there are men!" said someone from outside. He turned back.

Men were in the street, tall figures grouping in a column. A bugle was blowing the same hysterical notes over and over while the drums thundered.

A scout returned from the upper floors of the barn.

"They're gone, they're all gone."

"Not quite," said Thru.

A small mass of men, spearpoints flashing above their heads, was coming toward them. Mot archers tested a few long-distance shots, and they broke into open files and kept coming, shields up against the arrows.

At the rear of the files came a smaller group, centered around a flag bearer and the drummers. Thru studied them a moment. These were the officers and leaders. They would be better informed than the ordinary spearsmen.

Could they capture one of them?

As the men came closer it could be seen that many of them were weak, even stumbling a little.

Thru's faith in Toshak's hunch was confirmed.

The men began to chant, but their sound was weak and did not terrify the mots and brilbies. The men picked up the pace and came hurrying down the street, keeping the open files and straight lines while they spread out. Man was coming!

Thru shook his head to wipe away the strange, irrationally powerful terror of Man and flashed the signal. Every mot with a bow let go, and a storm of arrows fell on the men.

They kept their shields down and ran hunched over while closing together as they came to the corner of the muddy street. Here and there a man fell where an arrow had gone past the shield and through some chink in his leather armor. The rest came on with a steady, disciplined charge.

As they came to the end of the street, the mots and brilbies rushed out from where they'd waited along the barn wall.

The men turned quickly, with practiced skill, and presented a wall of shields and spears. The mots and brilbies could not hold back and, snarling with hatred, went in, sweeping aside the spears and crashing shield to shield against the line of men.

Spears and swords flicked and stabbed. The dreadful clatter of weapons broken by the hoarse screams and staccato grunts of men, mots, and brilbies rose up. The men were outnumbered and many of them were sick, but still they fought, and they were still hard to kill.

Thru found himself swept forward into the fighting when two mots just ahead of him suddenly went down, both thrust through with spears after their shields were knocked aside by a clever trick. The men would slip their shield edge around that of the mot and then pull sharply back. The mot shield would be pulled around to expose its bearer, and the spear would be rammed home. Nor did mots have much body armor, another thing they had to reinvent since the art for it had lapsed long ago.

Now Thru found himself in a whirling dance of lethal weaponry. He knocked aside the spear thrust from the right with his sword, and was fortunate to dodge the skillful thrust from his left that missed his thigh by a hairbreadth.

He slammed a foot into the right-side man's shield, sending him tumbling back. Thru's sword flashed down, the man jackknifed with a scream, and Thru was almost knocked off his feet by the man's legs. A spear from the left side almost got him again, but chipped off the bottom of the shield.

He spun, saw a mot go flying back, blood spraying from a ripped throat, and then countered the spearsman from the left with a kick to the shield that knocked him back a step. The man pulled back and dodged to one side to avoid Thru's sword thrust.

Something clipped Thru on the back of the head and he stumbled, seeing stars. Straightening, he glimpsed a man go hurtling over a brilby's shoulder to land face-down in the mud. Mots and men were rolling on the ground.

His right side was momentarily free.

The spear thrust again came from the left, and he barely knocked it aside with the shield and countered with the sword, but now he found an advantage, for his speed allowed him to keep the man on the defensive. Again and again he hewed into the man's shield and kept him from wielding his spear. Back he went a step, back another, and then Thru dropped down low, swung the sword, and clipped the man's ankles. With a howl the man went down, clutching his foot.

There was a moment to exult; two men he had taken down, his front was cleared. The weight of shame he'd carried since the defeat on the barricades at Harfield was gone. In the next moment he dodged a huge mace that swung low enough to have removed his head from his shoulders.

A giant of a man, almost seven feet tall and massively built, came storming through the press.

Hob was there to face him, but the brilby was hammered backwards a moment later as the mace flicked back with an unholy speed for such a huge weapon.

Other mots thrust with spears at the giant's back, but he was protected by men to either side. The giant was frighteningly supple for such a bulky figure. His shield was heavier than that of any brilby's. A string of victims lay behind him.

Thru didn't have time to ponder his odds of survival, because he was too busy dodging the backflick of that mace.

Hob darted in again at the giant. They met, shield to shield, and the brilby was borne back. Thru cut back in, swinging at the giant's knee, but the huge shield swung down just in time. The mace flicked toward him. His shield took the blow, but Thru was hurled off his feet to land in the mud. His shoulder and chest were ringing like a bell, and he couldn't get his breath for a few seconds. The giant stepped over to finish him, but was distracted by a huge blow from Hob swinging back with his sword. Another mot was coming in behind, where the men were too hard-pressed to stop him. The giant could not find the second required to kill Thru.

Another brilby came in, the numbers were telling. The men were falling back under the pressure. The giant was surrounded by them now, a string of mots circling him. There was an arrow sticking from his thigh, another from his shoulder.

But he was far from finished. A mot charged in too recklessly and was caught by the mace and hurled headlong, brains dashed into the mud.

The mace clattered back against other shields, knocking mots headlong. Two brilbies finally checked him, and he fell back a step.

Thru got to his knees and then, a little slowly, to his feet. His shoulder ached. He was still sucking for air, but there was no time. The fight came his way again. He warded off a spear with his broken shield and the spearhead flashed just over his shoulder. He struck at the spearsman and then both he and his opponent were knocked over by a brilby tumbling back from the giant's mace.

Thru rolled free onto his back. A huge foot stamped down and pinned his shield to the ground. The giant swung the mace, Thru dodged and thrust his sword up into the monstrous thigh beside the knee. The mace smashed into the ground beside Thru's head as the giant screamed.

Then Hob brought his sword down on the giant's helm. There was a flash of sparks, and the huge brute toppled to the ground right beside Thru.

"Many thanks, friend!" he said to the brilby as he got back on his feet. He noticed that he was trembling. Death had never before seemed quite so close.

The fight was over. Most of the men were down, dead, wounded, or simply too weak to go on. A few were running away, arrows darting among them.

The mots poured forward in pursuit.

"Prisoners!" shouted Thru. "Remember to take prisoners."

They coursed through the buildings. A few small groups of men tried to resist. None would surrender. Most had to be cut down or knocked unconscious.

In the end only a dozen or so were saved. The rest were slain, and their bodies piled up in the street. Many more bodies were dragged out from the buildings. When it was done more than a hundred dead men were counted, thirty killed in the fight.

Thru ordered a mass grave dug and then set about accounting for his own forces. There were eighteen dead mots, a couple of brilbies. Even men weakened by the fever had taken a deadly toll.

The mots' bodies were to be ferried to Sonf, then buried with proper honors.

"What of the buildings?"

"We will tear them down," Thru said.

Chapter 36

Simona had plenty of time on the gallery. The squalls and rain had driven the other women inside. She preferred it out there, in the wind and under the sun, and she could stay out there all the time if she so wished. Juguba Heuze's death had thrown the women's deck hierarchy into chaos. When it re-formed, it included Simona in a high position, because Filek Biswas had been made Surgeon General of the Fleet.

The death of the top admirals and the failure of Nebbeggebben to regain his health had created a leadership vacuum at the top. Admiral Heuze had vaulted into the leadership position.

Since they'd just consigned a third of their number to the deeps, Admiral Heuze had decided that Filek was the best thing the fleet could have as surgeon general. It was a great challenge, and he'd leaped at the chance to produce a revolution in medical practices. Admiral Heuze had backed him all the way in a cleanliness crusade.

From above her position on the stern of the great ship there came the thudding and wailing of the priests. In a frenzy they begged forgiveness from Orbazt Subuus. Their blood ran to the deck under the scourging. The priests were worried. They had thrown so many bodies into the sea that doubts about the power of the Great God had become widespread. Heresy was steadily growing among the discontented survivors. They whispered of the older gods, like the sweet Goddess Canilass, or the God of the Waters, Oonch. Louder and louder did the

red tops wail, but still the seditious questions were asked.
If Orbazt Subuus was really the Great God, then why
did his people suffer from this terrible plague? Why were
they dying in such numbers?

Simona had grown tired of the bloodthirsty Great
God, too. For years she'd been ambivalent about Him.
When she was in the temple in the midst of the shattering
emotionalism of His rites, she believed. He was Great
and Just and sat in judgment on sinful man and even
more sinful woman. She threw herself down before His
totem and begged for forgiveness. At other times, as she
read the forbidden history books and the even more forbidden philosophers, she found the whole thing ridiculous. An all-powerful God who saw everything
everywhere, and whose symbol was the Raven and the
eyeless face of Man, plucked while hanging on the pun-
ishment wheel? No it was too much, simply too tribal
with its bloodthirsty threatening quality. And why did
such a God, an all-seeing good God, demand blood sacrifice? The older gods and goddesses had not demanded
the deaths of their worshipers.

But He Who Eats needed blood on His altars. That
way He felt His people's love. He felt it in the death of
their enemies and those they anointed for sacrifice. He
was the Wise God, the One who ate His enemies. He
Who Eats demanded hundreds of hearts be tossed onto
His altars. All unbelievers were to be annihilated. That
was the first commandment given by Kadawak, the first
emperor of all Shasht. And despite the Reformation undertaken by great Norgeeben, unbelievers were still given
only one choice, convert or die.

But what, wondered Simona, if the believers became
the unbelievers?

"He bound them and he baked them and he sat right
down and ate them . . ."

Let He Who Eats strike her down dead if He existed.
That was her challenge, and so far she was still alive.

Which thought did not exactly cheer her. She stared
out, not really seeing the waters stretching to the horizon.

The fleet had moved offshore after the news of the loss of the settlement at New Hope Harbor. While the plague raged, the admiral had taken the ships out into deep water, well away from a lee shore. With their numbers severely reduced, plenty of running room was essential. They sailed up and down just as they had for months before, while the New Land was being spied out and the coastline mapped.

Despite the enormous improvement in her circumstances, Simona's heart was a desolate place. There was no message from Rukkh, and she had no way of sending him one. Filek was obdurate and would not listen to his daughter's plea that he have Rukkh brought to the *Anvil*. Filek would not even find out for her if Rukkh still lived. And while her status had improved aboard ship she was still a "red-mark girl," and no man of her own age and class would want her. But Filek's improved position meant that some older man might take her. Now he expected her to marry for his sake. He'd as much as told her so.

"You have to understand that whether we like it or not we have to found a colony. We have a duty to those who come after us. We must put duty above our personal feelings."

Duty? What he meant was establishing a dynasty. He had a position to protect. His daughter would marry well, even if it meant marrying some old fellow in his dotage. It was an appalling thought. Simona wanted a man her own age, not some filthy ancient with withered flesh and fumbling fingers. She wanted Rukkh, a man she could love. Filek would not listen.

So she would be the young wife of some aged admiral or other. She thought she'd rather die.

Oh, Great Nebbeggebben, you will have to do without me.

The cold blue water beckoned just thirty feet below.

Chapter 37

When Melidofulo and Toshak entered the room used to interrogate the men, they found that the prisoners were chained to their chairs. They had to be, for given their freedom they invariably sought to attack their guards and interrogators. They had shown unrestrained viciousness from the very beginning. Some had had to be tied down while their wounds healed to stop them pulling out their stitches to make the blood flow. One even managed to smash his own skull against the wall. He just suddenly stood up, snarled a few words to the other men, and hurled himself into the wall, facefirst with enormous force. He never came to, although he lived for three days in a coma.

The room had once been the royal racquet court, for a game that had long since gone out of favor. Since those days it had been kept in good repair and used occasionally for a party or royal frolic, with silks upon the wall. Now it was down to bare walls, with the light of a dozen lamps. Now it was a room for examining Man.

As the prisoners recovered from their wounds, so they were brought there and weighed and measured and poked and prodded while they hissed angrily and shook in their bonds.

Once they'd been measured, the men were put on comfortable chairs and Melidofulo and his team of mot questioners tried to get them to communicate. They had tried everything. The men would not respond other than through curses and spitting.

Melidofulo had finally resorted to the arcane arts of

the Assenzi, soft-spoken spells and hypnotic tricks, but these men were even resistant to that. Those that did fall under the spell spouted some gibberish, but did not respond effectively. After a while they would fall asleep, or just curl up into a fetal ball. None would ever accept that he was speaking to them, attempting to communicate with words to them. Using language, just as they did. Their disdain was clear. You are animals, no more worthy of speech than dogs.

In desperation they tried to communicate by writing on the blackboard, demonstrating the alphabet of the Land, and putting simple words up. They brought in objects that were surely common to all cultures, like shovels and a pail, and wrote their names. But none of this brought any response whatsoever.

Now, weeks after the battle at the Man-Place, they were still without any way of speaking to the men. And it was true that this group of men were an exceptionally uncommunicative lot. They rarely spoke among themselves, and that only sullenly and in few words.

More messenger birds flew north from Dronned to Highnoth. A few days later other birds brought answers from the north.

And so Melidofulo brought Toshak to the room again. Toshak was good at solving problems.

"All they have ever shown me is dumb passivity or furious rage."

Toshak nodded. He had been less than hopeful about this part of the exercise.

"They think of themselves as already dead. It doesn't seem that they accept the concept of surrender."

"They might respond to pain, to extremes of agony," said Melidofulo.

"We considered torturing them. But, well—" Toshak spread his hands.

"Mmmm," said Melidofulo. "You doubted that we could come up with tortures capable of breaking these men. There is a cultishness to their appearance, the patterns of shaving of their heads, the scars on their bodies that tells me they will attempt to sing their death song, even while we slowly burn their feet off."

"It is hard at times to understand how such a culture can succeed so well."

"Because it rewards aggression, craft, and cunning. These men are accustomed to cruelty and pain. They will laugh at us while we try to hurt them."

"They fought like demons, even though they were dying of that fever."

"And we know that it does not kill all of them. I am afraid that you are right, Toshak. They will never give up. There will be war."

Toshak's pulse jumped; Melidofulo had seen the light at last. He understood now that it was a fight to the death and not easily ended.

Melidofulo chewed his lip thoughtfully. War was such a waste of everything that Melidofulo believed in. He had thought it was something they would never see again, as extinct as Man or the dinosaurs of faraway Urth.

"By our count we deduce that the disease may have killed about a third of the men in the Man-Place."

"Well, we know a little more about our enemy, but there are still huge gaps in our understanding. We know there are forty large ships. There are at least twelve smaller vessels, which act as scouts for the main fleet. These small ships are very fast and have beautiful lines. All our fishing boat captains have commented on that.

"Their largest ships may hold as many as a thousand men, certainly they're big enough. There might have originally been thirty thousand in the whole fleet. Now, after the plague, perhaps only twenty thousand. Some of my staff think they might still be able to put an army of nine or ten thousand into the field, supposing that they have one soldier for every other person aboard the fleet. Right now we could not face anything larger than a force of perhaps three thousand."

Melidofulo had tented his slender fingers toward the tip of his long nose. Toshak didn't disagree. He had barely five thousand troops, of which half were still in the very earliest part of their training. They certainly could not match the enemy one on one.

"Let me say one thing here. If we are correct about the social status of the warriors, then we might expect that their armed force will not be that large. For every warrior there will be several noncombatants. We can see that these men are exceptional, they are all tall, powerfully built, all marked with scars and brands. Lesser men probably sail the ships and take care of menial duties."

Toshak nodded.

"So a standing army of perhaps only five thousand would be your conclusion?"

"Something in that region. The men we captured are all hyperrobust specimens, and cannot be the norm."

"How do we know that?"

"Assenzi memory is long. We remember Man."

"Well, five thousand men like these would be too much for our own forces to handle right now. We are still working on very basic drills."

"How long will it take before our army is ready?"

Toshak shook his head slowly.

"We will fight long before we're ready. The men will always be better trained than we. When we fight them, as I am convinced we must, we will lose many mots."

"And the Land will be saddened by their loss forever," said Melidofulo.

"One thing I cannot decide, is what kind of society these men have come from. I wonder if they are outlaws. Perhaps they have suffered some terrible wrong, and that has made them so savage."

"Oh, it is a great empire, Toshak. It can be nothing else. The size of their ships betrays that. They have the resources of a large society behind them."

"Then we have to learn their language and learn everything we can about them. They will come again and again, and we have to know how to defeat them."

"Do we have any idea where they might strike next?" asked the Assenzi.

"No common view has developed. I think they will come to Dronned next. They burned Tamf to terrify us, but then they used the ruins to build those sheds. They want to use our own cities as raw material for theirs."

"Then they might strike at Sulmo; that is the largest city in the Land."

"They might, but Sulmo is far south of here, and we know they didn't raid farther south than Bilauk. They moved steadily north after that, and after Tamf, Dronned is the next large city to the north."

"How will we face them?"

"We will have to meet them, shield to shield. If they do attack Dronned, we will give them a hot welcome."

Suddenly the door burst open and the King, himself, came hurrying in wearing nothing but a tunic, trousers, and yellow slippers.

"There you are, the two of you, both the fellows I wanted to talk to the most."

Melidofulo and Toshak looked at the King expectantly.

"Here," the King proffered a message. "There is marvelous news for you."

Toshak took the message, scanned it, and handed it to Melidofulo.

"A female?" said Toshak.

Melidofulo's eyes jumped wide open.

"Where?"

"Down in Creton."

"That is wo-man, the wife of Man."

"Woman," Toshak mouthed the unfamiliar word. "Excellent."

Chapter 38

Thru Gillo hastened south to Creton that same day with three companions. They were all veterans of the assault on the Man-Place: Onu Hamf, Beremel Padjaster, and Dunni of Tamf.

Onu was a hefty young fellow and the others slimmer, but all were capable of a fast walk all day. Dunni was said to have extraordinary skill with the bow. Their mission was to bring the female, the wo-man, back to Dronned.

Creton was a federation of villages and small city-states, owing allegiance to no king. Still, Thru was sure the folk of Creton would honor the wishes of the King of Dronned in this time of emergency.

They made good time. The weather was fine, and they passed through the ruins of Tamf on the second day out. They planned to spend the night with the Watch on Tamf, who were camped a mile or two farther down the road.

Tamf was a strange sight. Very little remained except for stonework here and there. Most of the walled city had been burned or pulled down. Piles of rubble and partly burned wood had been pushed together at the street corners. Here and there were houses that had been miraculously spared heavy damage and stood like sentinels to the devastation of the rest.

The walls remained, of course, including the ancient watchtowers and the gatehouse, but they were blackened by soot.

The South Road, where he had lived the winter before,

had had the misfortune to be on the side of Tamf nearest the Man-Place. Everything had been plundered for lumber for the huge Man barns. The laundry building where he had lived so happily had been torn down. Only the foundations remained.

The view up the road to the bridge was stark. There was just the city wall, the gate tower, and the bridge. All the graceful roofs and towers of old Tamf were gone.

Thru recalled the happy time he'd spent there, working during every scrap of daylight producing his best work. Those wonderful evenings with Nuza. Eating by the fire, making love on the big bed he built in the corner of the space.

Thinking of her brought on the pain of loss and separation and left him with a weird ache in his heart.

The walls of Tamf were all that was left of that time.

He looked down the road. Grey clouds were coming in. It would be best if they stopped the night here with the Watch on Tamf.

The camp was now a solidly built fort set on a bluff overlooking the Tam River. Most of the materials, former beams and rafters from Tamf, had come from the now-reclaimed Man-Place.

They were met with a warm welcome. Thru and the others were well-known to all the young mots in the current Watch force. The capture of the Man-Place had set off an explosion of activity in the Land. The terror had given way to the rage in the hearts of the folk of the Land.

There was sad news too. King Rolf of Tamf had finally succumbed to his wounds. In the woods of Sonf, he had breathed his last. The succession would pass to his son Sudu, who had already been anointed. The folk of Tamf, meanwhile, had evacuated the coastal regions. The mots there had gone to the muster in Dronned.

Thru and his companions made a quiet supper of bushpod and mealpuppies washed down with some thin beer. They slept in bunks like the rest of the Watch.

The next day they set out for Creton.

Wagons laden with building materials pulled from the Man-Place were rumbling slowly eastward into the interior as they went past. Tamf was going to be rebuilt, eventually. But for now, nothing was to be wasted in a place where the enemy might return. The coastal cities had emptied of valuables and furniture. Inland, in the towns along the edge of the Drakensberg, the price of storage for furniture had jumped fourfold overnight. And still the wagons were heading east.

Thru, on the other hand, was going west and south, out into Creton once more. Most of the folk had fled these parts, and at night the wolves howled after detecting the presence of Thru and his fellows.

Through the vale beneath Mount Nippi's grey peak they went, under the eaves of the gracious beeches along the Fwaan River. They found small villages abandoned, the polder still being tended by small groups of mots who camped in the woods. These mots were hungry for news of the world outside. The emergency had brought traffic on the roads through Creton to a complete halt, and most of the local folk had fled up into the Coal Mountains.

Thru and his party did their best to answer questions. The men had made no further landings. Meanwhile, there was a lot of training in progress. The army was quickly taking shape. Units had been formed up, officers appointed or merely confirmed in some already-existing units, and it was now fumbling its way through the process of learning to fight as an army. Indeed Thru had had to leave his own regiment just as they were beginning drills in line combat.

Everyone they spoke to had finally come to the realization that life as they had known it was over. War had come, and unless it were won, there would be no future for any of them.

The following day they came out into the coast country. In the afternoon they saw the sea and they had reached Meulumb, a town a little up the coast from Crozett by evening. There were two messages waiting there for Thru. One, dated three days before, was from Mies Aglit, the royal agent in Crozett. It urged Thru and his "force" to hurry to Crozett where the "woman" was being held prisoner. The second was dated the day before and urged Thru even more strongly to hurry his progress. Crozett had many angry refugees from the devastated villages, mots who had seen their families slain by men. There was a danger that the woman might be killed by a mob.

With the moon lost in cloudy skies there was very little light, so they rested, rose before dawn, ate a hurried breakfast and got on the road within minutes of the sun's breaking the eastern horizon. By late afternoon they were entering Crozett.

They couldn't fail to spot the changes. Crozett had a wall and guards now. Thru also noticed that the moat had been deepened and filled to the top. Crozett was not about to join Bilauk in the list of places taken by surprise.

The guard carefully perused Thru's documents, checked the Royal Seal, and sent them on at once to the Guild Hall.

Inside they found the town constable, Iras Bafuti, who was struggling with a thousand requests from refugees for help in looking after their houses or their polder while they were absent.

Bafuti rose from the table with a sigh of gratitude. His clerks continued to open messages and pile them up on the appropriate stack.

"Welcome to our city." Bafuti clasped each of them by the hand. "I take it you come on official business."

"Yes," said Thru, fumbling in his pack. "Here are letters Royal from King Belit describing us and our mission."

Bafuti wasted no time in opening and scanning the scroll.

"Ah hah! Yes, that would be a very good idea." He looked up at Thru.

"You will be taking the prisoner back with you. You

will need guards, I think. There are many very angry mots in the town. They want to kill her."

"What is her physical condition?"

"She seems well. We have fed her buttered oatmeal, and she takes some seaweed and podwater. She is kept in a guarded room, but she is no longer kept in bonds. She hasn't shown the slightest trace of violence toward us."

"That is good news," said Thru, who had been hoping that the female version of Man would be more tractable than the males.

"I have to say that you've come in time to save me from a very difficult situation. My support among the mots in the town is dwindling with each day. There are a lot of folk who want this woman dead."

"No doubt. They have suffered grievously at the hands of Man."

"So we shall have to make your exit a quiet one."

"We could be on our way by first light."

"That might not be soon enough."

"Then we shall prepare to leave at once. Can you provide us with guides so we can take backcountry roads and paths?"

"I can and I will. Let's get you on your way before the mob arrives. I'm sure that the news of your arrival will have spread beyond the guard at the gate. They will know why you're here, and they will not want her spirited away."

Thru gulped a cup of hot guezme tea and went to inspect the prisoner. At the last moment he decided that he should go alone. There had been repeated mob scenes outside the Guild Hall in the past couple of days. She would be frightened enough at seeing a strange mot up close, let alone four of them. There was difficult work ahead; it would be best if she was cooperative. By daybreak Thru wanted to be ten miles from the city.

Onu and the others went with Bafuti to plan their getaway. They would use a postern gate on the northern part of the wall. There was a private road that ran through a plantation just outside. A map of the city and its environs was rolled out on the big table in the Guild House.

Thru was taken down a flight of stairs to an underground floor. A low-ceilinged corridor took him past a series of storerooms. At the end was a room that had been emptied for use as a cell. A pair of guards stood outside the door.

Thru knocked, waited for a count of three, and went in.

It was uncanny. In the lamplight he took her for a mor. She was wide-hipped and full-breasted in the same way, but her face was bare of fur and her skull was covered in long hair like a horse's tail.

She was standing behind a small table, her hands pressed together in front of her body in a universal gesture of anxiety. Thru was thankful he'd come alone.

He raised a hand out to her with the palm forward while keeping his other hand on his stomach. Being this close to a human made him shiver a little, and he tried not to let it show.

Her eyebrows shot up momentarily, she blinked a few times, while he studied her with his eyes. Her nose was much longer than that of a mor and her eyes were wide-set and darker than those of his own folk. And still it was astonishing how much like a mor she was. All she lacked was the pale fur on her face.

He pressed his fingers to his chest and gave his name, repeating it a couple of times. He hoped fervently that his voice didn't crack. This was an oddly emotional moment, and he was still fighting down his instinctive fear of her.

Then to his surprise, she said, "Thru Gillo," and bowed to him. Then she raised her hands to him palms forward and pointed to her self.

"Simona Gsekk," she said with another bob of her head and a little smile.

Thru had never seen a man smile. The fear had lessened suddenly, and he saw again how wise Toshak had been to send him to rescue this woman. She would communicate with them. Now their very survival might depend on whether he could bring her safely to Dronned.

He beckoned to her to approach. She did not hesitate, but came around to his side of the table. The clothes they'd given her didn't fit very well; the leggings were cut for a mot and were tight around her hips.

"We have to leave, now," he said while gesturing to the door. She understood the gesture, even if she didn't understand his words.

She walked out the door and he followed. The guards fell in on either side and escorted them back through the building to Bafuti's headquarters above. As they came up the stairs they heard angry voices shouting in the streets.

At the sight of her the clerks stopped working. Every eye was on the woman.

The word had gone all over Crozett by then. Mots from Dronned had come to take the woman away.

Even Bafuti showed surprise on his face. He'd thought that the woman would surely be shackled in some way, but here she was completely unimpeded.

"I'm afraid a crowd has gathered," he said. "Your arrival has upset the beehive here, I fear."

"How many?"

"At least fifty, and more coming all the time. It's the worst yet."

"How many doors does the building have?"

"Three, there are two doors leading onto the yard at the back."

"Then I will talk to the angry ones while my companions escort the woman out the back."

"Are you sure you should try and speak to them? They're very angry, probably been drinking, too."

"I know, and I understand their anger, believe me. I saw Bilauk, and Hurves. I fought the men at Harfield and the Man-Place. I can tell them the best way to gain revenge."

"Well, then. No fur off my neck though if they don't listen to you."

Thru looked outside. The throng was gathered outside the big front doors of the Guild Hall, mots dressed in country boots and wool trousers, stout jackets and small square hats, brilbies in long coats and big wool hats. When they saw the movement at the shutters they erupted with a roar.

Onu and the others clasped hands with Thru, then they led the woman out the back. Thru could see that she understood the situation. She heard the anger in that crowd and understood why it was there. Her eyes caught his again, eyebrows arched in question. He gestured for her to go with Onu. Then he pointed to his chest and then to the outside.

Something like panic came into her eyes, then she was gone. He waited until they were at the back door, then he went out the front and onto the porch. The roar went up again and slowly subsided as he held up his arms for quiet. Eventually it was down to just an angry growl from here and there.

"Who the hell are you?" said one brilby in the front.

"My name is Thru Gillo, I came here on a command from the King of Dronned, whom I serve."

"Dronned, huh? And what is Dronned's business here with us?"

"The woman, of course. Right now the King is mustering an army in Dronned. He calls on anyone who wants to fight the men to come to Dronned now and join the army."

"We are Creton, not Dronned."

"That does not matter. We will have to come together to fight the men; only if we are united can we survive."

"Since when does Creton go to fight for Dronned?"

"Since now, because Dronned will come to Creton to fight if that is where the men are. Listen to my words. The men will land an army that numbers in the thousands. We have to meet them with an army that can hold its own against those numbers and defeat them."

They digested this.

"What do you know of men?"

"I fought them at Harfield. I saw what they did at Bilauk. I have walked through Tamf. I fought them at the Man-Place when we took it back."

Some of the mots gave a cheer at these last few words. Others were not satisfied.

"What does that have to do with the woman? Why shouldn't she die? My wife is dead. So are my children. Why should I be denied revenge?"

More angry shouts. Thru waved his hands.

"For good reasons. We need to know a lot more about them."

"Why do we need to know about them? We just want to kill them."

"Yes, of course, but we need to know things like, where are they from? Where is their homeland?"

"Hell is their homeland, of course, and we have to send them back there with a spearpoint in their guts!" shouted a fat mot in the second row.

"Listen to me, people! These invaders came from somewhere on this ocean, or from another ocean beyond it. They came from land like ours. We need to know how far away that is. We need to know how big their land is, how many people it holds. It is vital to know everything about that land. Do you see?"

"I see it all right," said the fat mot in the second row. "I see Dronned mots coming down here and trying to take our prisoner. You want a prisoner, you take your own. This one is ours."

There were angry shouts of assent at that. Thru put his hands up again for order.

"And what are you planning to do with her? Kill her, that's what. And waste a precious asset that has fallen into our hands. Listen to me, will you? We're talking about our survival. When we took the Man-Place we captured men. Not one of them has ever given us anything but curses. So we learn nothing from them."

"So? That is Dronned's problem, then."

"You think it is only Dronned's problem? You intend to fight the men all alone? There are forty ships in the fleet, and they will land an army of thousands. What good will the walls of Crozett be then?"

"They burned Tamf," said someone else.

"King Rolf is dead," shouted someone at the back.

"They burned Tamf because we do not remember how to fight. But in Dronned we are learning all over again, and the surviving mots of Tamf will fight alongside those of Dronned. Mots are coming to the muster in Dronned from every realm of the northland. The army will train at Dronned, but it will go wherever the men land and it will destroy them. It must. Or we are all doomed to die as meat."

There was a silence.

"The woman is different—I believe she will learn to talk to us. We can learn something of their language and of them. Then we will know what we are dealing with. And mark these words, we have to know where they come from, because then we will know if they're likely to be reinforced."

After hearing these words the mob lost its edge. The anger was still there, but there was too much obvious sense in Thru's words. A few hotheads still called for the female's death, but they were unable to stir the rest of them.

Thru answered questions about the muster in Dronned. Were mots from Creton welcome?

"Of course. We need every mot who can lift a spear! If you want to gain revenge, then join the army in Dronned. The King will see to your weapons and your keep while you're in the army."

Mots at the back of the crowd were leaving. The anger had gone out of the situation. A few called out that they were going to Dronned to join up. Others simply turned around and left. Thru noted a handful of angry faces muttering together to one side. They weren't safe yet, not by a long mark.

Thru went back inside. Bafuti was looking at him with a degree of respect. So were the clerks. After a second or two, Bafuti found his voice.

"I think there are still a few diehards out there. You had best be careful."

"All the way to Dronned," said Thru as he went to the back door.

Chapter 39

The scarred one caught up to them after they'd been walking for about half an hour.

By the time he reappeared they were on a muddy path that wound between clumps of trees and what appeared to be neatly kept vegetable plots. The light was poor and occasionally the big one, the one called Onu, would shine a beam from his dark lantern to show the way. Then she caught glimpses of the neat rows in the plots.

They heard the sound of someone approaching from behind. Onu motioned them to stand back off the path, under some young trees. A figure came hurrying up the path, dimly visible. Onu stepped out and briefly flashed the light from his dark lantern. By that light she saw him. It was the one who'd come to her room, the one with the scars on his face, the one who'd stayed behind to confront the mob baying for her head.

"Thru Gillo" was what he'd named himself. She had said it back to him, and he'd reacted with what seemed like both surprise and a spontaneous joy. For some reason her own hopes had soared when she'd seen his face light up like that.

We can communicate, she thought. *I am not alone among them.*

He was the first of the monkey-folk that she had met who seemed inclined to try to talk to her. The others had stared at her with wide-eyed expressions while talking among themselves in a ceaseless babble of incomprehensible sounds. To her ears their language seemed top-heavy with vowel sounds. But she had no doubt that

it was a language. They were civilized. The priests had lied.
The priests had ordered the extermination of the monkey-
folk knowing they were a civilized, intelligent people.

She shuddered inside at the thought of how the Shasht
warriors had attacked these folk and slaughtered them
as meat. She'd had this sickening understanding ever
since that first strange, terrible moment when the fishing
boat hove up beside her, just as her strength was leaving
her. The faces that looked down at her were not exactly
human. They were covered in fur, from chin to forehead,
with only a patch around the nose, eyes, and lips that
was bare. Their heads were covered in the same short
fur, not in hair. Monkeys were well-known in dry, hot
Shasht, where they were eaten like everything else that
walked, flapped, flew, or crawled. But these were people,
and she had eaten of their flesh.

Thru Gillo exchanged words and handclasps with the
other mots. Then he turned to her and said something
in urgent words. His voice had a slightly triumphant note
to it, and she understood that he was telling her that
they had gotten away cleanly from the mob.

"Thank you," she said in the tongue of Shasht. She
sensed that he understood, he bobbed his head and
turned back to the mots.

They did not tarry, despite Thru's confidence in a clean
getaway. They knew there would be pursuit from some
of the remaining diehards. Several times they paused to
listen carefully for sounds of pursuit.

Then after a short conversation between Thru and
Onu, sometimes with contributions from the other two,
they would move on, still trying to keep up a very quick
pace despite the darkness.

Fortunately the muddy path soon came out onto a
wider road that was paved with long slabs of stone. She
marveled at the quality of this road, pale grey in the
dimness as far as she could see.

A breeze stirred the poplars above their heads.

Onu and Thru set off again with a certainty that was
reassuring, and Simona set to keeping up with them.

There was no slackening of the pace. One of the others, the tall one, as she thought of him, loped off ahead and soon disappeared into the murk.

They kept on down that road, the poplars rustling above them, and the miles soon slipped away. The road stretched ahead, beckoning Simona on into the utterly unknown. She was lost, but not in the land of the dead, not in the Kingdom of the Great God, but in the Land of the monkey-folk. She wondered, briefly, if her father was still grieving for her. He had betrayed the trust between father and daughter, now that he was the admiral's favorite and he had to "consider his own political position." It was the dismal end to her hopes and faith in him. Still, she hoped he grieved for his lost daughter, and not merely a marriageable pawn.

They went through a stretch where the road was surrounded by garden walls, and then the rows of trees returned. Quite suddenly the tall one who'd gone ahead reappeared, stepping out of the shadows beside the road.

There was a whispered conversation between the monkey-folk, and then they left the road and entered the trees. Progress became much more difficult as they worked their way through the woodlot. Simona tripped and fell, not once but several times. Each time she felt a small, strong hand grip her arm and help her to her feet. That encouraging voice said something in its unknown tongue, and she recovered. They went on.

After a while they came out of the tangled trunks and roots onto another road, this one paved with small rough stones and rocks. Now and again they passed small stone walls leading off into flat fields of some sort. There was a dank, earthy smell in the air.

They crossed several streams on stilt bridges. The water was slow-moving, dark beneath their feet. It was reassuring to regain solid land after each of those spindly bridges.

Eventually they came to a crossing of roads. Her companions gathered to discuss their options. She gazed around. The clouds had thinned and let a little more moonlight onto the scene. She dimly perceived hills lying nearby to one side. A wood stretched along the road, a stream ran down on the other side. She could hear the water, catch a sparkle from its dark surface.

They went straight on, through the crossroads and down into the woods that bordered the stream. They continued on for a while until suddenly there was a whistle in the air just above her head. A strangled cry came from Onu, and she saw an arrow suddenly jutting out of his chest.

Thru grabbed her wrist and pulled her off the road, through some trees, and down to the waterside. He hissed something short and fierce in her ear and pushed her toward the water.

There were cries and the sound of blows coming from the woods. Mots were there, mots who wanted to kill her.

She took a few steps and dived into the stream, was shocked by how cold it seemed as she came to the surface. Then she struck out in a breaststroke, just as she'd learned it at Shesh Zob when she was a girl. She'd always been a good swimmer, and after kicking off the clogs they'd given her she moved out into the stream at a steady pace.

She became aware of someone else in the water close to her, splashing toward her very quickly. A hand caught her hair and jerked her head back sharply, another hand pushed her down under the water. She struggled, broke free and came to the surface for a gasp of air.

The hand caught her hair again and pulled her back. Another hand came up above the water. She saw a glint of metal. Instinctively she raised an arm to ward it off and felt something sharp bite into her flesh near the elbow.

She screamed and flailed out in the water with her legs. Her shin collided sharply with someone's body and she kicked away furiously, then turned to swim. She could hear her enemy in pursuit. A few seconds later a hand grasped her shoulder and turned her; she ducked under and the knife missed her back. She surfaced and glimpsed a hand that landed on her face and thrust her down. She drove herself up, cannoned into him, and surfaced again. Her assailant took a stroke and reached out for her again when he was suddenly interrupted by another swimmer who pulled him around in the water. She caught the sound of a heavy blow.

Another arm took her shoulder and she wheeled around in the water with a cry, but it was the scarred one, Thru, and he waved a hand at her for quiet. She stifled her cries and trod water, gasping for breath.

He pointed and swam for the farther bank of the river. She followed him, and they emerged, wet, shivering in the shallows. They scrambled up the bank and into an orchard.

She was holding her arm when Thru stopped her with a gentle touch on the shoulder. He examined the wound carefully. She felt a ferocious sense of concentration from him. She heard something rip a few moments later and he tied a length of cloth very tightly around her arm above the elbow. A tourniquet! *Then I am bleeding,* she thought, glad to have it at least confirmed.

They continued walking through fruit trees and then down a narrow lane past low walls. There was a scent of jasmine blossoms on the air. It would have seemed a magical night to her, after so long in captivity aboard the *Growler,* except that there were creatures like men who wanted to kill her.

Much later they waited, shivering a little, in a hollow at the base of a tall cliff while dawn broke over the hills. They slowly warmed in the light as it strengthened. Off to the east wolves were calling to the sun. She shivered at the sound of their calls, which she had heard before only when her family had visited Uncle Direkk, who lived in the mountains of central Shasht, where wolves and were-cat still roamed. She'd been twelve that summer, and first aware of how crushing the embrace of purdah would become. Her first menses were only months away, and as soon as they came she would be a woman and therefore restricted to the world behind the screen and the veil. Those days with her father and Uncle Direkk had been wonderful, but tainted by her fear of what was to come.

When the light was strong enough Thru inspected her wound again and then disappeared into the trees below the cliff for a few minutes. He returned with some leaves which he wove into an impromptu bandage that he tied together with strips of bark peeled off a tall tree with brown-and-yellow bark. Simona was simply astonished by the dexterity and skill displayed in his work.

"Thru?" she said when he had finished. She felt very daring for a moment.

He turned to her, the big eyebrows rising in a way that suggested a monkey's face again. And yet he was more like a man, by far. Perhaps that was the effect of those scars, running down his face. In his eyes there was an open door to another world.

"Simona," she said, pointing to her own chest.

He nodded. "Simoan-a," he said with exaggerated care.

She pointed to her arm. "Arm," she said.

He broke out into a huge smile.

"Arrrm," he said in response. She giggled, enthralled suddenly with this wonderful thing, the opportunity to converse with another kind of intelligent being.

Later, when the sun was above the trees, they left the cliff and went on across a landscape that struck her as being utterly wild. They were between two hills, each of which showed bare rock surfaces in several places. Trees struggled to survive on every exposed surface, their roots coiled into cracks along the rock. A stream splashed down through a field of stones and boulders.

They continued through a tangled world of fallen trees, patches of dense undergrowth and stands of great trees, taller and more robust than any she recalled from Shasht.

As they went they continued to trade words.

Water was la'am. There was a little catch in the middle of many mot words. She had already learned that Thru was a mot, that she was like a mor, but mors didn't have "ga-an"—hair or perhaps long hair. She was still not sure. She had named herself "woman" and she thought Thru understood that clearly enough. He said, "Mor, woman," several times.

And so the lessons went.

Chapter 40

After sleeping out under the stars for more than a week, Thru and Simona reached the outskirts of Dronned without further evidence of pursuit. They had not seen Onu or the others after the fight in the woods. Thru had left one of the attackers for dead and others had been wounded or killed in the fight on the shore, but he knew not how many or how badly. All in all it was a bad situation; to have more mots killed in this business was only likely to inflame the hotheads in every community.

So, since he was determined to keep Simona safe at all costs, he struck away from the roads and took hunting paths. They skirted Tamf, avoided the big camp, and took a broader trail that passed through woodland for miles. They saw very little traffic and when they did they usually hid in the woods until it passed. For food he went into villages along the way and bought what available supplies he could get with promissory notes on the Crown of Dronned. This meager supply he supplemented with a rabbit or squirrel if they came across any. In the wildwoods game was plentiful, so most evenings they had something for their fire and their bellies. Still, they grew lean on this diet.

Simona understood that Thru was keeping their path away from civilization. Apparently he feared more violence from mots who wanted to kill her in revenge for the raids on their own folk. Beyond that she had no clear idea where he was taking them; they lacked the words yet to express such things. Still, she found it easy enough simply to trust him.

He was her savior in a foreign land, and he was also her demanding language instructor. He never rested, it seemed, and was always pushing for more words, more usages, new verbs, adjectives, and ways to say things. He was starting to get the hang of the declensions of the common verbs in Shashti, which surprised her a little, since all of them were irregular verbs with very different systems.

They had begun to speak to each other though in a weird gabble of both languages together. It was ugly, but it just about worked, and it even helped them learn new words since they came at things from both directions, like "tree" which she learned was "avasar" while the "forest" was "avasari." Generally the language of the monkey-folk seemed very regular, quite easy to learn. Still there were many things beyond immediate comprehension, such as the proper word order in a sentence. And yet, despite everything, each day they added dozens of new words and their use of the verbs and adjectives grew steadily more accurate.

Along the way she had tried to tell him something about the world she came from.

"Shasht is the city, the great city. It is built of stone. Many thousands of people live there, perhaps a million. No one has counted in a long time. It is politically difficult to count."

It took them an hour or so before they were both confident they understood what "politics" meant. The harsh repression and use of informers that governed Shasht was also difficult for him to comprehend. Why would the great king need to hear every word his people spoke? What good would it do him to know that they hated and feared him? He must know that already. The system seemed nonsensical.

But Simona explained that a great many lives were lost every year because of informers ferreting out traitors. "Traitors" was another word that was difficult to explain satisfactorily.

From these exchanges Thru gained the impression of

a huge society, much, much bigger than Dronned or even Sulmo, both wider and deeper than his own, with layers of oppression holding it all together.

Never had his mission seemed more important. He had to get Simona safely to Dronned. Thankfully they were finally in sight of the turrets of the Guild Hall. But he wanted to make sure of her reception. He led her off the path and left her hidden in a thicket at the bottom of the great dunes that skirted the beach.

"Wait here, Simona. I go to see our King, make sure all is safe. Understand?"

Impulsively she reached out and hugged him. "Understand," she said.

He left her then and hurried away through the undergrowth. After a few minutes he reappeared down on the road, a small figure hurrying north. Simona watched him disappear up the straight road. There was other traffic, a few donkey carts, other figures bent over under objects carried on their backs. The walls of the city were close enough that she could see the towers and steeples inside, signs of a good-sized regional capital back in Shasht. This, then, was the sort of place that the warriors had captured and burned to the ground on the orders of the priests.

The priests had always claimed that the New Empire was different, that since Norgeeben the Great's reformation, the bloody ways of the Old Empire were no more. But here, with this dismal slaughter of an intelligent other race, the priests of He Who Eats had shown that they were in no way advanced over their terrible forebears.

It was strange, she realized, but all thought of wanting to end her own life had gone. She guessed that it had vanished the moment she hit the water off the stern of the *Anvil*.

That water was so cold! The shock had just changed everything. Suddenly she had wanted nothing more than to live!

She had swum after the ship, but it had continued

sailing away from her, and no one responded to her cries
for help. And then, alone in the sea, she had swum until
she could swim no more and she simply floated, tossing
up and down on the waves while lying on her back and
using her hands and legs as little as possible. She understood that death was closing in.

And then the miracle, a small boat under a triangular
sail. Rough hands had hauled her out and wrapped her
in that warm blanket, stinking of fish.

She'd stared at them, and they had stared back at her,
both sides appalled by the differences they saw in each
other. But they did not kill her or throw her back in
the water, and later she slumped into the sleep of utter
exhaustion. When she woke up they fed her a bowl of
hot porridge and sour butter. She'd slept again, and finally she had awoken at dockside and entered a new and
completely strange world.

In a brief time she had seen so much, the buildings, the
streets of a town that were obviously ancient and well
made, that she was left overwhelmed. Then they had
brought her to a dark room, and all she was left with were
the memories, those images! Those buildings, with their
fantastic detail. Each housefront was faced with stone set
in exquisite patterns. The amount of work involved was
simply enormous.

Since all she'd had on when she jumped ship was a
shift, they brought her clean, dry clothing. They opened
seams and reworked them on the spot, and she watched
them with absolute fascination. She liked their neat,
quick ways of moving, their big-eyed expressions. Once,
at Uncle Direkk's ranch in the mountains, she had seen
monkeys taking ripe grain from a field. Their hands and
fingers went through the grain with the same speed and
meticulousness.

Most of the time she dozed on the little pallet they
had provided. They freed her hands after a while and
brought her food twice a day. Usually it was more porridge, with butter and salt. Sometimes they brought
steamed vegetables and seaweed. They were not hostile,

nor did they try to talk with her. For elimination they provided a bucket with a tight lid. She was forced to reflect that they were in every way the civilized equals of her own world.

While she was there she had become aware of a slow-building tension outside. Then had come the first angry crowd. She'd heard them, shouting and banging on the door. It sounded like there were a lot of them, and it didn't take much imagination for her to guess what they wanted. More guards came and went outside her door while she crouched in that room, terrified.

When she thought of what the warriors had done to these folk she wanted to weep. And the memory of the hot, roasted meats brought down to the women's deck made her want to vomit.

She would never believe in the Great God again. He Who Eats was a disgusting atavism, and she renounced Him completely.

The priests were all liars.

Then came that long night when the mob came back and raged outside the building for hours. She had expected them to break in and kill her, but they did not. After hours of shouting and banging on the door, the mob finally quieted and left.

And then the next day Thru Gillo came to her cell, and everything had changed.

She sensed a strength in him which only intensified while they fled through the wilderness. He was a quiet one. The guards outside her door had talked all the time, great chatterers she thought. Thru was not like that, but he was persistent in working on learning new words. She felt an enormous thirst in him for communication, and she wished to respond.

Thru returned after a couple of hours, breaking into her ruminations. He brought a donkey cart, which he pulled off the road down below her position in the scrub. She climbed down from her hiding place.

"Come, the King wants to see you."

She climbed into the back of the cart, lay down, and

he covered her with a blanket. Back at the city gates the guards paid him no mind.

Through the city they went. She heard the sounds of many citizens at work, the clop of donkeys and the rattle of cart wheels, some hammering and a loud roar from some unknown source. Then these sounds died away and were replaced by echoes as if they were in a large walled enclosure.

The cart came to a halt. The blanket was pulled back, and Thru helped her out and guided her through a door and up some stairs. There was a narrow passageway and a door to a large room, plastered and painted white. The red-tiled floor was covered with large woven mats. Furniture of a consistent, neat design stood here and there. Figures stood up, pushing back their chairs.

There was another mot, who looked older and fiercer than Thru Gillo. His eyes were extraordinarily piercing.

"D'thaam," she said, using the term for "greetings" that Thru had taught her. The fierce-looking mot smiled at that, and his eyebrows bobbed up and down.

Then she saw the other two figures, and her eyes bulged and her blood ran cold. They were not mots, and they were certainly not men.

The bodies were lean and frail-looking, the heads seemed overlarge and in the heads the eyes seemed even more out of scale. Those eyes! The way they peered at one . . .

They were the demons, just as they were described by the priests of Orbazt Subuus. Narrow faces, large protruding eyes, the V-shape to their foreheads, the narrow ears. It was exactly as they were painted on the Hell Wall in the temple of He Who Eats. They were of the cloven hoof, the taint of other, the workings of evil.

She stood there shivering, struck dumb. Could it be true? All of the tales of the priests? No, it was not possible!

"D'thaam," they said in quiet, whispery voices.

She turned to Thru Gillo with beseeching eyes.

"Will they kill me?" she said.

"No, no, no!" He put his hands up. "No kill you. Talk to you."

She whirled back to the demons.

"Talk to you," they repeated.

Chapter 41

Filek Biswas sat at the lower end of the admiral's table and listened patiently to the wrangling between generals and admirals. It was late in the day, the sixth bell had rung a while back and Filek was very tired. Organizing an army's medical arm in the wake of a plague was quite an onerous task.

The meeting had been running for more than an hour, and little had been accomplished. Filek knew that Admiral Heuze was playing his own game, allowing the lesser commanders to exhaust themselves against each other before he moved in to lay down the law.

Heuze had been flattered by fate, Filek believed. With the Imperial Scion, poor Nebbeggebben, reduced to an invalid by the plague, Heuze had a free hand. Only the yellow tops could challenge him, and their position was much weakened. The pestilence had also carried off Admirals Neg and Jamaillo, who had outranked Heuze.

Heuze could not have asked for more, but he got it anyway, when his old wife died as well. And since he had deliberately not brought his sons on the expedition, so they wouldn't be killed by the watchful and suspicious Scion, he posed no threat to Nebbeggebben's New World dynasty.

Heuze understood his situation very clearly, one reason he had raised Filek to surgeon general for the fleet. Heuze needed smart men around him, and he had met few that were smarter than Filek Biswas.

For his part, Filek had never imagined that he might rise in the world like this. He had resisted the urge to think himself exalted in some way, but it was hard to resist, when you were surrounded by a group of such utter dolts. The generals, from Uisbank to Raltt, were uniformly stupid. They had risen in the world by surviving while their cleverer counterparts had been weeded out by the Hand of Aeswiren, which constantly monitored the upper classes of the empire.

The admirals were slightly better, but Heuze himself was unusually learned. He came from a good family and had received an adequate education.

Filek could sense that Heuze knew that he had an opportunity of historic scale. With no real rivals he would eliminate the monkeys and set the colony in place. He would be there beside the crippled heir of Aeswiren and would rule through Nebbeggebben's authority. It was perfect, and with no heirs of his own in the colony he did not threaten the dynasty, so the Hand would leave him be.

Heuze spoke up, breaking into the old quarrel about numbers.

"We will land three thousand men on the first day. We will replace them with a second three thousand on the third day. We will hold two thousand in reserve."

"Exactly," said Sub-Admiral Geppugo, hurriedly switching his position.

"We will land three thousand and their supplies," Heuze said next. General Uisbank, who had been frowning, settled back a little. It was Geppugo's turn to frown.

"Two days' worth?"

"Of course. If the wind changes, we might have to pull away from a lee shore, so we must land enough food for at least two days."

"What did the leadsman find?" said Geppugo, clutching for one last hope.

"They have charted the northern approach and found it hopelessly riddled with shoals. Only the south is usable for vessels with our draft."

"If we're restricted to the south side of the estuary, that will keep the number of ships we can deploy to a minimum. We can land the men, but not with all their supplies."

"We will send in the supplies in longboats, from all across the fleet. Every ship will contribute."

"That breaks with the rotation that was in use before."

"The situation has changed. We have a third more supplies than we thought we'd have. All ships can afford to contribute."

Quartermaster General Scupp frowned, but said nothing. Under Heuze his position was uneasy anyway. And what Heuze said was actually true, though Scupp had wanted to wield a little patronage from his position. Ah, well, he'd done well enough from the voyage. No need to stir the pot too much.

General Raltt, Uisbank's second-in-command, raised the question of priests. There was an audible groan from several throats.

"They are demanding at least fifty red-tops be landed, with all their regalia."

Tilgo Lupabusil, the only ground officer with a brain, in Filek's opinion, spoke up. "I say we don't land any. The men will fight better without 'em."

"Tell them we only land yellow tops. They can show their appetite for danger."

"Danger?" bristled Uisbank. "The monkeys are no danger; how many times do I have to tell you?"

Seeing the questions in their eyes, he went on. "Look, just because a swarm of them got in and overran the settlement at First Landing doesn't mean they can fight. We will land our force in front of the objective and storm its walls."

"And what if the plague recurs?" said Geppugo.

"Then we withdraw at once. We do not leave men, outnumbered and hopelessly sick, to face a swarm of vicious monkeys."

Heuze turned to Filek.

"Surgeon General Biswas, what do you think we should do in regard to a recurrence of the plague?"

"I doubt that the same one will recur, at least not

immediately. But there might be other new diseases. We are far from home, and everything here will be different in some degree or other. But in the event that another fast-acting fever breaks out, I would suggest that rather than reembark the men to the fleet, they be ferried by longboat away to a safer location and kept there for as long as possible."

"Is that to be our rule?" Uisbank turned back to Heuze, who pursed his lips thoughtfully.

"And if the men get sick, they will have to remain onshore, on foreign land, under the threat of attack?"

"We will guard them. Put them on an island. There are several out there with no inhabitants."

"Oh that will be wonderful. Sick of some plague and left on a deserted island."

"Better that than infecting the rest of the fleet. We cannot afford to lose another third of our numbers, and we have but a few months left before winter. We must use that time to cleanse the land of these monkeys. We must also find and confiscate their food caches. Our strategy all along was to mobilize them with the initial terror and send them fleeing inland. Then we would hold back while they set up food caches inland that we could locate and rob later. Then in the winter we would attack again and again, using their hunger as another weapon to destroy them with. This is what we must do, even now."

Uisbank sniffed and arranged a pointer carefully in front of him. The other generals looked askance, but even they could see the sense of it. They had to defeat the monkeys and capture their food caches before the weather turned bad.

At last the meeting came to an end. Heuze and Filek were closeted alone in the admiral's private cabin. On the wall hung the gorgeous woven mat of monkey manufacture. More of these kinds of works had appeared elsewhere in the fleet despite the fulminations of the priests. There was a kind of craze for them, as well as for other types of monkey crafts. The work shimmered with color and a magical sense of design. Filek gazed at it again with something akin to awe.

"So?" said the admiral, breaking into his reverie.

"I think it goes as you expected. Uisbank is eager to get ashore and into his command. He'll agree with anything to speed things up."

"I feel a great responsibility, Biswas, you cannot imagine the weight of it. Sometimes I cannot sleep. It is as if the entire future of the colony rested on my decisions, and to tell the truth, it does."

Filek nodded without great enthusiasm; since Simona had vanished overboard, his own contribution to the future had become moot.

"Indeed, sir, indeed."

The admiral droned on about his anxiety and how it contributed to his difficulty in sleeping. While listening with half an ear Filek pondered his own situation. He would have to marry again. It would be expected of him in his new exalted position. It would be very difficult to find someone like Chiknulba among the women on the ships, a woman who was well-read, who treasured the arts and culture. That was what he liked to discuss, that was the world he knew. Together they had shared the passions of a small, surreptitious elite who supported the arts and circulated banned reading materials.

Would he find a woman like that among the widows aboard the ships? He doubted it. The learned, well-read elite did not choose to emigrate. It was the less fortunate who left Shasht. So he would find someone young, and he would simply impregnate her a couple of times. He would never re-create the wonderful family life he had had with Chiknulba and Simona. Oh, Simona! How his heart ached for his wonderful, wayward daughter, more intelligent than anyone else he'd ever known. He had to turn his thoughts away to avoid being overwhelmed by emotion.

"How goes your own campaign, Biswas?" the admiral, head filled with the fumes of the victory he sensed in the near future, had not noticed Filek's blinking eyes.

Heuze referred to the drive to put cleanliness to work in every surgery in the fleet, and to ensure that all surgery was done on anaesthetized patients.

"It goes well, perhaps slightly ahead of schedule. The most resistant dolts have been turned out into other lines of work."

"Heh, heh, nothing like a change of job to wake up their ideas, eh?"

"Some of them will end up scrubbing floors. There is an obduracy about some men that comes close to idiocy. Anyway, the next step is to ensure that the medical teams for the army are ready to do their job. When last I checked there was a shocking laxness about them. There were even claims that such habits were normal for the army. I hastened to assure them that they were wrong and that I would remove anyone who fails to do his duty to the maximum. I have summoned three for sentence this afternoon."

"Indeed, indeed, well the slave ranks were thinned by the plague just as the rest of us were. That's all you hear from the slaves now, how overworked they are because they are so few."

Heuze scratched his belly. "Discipline always improves a little throughout the fleet, when the tongs are wielded publicly like that."

After Filek left the admiral's cabin he hurried two decks down and well forward, to reach his own domain, the grand surgery of the *Anvil* and next to it his office, his storeroom, and a separate office for fleet matters. The surgery itself consisted of three rooms, a sawing and cutting room, and two recovery rooms.

It was in one of the recovery rooms that he had set the review of sentence for the three former ship's surgeons.

They were waiting, seated on a bench under guard. They bore the marks of a light questioning by the red tops, their broken hands wrapped in bandages. The report was laid out on the desk, but Filek had already read it.

He sat down and stared at them grimly.

Zuik was among them. Not because Filek had sought
to place him in this position. He hadn't gone after his
former tormentor. No, Zuik was there because he simply
refused to stop drinking the alcohol meant for sterilizing
tools and needles.

Next to Zuik were a couple of other alcoholics, Petragga and Kudak. They wore the air of complete defeat
that was common for men in their position. Even a light
questioning by the red tops involved terrible, brutal acts.
Few men were the same afterward. And ahead of them
lay public castration and life as slaves. They were im-
ploded, their faces leaden.

Zuik was more complex. His face rippled with emotions barely suppressed, rage foremost.

Filek called the session to order; the scribe began to
copy.

"I have reviewed your cases. You are all incredibly
stupid. All you had to do was to stop drinking quite so
much alcohol. Perhaps reduce your consumption by half,
or two-thirds, and learn to live on that. And while you
were at it, you could clean up your surgery and adjust
to the new rules. But no, not for you three prizes. You
kept on guzzling the spirits, and your surgeries were
filthy when inspected. You were insolent and refused direct orders to clean them up. And so, here you are, about
to lose your future as men."

He stared each of them in the eyes.

"You, Petragga, I find guilty as charged. You will be
castrated in public and sold into slavery. Kudak, why did
you attack the inspector with a scalpel? What got into
you, to do something as stupid as that?"

Kudak's head hung a little lower.

"You, too, will be castrated before the fleet and
pressed down into slavery."

He turned to Zuik.

"You, Zuik, have been less offensive than these two.
You have simply continued to abuse the alcohol store.
You and I have a history, Zuik, but I want you to know
that that has nothing to do with my decision here. You,

Zuik, I sentence to serve in the army. You keep your manhood. However, you are on probation, and if your surgery is found filthy and if you continue to abuse the alcohol ration, then you will most definitely lose your masculine status."

Filek did not want to enjoy this moment, but he couldn't help letting go a little. He did not smile, however, or give any other sign of emotion.

Zuik's eyes, so dull a moment before, now glistened. He was spared! He was still a man! And—dammit—he owed it all to Filek Biswas!

Chapter 42

It was raining softly in Dronned, a summer rain that promised good things for the ripening crop of waterbush. Master Utnapishtim paused by the window to look out at the city, a pleasing cascade of greys and green, with the darker stone of the street at the base. Wagons continued to rumble toward the gate. How often had he come to this ancient town with joy in his heart? And now he was here to fight a war, a war that had to be won if the folk of the land were to survive.

From the first terrible news Utnapishtim had known it would come to this. He and Graedon had immediately hurried south to Dronned and thrown themselves into the work. Graedon took over the small ironworks inside the city and began expanding it immediately. He had a team of sixty mots working around the clock building new structures. The coal reserves were examined, and more coal and coke ordered. A readjustment of trade routes was required since the coastal trade was paralyzed because of the presence of the enemy fleet. Fortunately there was the south riverway into Pelej from Ajutan. More barges were collected to handle the increased traffic. The smelters worked day and night fed by an army of soot-covered mots.

Meanwhile Utnapishtim was working on a number of fronts. With Melidofulo he worked on supply problems, particularly food. Caring for the polder had fallen to the soldiers and teams of loyal chooks, who were bravely working the fields once again. Utnapishtim assembled wagon trains, and spent a day sorting out the rotation of the available force of donkeys in the town.

The King was a source of strength. Belit the Frugal had risen to the challenge well. He was pleased to see Utnapishtim and Graedon, sensing at once that they were more deeply committed to the war than was Melidofulo.

The ironworks was soon putting out a vastly increased flow of arrowheads, spearheads, bars for swords, discs for shield bosses. Working with Master Graedon were young designers from the Metals Guild of Dronned, who had come up with simple, economical designs for swords and spears.

Their designs had all been passed by Toshak, who was at the center of the whirlwinds that rattled through Dronned in those frantic days. Utnapishtim gave a last glance toward the gate. Out there, in the royal park, Toshak would have his small army drilling. The King would be there, with all his court, drilling with the rest. The impact on morale of seeing the King and his retinue with swords, spears, and shields had been wonderful.

He turned back into the room. A long, narrow chamber in a drafty tenement in central Dronned. Graedon was writing at a bench. Melidofulo, with his long, grey face and mournful eyes, came in, agitated as he often was these days.

"This is the one crisis I never dreamed would occur. Not once since the day we buried the last of the High Men. I thought they were all gone, every one of them. I thought the world could live in peace at last."

"You were not alone in that, my old friend. This is the one nightmare that none of us predicted."

"Yes," said Melidofulo, though he knew well that Utnapishtim had. In fact, he advocated a greater degree of awareness of danger. "We should have kept our weapons sharp, our watch on the sea alert."

Utnapishtim said nothing. Graedon was busy with his papers, and did not look up.

Melidofulo shrugged. "Well, at least I think we can

say that the folk of the Land have begun to respond
effectively to the threat. Even the chooks have come
back from the hills and are working in the polder. The
harvest will be good."

"But only if we are still here to harvest it. The enemy
will attack before then. We will have to hold them away
from the polder."

"It will be difficult to protect the polder with only a
few thousand mots."

"Fresh polder will have to be created in the higher
valleys," said Graedon, looking up from the papers.
"Hard work, building high-country polder, and difficult
to do over the winter. Hunger is certain, starvation is
not. Fortunately, we know so much more about our
enemy now, we can predict some of his actions."

"The Spirit be praised for sending us that young
woman. She confirmed that the fleet is hungry and has
been for a while. Even with the loss of a third of their
number, they will run short of food before winter's snows
are upon us. So we can be sure they will land and go
after our own stores of food."

"So we cannot avoid meeting them in battle. There is
no other conclusion possible."

"Yes," said Melidofulo. "We must go through with
this madness of turning our society into an armed camp."

Utnapishtim allowed himself a tiny tremor a smile.
Melidofulo, like the rest of the Assenzi, was struggling
to overcome the mental habits of a lifetime spanning tens
of thousands of years.

"Undoubtedly true, my friend."

Graedon saw his opening.

"I can report completion of the second order for arrowheads. We've put ten thousand steel points into the
hands of the fletchers. That's with five thousand spearheads and more than three thousand sword bars."

"There, you see Meli? We have already been trans-
formed into an armed camp, and neither of us was aware
of it."

This mild sally produced a tiny grunt from Melidofulo before he turned back to his greatest source of anxiety.

"The more we learn about the civilization that the woman represents, the more I fear for our future."

Utnapishtim tried to reassure Melidofulo.

"Shasht lies on the far side of the world. It took this fleet more than a year and a half to reach our shores, and it would take a similar length of time to return. They will not be resupplied very often. That gives us our chance for survival. But we must still defeat them before winter if we are to save the harvest from the coastal polder and seaponds."

"It is time for Thru Gillo to report," Graedon commented.

"Good," said Utnapishtim. "He can usually be relied on to bring some fresh food for thought." Graedon was usually right almost to the second when it came to these things. Sure enough, Thru Gillo knocked on the door a few moments later.

"Ah," Utnapishtim waved him in. "Welcome, Thru Gillo, it is always good to see you."

"Masters." Thru bowed to each of them.

"What news have you for us?"

"Well, vocabulary has increased by thirty words today, but it is still difficult, because we ask more detailed questions now."

"That will continue for a while. There's a lot we need to know quickly."

"She understands the position we are in and remains cooperative. She has told me many times that she was horrified by what happened. She will help us if she can."

"And how do you find her spirits?" asked Melidofulo.

"They vary with the days. She is in the grip of strong emotions. As you know she tried to kill herself by throwing herself off a ship. Now she feels completely cut off from her own kind."

"The Spirit meant for her to do this work," said Melidofulo.

"That's what I tell her, myself," Thru agreed. "It is

surely the Spirit that sent her to us, nobody else would have been half so well informed. She tells us everything that she knows about their cities, their arts, their festivals . . ." Thru was waving his hands, caught up with enthusiasm. He saw the look on their faces and stopped.

"Their world is terrifying, Masters. They are governed by little more than their greed. They have exhausted their land with their numbers. She describes areas that are now desert, where once there grew forests and farms.

"Shasht is dying." Just saying that name was enough to send a shiver through Thru's bones. "They have no large animals like our elk and moose. There are no bears, not even many wolves, and the cultivated area covers all the land. They cannot spare anything for the creatures of the wild."

"Did you ask her about the origins of the official religion?"

"Yes, Master Utnapishtim. The Great God was set in place by the first emperor, Kadawak."

"Ah, as we thought, Graedon. The religion came with the state." Certain suspicions were forming in Utnapishtim's mind.

"What did she say of the older religious beliefs?" asked Melidofulo.

"She says that the priests of Orbazt Subuus preach that the Great God came and devoured the other gods. He was hungry, and he cut them down and made food of them."

"It is a strangely bloodthirsty society, from what we have learned, is it not?" murmured Utnapishtim.

"Horrible," said Melidofulo. "Their priests sacrifice thousands of people on the altars of this dreadful god."

"Yes, exactly. Not unheard of in the ancient histories of man, but in this case there seems to be an edge to it." Utnapishtim's suspicions had hardened completely now.

"Graedon?" he said suddenly. "What do you recall of the last days of Karnemin?"

"Karnemin?" Graedon and Melidofulo's heads came up with a jerk.

"That is a fell name to bring up at this moment," said Melidofulo. "Karnemin has been dead nigh on ninety thousand years. He was seen to fall into the crevasse, was lost in the ice."

"So it was believed by most of us at the time. But not by all. Some of us have long harbored a suspicion that what we saw then was an illusion, perhaps a slave of Karnemin's tricked out to appear like him. Long have I wondered if he had somehow survived and escaped beyond our reach."

Graedon was nodding slowly. "Yes, Master Utnapishtim, I also sense some extra hand at the tiller of this engine of destruction. If he lived, then possibly he guides it."

"We need to know much more." Melidofulo was frowning.

"This young woman is very well-read. Indeed we are fortunate that her knowledge of her own world is so extensive. We will want to know everything she knows about the history of the empire."

"Well," Thru began. "She has told me before that the empire began with Kadawak. He was also the High Priest of the Great God. When he died they slew a thousand captive warriors and drenched the stone of his pyramid with their blood. . . ."

The questioning continued for a while until Thru had passed on everything he had discovered in the last day or so.

Eventually Thru left the Assenzi and hurried out into the rain. His path took him to the Laughing Fish in search of some of the evening chowder. There, he found Toshak, but both of them were too late for dinner.

They took mugs of ale and sat together in a corner. Other mots, seeing who they were, left them alone.

"How is our prisoner?" said Toshak after a moment.

"She tries very hard. Sometimes I think she despairs, but at other times she is almost happy."

"It must be difficult for her." Toshak set down his

mug. "Well, so it is for all of us. Our army progresses, but by the Spirit we have a long way to go."

"Can we meet them in battle, when it comes?"

"I hope so, young Thru, I hope so. If we can face them on favorable ground, perhaps."

They sipped.

"It is strange how fate has thrown us together, Thru Gillo. I want you to know that I wish you and Nuza well. Someday I hope you two can wed."

Thru felt his eyebrows zoom upward at hearing this.

"Well, I thank you, friend Toshak."

"And meanwhile we have a war to win."

Chapter 43

Through the night there was a steady rain, and heavy clouds were in motion at dawn. Later they began to clear, but the wind died away to almost nothing, and a thick mist rose from the sea.

Admiral Heuze decided it was time.

The ships moved into the bay and began to work their way cautiously shoreward. Six ships were involved in the operation, led by the *Anvil*. Heuze wanted the glory of this action firmly attached to his own name. Behind *Anvil* stretched *Grampus, Crusher, Growler, Tooth,* and at the rear *Sword*. The mists covered them well, and they were within a mile of the shore before the beacons blazed from the tops of the headlands.

The ships hove to immediately and set down their boats. Hundreds of men climbed in, and the rowers took up their oars and drove the boats toward the shore. As they came, the warriors chanted a rhythmic war song, seeking strength from sword and spear. Each man swore to the Great God to use them well upon the enemy.

The boats sliced through the water while the chant went on, its harsh sound designed to terrify the enemy before the soldiers of Shasht even showed themselves upon the field.

The red tops began to pound their drums, and the boats surged forward, over the last few hundred yards.

As the boats came in toward the beach, Rukkh noted that it was a remarkably still day. The mist obscured the beach and made the town invisible, though he could see the sand dunes that rose behind the beach as a series of pale yellow curves with no outlines. The alien strand, a curve of sand and pebbles, awaited him.

He stopped chanting to take war snuff, caressed his snuff-egg, and pressed it back inside his tunic. On his arms and legs he wore leather armor, and in the middle of the chest a small breastplate of steel. These precautions were the result of the previous fighting with the monkeys, who had shown that they could be dangerous with sword and spear. The high command were worried about casualties now. The plague had run a scythe through the ranks of the warriors, so the survivors were unusually precious.

But Rukkh had fought the monkeys. He knew what they were capable of. Relatively easy meat to kill, compared with men. He still didn't feel he needed this much armor.

The chanting continued right up to the moment they beached and jumped over the side, while the rowers crouched down to get out of their way.

The dunes at the top of the beach were more clearly visible. Sandy yellow masses, they were topped with fringes of long grass. For some reason the sight brought up old memories for Rukkh, of the dunes behind the farm where his father fought the dry, ruined land for their living. He was running barefoot on the dunes, making sure to escape his older brother. Scmakkh was not a nice brother to have, especially when he was fourteen and Rukkh was only nine.

He laughed bitterly inside at the memories. He had killed his older brother when the time came. He had never regretted it.

The water was cold around the ankles, but they were soon past that and scrambling up the beach in their hobnailed sandals. When they came out on a level part of the beach the red tops started banging the drums again and the chant for Orbazt Subuus came rolling forth once more and echoed off the face of the dunes.

The men quickly formed up in companies. Emjex was the new company captain, Cauta having died in the plague. Burok and Hugga were the same sergeants they'd always had. Why was it that so few sergeants had died of the damned plague? If they could have lost anyone else, Rukkh would have nominated Burok for the honor.

Forjal was on his right, as always, but poor old Hukkit had died in that fight with the monkeys. There were lots of other missing faces, mostly from the plague.

Burok was shouting for them to close up and get in line. They already were in line, but Burok wasn't looking at them, he was looking to Emjex, making sure the new captain heard old Burok roaring.

They marched up the beach in files set six feet apart, shields deployed, spears held ready. Burok stomped by, scattering shingle, his heavy shoulders heaving under the dogskin he wore over his helmet.

Burok roared again, demanding more zest in their step. Rukkh increased his pace and kept abreast of the line as they double-timed up the slope. Behind them more boats were beaching and more sergeants were bellowing as their men formed up.

Scouts had gone ahead into the dunes. One of them appeared briefly on top of a dune to wave his red semaphore sticks. More orders came immediately.

The men turned to their left and began to double-time along the beach, parallel to the dunes, through the thick mist. Burok had told them that they were going to capture a big monkey place that day. Opportunities for loot would be plentiful.

Scouts came running by, bows over their backs, semaphore sticks in their hands. A minute later they heard more orders being relayed down the chain of command. Burok bellowed for the squad to halt and form up ready to receive the enemy from the direction of the dune.

They turned and dressed themselves right on the new line, six feet between each man in every direction. Burok snarled imprecations at Catlonga, who was slightly out of position. There was nothing new about this, and it was even vaguely comforting to hear the familiar cadences of Burok in full flow.

The first arrows, looping out of the fog at them, were still a little bit of a shock. It was always the case. Having arrows and rocks directed your way was never a comforting thing.

The arrows fell among them with a soft collective whistle. Burok's voice roared again, and their shields snapped up at once while they readied their spears.

Captain Emjex was bellowing about somebody's God-damned, fornicating, useless sense of position. Lieutenant Chaff relayed the complaints. Sergeant Hugga took them to the source and commenced yelling in the face of Blukubo.

A few more arrows fell among them, mostly lodging harmlessly in the mud.

Their own archers were holding fire, not having targets to aim at.

They remained halted there while scouts loped ahead up into the dunes. They vanished from sight. A little later they reappeared and waved red sticks.

Orders rang out. They turned left, re-dressed to the original line, and went forward again, shields up, spears ready. The mists thickened as they moved north along the beach. They crossed a patch where seaweed in considerable quantities had washed ashore and was being dried for harvesting. The stuff crunched and crackled under their hobnails and for a while the smell of it filled their nostrils. Then they were past it and also beyond the end of the dunes.

Quite suddenly there came a sharp whistle on their right and the scouts could be seen signaling.

"Prepare to receive enemy from the right flank!"

They formed up, turning and flexing their lines to be able to receive an assault from the dunes.

Then they saw monkeys, lots of them, clustering along the top of the dune. Arrows flew in both directions, but considerably more were falling on the men. The top of the dune gave the monkey archers a good position for aiming a plunging fire down on them.

Rukkh felt an arrow thud into his shield. Another one

clipped the edge and caromed past a few inches from his face. He heard a curse behind him as it struck someone.

More arrows were coming.

Captain Emjex was requesting permission to clear the dunes of the enemy. A few moments later orders came down and Burok sent his men running forward, up the sandy face of the dune. For the first time that day they climbed that hundred feet of sand.

The drums thundered, and they screamed their war cry.

Arrows flew among them. Here and there someone stumbled and went down, but the rest kept going. Rukkh had arrows sticking out of his shield, but none had harmed him yet.

It was tiring work, though, driving up the slope through the loose yellow sand.

At last they reached the top and found the enemy gone. A shout came from Forjal, who pointed down the far slope. A few figures were still visible taking to their heels into the heather, which was braided by ancient game trails.

Burok halted them on the top, and they formed up, dressed their lines with habitual efficiency, and waited. Burok was very unwilling to enter the tangled heather on the inland slope of the dunes.

"Can't keep formation in that!" he pointed out to Lieutenant Braz.

Officers were conferring. Semaphores were flying, red, then blue sticks.

They remained in position, holding the top of the dunes at their northern tip. The Blitzers had a fine view of the battlefield.

The mist was fading by that point. A light breeze from off the bay started clearing the air. The walls of the city appeared, with its towers and steeples within. Rukkh could see that it was a big place, easily as big as the one they'd burned before the plague. Hell, there was a moat, full of water. This city would be harder to take. Rukkh counted three gates on the near side of the city, a small one just above the beach and two larger ones from which came roads. The space in front of the walls was completely clear, right up to the edge of the moat, though farther back, beyond bowshot, the ground was covered in walled-garden allotments and a maze of small paths that connected them to the roads. Inland, to the right of their line of advance, grew a strip of forest, and beyond the forest were small fields, bright green with the burgeoning crop.

Generals wanted to take a look at all this with their very own eyes, and so they waited there while Uisbank and his retinue climbed the dune. By then the mist had receded almost completely. They could see the organized masses of the enemy marching out of the center gate about a mile away. Rukkh's practiced eye took in the loose, but not completely sloppy formations. Regiments of perhaps a thousand individuals, he judged, marching in column. At the head of each was a trio of officers and a standard-bearer. For standards they used small bright pennons in different color combinations.

Uisbank watched the monkeys with their amusing little display of disciplined marching. Regiments of the little creatures? It certainly wasn't what he'd expected. At the fight at Tamf, Uisbank had been on the staff of General Ruus. The monkeys had never tried to do more than hold the wall, and they'd been easily outmaneuvered there. Now they thought to imitate men, did they? Hah! He'd soon show them about that.

Uisbank called his officers together. He planned to use the classic slanted front attack that had won the battle of Kaggenbank and put Aeswiren III on the throne. The army would line up with three regiments in line, facing the monkeys, who were in line along their road. The Blitz Regiment, famous for frontal attacks, would be the closest to the city while the Fourth Regiment would fill in behind it. The remaining Fifth Regiment would be held back in reserve.

The regiments closest to the wall would move off first, pitching into the monkeys around the gate. If at all possible, they would seize the gate. The other two regiments would advance a little later and thus the line would trail back from the left to the right. The monkeys should be forced away from the wall and then compressed and encircled before being slaughtered.

The regiments stepped forward to begin the maneuvers. Rukkh's company went downslope to rejoin the regiment, which would be the lead regiment in the coming fight. Often that was all a battle required, a single clean thrust by the Blitzers through the enemy's belly. They were justly famous for the power of their attack.

The company quick marched down the dune and across the flat ground in front of the walls and took their position in the regiment. They faced inland, with the city walls about two hundred feet to their left. There were monkeys everywhere. A line of them on the walls, keening and wailing, and a great mass of them arrayed along the road near the gate.

On the dune top, General Uisbank decided against sending a force to clear out the monkeys in the heather. His priority was just to hit the damned monkeys on their right flank and push them away from the gate. Then he could be certain of massacring the lot of them.

Skirmishers on the dunes could be attended to later.

The regiments lined up in smooth array, watched by the monkeys from a distance of a thousand feet. A few long-ranging arrows came hurtling out from the walls, on their left, but it was a little too far for them. The shafts sank into the soft ground. Rukkh noticed that there were lots of muddy places ahead, where the night's rain had softened the earth.

The trumpets blew the charge as soon as they'd dressed their lines. Forward at a trot went the men on the left, closest to the wall. At the same moment there came a loud crack from the walls, instantaneously followed by a whining shriek, and a rock as big as a man's head was hurled off the wall to land in the middle of the regiment. By a miracle it simply slammed into a muddy slough and rolled away down the aisle between their lines.

Unfortunately the second one hit poor Blukubo square in the chest.

The loud *crack-whine* sounds kept coming, and with them more rocks. Men went down like skittles as these rocks slammed into them. Without any orders, the pace of their charge was quickened. Arrows from the mass of monkeys ahead began falling among them in drifts. Here and there they brought forth cries of pain and curses. Another rock bounced short, then flew through the squad's ranks at chest height, until it caught Wiggi full on the shield. That wasn't enough protection, and Wiggi was hurled to the ground.

"Close up that file," screamed Burok, and they stepped over poor old Wiggi and went on.

At about that moment there came a blast of trumpets behind them. The men didn't look back; that was for officers to do. They kept going forward until new orders came down to them.

What they didn't see was that the small gate close to the edge of the beach had opened, releasing a force of monkeys that was charging headlong at the rear of the Fourth Regiment, backing up the Blitzers.

Orders were being bellowed. The last two lines of men in the Fourth were halted, turned about, and set to receive the enemy assault.

The rest continued the quick-step charge toward the enemy.

But now the enemy's two other regiments had turned and hustled closer to the one directly ahead. They were shortening their line and deepening it opposite the onrushing assault column.

Rukkh noted the raggedness of the movements, but the end result was still a dramatic thickening of the line ahead of them. And now there was a threat of a force coming in on their right flank as they attacked.

More trumpets were blowing as General Uisbank made corrections, calling on the other regiments to close up formations and accelerate their approach to keep the fornicating monkeys from falling on the right flank of the attack column. His echelon attack was blurring.

With a roar and a clatter, the fight behind the Blitzers began as the enemy came up against the rear guard. More rocks whistled into their ranks and bounced on and then they were moving over the last hundred yards, speeding up to a run but keeping their lines straight. The war cry was rising high and the red tops were still hammering away on their drums.

The enemy gave a great cry of their own and surged forward, and in a moment the forces came together. Rukkh found himself confronted with a row of long spears and behind them oblong shields painted with a number of animal motifs. He tried to deflect the spear ahead, it struck his shield, pulled back, and stabbed at his legs. He cut down with the shield and drove the spearpoint to the ground, but another spear jabbed at him, and he was forced to step sideways.

The monkeys were keeping a forest of spearpoints in their faces. It was hard to go shield to shield and use one's momentum to smash them back.

Rukkh thrust with his own spear, its point leaping and flickering as he stabbed at the monkeys in front of him. Rukkh was impressed, despite himself. They were fighting well, much better than they had in the fights he'd taken part in before. He dodged another spear thrust. An arrow clipped the side of his shield and struck him on the breastplate with considerable force. He struggled to get his breath for a moment, and the enemy spears thrust at him from both sides together, forcing him back a step and exposing Forjal, who gave a curse and stepped back, too.

The whole line of the squad was peeling back, stepping into the men behind them, who cursed them for being weak-willed sons of whores. The regiment was bunching up.

Meanwhile the pressure on the right was growing intense where the attack was flanked. The monkeys had closed around on that side, taking men on two sides. Inevitably the lines had curved back and knots had formed in their formations.

Burok was cursing Rukkh's sodomistic parentage for letting the lines bunch. Then a stone struck Burok on the helmet with a loud clang and he pitched facefirst into the mud. The monkeys were pressing them. More spears were thrusting and jabbing. Rukkh deflected spearheads, felt one stick in his shield, then tug furiously as its owner tried to pull it free. He held on, trying not to be pulled out of line, another spear struck at him, and he pulled his hip aside. He couldn't move the fucking shield.

"Nooooooo!" screamed Rukkh, and Forjal somehow knocked up the spear coming at Rukkh, but also managed to flick his spearpoint back into the monkey's face, sending it over in a fountain of blood. Rukkh's shield came free as the spear snapped.

But then Forjal was tripped up by another monkey's spear and fell backward with a loud curse. Rukkh nipped in, used the shield to clear away the spears pointed at him, and thrust overhand into the breast of the nearest monkey. The armor took most of the blow, but gave enough for blood to run when he pulled back. The monkey fell back, but others pushed forward.

Forjal had regained his feet, but now his spear had stuck in a monkey's shield. There was no time to pull it free. Forjal let go and drew his sword while his shield knocked away one spear thrust and he ducked another.

The monkeys were pressing. There seemed to be more and more of them. The line was buckling. There was a loud scream to Rukkh's right. Yegeb in Hugga's squad had gone down with a spear in his guts. Monkeys broke the first line back around Yegeb's body.

Forjal, now cursing in a continuous roar, was slashing back and forth at the spearpoints in front of him, while Rukkh and Oggi pushed in on either side, trying to halt the monkeys and set them back.

They were halted at spear's length, jabbing away again

at a line of monkeys that would not give ground. They were dying, but they were not bending.

Among the monkeys there were some bigger ones, like he'd seen in the previous fight. One of these was opposite now, and for the first time, Rukkh felt that he was the smaller of the combatants.

The heavyweight monkey slammed shields with him, and Rukkh was driven back a step. He cursed, jabbed at his foe's face, and darted to the side. The monkey was quick with the spear, but unskilled. He lunged too far and overbalanced.

"Forjal!" roared Rukkh. "Grab it!"

Forjal had seen the opportunity and he dropped his sword and grabbed the spear shaft. A powerful tug jerked the monkey farther off-balance, and Rukkh thrust home into its side, at the point where the leather plates were tied together. The big monkey jackknifed with the agony, Rukkh got a foot up on the brute's chest while he tore the spear free. Then he had to protect himself from monkeys to his right, who were stabbing at his face. Another monkey had closed up in front.

Forjal tripped over a body and went down on one knee. Oggi covered while Rukkh dueled with the monkey on his right. The problem on the right was Glukk, who had gotten his shield wedged tight against a trio of monkeys there. They were stabbing over it at him, and he was fending them off with his sword. He'd lost his spear in the press. The flanking attack had choked off their assault, and the line was caving in from the right.

Now the inevitable came, and Glukk took a spear thrust in the thigh. He heaved back with a final effort and broke his shield free. Two monkeys were pulled off their feet as he came. But big Glukk was down, leg pumping out bright arterial blood. The monkeys swarmed over him.

Rukkh dodged a grounded monkey's spear as it flashed around his ankles and slapped it with his shield.

Another man went down. Rukkh evaded spearpoints, felt his shield take a heavy blow, and then something rapped him hard across the front of his helmet and he saw stars. He could feel blood running down his lip to his mouth and thought his nose was broken, but there was no time to check.

Shields slammed into his own, spears thrust at him. Then more men pushed up and drove the monkeys back. Lurgi came up from behind along with Chazz. Rukkh slipped back a few paces to regain his breath.

Burok had gotten back to his feet, but he was still shaking his head. Rukkh had a second to think how incredibly hard Burok's fornicating sergeant's head must be, and then there were orders being screamed behind them.

They were taking unacceptable casualties.

Sergeant Hugga had taken over Burok's men for the moment, until Burok either recovered or was replaced. He roared at them to retire, spears front, stepping backward smartly in good order!

They retreated in proper fashion, parade-ground style, except that they left a litter of their brethren lying among a heap of the sodomizing, God-damned monkeys.

The fronts separated. The regiments retired and dressed rightward to move out of range of missiles from the wall.

Uisbank was left to chew over the fact that his thrust along the wall had failed. The damned monkeys had—somewhere, somehow—learned to fight.

They were still crude, and they'd lost more heavily than his men had, but still they'd stopped the charge of the Blitz regiment, something that few human armies had been able to do since Aeswiren began his rise to the summit of power.

The casualty list was going to be far too long. Uisbank felt a clutch of fear. More than forty left behind, most of them dead. The stones from the catapults had done some heavy damage. Uisbank had never thought the monkeys would be capable of something like that. Catapults? The monkeys were just animals; how could they come up with catapults? And who had taught them how to hold their line like that and wield spears like men?

Meanwhile, the force of monkeys that had sallied out of the waterside gate had retreated back to it and were passing in, while the men pulled back out of range of the rocks from the wall.

The Fifth Regiment was sent forward to take the place of the Blitz and the Second, Third, and Fourth Regiments were ordered to lengthen their line and threaten to flank the monkeys lined up on the road.

The maneuvering began after a few blasts on the bugles.

"While we stretch out their lines," said Uisbank to his staff, "we'll take a good look at the field."

If the monkeys had learned to fight, at least a little bit, then he needed a new strategy. The men under his command were mostly veterans. They could be trusted to pull off the most complicated maneuvers. Perhaps it was time to dazzle the monkeys with some military artistry.

Damned monkeys had upset the timetable though. There'd be no triumphal dinner that night. Nor would they take the city easily. At least, not yet, not today, not at the first blow, which was the sort of thing that had a chance of making it into the history books as they would be edited by the Hand of Aeswiren. Uisbank shrugged inwardly, uncomfortable with the thought of Admiral Heuze's smirking reaction to this news.

Phaugh! Uisbank hated that whole world-weary, semitreacherous state of mind that the admiral personified so completely. People like the admiral loved art and poetry and disdained the common people's love of the bloodthirsty games in the arena. Uisbank hated all the bastard, sodomistic softies, who would end slavery and abolish the blood rites of the Great God. A knife in all their hearts!

Uisbank was true to the faith, true to his core belief in the majesty of Aeswiren III. No trace of disloyalty had ever slid across his mind. When he bowed low to the Great God, he bowed low in purity of soul.

The priests all knew this, and the red tops left him alone.

Heuze, on the other hand, had run up a high mark in the books kept by the priests. That had been unwise. And what the priests knew was almost certainly well-known to the Hand of Aeswiren. It could strike at any moment, and that old bastard with his smirks and witty remarks would be given to the red tops for "correction" before his interrogation began.

It would be what he deserved, thought Uisbank, before summoning his scouts across.

"What lies inland, beyond the roads and those gardens?"

"More gardens, orchards. All the way to the next road and the road beyond that."

"And what lies inland down the coast?"

"After three miles the cultivated land stops. The road goes on through wild woodland."

"And on the far side of the city?"

"First there is a stretch of water paddy about a half mile across with the river in the center of it."

"Bridges?"

"Lots, but all small."

"Without bridges, how difficult to negotiate?"

"Moderate difficulty. Ditches and canals are frequent. There are narrow lanes, walled enclosures, ornamental statuary."

"What?"

The scout shrugged. "Well, they're carvings in stone, about life-size I'd say. They're usually of monkeys carrying farm implements."

Uisbank's eyebrows rose.

"Statues of farmers?"

"I suppose."

Uisbank flashed his teeth as he let out a great laugh.

"Now we know we're fighting idiots."

The scout laughed, too, of course, but in his eyes there

was still puzzlement. The monkeys carved statues of themselves? How could animals do that? Something very basic in his worldview was coming apart at the seams, and the scout could not completely hide this from himself.

Chapter 44

"All right then, I'll run through this one more time."
Uisbank turned back to the sand chart they had drawn
of the battle. The city sat at the center with a strip of
flattened sand around it.

"By the grace of Aeswiren and the gift of the Great
God, we are here and our force is together and ready
to fight."

The red markers of the army were lined up facing
inland with the city wall on their left. One regiment was
held ready to counter any sallies from the city. The monkeys were indicated by blue markers.

Watching the proceedings were the line officers, almost
all of them.

"The first phase of our battle is over. We have blood-
ied the monkeys and taught them to fear us."

Uisbank stared at his officers, looking for any signs of
lack of heart and passion. Any slackers would talk to the
Hand, he'd made that plain.

"Now we move to take control of the battlefield. We
swing inland, shift our strength across to the right, and
move past the enemy. He will have to face us with the
walls at his back. We will stretch out his line, and then
we will attack.

"We will give him the horns of the bull."

Their faces broke into smiles and a rumble of amuse-
ment went round.

If the enemy turned to face them, as he must, Uisbank
would thin the center of their own line and bulk the
wings. Then they would attack with both wings slanted

forward to catch the enemy on the flanks of his formation. The center would not engage until the enemy's flanks were both impacted. Then the encirclement could begin and the enemy's destruction completed.

But the flanking action had to be quick.

"I want to see good work by our men. They're veterans, they know how to do this better than anyone. Let's show these stinking monkeys how men put in the bull's horns."

By going inland, Uisbank wasn't going to worry about the monkeys cutting him off from the beach. If they tried to get in his way, he'd knock them aside. This time he was determined to set the field properly and let his men's strength and skills crush the monkeys once and for all. He'd kill them all, right in front of those walls, and let the defenders see their own doom coming!

Uisbank was gratified greatly by the fire in the eyes of his listeners. They all wanted to do whatever they had to to smash this mockery of an army that the stinking monkeys had put out there on the field. They all still felt the shame of their failure to smash the monkeys with the first charge.

The Blitzers couldn't explain it either. They always broke through, but this time they hadn't. The monkeys were too quick with their spears, and then they'd broken in on the right flank. They'd left forty dead back there and there were twice that many with wounds. A dozen of those now being ferried out to the ships might die. No, the Blitzers were in a sorry state of disbelief. They were left standing in reserve while the Fifth Regiment had their place.

And still there was anger in the army over the regiment's failure. A few voices had been heard suggesting they be dealt with the way the Old Empire would have, with a decimation by crucifixion. What Kadawak would have done.

"What Kadawak would have done is feed us to the ants," growled Uisbank. "All of us. No mercy would be shown. But we serve Aeswiren, not Kadawak, so we are

fortunate. We will get the opportunity to atone for ou
error and to show the Emperor what we are made o
and how much we venerate his glorious name."

"Aeswiren!" they chanted with right-hand fists presse
to their chests, left hands raised high.

Uisbank began to issue specific orders. Second an
Third Regiments were to hold their positions for the mo
ment, while Fourth and Fifth march around them an
extend the line inland facing the walls, but out of rang
of those damned catapults.

Colonel Bok of the Second had just received his writ
ten orders from Uisbank's clerk when there came a sud
den shout, followed by another shout that had almost ;
sense of panic to it.

More shouts followed. Men were moving.

"What is happening?" snarled Uisbank, peerin
toward the commotion.

"Look!" yelled an excited staffer.

Coming at them out of the heather was a mass o
monkeys carrying shields before them. They ha
emerged unseen with amazing stealth. No one had no
ticed them until they were well on their way.

Arrows started falling among the officers and Uis
bank's staff. An aide gave a plaintive yelp as an arrow
sliced into the edge of his forearm.

Isolated on top of the dune, the officers were expose
to a swarm of hundreds of monkeys with just a detach
ment of thirty men to protect them.

Uisbank dropped his pen, felt his jaw slacken. Wha
was the world coming to? Here were these filthy mon
keys actually daring to attack!

"Bugler!" roared Emjex.

The bugle began to blow for help.

Bugles were instantly blown down below, where the
mass of the army was laid out north of the dunes on the
open space. Orders could be heard being barked, and
men turned and began to hustle toward the northern end
of the dunes, but it would take them a few minutes to
get there.

And then the screaming monkeys were on them. General Uisbank and his commanders found themselves fighting for their lives with their own swords and whatever they could find as shields. The monkeys drove in with no sound, no cries, nothing but the fire in their eyes. As they came, some slipped around the men and encircled them on top of the dune.

The monkeys pressed hard, and they were on all sides now and the fight was unequal. Arrows had ceased, this was all spear work now.

Colonel Bok went down, Lieutenant Greevis was spitted by a spear that passed through his leather chest armor. There were only twelve of them left on their feet when the monkeys drew back.

Uisbank had taken a knock on the head from a shield and a couple of jabs from spears and knives. It was a shockingly fierce fight. These monkeys were quick. Uisbank had not quite appreciated how important that was until this moment. His head hurt, and there was something in his eye, and he was afraid it was his own blood.

The monkeys were on fire; you could see it in their eyes. They had the advantage and the numbers. The wall of shields and spearpoints was going to rush in and overwhelm the men standing at bay, while the rescue parties were still struggling up to the halfway mark on the dune.

"Surrender!" called a voice from the monkey side in clear Shashti.

What? Uisbank was stunned. Had he heard that voice correctly?

"Surrender!" it shouted again, quite clear. "Surrender and your lives will be spared."

Uisbank felt his jaw drop.

The fucking monkeys were speaking Shashti? What the hell was going on? The surviving dozen men, ten officers and two soldiers, exchanged looks of wide-eyed amazement.

"Go fuck yourself!" screamed Captain Emjex in a spasm of rage.

It was perhaps a bit peremptory, considering the situation. Then before he could waver, Uisbank waved his sword and roared, "We will never surrender!"

There was a long, silent moment.

"Bugler, hurry that relief!" But there was no way the men down below would reach them in time.

The bugle blew, and the monkeys surged forward and the fight renewed. A roaring sound rose up composed of grunts, oaths, and the racket of wood and steel slamming on shields.

When it was all over, Uisbank, still stunned, was walking down the slope on the end of a rope attached to the cuffs on his wrists. He was limping badly, but his captors didn't seem to care.

The other captives were the bugler and Uisbank's clerk, Fee-id, a slave. The rest, so far as he could tell, were dead.

Chapter 45

With hundreds of men charging the top of the dune, the victorious mots did not linger. They ran, they scampered, back down the inland slope and into the tangled heather. This was what a victory could feel like! They fairly danced into hiding once more.

Behind them, a horde of red-faced men, panting from the exertion, came up onto the top of the dune. They found a handful of survivors, wounded and lying among the dead. They found no trace of General Uisbank and had to accept the horrific likelihood that he had been taken prisoner. Messages were sent back down to the lieutenants who were clustering behind the Third Regiment, wondering what was going on.

On the other side of the dune, Thru made sure that their captives were dragged down through the heather at a smart pace and then under the trees of the woodlot that grew along side the road. It was a triumphant moment, but Thru knew they had plenty yet to do that day.

And the first thing was to find the Assenzi. This he did, almost immediately, when they appeared from behind a tree like three small black storks, stalking over on spindly legs to confront him. Thru had to stifle a laugh at the sight of them. He realized he was still a little light-headed from the events of the last ten minutes.

"We took them by surprise, Masters. Your spell had them completely in its grip; they never saw us until we were on top of them."

"Your casualties were light, they tell us," said Melidofulo.

"Yes, Master."

"Congratulations," said Utnapishtim. "Thru Gillo, we see you brought in some prisoners."

"One of them was wearing this on his helmet." Thru showed them the red plume he'd snapped off General Uisbank's helmet.

"Excellent, a commander of some high rank. We will interrogate him immediately."

The captive men were being led rapidly up the road toward the gate. They passed behind the mot regiments set out on the plain in front of the walls. A lot of unkind comments came their way, which they understood all too easily, despite the different language. Ahead of them the city gates were half-open. Within they saw a city street, buildings, a crowd of monkeys.

Thru Gillo had moved on. He was studying the men on the top of the dunes. A line had been formed up there at least one hundred men long. But it didn't seem to indicate an imminent attack. The men seemed content to hold the top of the dune. It was just as Toshak had predicted.

"Cut off the head, and their army will fall onto the defensive. The initiative will pass to us."

And indeed, that was what was happening to the army of Shasht. By some strange and terrible circumstance, the ranking officers of the army had been caught together and slaughtered.

The army had been decapitated. General Uisbank had even been captured. General Raltt, who had been organizing the food supply on the beach, was now the ranking officer. Frantic signals were sent posthaste to the fleet command.

Thru had to take a few deep breaths and concentrate. The feeling of triumph was just a little too intoxicating.

"Well, Thru Gillo, you're in command. Shall we attack them again?"

It was the Grys Norvory, titular commander of the regiment they had readied for the attack. For a bare second or so, Thru felt the old bitterness; then he dismissed it. There was a war to win, and personal feelings had no place in it.

"No, Toshak said to wait."

"But there's just a hundred of them up there. We could take them like we took the first lot."

"There's a hundred we can see. I would rather trust to Toshak's instincts. He understands these things. He was trained at Sulmo."

"I have received training as well."

"And Toshak is our commanding officer. We will wait on him. That is an order."

The Grys looked at him, and something hard glittered in the eyes for a moment. The others, a mixture of officers who were elected by the mots of their commands or appointed by the King's Commissioners, looked on with interest. The Grys had chafed before at being subordinate to Thru Gillo.

That hard feeling in Norvory's eyes provoked something in Thru. He was ready to drop everything and punch the Grys silly, right there.

And then Toshak appeared, breathing a little hard from having run most of the way. His staff were still toiling up the path through the woods.

"Congratulations, Colonel Gillo. Your attack went perfectly."

"Thank you, sir!" Thru went to attention and saluted, far from expert in either activity.

The Grys stood there stone-faced.

"Whatever is wrong with you two? You look as if you were about to attack each other when I came up."

"Uh, nothing sir!"

For a moment Toshak stared at them. He looked to Thru for an explanation, then motioned to the dunes.

"Must take a closer look." They set off up through the heather to a vantage point on a rock that broke above the tangled vegetation. Toshak studied the top of the dune with his spyglass, then he turned it on the plain off to one side. The regiments of men had retreated and formed a defensive position across the plain from the bottom of the sand dunes to the top of the beach.

Toshak returned his gaze to the line of men atop the dune. Clearly there were more men waiting just over the top of the dune.

"I think it's clear that those men up there are supposed to be a lure. They are hiding several times that number on the farther side of the dune, hoping we will attack when they can crush us."

The Grys Norvory stared at him. Then he looked back to the dune top and studied it more carefully.

"I have a better idea," said Toshak in the quiet voice that Thru had begun to recognize as signaling something important.

"We will attack, but not just yet. Better to let those men wait up there for a while. Make them get impatient. Make the others behind the dune relax. Give them an hour or two. Meanwhile, we bring up some catapults, then attack under cover of their fire."

"The mots are fired up, ready to go now. We can take them," said the Grys Norvory.

"We can't risk failure. We'll use the catapults to break up their line and attack at the same moment. The Assenzi may be able to help us again with a spell. They seem to distract these men very well."

And so the battlefield remained quiet. Boats rowed to and fro the big ships and the beach while the men held their positions, keeping about three hundred paces from the line held by the mots along the road.

The mots were still eager to attack again. Their first heady victory had taught them that they could wage war, and there was a fire now burning in them, a fire that cried for vengeance.

Four of the small-size catapults, capable of firing seven-foot spears a distance of four hundred yards, were brought up by a sweating army of youngsters now working in Graedon's Engineering Corps.

While the catapults were reassembled in the heather, Thru made sure that the mots in his regiment received some food and water. He took the opportunity to check with his scout parties set out to the south near the hamlet of Welgen. Parties had ranged well out on that flank, climbing to the top of the dunes about a half mile farther south, where they began to decline in height and mass. Thru understood that the enemy was holding his positions defensively. His main force had moved back to form a line with the force on top of the dune. There were still boats plying to and fro the shore, and the ships could be seen, lined up out into the bay.

Other scouts reported back from the southern end of the dunes. There was activity aboard the ships, one of which had moved closer inshore. There were no men on the southern dunes, and it did not appear that the men were concerned about attack from that direction.

All four catapults, along with two dozen spears apiece, were hidden in the heather within two hours.

Still they waited while Toshak studied the positions from the wall and discussed the targeting with the catapulters.

Chapter 46

The ancient beings came to her once more in the little room where she was kept under guard.

"Good day, Simona, we hope we find you well." They spoke perfect Shashti, better than Thru, and they had learned it from just listening to her. Such ability was faintly terrifying.

They still seemed like the demons on the Hell Wall, but she had learned how different they were from each other. The one named Utnapishtim was the take-charge one. His huge eyes were very pale, and he wore the glowing blue gem at his throat. Melidofulo wore black, and his thin face was a beacon for anxiety. The other one, called Master Graedon, wasn't with them this time. He only rarely appeared; Utnapishtim always excused him at the beginning of the conversation, saying that he was busy on some project or other.

"Yes, ancient Masters, I am well. I heard there was fighting today."

"Yes, dear, the Shasht fleet has landed an army outside the city."

It was what she had feared. And when they conquered the mots and found her in this cell, what would they do to her?

She could see the priests with their knives all too clearly in her mind.

"We have come to you, Simona, in the hope that you will be able to help us identify a prisoner."

She hesitated. Were they asking her to betray her people?

"I would like to help, but I cannot be a traitor."

"We understand that. But you know that many men will die before this war is over."

"Yes."

"We want to bring it to an end as quickly as possible. That will save lives."

"Yes, I see."

"If we know this man's identity, then it may help us in getting him to talk to us. So far he refuses to speak."

Simona nodded. The arrogance of the men of Shasht was boundless. If all they wanted was to talk to this man, then that she could do.

"I will help. I would do anything to stop this senseless fighting."

She followed them through the corridors and staircases that filled the building. They paused outside a door two floors up. Utnapishtim pulled something out of a pocket in his robe.

"The battle has not been decided, but we were fortunate in capturing this man. He had this plume on his helmet."

At the sight of the crushed red plume Simona shivered.

"It is from either a colonel or a general, but I'm not sure which."

"Would you come in with us and take a look at this man? Do not fear, he will not be able to see you."

For some reason her heart pounded at this thought. To see a man of her own people, after these weeks among the mots and brilbies?

"Yes," she heard herself say, but fear left her trembling.

"Come, my dear, wear this raiment. Cover your head and hair. He will not know you."

Utnapishtim handed her a cloak made of fine wool, very soft and light. The hood came over her head and she wound a flap across her face.

"It will only be for a moment," said Melidofulo. "Do not fear. He is restrained."

Utnapishtim surveyed her before opening the door.

"You will appear as no more than a strangely dressed mot."

General Uisbank's head jerked up as the door was opened. His guards stepped forward a moment and stepped back when they saw it was the Assenzi. Uisbank was sitting on a stool with his hands bound behind his back and his ankles tied to the legs of the stool. A lantern hung directly over him, bathing him in light.

Uisbank saw that the demons were back. They spoke Shashti with a lack of accent, but they spoke Shashti. He didn't know how—unless some prisoner had talked. But that was close to unimaginable. Any man taken would have preferred to die in the grace of the Great God than teach these demons Shashti.

The usual pair of demons were there, accompanied by a third figure, covered head to toe in brown. God damn! The fucking monkeys wore nothing but brown wool. They were so goddamn primitive they hadn't got around to putting a little color into their clothes.

Uisbank looked down at the wide beams of the polished wooden floor. Why didn't the God-damned, fornicating monkeys just kill him and get it over with!

Then his head jerked up again. There was something odd about the figure in the brown robe's movement, something that spoke to him on a level below conscious thought. And a moment later he knew.

"Traitor!" he screamed. He tried to leap to his feet and attack, and the stool rocked violently in place. The guards moved to hold him down.

"Filthy, fucking traitor, the priests will have you! They will flay you alive. You will die screaming for the mercy of the Great God."

Despite the priests, Uisbank was rocking the stool up and down, it fell with a crash, and he rolled back into the wall. The guards bent over him.

Simona turned and stumbled out of the room, barely able to see, shaking with terror.

He had seen her. He was a man of Shasht; he would

always know a woman of Shasht. The priests would have her! There was no mercy in their world.

His name was Uisbank, she was sure. Of the Gofft clan, and recently promoted to command of the landing army. Filek had told her that he was a complete dolt, promoted because he was completely trustworthy. She had seen him on the women's deck of the *Anvil*.

Outside, in the hall passage, she leaned against a wall and shivered.

"He sensed you in some way that we do not understand," said Melidofulo stroking his tiny chin.

"He is a man, I am woman. That is all it took," she said bitterly.

"Ah," said Utnapishtim. "Sexuality is an area in which we are weak. Being nonsexed ourselves it is a thing we can only guess at. However, he still does not know your identity, and he is still our prisoner and so he will remain."

She felt a tiny flash of sympathy for poor Uisbank. No harder fate could she imagine for a leading warrior of Shasht. How he must long for death!

Chapter 47

"Go!" said Thru and, with little more than whispers down the line of command, they did.

Once more the Assenzi had laid a spell over the scene. The men lined along the top of the dune were distracted by distant birds circling over the city, pointing to the dozens of white birds and crying out to each other that it was an omen.

An omen that they misunderstood, to their cost.

Nine hundred mots, organized in three columns, twenty mots abreast, were churning up the dune. At the front of the columns were teams of the strongest brilbies and mots.

Most of this front rank had acquired steel helmets and heavy shields. They were armed with two spears, one a lighter weapon for throwing, the other a heavier spear with a long steel head designed to be wielded overhand, thrusting and jabbing for the eyes of the opponent.

Behind them the catapults were armed and ready, just waiting for the command to fire.

For Thru, in command of this amazing moment, it was agonizing. How long would they have? For second after precious second the columns charged up the slope unseen. Willing them on, he watched while each stride they made ran off his tongue,

"Nine . . . ten . . . eleven."

Still the whirling white birds above the city caught the men's eyes. Not one had spotted the massed columns of mots running up the slope toward them.

Thru kept counting, kept praying, and the spell held

while the columns covered three hundred feet of clump grass and compacted sand.

There were maybe a hundred feet to go, when someone looked down from the birds and gave a shriek.

The men had barely time to pick up shields and yank spears out of the ground. Officers were screaming the first orders, something about "forming up," when the catapults let go and seven-foot-long spears hurtled through the line atop the dune. It was a shock to everyone's system, the last thing they'd expected. One spear missed, going too high by a foot, but the others struck men and hurled them back off the dune.

"Close up!" roared a sergeant.

There was something terribly sinister about the silence with which the monkeys came on. They came at them like assassins, on silent feet.

At ten feet's distance the leading line threw their javelins, then slammed in with shield and spear. The massive impetus of the brilbies and mots was enough to drive the men back before them while the harsh sound of war rose up and bugles started shrilling.

The men on the farther slope had been waiting quietly out of sight for hours. They only awoke to the peril when the fighting started above their heads. Suddenly, with loud crashes, a couple of men were hurled back down the duneside. There was a glimpse of something whirring by above them. One of the fallen men had been spitted by a prodigiously large spear.

They came to their feet, grabbed their weapons, and started up the dune to reinforce the line while the bugles screamed.

But the line had already shattered. The young brilbies had smashed open further gaps in the line, and behind them came mots and brilbies boiling with a rage to avenge the dead of Tamf and Creton.

The line of one hundred men dissolved, and the columns surged over the top and down into the three lines of men who had been waiting below. The impact came almost before most men had recognized that it was coming. There was barely time to do more than get the shield up and take the blow.

A shattering crash rang up and down the dune top as the columns bit into the lines of men. Most men would have broken and run for their lives, but these were the Blitzers, rested from the fight that morning and angry about how it had gone. Their pride sent them toe-to-toe with the onrushing hordes, and they knocked aside spears and turned shields and thrust home with their own weapons. For a few seconds the fight teetered there, but then over the dune came the third column, falling right on the men's right flank. The flank collapsed, the lines bent back farther. The slope of the dune completed the disaster because there it grew much steeper for a few feet and the men could not hold their footing. The lines fell back downslope with roars of rage and bafflement, but despite everything the mighty Blitzer Regiment could not hold its position.

Behind, on the top of the dune, they left twenty cut off, still battling.

"Surrender!" shouted a voice in clear Shashti. "Surrender and your lives will be spared."

"We will never surrender!" bellowed several men.

"Is that your answer then?"

"Go fuck yourself with a javelin's end you filthy, fucking monkey!"

"So be it."

Archers shot some of the men down, the rest were buried under a wave of spears and shields. None of the twenty survived.

Only on the shingle top of the beach did they finally make a stand. And as if by a miracle they were greeted with the sight of a dozen boats putting in with the first reinforcements. Red tops were drumming frantically while hundreds of men formed up on the beach.

With a great shout the Blitzers greeted these reinforcements.

"For the wrath of He who Eats!" screamed a voice.

"Kill!" they roared back.

And they went back at the monkeys who were coming right up against them. This time the charge was disorganized, and instead of columns it was as two broad masses that they came.

The impact came with a solid ringing *crunch* up and down the line, and the familiar roar of war arose. The men of the Blitz Regiment set to showing the monkeys how men really fought.

In a few moments the onrush lost impetus and came to a halt. Two walls of shields faced each other at spear's length while rocks and arrows flew overhead. Thru, at the same spot on top of the dune where General Uisbank had once stood to survey the city he intended to capture, saw at once that the charge had died out.

He ordered a retreat to the top of the dune, which they would hold. Catapults would be brought up to fire on the beach below. Unfortunately, his regiment had dissolved into a roaring mob with no sense of organization at all. And now the men from the boats came running up the shingle and pushed through the Blitzers to get at the monkeys.

"Make room for the Veteran Sixth," bawled sergeants.

The famous Sixth Regiment had arrived on the field, ready to save the situation as they had done so many times before.

Grudgingly, the Blitzers gave the Sixth some of the line, and the men fresh off the ship went in hard. They hurled javelins, then smashed into the line of mots and brilbies, stepping over a dozen dead monkeys while others broke away from the line and fled back up the dune.

Thru sent more orders for withdrawal. They needed to reorganize before the fight turned completely against them. Again the orders were sent in vain.

Disaster loomed. Thru could see that his line was about to break. The men were already through in several places. But he could not recover control; the mots and brilbies were lost in the chaos of war. They fought in a dense mass, with spears jabbing at the gaps between

shields while they pushed back and forth in a heavy
scrimmage.

The men, however, responded to orders and bugles.
They were exploiting the openings in the lines, turning
the flanks on either side.

And then he heard the clatter of equipment and the
thud of feet, and Toshak arrived with two more columns
of mots and brilbies, brought up at the run from the
nearest regiment.

"More are coming. We must hold them here. This will
be the vital point of the battle."

Thru nodded, and ordered the catapults brought up to
the dune at the double.

A defensive line was formed. More orders were sent
down to the struggling masses below, and finally a large
group broke away from the main battle and started back
up the dune.

They were immediately targeted by the rows of Shasht
archers lined up behind the battle. Climbing the dune,
watching out for interloping men, and dodging arrows
was a difficult task. Many failed, and their bodies rolled
to the bottom and built up in drifts.

The first fugitives reached the top of the dune and
were welcomed through gaps in the new, disciplined line
that had formed there. Behind that line they found Thru
and some of the other officers waiting. Among them was
the Grys Norvory, who had blood streaming from a
head wound.

More fugitives came back, but they were taking terrible casualties as the men pressed them hard. Perhaps two
hundred were down, and others were bearing stab
wounds and arrows in backs and shoulders. They retreated up the steep part of the slope with the men stabbing at their backs, and threw themselves into the gaps
in the waiting line of mots.

The gaps shut behind them and the men came up
against the new wall of shields and disciplined stabbing
spears.

The Sixth Regiment were determined to show the

Blitzers a thing or two, and they hurled themselves into it. Once again a real roar of battle went up as the two sides clashed. But most of the men were without their throwing spears, and they were fighting up a slope while standing on sand that gave way beneath their feet.

It was a near-suicidal task. Men staggered back, again and again with stab wounds to their eyes and faces. Then catapults were pushed forward and fired down into the ranks of men while bodies were hurled back, spitted like chickens.

It couldn't go on for long, and soon the men of the Sixth Regiment, like the Blitzers before them, discovered that they could not necessarily break a line of monkeys behind shields. The men fell back a few feet. Their disadvantage on the slope was too much for even their skills and experience to overcome. The damned catapults let go again with that chilling *crack-whine* noise, and there were brief shrieks as the long spears hammered home.

General Raltt was the new commander of the army, and a nervous fellow. The situation he'd inherited from that oaf Uisbank was not good. Standing on the beach looking up the dune he could see that the Sixth Regiment was just taking casualties up there and not gaining a yard. He ordered them back, then moved on to take a look at the disposition of the other regiments.

The Sixth were veterans and they accepted that there was just no getting around the fact that they had to retreat. So they withdrew in good order, disciplined lines moving backward while keeping shields and spears up toward the enemy.

At the bottom they passed through the re-formed Blitzers, then they turned and re-formed behind the Blitzers.

Sergeants bellowed for silence as the two units exchanged a few insults here and there. In truth, the Sixth and the Blitzers got along well, and often fought side by side. It was the pestilential Third and Fourth Regiments that they hated.

All of them stood there, shields resting on the ground,

spears in hand, and looked up the long slope of sand and swore to the Great God that the battle was going to be won. The sodomistic, fornicating, ass-wipe monkeys were not going to get a victory on this field!

Unfortunately, the damned monkeys had those catapults up on top of the dune, and they could range over just about the whole fornicating beach.

General Raltt was careful to set up his command post farther toward the city, at a point that was out of range of both the catapults on the dune top and the stone-throwing catapults on the battlements. He discovered that only an uncomfortably small area was safe from both, and stones could still skip and bounce right into the center of the command post. Twice in the first hour, Raltt and his staff had to jump up and scatter when a rock the size of someone's head came rolling through at high speed. On the second occasion it smashed the map table and ruined the map on which they'd drawn up the battle plans.

A new table was brought up and a fresh map begun at once by the mapmaker. But the incident left everyone nervous and uncomfortable.

Raltt cursed vehemently. There were three thousand men ashore, and they were boxed in on the plain between the city walls and the tall dunes above the beach. The monkeys effectively controlled the right and left side of the field. In front was a line formed by three regiments of monkeys, all armed with spears and shields and capable of putting up a stout resistance to a charge.

It was going to take some miracles from Orbazt Subuus and some huge efforts by his devoted servants, the officers and men of the army of Shasht, to get them out of this one.

At about the same time, up on the dune top, Thru was rejoined by Toshak and his exhausted staff, who had run back and forth to the city battlements and this dune many times, covering more than a mile on each trip.

"They've just been standing there while we shoot at them."

"Having success?"

"Every second arrow seems to strike amongst them, but they have spaced themselves out, and most of our shots don't hit anyone."

"Slow the rate of fire, conserve the spears. We've halted them for now. I doubt the new commander down there will risk another attack today."

Thru nodded; as usual Toshak made sense. Thru passed orders for the catapults to slow their rate of fire.

Toshak studied the enemy down below, drawn back into a hunched beachhead.

"Look! They're entrenching on the plain."

Thru saw that behind the line of spearmen other men were digging a ditch.

"What will happen tomorrow?"

"We will watch them leave."

"How can you be so sure."

"You will see, everyone will see, tonight."

Toshak turned away with a mysterious smile. His staff rose with a few groans as he set off once more for the city.

Chapter 48

That night, with the army's first wave ashore and holding a beachhead, Admiral Heuze dined with some regular companions in the admiral's cabin. There was Captain Pukh of the *Anvil*, there was Chalmli, chamberlain to Nebbeggebben and an invaluable source of advice concerning the Imperial Court and its agents. And there was Filek Biswas, the Surgeon General of the Fleet.

Pukh was an excellent seaman and a fine fellow, with an interest in the arts, who had sailed with Heuze on many a voyage in the cold south seas. Most important he and Heuze shared a similar sense of humor. Much of the world they found to be simply so absurd that you had to laugh.

Both the admiral and the captain listened agog while Chalmli described events at a feast Nebbeggebben had held just before setting out on the voyage.

"So they opened the first cake and out came the maiden. A very pretty little thing. And not a slave, oh no, she was actually wellborn, and had been tricked into thinking she was going to meet the prince afterward. Such wickedness can hardly be imagined."

And indeed, the vicious goings-on at Nebbeggebben's court were not for young things with starry visions of bedding a prince.

"So, then they popped the second cake and out came this huge cretin from some slave farm in Pangifica."

The captain's jaw fell open.

"What?"

"Oh yes, and of course the maiden is bound by silken

cords at the knee so she can only take tiny steps. The cretin was all over her like some cheap gown in less than a minute. I swear everyone laughed for the next ten minutes while it went on."

The seamen roared and pounded the tabletop.

Filek Biswas winced. The traditional wedding feast was supposed to feature the two cakes, which when cut into would reveal a man and a woman, a married couple who would merely kiss and hug before stepping aside to polite applause. This degrading spectacle of Nebbeggebben's merely showed the depths to which the imperial family had descended. Aeswiren was a bloodthirsty thug, but all his progeny had been even worse. The city of Shasht had no doubt breathed a sigh of relief at seeing the last of Nebbeggebben. Only now, of course, they could await the eventual reign of Aurook, the second son of Aeswiren. Aurook liked to kill drugged gladiators, and boasted of killing a hundred men before his nineteenth birthday.

"And how fares the Lord Nebbeggebben, my dear Chalmli?" said Filek after the laughter had died down.

"Ah, well, 'tis good of you to ask, Surgeon General, but he remains weak and fretful. His appetite is low; he eats very little and keeps even less of it down."

"I do wish he would allow an examination." Filek wondered what sort of poisons the witch doctor was giving the prince in the name of medicine.

"He will not. Like his father, he distrusts modern medicine."

Filek smiled and dissembled. "I understand, of course, perfectly natural response considering some of the things that go on under that name. Often the term 'modern' in today's medicine is a complete joke. There are new understandings of the body and disease, but many so-called medics ignore them."

Chalmli nodded agreeably, full of good humor and spiced dumplings.

"Every discipline seems split by a group that refuses any change to established procedures even though they're far behind the times. In the magics it has become a scandal. In the Arcana League the Obdurates remain in command, and will not allow any rewriting of the First Ten Words. What makes it so ridiculous is that everyone has ignored the First Ten Words for a hundred years. Thus it doesn't matter if the Obdurates give way or not, since nobody obeys the dictates anyway."

"How does that sit with the holy priests of the Great God?" said the admiral with a roguish smile.

"Well, of course, the priests are allied with the Obdurates. Anything that cripples the magics serves the priests well. But try as they might, they have never broken Aeswiren's links to the magic schools."

"The priests also know that attacking the Schools of Magic upsets the witch doctors."

"I cannot believe the priests are worried about the witch doctors. The priests have all the power now over such matters," said Filek.

"Ah, but not in the colonies," said Captain Pukh. "We see some wild old things in the colonies. The witch doctors have the power out there it seems to me."

Heuze chuckled. "Anyone who has been to Seducer's Island in the open season has seen things beyond the realm of the normal!"

Captain Pukh roared, almost knocking over his goblet when he banged down a huge hand on the table.

"Seducer's Island in the season, oh my! Oh yes."

Heuze's servant poured more wine, and then the meal was brought in. Some porpoise had made the mistake of straying too close to the bows of the tender *Slicer* and had been gaffed and hauled aboard in no time.

"Do have some of this excellent porpoise, Biswas." Heuze was happily carving thick slices from the fillet. It had been marinated in wine and then baked briefly before being flash-fried in a skillet to brown. Finally, brandy was poured over the skillet and set alight to glaze it. It was superb, medium rare with a delicate crust on the meat.

A toast to Admiral Heuze was proposed by the captain.

Then a toast to Nebbeggebben was made and Chalmli smiled on Heuze.

"And what will General Raltt do tomorrow?"

"Oh, I expect he'll break out of this beachhead and invest the monkey town."

"Do you really think it's going to take a siege to capture the place?" said Chalmli.

"I do."

"It seems extraordinary to think that could be possible. They're only monkeys."

"Well, they stopped the army cold this day. You've seen the report."

Chalmli hesitated. "Well, yes."

"We attacked their line in the morning and were beaten off. They struck lucky at midday and captured that fool Uisbank. They attacked in the afternoon, broke through but were stopped on the beach. They now hold the high ground south of the city."

"I've heard they've got catapults up there."

"That can be confirmed," said Filek emphatically. "Today was a very bloody day."

"Well, we can't afford that," said Heuze, leaning forward suddenly. "We don't have the margin to allow for error now. My timetable is to get this colony ashore and in decent housing by the first snows."

"Then a lot is resting on General Raltt's shoulders," Chalmli said before taking a sip.

"Indeed there is. But the rest of us must do our bit, too. I know the men will make short work of them once we break up their formations and get to grips."

"Aye, aye, absolutely, sir." Captain Pukh raised his goblet.

"And tomorrow we will land the reserves and use our combined strength to break their lines and bring this to an end."

"Of course, exactly what the prince would have done in your position, Lord Admiral." Chalmli raised his goblet and drank a toast to the admiral.

"Thank you, thank you, friend Chalmli. And let me

respond by toasting His Highness, the Prince Nebbeggeb-ben, long may he live."

None of them could mistake the honest fervor in Heuze's voice when he said this, but they understood. Nebbeggebben's survival kept the Hand away from Heuze.

"So, tomorrow General Raltt will be given fresh troops. Then we'll winkle them out and drive the rest of them into the hills. Then we can get on with building the colony."

"There is something that's been troubling me," said Filek.

"And what is that?" said the admiral.

"Are we going to eat them this time?"

"Of course, they are good meat."

"But they are not just animals, they are intelligent."

"Oh, come now, surely not?" Chalmli's thick lips had drawn together in a pout.

"I think they demonstrated it today. Did they not capture General Uisbank? Last week the general dined with us, tonight he dines at the pleasure of those monkeys."

"If they haven't baked him on a bed of onions and eaten him, the stupid fucker!" roared Admiral Heuze.

Captain Pukh convulsed with laughter, too, and the pair of old salts raised their glasses to each other.

"Winning a flukey fight is not necessarily a sign of genuine intelligence," said Heuze. "After all, other creatures fight; look at army ants. Are they intelligent?"

Filek sighed. "These creatures build cities and defend them, they make objects of such beauty that all of you are participating in an illegal market in them. How can they not be intelligent?"

"Well now," rumbled Chalmli, "we don't know that they built anything at all. They're just living in these structures. They probably inherited them from proper men who seem to have died out in these parts. The same goes for the rugs and plates and fine things we've found. They're animals; they don't even know the value of these things."

Filek shrugged, wishing he could believe this.

"It doesn't matter, Biswas," said the admiral. "It doesn't matter if the monkeys made these things or not. I know you mean well, my friend, you've got a generous heart. This is not a criticism of a surgeon. You are the best surgeon in the world, Filek, you know my opinion there. But a kind heart clouds the mind's eye, see. There are always practical difficulties to consider. Our very survival depends on our landing here and seizing this land. There won't be room for both the monkeys and us, and we know that if we don't eliminate them entirely, then later on, in a century say, they'll haunt our descendants. We need to remove them from the landscape. Since they have to be slaughtered, we might as well not waste 'em, eh?"

The admiral and captain guffawed again and thumped the table.

"Very droll, sir, very droll," Captain Pukh toasted the admiral's wit.

Filek knew he could not show annoyance.

"Well, of course." He forced a smile. "That is a consideration. But surely future generations will curse us for eliminating the source of this incredible art of theirs."

"Oh we don't know that. Art has its fashions. And anyway, we'll have been dead a long time by then. And so will the damned monkeys."

More laughter rocked the table and Captain Pukh called at once for more wine.

Out in the darkness beyond the line of ships there was a cog, square-rigged with a full set of sails. But her sails were daubed with black pitch, and she was virtually invisible without moonlight.

It was old *Pebbles,* a boat that had traded up and down the coast for twenty-five years. Now she was making one last trip, a short one.

Aboard her were a crew of six, and behind her she towed a boat.

Her hold was stuffed with bales of bush fiber, soaked in paraffin. She nosed toward the line of Shasht ships, all of them giants compared to her.

The wind was on her beam now, and she was making good speed, moving toward the center of the line of ships. They had chosen the center in case their first target got away, in which case there would still be others inshore and within reach.

The wind gusted a little and the rigging creaked as the sails pulled hard. The dim outlines of the ship they were aiming for became clearer, sails furled, at anchor. The crew of *Pebbles* kept to their grim task, certain of success.

Aboard the *Growler* the lookouts were too busy talking among themselves to notice old *Pebbles*. After the excitement of the day's fighting, the quiet of the night with nothing but a handful of lights in the distance to look at was disappointing. They talked among themselves about the fighting and how what had happened to Uisbank had been foretold. Wasn't Uisbank one of those God-damned priest lovers? Always calling on "He Who Eats" for guidance and all that. It just went to show that the heretics were right. "He Who Eats" had less power than the older gods.

Wrapped up in such concerns, their first intimation of trouble came from the sudden odor of paraffin wafting in on the breeze.

Heads came up, and they stared out into the dark.

"What is that smell?" said a voice.

"That be oil of black tar. I remember it from Pangifica."

Out on the starboard side, something dimly visible was in motion.

"Ahoy there, what ship?"

A dark shape was appearing, a small vessel, less than a tenth *Growler*'s size. She was just a couple of hundred yards away, and her sails were painted black.

"What ship goes there?" roared the lookout.

"Away on the starboard side, a ship!"

By then Captain Shuzt was on deck and had grasped the peril.

"Cut anchor!" he bawled.

Feet thundered on the deck.

"Cut that anchor, get on with it now!" The officers were frantic.

Old *Pebbles* was close enough to be seen, so close that her embrace was inevitable.

That was why the Dronned shipwrights had spent the day working on *Pebbles*'s prow, where she now sported a sharp beak covered in a sheet of steel from Graedon's furnace.

A lantern had been run up the yard to throw more light out onto the dark stranger, and they saw that it was too late by far. Long before they could saw through the anchor cables, the cog was going to strike amidships.

"Belay that order, leave the anchor cables. Prepare to board the enemy."

But it really was too late. A few moments later the cog arrived, and a sharp shudder ran through the bigger ship as the ram stove in the timbers at the waterline with the suicidal fury of a bee.

"Man the pumps!" was the cry, and crewmembers were already in motion when it came.

The enemy crew was diving overboard and swimming away, all but one, who bent down and pulled out a darkened lantern, opened it to expose the flame, then lit a length of oil-soaked rope. He tossed the rope into the hold. Almost instantly the paraffin vapor in the hold caught fire and a blue flare of flame shot up. Then the bales ignited.

The pitch-covered sails caught next, and in a few seconds were a sheet of flame. The rising conflagration bathed the ends of the yards of the mainmast. The furled sails caught fire while men climbed screaming into the rigging to try and douse them.

Meanwhile, the roaring flames from the cog's hold were scorching the side of the *Growler* in the most villainous way. The paint had peeled away, and the timbers were blackening.

Desperate men threw buckets of water down the side, but it was too little too late.

The main yard was well and truly alight. A man fell, screaming from the yard and slapped the main deck. Flaming fragments fell from the yard and men ran hither and yon with shrieks as they stamped them out.

Now the side of the ship was catching fire. Black smoke was filling the carpenter's walk inside the hull and seeping into the cabins and storerooms belowdecks. More men were there throwing water on the timbers.

And the cog still burned with unlimited fury. The *Growler*'s upper yards were alight, and men were scrambling down, trying to avoid the fire that was consuming the mainsail. Some rigging fell with a crash of tackle and blocks. A man was knocked off the siderail and fell to the sea with a wail.

Then came a loud, horrified shout. The flames had taken hold on the top yard of the mizzenmast. More men went scrambling above to try and stop them.

Men ran, scrambled, hurled buckets, and ran again, but still the cog's deadly cargo sent up sheets of scorching fire that had not only blackened *Growler*'s side but had ignited the hatches and their frame timbers. Now fire exploded out of a stores locker on the main deck, where an ember had set light to dried, folded sails. Captain Shuzt howled for help as he ran to fight the fire himself with an ax, knocking down the blazing planks of the locker and hauling out the sails and hurling them overboard, still blazing and smoking.

The fire on the main yard was out of control though, and it set the mast above it alight. In moments the yards on the foremast caught, too, and the disaster was complete. A wooden ship is always vulnerable to fire, her masts and rigging can easily catch and her hull is by necessity dry and waterproof.

Now the *Growler* began to go, and though the fire that scorched her side timbers never actually went past that, the flames that fell from the burning masts took hold first here and then over there, and before long the ship was ablaze from one end to the other.

Old *Pebbles* was by then consumed; her timbers sank, hissing into the waters of the bay, but her mission was completed. The rest of the fleet could do little except put down boats to pick up men and women who hurled themselves into the sea for survival. Unfortunately, many could not swim.

The ship's fiery death throes were visible for many miles up and down the coast.

Growler burned to the waterline. A thousand men and women perished, and Filek Biswas had a huge emergency in treating hundreds of survivors with burns and broken bones.

Admiral Heuze wasted no time on pulling his fleet out of the bay. *Anvil* hauled her anchor and ran down the line and started beating her way out to the freer waters beyond. He wasn't going to be caught again by some damned cog full of pestilential monkeys and oil. The other ships, led by *Sword,* fell in behind, and through the hours of darkness the fleet worked its way out of the bay and ran south on the wind.

Chapter 49

It had been a difficult night for the Blitzer Regiment. Their failures on the previous day had been deeply disturbing. Twice they'd been bested by the pestilential monkeys, and the very name of their regiment had been called in question.

Then came the fireship attack on the *Growler* and the night was lit up with flames and filled with the distant shrieking of the doomed. This was hardly reassuring, and afterward they struggled to get any sleep at all on the shingle beach.

Later, when the moon rose, they realized that the fleet had gone. Officers went around to assure everyone that the fleet would be back and that the rest of the army was going to be set down beside them. They would spend the day resting up, letting the monkeys stew and worry, and attack in the afternoon with double the strength of the day before. But still there was a feeling of abandonment, and some men began to mutter against the sailors and the priests, too.

Since the plague there had been a great deal of muttering. Rukkh tried not to listen to it. He hated the priests like everyone else, but complaining did no good. At one point he felt physically sick to his stomach. The thought that the army could actually be in any danger in this position was still close to unthinkable. How could they be in danger from the fucking monkeys? No, the day before had been a fluke. Tomorrow the men of the Blitz Regiment would go forward, and this time they would succeed.

But still . . . What if the fleet couldn't get back in? What if no reinforcements came? How many monkeys might actually be out there? They'd seen an estimated five thousand enemy the day before. What if there were ten thousand more coming? How great might the odds become? All were uncomfortable questions.

In the hour before dawn they kept up a very keen watch, absolutely determined to make sure the monkeys didn't creep up on them. Nothing that moved, even down to some crows, was ignored.

On the right of their front the open ground ended and there was an area filled with low-walled gardens edging the road that lay behind. Then the soil became sand and the ground rose into the sand dunes that skirted the beach farther down on their right. That was where they'd been whipped the day before. Now that section of the line was held by the Sixth Regiment.

Just thinking about being rescued by the Sixth Regiment was enough to make any Blitzer burn inside.

Unfortunately, their careful scrutiny of the ground was wasted. The monkeys had made their move hours earlier, while the *Growler* was burning out in the bay and every eye was glued to it.

Now there was a mot regiment crouched in the garden allotments, just two hundred feet from the top of the beach where the Blitzers had their line. It was a bold gamble by Toshak, but since the men had lost the top of the dunes they could not see into the gardens, even though the walls were barely three feet high.

The mots waited through the darkness until the light broke in the east. They watched the men relax and stand down. After a minute or so, as the light became stronger, most of the men who'd been keeping watch behind their frail palisade of sticks left the line and went down to the cook fires to try and get some early breakfast. It was hungry work, standing in the cold before dawn staring into the darkness, looking for enemy movements.

The commander of the mot regiment, Nusi Climoth, judged the moment had come. With as little noise as possible the regiment stirred, stood up, and rushed forward. With shield and spears in hand they ran flat out for the ditch and palisade. Speed was vital, that was what Toshak had emphasized in his address to them the night before.

The first Rukkh heard of it was the sudden explosion of noise when the charging monkeys were finally spotted. Shouts, almost in disbelief, then in anger rippled off the line. The shingle beach was suddenly alive with men jumping to their feet.

Rukkh had only dozed off in the last couple of hours, and he felt somewhat logy and sleepy as he staggered up. His spear and shield came to hand without conscious thought, and he joined the column of figures heading up the beach. They moved at a quick step, shaking heads to clear them in preparation for fighting.

How had an attack arrived so quickly? The enemy lines were half a mile distant, and the watch had been so keen. It seemed impossible.

The men ahead of him had stopped. Something had held up the whole column that was moving up the beach. Sergeants were bellowing on the right, and then, shockingly, there were men, mixed up with monkeys in a thrashing mob coming back down the beach.

Beyond that there were monkeys all over the place. Clearly the line, with its prepared ditch and stockade, had been overrun.

One of the men directly ahead of him gave a scream and a spearhead seemed to explode through his back. He went down, and Rukkh found himself fighting one of the larger type of monkeys, a hellishly strong one, too. The spear stabbed at his head. He jerked up his shield to deflect and the enemy smashed his shield against Rukkh's before Rukkh could use his own spear. Rukkh felt himself jerked back a step and almost went down.

The monkey's spear sliced down his cheek and slid off the cheekpiece of his helmet as he jerked aside. By the Great God's wrath that was too fucking close!

Rukkh cut up with the shield edge, caught the monkey's shield, and turned it. He lashed out with a foot before the monkey could recover and felt his blow slam into the monkey's crotch. It buckled, and Rukkh stabbed down with his own spear, but the monkey's shield blocked him, and then the damned thing stabbed back. Again Rukkh had to defend with his shield.

To his right there came a sudden movement, and the whole line buckled from that direction and men came falling and stumbling into him. Rukkh felt a spear lance into his side and then he was down with his shield lying on top of him and someone on top of that scrabbling around while someone else was lying on his legs.

The shouts, screams, and constant keening from the fornicating monkeys was all deafening. Rukkh struggled to move, terrified of being buried alive under so many bodies. His side stung, and there was wetness on his hip so he knew he was cut.

Someone trod on his back, ramming him facedown to the shingle. There was a very loud shriek, someone else fell over the pile, and Rukkh struggled to breathe. Other men were trying to move; he kicked out and dislodged the one on his legs and then shoved and wriggled until he got his knees under him. Lastly he heaved the weight off his back. As he got up he found that his leather breastplate had saved his life. There was a gouge down the side of it and a shallow wound in his side above his hip.

Monkeys were everywhere. Their screaming noise filled the air. Knots of men were surrounded by the sheer mass of them. The Blitz Regiment's position had broken up completely.

"By the Great God, Rukkh, I need a hand."

Rukkh got hold of Forjal and pulled him to his feet. Forjal's belly was open and he was literally holding his guts inside. Standing up made that hard, but Forjal was tough. He kept moving.

"Gotta make it to the water," he gasped. "There'll be boats to take us off, right?"

Rukkh knew there were no ships in the bay, therefore no boats either.

Oggi came up and helped cover them. Monkeys veered away from their spears. The situation was completely chaotic.

A bugle sounded, off to his left, another to his right. The army was responding, finally. Forces would move in to cut off this attack and restore the line. But for the time being the hellish, deafening keening and ululating of the monkeys was all around them.

Other bugles were calling. A lot of men were in motion. Lurgi and Chaz went by with shields up. Rukkh saw Sergeant Burok run past, too, bellowing something about forming in fours. Forjal was still walking, somehow.

But the monkeys were also moving. Rukkh heard a new shout and looked back to his left. The fornicating monkeys were pouring down the sand dune and attacking the Sixth Regiment's line.

"By the stinking shit of He Who Eats, what is going on today?" said Oggi in despair.

Rukkh didn't have an answer to blasphemy like that. But he kept a firm grip on his spear and held his shield up as they edged back down the dune while monkeys came in at them from all directions. Rukkh swung right, spun a bit until his back was to the sea, and jerked his shield behind the edge of the leading attacker's shield. He pulled back and exposed the monkey to his spear thrust. As the spear went in below the leather breastplate, the monkey made a little sound and folded up.

He had to heave the spearpoint out and that slowed his response. A spearhead just missed his eyes in the next moment, clanging off his helmet. Something else nicked under the edge of his shield and hit him hard in the shin. But for the leather greave, it would have broken bone. As it was, he went down, rolled into someone else, and came up again behind Oggi. The monkeys had stabbed Mushukk, who'd fallen over him as he rolled.

This was rapidly turning into the worst day in Rukkh's entire life.

Forjal had broken free and was running, somehow, in a slow crazy tilt down the beach. Sergeant Burok was steadying a small but growing line of resistance. Rukkh saw Chaz was there. Big Uruk was there, too. Half a dozen others, all with shields up and spears ready.

"Get in line, Rukkh!" roared Burok. They were dressing right automatically and spacing out at shieldswidth.

And then the monkeys were on them again. Spears flicking and stabbing, shields slamming and cracking against the oncoming tide of the fornicating sons of sodomites. The monkeys came on, but the monkeys died there, because these men had their backs to the sea and were fighting with all the terrible skill of their kind.

Soon the line had thickened further; more men had struggled through the throngs of keening monkeys. The initial assault had broken the Blitzers completely, but now they were able to re-form because the monkeys had no battle discipline. Their formations broke down into mobs as soon as they engaged.

Soon the monkeys were streaming back up the dune while archers shot them down. And then the two flank forces came in and joined up in front of them, reknitting the army's line of battle.

Burok was there to help steady them. More men joined up, coming in from all over the beach.

"Forward, let's kill the fucking monkeys!" shouted Burok.

Rukkh and the others roared the war cry and hurled themselves forward.

Now they were taking the monkeys in the flank and the killing was easy. Soon the monkeys broke and ran. Back up the shingle beach they went, across the short strip of sand at the top and on to the low walls of the allotments.

After them came Rukkh and the rest of the surviving Blitzers, their war cry on their lips.

At the wall a fresh force of monkeys stood up. Hun-

dreds of bows let fly, and a swarm of arrows fell on the
Blitzers. A loud *crack-whine* from the top of the dune
signified another of those damned seven-foot-long spears
and it zinged into their ranks a moment later, but missed
and slammed harmlessly into the sand.

Big Uruk hauled it out and waved it at the pullulating,
pestilential monkeys, and they all cheered.

Then they were up on the wall and fighting toe-to-toe
with a solid line of monkeys.

The fight teetered there for several minutes as the two
lines stabbed and hacked at each other. The Blitzers gave
it everything, but the monkeys would not step back.
Dead bodies heaped up on both sides of the shallow
walls. The little vegetable gardens were smashed to pulp
beneath the feet of the combatants.

Then, just as the monkeys were starting to give—big
Uruk had thrown one bodily through their shield wall
and Chaz had exploited the gap with a beautiful thrust
of the spear—there came a lot of noise from the left and
another mob of monkeys came running up and threw
themselves into the fight.

At their head was one who wielded only a sword. He
fought with such speed and grace that men's bodies tum-
bled away from him to either side with a steady, relent-
lessness that was terrifying to see. There was something
familiar about him to Rukkh. And then he recalled him
from a fight in the streets of a small place they had taken
and burned.

Oggi was on Rukkh's right. He was the next to engage
the monkey with the sword. Rukkh was squeezed between Oggi and Konigswat and he missed the next series
of motions, but it ended with Oggi's scream, a last shriek
of hate and anger. Then, as the sword flashed and Oggi's
head flew away, the shriek cut off instantly.

Rukkh slammed his shield into the side of the monkey.
It was caught unprepared and went down on its knees.
Rukkh fell on top of it, pushed from behind by Konigswat, who was struggling with another one of the really
big monkeys.

Rukkh kicked out, knocked the enemy away, and got back on his knees. At which point something hard and heavy came down on the back of his helmet and just about brained him.

When he came to, he was being dragged across the ground. His head was still ringing like a bell. Then hands released him. Feet trampled him. He struggled to sit up. His head was still not right, but he was alive. He found a shield, then a spear, and moved to regain the line.

They were at the next low stone wall, and the fight was just as it had been. Spears stabbing back and forth while shields smashed together. The monkeys just would not give ground any farther. They died there by the dozens, and the bodies mounded up, but they would not break. And the men were dying, too, and they could not take these kinds of casualties for long.

Suddenly the bugle was blowing for a retreat, and Burok was bellowing. Sergeant Hugga was roaring, too, and the Blitzers backed off, disengaged, and retired to the first stone wall.

The monkeys had lost all organization, and they, too, were not ready to resume the fight. But the Blitzers' position was untenable, because to their immediate right rose up the tip of the sand dune. A hundred feet above them there were monkeys and those damned catapults.

Another huge spear flashed down, and there was a shriek on the line and some poor bastard was skewered. It took him ten minutes of agony to die.

Again the bugle blew and they withdrew and moved back in good order to the previous front line. The monkeys were not ready yet to reengage. The casualties had been too many, and their formations were completely disorganized.

They stood there, panting, chests heaving, then they looked to wounds. Everyone had some by then, from what had turned into the biggest fight they could remember. The monkeys held their ground, the giant spears were the only threat for the moment. After a while even they ceased to fire.

The Blitzers realized the fighting was over. The lines stood down. Burok went round to count casualties, and men with wounds were told to assemble for treatment.

Rukkh heard that Forjal had been taken off in one of the first boats. Good old Forjal was one tough bastard of a soldier. Must have run two hundred yards holding his Goddamn guts in. Rukkh sent up a prayer to the Great God.

Give your grace to old Forjal, He Who Eats.

About then the ships appeared at last, tacking into the bay and dropping their anchors. There came a ragged cheer from the army on the bloodstained shore. The ships, however, remained much farther from the shore than on the previous day, so the boats took far longer going back and forth.

A medical tent was set up just for the Blitzers, some food was brought up, and they gathered around the cauldrons. Everyone was pretty quiet. The sun was barely over the horizon and already they'd fought a major battle and lost more than a hundred men. The mighty Blitzers were now reduced to fewer than four hundred men capable of fighting.

Chapter 50

Admiral Heuze was finding it harder and harder to take the repeated shocks thrown up by the battle. The monkeys were proving themselves to be tough opponents, against all predictions, they were many thousands of miles from home, and there were no reinforcements in the offing. The situation, in a word, was precarious.

All through the morning hours the fleet beat its way back up the coast against a stiffening north wind. When they finally slipped into the bay, reduced sail, and lowered their anchors, they found the army in a state approaching complete disaster. Heuze felt his head begin to pound as soon as he read the reports.

General Raltt had been surprised by a dawn attack and had fought a desperate rearguard battle back and forth over the beach in the first hours of daylight. Hundreds more good men had been lost. Now the army was just sitting there, pulled into a defensive arc on the beach while suffering constant harrying fire from enemy archers and catapults. Casualties in the first full day of this campaign were approaching a thousand, half of them fatalities. That was unacceptable. Who knew how many such battles they might have yet to fight to subdue and destroy the pestilential monkeys?

Heuze could hardly believe that Raltt had let himself be surprised and pushed back to the water's edge. He sent a message requesting Raltt's appearance on the flagship at once. Raltt sent a message back saying that his presence was required on the battlefield. The monkeys might attack at any moment.

After counting to a hundred to try to calm himself, Heuze ordered his personal barge and went ashore. He had the sense that the expedition itself was hanging in the balance. He had to intervene here personally to turn things around.

Filek jumped at the chance to accompany the admiral, filling the barge with extra medical supplies, which he was sure would be needed.

The admiral's barge surged over the water, impelled by twelve strong men. Filek admired the coastline. What struck him every time was the lushness of the place. Above the shallow cliffs and sandy beaches grew enormous trees in wild profusion. It was uncanny to one more familiar with the barren lands of Shasht.

Ahead was the line of the beach, waves crashing on the shore. Yellow sand dunes rose up beyond the beach. On their tops was a dark mass that had to be monkeys and their shields. Filek shivered. There were the weavers of those amazing mats. There were the potters and wood-carvers whose work he had marveled over.

Then he saw the beach. By the Great God's Wrath, the place was a slaughterhouse. There were dozens of bodies washing in the surf, some of them women from the *Growler*. Filek shuddered with disgust. To think of the women of Shasht dishonored by public exposure in this way was horrifying to his soul. And he breathed a prayer to the Great God that he didn't even believe in, because the disaster could so easily have befallen the *Anvil* rather than the *Growler*.

The barge was run ashore, and the admiral was lifted out by the bargees and set on the shore. He dug his crutches into the shingle and heaved himself up the beach. There was no one to meet him, and he was furious at the lack of respect.

While Heuze stormed off to see General Raltt, Filek oversaw the unloading of the supplies he'd brought and had them taken to the medical tents. The tents were virtually madhouses, the surgeons working flat out for hours on the horde of wounded that were camped around them. The wailing, the stench, the baskets of amputated limbs, it was all stomach-churning.

One of the first serious cases Filek was confronted with was Forjal from the Blitzers. The medics had pushed his innards back inside him and sewn him up. The man was pale, there had been considerable loss of blood, but his heartbeat seemed perfectly regular. Filek noted that the man's body was already covered in scars. He was obviously a hell of a fighter. Filek had Forjal put at the head of the list to be ferried out to the *Anvil*. He would take that case himself out of sheer curiosity. It was unusual for a man to live so long after being partially eviscerated. This Forjal must be incredibly tough.

Meanwhile, farther along the beach Admiral Heuze had found General Raltt and his staff standing by a field table poring over the scouting chart. Forewarned of Heuze's approach, Raltt was working furiously on a "plan." There were still details to try to work out, though, lots of details.

Heuze swung himself past the adjutant and right up to Raltt's map table.

"General Raltt, what is the meaning of this?"

"Excuse me, Admiral, but I'm in the middle of something important."

"You'll be in the middle of a trial before the priests if you don't stop this insubordination and start listening to me."

"Admiral Heuze, do you think that by pulling rank at this moment, when our forces are locked in combat here, that you are helping the situation?"

Heuze looked around himself slowly.

"You are not locked in combat, General. There has been a battle, and I see that you have lost much of our army. But you are not fighting right now. And our army is hemmed in on the beach where it landed, a full day and a night after it was put ashore. What is going on, General?"

Raltt sighed. He knew he would have to give in. Heuze

outranked him, and the Hand of Aeswiren would enforce military discipline.

"I'm sorry, Admiral Heuze. I apologize for not being able to greet you personally as you stepped ashore. I am busy trying to come up with some remedies for the serious situation we find ourselves in."

"Why in the name of the purple ass of He Who Eats are we in this so-called 'serious situation'?"

"It's, ah, hard to say, Admiral Heuze." Raltt was a little shocked at such open blasphemy. Things were obviously a bit different in the fleet. The army was more straitlaced about this sort of thing.

"When I assumed command, the line was pretty much where it is now, but we were fighting off an assault from the sand dunes. Since then we've fought off another assault during the early dawn. We counterattacked and drove the enemy back to his lines, but we could not hold our position there because of enemy missiles from the top of the dune."

"General Uisbank was responsible for the loss of the dune top, correct?"

"Ah, yes, Admiral Heuze."

"So what we have here is a complete failure by the army command, correct?"

"I wouldn't say that, Admiral. General Uisbank was taken by surprise."

"And what happened at dawn?"

"Well, I don't know how they did it, but the damned monkeys crept up on the Blitzers' front and weren't noticed."

"So it was the fault of the Blitzers?"

Raltt stiffened. "You will find everything in my report when it's done. Right now I have to win a battle."

"Yes, of course. Enlighten me; I would like to know how you plan to do it."

Raltt gritted his teeth. "Then watch, but please don't interrupt while I explain things to my officers. Clarity is very important right now."

Heuze gave an angry snort as they both turned to the

big chart spread out on the table. He would have the general's hide pegged out under the sun eventually, but for now he needed to win this battle.

There on the chart it was all laid out quite plainly, a complete military nightmare. They had landed, been stiffed in their attack, and pushed back into a shallow salient on the beach and the plain in front of the city walls. The enemy had the high points of both ends of the field. To the left they held the city walls and on the right they held the line of dunes that sat back from the beach.

Raltt fought to control the nervousness he felt. This was his first major command, and he had been dealt an atrocious hand.

"All right, listen up. We will strengthen our right and force the top of the dunes farther down the line. Then we will push the enemy off the dunes entirely and regain control of the situation. Understood?"

They nodded as if impressed by his military genius, though anyone could see that they didn't have a lot of choices.

"So units of the First, Second, and Third Regiments will detach and move along the line to the right. I will leave it to unit commanders to select which sections they wish to send, but remember we want the men who are freshest and ready to give it their all today. All right? Any questions?"

There were none.

"Good. Orders will be drawn up."

Heuze stilled any critical thoughts. There were more important fish to fry.

"Well, General, it looks like the best thing available. I will land more regiments on the southern part of the beach, and that will help speed things up."

"Admiral, that would be wonderful. If we could have the five regiments still aboard ship, I think we could guarantee to sweep these dunes clear of the enemy."

"Of course it is going to take an hour or two to get

those men ashore. I daren't come in too close, not after last night."

Raltt pursed his lips. Naturally, the fleet commander was nervous, after the previous night's fireworks. However, from the army's point of view, it was essential to get some reinforcement on that right wing and force the monkeys off the high ground on the dunes. More than ever, Raltt regretted Uisbank's cavalier refusal to fortify that dune top when they first had it.

The officers milled there for a few moments while the clerks wrote out their orders and stamped them with the general's seal.

Raltt and Heuze looked over the map while Raltt tried to get Heuze to put the men aboard one of the smaller ships and send them in at once.

"Even an hour might make a great difference."

Heuze was about to respond, but at that very moment one of the admiral's bargees came running up, face filled with fear.

"Admiral, begging your pardon for interrupting, like, but Lieutenant Kligg says you should take a look at the entrance to the city harbor."

Heuze snapped up his spyglass. His blood ran cold as ice.

"Another God-damned fireship!" he exploded. "Look! Sails all filthy brown and she's coming out as proud as you damned well please."

Heuze turned back to the bargee.

"Ready the barge!"

Then to Raltt.

"I have to get back to my ship; we may have to maneuver until we can destroy that filthy little cog they're sending out."

"What about the reinforcements? I need to build up that right wing."

"As soon as possible we'll set them down."

"What does that mean?"

"Just that, as soon as possible."

And then with a sudden blare of bugles they became aware that the monkeys had started another attack. This time it fell on the First Regiment, which was on the farthest left of the line, facing the walls of the monkey town. The gates there had opened again and a column of monkeys came charging out, straight along the top of the beach toward the First Regiment. At the same time a pair of trebuchets, located behind the city walls, began to throw huge rocks over the walls, high into the sky and down on the First Regiment's position. The rocks weighed hundreds of pounds, and where they landed the First Regiment broke aside in disorder.

Raltt and his staff swung their attention to the new threat. The left flank had to be held. Further thoughts about strengthening the right wing were forgotten for the moment.

Heuze hurried over to the medical tents, where he found Filek already stained red from neck to waist.

"We should get back to the ship at once. The enemy has another of those damned fireships."

Filek's eyes widened. He took off his apron and followed the admiral. Something told Filek just then that he did not want to be left behind on this bloodstained beach. It was possible that he might never get another chance to leave it.

Back they went, through the throngs of wounded men, while Heuze said nothing, but kept looking anxiously over to the harbor where the dark brown sails were filling. The small monkey ship was clearly visible now, a small bow wave breaking white before her.

Filek stared for a moment. All that talk about how stupid the monkeys were seemed painfully incorrect.

However, poor Filek was in for another unpleasant surprise. For with everyone's eyes on the fireship and her nasty brown sails, no one had noticed the swimmers in the water off the beach.

Two dozen brilbies, the best swimmers in all Dronned, were swimming across the water from the end of the harbor mole. They used a careful stroke and avoided kicking up the water. As they got closer, they moved quietly in toward the admiral's barge where it waited on the shore. The bargees, meanwhile, were drawn up in two lines on the sand, waiting for the admiral, who was approaching on his crutches.

Suddenly the brilbies swarmed up out of the water on either side of the barge, flourishing swords and clubs, and took the poor bargees completely by surprise. In a matter of moments five men were down, and the rest were running away.

The admiral gave a weird little scream as he saw the big-shouldered monkeys heaving the barge off the shingle and back into the water.

"No, you fools," he screamed at his men. "Stop them! They're taking the barge!"

The bargees halted, spun around, and with a collective roar of rage sprang back to recover the barge.

For a moment it seemed that a disaster would be averted. Filek even felt a cheer begin in his throat.

But at the waterline a row of even grimmer brilbies turned back and took sword and club to the bargees with a will. Two more men died then and there. The others could do nothing but retreat out of the water, stand on the beach, and throw rocks at the barge. Then the monkeys turned and swam out.

Some soldiers had come up by then and arrows and javelins were hurled out at the swimmers. Just one of the fornicating monkeys was hit and fell off the barge. Another dived in immediately to rescue it and both were pulled from the water. The monkeys worked the oars as if they had been born to them, and the barge swiftly pulled away toward the city harbor. More arrows pursued it, and some hits were claimed, but it did not waver in its progress toward the harbor.

Admiral Heuze was left stranded, a couple of miles from his flagship, while a fireship was sailing out to attack the fleet. Along with him was Filek Biswas, an enormous mass of dismay cooling in his belly.

Suddenly bugles started blowing urgently over on the right wing, where more monkeys were massing on the tops of the dunes, well south of the end of the Shasht

army line. In fact they had occupied the exact part of
the dune that Raltt and Heuze had intended to seize
with the reinforcements.

Admiral Heuze's eyes had a strange look as they
glanced up to Filek. *It's fear,* thought Filek. *He's afraid.*

Chapter 51

The day was coming to an end, and Simona knew that the fighting was over. The distant roaring and screaming had stopped, so had the strange, ominous thudding sounds made by the huge, unseen trebuchets placed in the streets near the palace where she was confined.

Her eyes were red from weeping, her hands sore from being wrung together. Men and mots were being killed, and she was torn by her feelings as a woman of her race and also by her concern for her newfound friends. The combination left her confused and fretful.

Try as she might to shake it, the fear of a total defeat for the colony gripped her. And yet she could not in her heart wish for a victory for the men of Shasht, either. How could she wish such a horror upon a folk like the mots of the Land?

She shuddered when she thought of the teachings of the priests. The "monkeys," they said, were just animals to be slaughtered and displaced. But she had seen their world, and it was as fine as anything in Shasht. The palace was small, especially compared to the grandiose structures of Aeswiren, but it was beautiful. Carvings in dark wood of fantastic quality covered many walls. Beautiful mats decorated the floors and other walls. Everything was clean and freshly painted and lovingly cared for.

And this ancient civilization was to be simply brushed aside and destroyed to make way for the colony? She could not accept that. There had to be a better way than just out-and-out murder.

Thoughts like these had run through her head all day while she listened to the distant sounds of the fighting. Sometimes she heard vague crashing in the distance, like storm waves on a beach; at other times there were bugles blowing near and far.

At times she wondered if poor Rukkh had been slain. Of course, going back to her own people now was likely to lead to a death sentence. She recalled the hysterical hate in the general's voice when he penetrated the disguise and called her "traitor!"

And then, at last, Thru had come.

"Thru! Thank you for coming. Thank you so much. This has been very hard today."

"I came as soon as I could."

"I heard fighting, but the guards will not speak to me. Will you tell me what has been happening?"

"Well, there has been hard fighting. But we think they are beaten now. Tomorrow we will make them surrender, I think."

Simona was shocked. "How?" she began, one hand to her mouth, her lip trembling.

"Well, on the first day we stopped their attack and eventually pushed them back to the beach. Today we stopped two attacks and pressed them back into a smaller space. They have lost many men. We sent them a message to offer them the chance to surrender and avoid further bloodshed."

"Oh!" Could it be possible? A surrender would surely end the war.

"They killed the messenger and threw his head out onto the battlefield."

"Oh."

"And last night, we burned one of their ships. Sent a fireship."

"Oh, by the Great God, that is awful."

"Yes." Thru was nodding in agreement.

"What happened?"

"The ship burned and sank. Many men, many women died. Their bodies are washing up all along the bay."

Thru gave an eloquent shrug. "But this is not a war that we began. We are not trying to invade Shasht. We would not kill any of your people unless we had to."

Simona gulped, swallowed. Oh, by the Great God she was such a traitor, such a vile wretch. But at the same time she knew that he was right.

"Which ship was it?"

"It was the fourth one in the line, counting from the nearest one to the city."

"The fourth?" Simona's eyes grew wide. "It was the *Growler* then." She broke down then and wept for the people she had spent a year's confinement with. Poor Aunty Jemelm, to survive the plague only to die of fire. Unless, poor thing, she had drowned.

Thru understood something of Simona's pain. They had spoken of their families, he knew her mother had died in the plague and that her father still lived. Through no fault of her own, she was now caught in a strange and frightening position.

He took her into his arms and comforted her as if she were a mor while she rested her head on his shoulder and wet his fur with her tears.

When she spoke again it was with a husk to her voice.

"My mother and I lived on that ship for the whole voyage. We transferred only recently. All those people I knew, to think of them drowned like that, is awful."

"Yes, it is terrible. I am sorry for it, but we have to strike back at them with every weapon we have. We have no choice if we are to survive."

"But what of our survival?" she said. "If we cannot have the colony, then I don't know what will become of us all."

"You will have to go back to your homeland."

She sighed. The wrath of Aeswiren III was all too easy to imagine.

Sometime later, Thru made his way to Toshak's command post, now set up in the south gate. The initiative had passed completely to Toshak, it seemed. The enemy had tried to break out and had failed. His fleet had quit the bay and not been seen since. Thru found Toshak enjoying a light meal while contemplating the map of the battlefield that had been set up on the wall of the command post, his head bandaged like half the army.

"Come, Thru Gillo, will you eat with me?"

"Of course, General Toshak. Has anything changed?"

"Not since darkness fell. The enemy stay inside their trenches and lick their wounds. I think they may be running short of food and water. The fleet meant to resupply them today I would imagine, but it has not been seen."

"The winds outside the bay are unfavorable, I heard."

"That is what I hear, too, altogether too fresh and lively."

Thru tore into the fresh bread. A mussel stew thickened with seaplums was brought out.

"They pressed us hard today."

"They were desperate. Those were the attacks of a force reaching the ends of its strength. Both times they put far too much of their force into the assault and left themselves open to attack on the rest of their line. On both occasions it was our ability to flood their line and threaten to cut them off from the beach that ended their assaults on our lines."

"And so they are beaten?"

"I think it is close to that. They occupy less of the Land tonight than they did in the morning. And they have left many dead on our sands."

"What do you expect, tomorrow?"

"They will probably make us kill them. I do not expect them to surrender." Toshak spoke with the certainty of a trained warrior. Thru hoped he was wrong.

"They are brave, but their commanders are stupid."

"Perhaps they underestimated us. They will learn."

"Does that mean that it isn't over?"

"The fleet still exists. They have more men. What other choice do they have?"

Thru tore off more bread and chewed in silence.

Chapter 52

Darkness lay over the Land. The great red star had risen in the southeast and cast its baleful light across the beach south of the monkey city. Admiral Heuze, sitting with Biswas and a few surviving members of his barge crew, struggled to contain his rage and anguish.

"We're barely hanging on here," he muttered to Filek.

The wind had come up a little bit, and small waves were breaking on the beach.

The army now controlled only a shallow salient on the beach, with a small extension northward onto the city plain. Twice they had failed to break the lines of the monkey army, and twice the monkeys had fought them back to the beach. Now they were done. There were fewer than nine hundred effective soldiers left. More than a thousand dead lay on the beach or washed to and fro in the shallows. Thousands more were hurt or just worn-out. They had run out of water long before, and their food supplies were very low.

The medical tents had been overrun by the monkeys during the frenzy of the second counterattack. The monkeys took away most of the tools and metal things they found. Filek's work had been severely hampered. Among the things stolen had been the surgical-thread cache.

Men with terrible wounds could no longer be stitched up. But with the lack of surgical alcohol, most of the seriously wounded men would die anyway.

"It looks bad," Filek had to agree.

"This has been a pitiful performance," snarled Heuze. "These are some of the best troops in all of Shasht. They earned the right to be in this colony. It was their chance to raise their social status."

"The enemy is clever enough to take advantage of mistakes, that's for sure."

"Oh, thank you, Master Biswas, for that helpful remark."

"I'm sorry, Admiral. We all underestimated them. Who would think they would know to take our surgical spirits and our knives? Half these men around us will die."

Nor did it help that the admiral had understood from the beginning the depth of his error. He'd advertised his presence to the watching enemy, coming in on his big barge. The enemy had struck at the barge and thus cut him off from returning to the fleet before the fireship got out. The fleet then slipped anchor and ran out of the bay, determined not to allow a repetition of the *Growler* fiasco.

Just like Uisbank, he'd allowed the enemy to decapitate the command. Now he'd be lucky if he didn't join General Uisbank in the custody of the sodomizing monkeys. By the bright blue ass of the Great God, this was getting to be a desperate situation.

"If they attack in the morning, they will overwhelm us," he moaned.

"Then we must kill each other. If you like, I will open your veins tonight, and you can die relatively painlessly."

Heuze grinned at him. "Not yet, my friend. Not yet. I think I'll wait until the end for that."

But inside, Heuze was not grinning. He was the admiral of the fleet, in command of the entire expedition. He wasn't supposed to go out like this, trapped like a rat on the beach.

And at the back of his mind rose the thought, over and over again, that Captain Pukh and the rest of them had betrayed him. They had decided they might as well let the army be destroyed, if it got rid of Heuze and left the command open to them. Heuze sighed heavily. Then they'd start fighting each other, and the Hand would try to kill them off, and it would all end in bloodshed and the demise of the colony. Heuze's name would go down in history as a dolt who'd lost his fleet.

"Look, a light!" A soldier was standing up, pointing out to sea.

"Where?" growled Heuze, getting painfully up onto his good leg with a crutch jammed under his arm. His back was sore from spending the day standing and crouching on this damned beach, but the sudden hope quenched the pain.

There it was, undoubtedly a light.

"Quickly, raise the lantern and then lower it slowly."

Men scrambled to obey and a lantern was lofted up and then lowered slowly down again.

The light winked back a message at once, using the naval code of long and short blinks of the light.

Heuze gave a cheer as he read the blinking light. It was good old Captain Pukh, who'd brought the fleet back.

He ordered the smaller, swifter ships to enter the bay and set down boats to take them off immediately. The larger, less nimble vessels were to stay outside, away from the potential damage from the fireship that was still in the harbor.

Then he passed on orders for water and surgical spirit and tools on Filek's behalf. General Raltt had joined them by then.

"General," said Heuze with a smile, "the fleet is back, and I've ordered three ships to come in and pick us up tonight."

"Thank the Great God, we may yet get out of this alive."

Heuze smiled unpleasantly. He would attend to Raltt's trial himself. Then he would cure the skin carefully, and have nice little moccasins made of it.

"Ready your men. We will need to move some of the wounded first. We must uphold discipline here."

"Of course, Admiral." General Raltt seethed at the implied insult to his troops. "They are warriors of Shasht; they will hold the line until the end."

"If the monkeys attack while we're doing this, we have to hold them off."

"We will leave their heads on the sand if they attack."

"That'd be good. Because we've left enough of our own."

Raltt bowed his head. There was nothing to be said.

He withdrew and prepared orders for the evacuation. They would begin with the walking wounded and the serious cases that could be moved. Then they would take the lightly wounded, starting with the First Regiment and going through to the Blitzers at the end.

Meanwhile Heuze was waiting impatiently for a barge to take him off. As it came he hummed to himself Kadawak's "Song of Triumph" from Hugel's great opera, *Blood and Iron.*

This was the moment when Kadawak came upon the maidens and captured them for his fire. Heuze was very fond of the scene with its slow-mounting music of triumph as Kadawak stalked across the stage, and the drums began to thunder.

They had taken a licking, no doubt about it. But he, Heuze, would survive, and he would take this lesson to heart. The monkeys were no fools. Whatever the priests said they were, they were smart enough to have learned how to fight somewhere.

At last the barge grounded in the slight surf and Heuze hurried to it. Filek went with him. There was a lot to do to prepare the fleet surgeries for the onslaught of the wounded. Filek was thinking purely about the logistics of lifting the worst wounded out of the boats and down to the surgery. A sling of some sort hung from the main yard might be the best way. The bosun would come up with something ingenious. You could always trust the sailors, they were a remarkably competent group.

Meanwhile, on the tower above the south gate of Dronned, Toshak conferred with the Assenzi.

"Three ships have entered the inner part of the bay. They appear to be the smaller, more maneuverable ships."

"So they're still afraid of the fireship," said Melidofulo.

"That ought to hamper their efforts," murmured Utnapishtim.

Toshak had moved small markers on the map to show where the frigates had anchored.

"We assume they intend to take off their forces in the night. The question is whether we should risk attacking them in the dark or not."

"It would be more merciful to just let them go," Melidofulo said.

"Yes, of course," said Utnapishtim. "But we must carefully evaluate this. The more damage we can inflict on them here, the more likely they will leave and not return."

Old Graedon broke in. "The question might be better phrased, 'What can we do to them?'"

"Exactly. Trust you, old friend, to go to the heart of the matter. What can we do in this situation?"

The Assenzi looked to Toshak, who considered his words carefully.

"We could attack them. But I don't know how well our units would perform in the dark. They have enough trouble keeping a disciplined front in daylight. After the first command they turn into a mob."

"We could bring out the trebuchets and hurry the enemy along," Graedon suggested.

"Yes," said Toshak, "that's what I was leaning toward myself. Too much risk of heavy casualties in a night assault, and we have already taken too many."

"Yes, that is true." Utnapishtim agreed. The day's toll had been awful, more than fifteen hundred dead and another thousand with serious wounds. The only saving grace was that the enemy had suffered as badly. But could there be any grace in a situation with so much bloodshed? Utnapishtim doubted it.

"How long to dismantle them and bring them outside the city?"

"I believe the youngsters who do that job would surprise us all."

Utnapishtim accepted this. "All right, let's do that for now. We've inflicted a strong check on their ambitions; Spirit willing it will be enough."

"The young woman told us that they face starvation unless they can land here."

"Then they will starve somewhere else, for we will not feed them, and they will die if they land here."

"There is more we could do," old Master Graedon spoke again.

Utnapishtim nodded. "It is savage."

"Agreed, but it could be very effective."

Toshak understood, too.

"Yes, we do have the other fireship. We could strike when the ships are loaded down with men. If we can destroy another ship, it will surely drive them away forever."

Melidofulo made a grimace of disgust.

"Surely this is the way of our enemy, to attack the wounded, the females, and children?"

"Yes, that is perfectly true," said Toshak. "The question is, should we do this to ensure their complete defeat, and our own safety?"

Melidofulo looked to the heavens for guidance. Red Kemm glared balefully over the southern hills. To condemn so many, now that they were already defeated and driven from the field. Was it not against the will of the Spirit?

"I wonder what Cutshamakim would say," he said at last.

Utnapishtim looked to Graedon; both of them shrugged. The great spiritual leader of the Assenzi was far away in Highnoth.

"In my experience," said Utnapishtim, "Cutshamakim has always stressed practicality. I expect he would see how strong our need is. He would understand the tragic aspects, but I think he would go forward."

"They must be taught a lesson," said Graedon. "And we have already taken too many casualties."

Melidofulo sighed. "If it must be, so be it."

Admiral Heuze and Filek rode off the beach of the damned on the first boat. After them came the worst of the walking wounded, then the nonambulatory wounded who could survive such a trip. Meanwhile, the rest of the wounded, who could not be moved, received the knife of mercy.

The boats kept moving to and fro. The red star set well before moonrise and then the sky filled with clouds as a breeze sprang up from the southwest. The frigates were dimly visible out on the water. On the shore, men waited in lines for evacuation while boats came in and went back out at a steady rate.

Suddenly there came that awful thud of the giant stone-throwing catapult.

"Watch out!" shouted a voice.

And then out of the night sky fell a rock the size of a man, plowing into the beach at the waterline and throwing up a splash of sand and water.

It fell ten feet from the nearest boat, causing no damage. But every man's heart skipped a beat.

There was another thud almost immediately. The motion toward the boats had halted and every eye was looking up into the dark sky.

Rukkh was in the shallow water by then, about to get aboard a boat. Some sixth sense made him jump back a step and the next moment the stone struck the prow of the boat and flipped it up on its endbeams and over, hurling screaming men in all directions.

Rukkh fell over and a wave washed over him. The wounds on his hip and face stung from the salt. The boat was upside down, several men trapped underneath.

Rukkh got back on his feet, pushed forward, and helped turn the boat back over.

The front of the boat was stove in. Some of the oars had been smashed. With cries of disgust the men stood back from the useless thing. Another thud came, and they all looked up. The stone was visible for a fraction of a second, a dark mass poised against the night, and then it fell on the shoreline harmlessly, throwing up a big splash in the shallows.

From then on the evacuation became much more chaotic.

Toshak and Graedon had organized a regiment of donkey carts that ferried rocks from the seapond walls down to the line of trebuchets that had been set up on the plain. Two or three stones a minute rained down on the nervous men inside the shield wall. Most missed, but the occasional hits produced spectacular carnage.

As soon as he was aboard *Perch*, Admiral Heuze took steps to regain control. *Perch* was a swift frigate and her captain, Hujuk, was an able type. The other ships in the bay were *Shark*, another frigate, and *Grampus*, the smallest of the great ships, in the same class as the *Growler*.

Waiting for him was a private message from Pukh. The situation was not quite as good as he had hoped. Captain Kuhgo had mutinied, or something very close to mutiny. On hearing that Heuze was stranded on the beach, he had declared an emergency and taken the big ship *Crusher* out on her own.

There was some sentiment in the fleet in Kuhgo's favor. Nebbeggebben was rumored to be considering siding with Kuhgo.

Meanwhile, aboard *Anvil* Captain Pukh had put Sub-Admiral Geppugo into irons because Geppugo had tried to take control and move the entire fleet back out to sea. Geppugo had declared that they should abandon the attempt to colonize the monkeys' land and go south to the wider oceans and search for easier opportunities.

Heuze's blood boiled when he read all this. That treacherous swine Geppugo would go to the priests at the soonest opportunity, while Kuhgo would hang, as soon as a court-martial could be held.

To calm himself Heuze bathed, put on clean clothes, and took some dinner with a mug of mulled wine. He sent for Biswas to keep him company.

Biswas came in, also wearing clean clothes and with the blood washed from his face and hair.

"There you are, Filek. Have some wine. Pretty horrible work you've been at I expect."

Filek took the wine eagerly. He had long since become
immune to the horrors of his work, but the sheer volume
of it on this day had been overwhelming. He had sewed
dozens of men back together, three men dying even as
he operated on them.

The wine was sweet and warm, and he knocked back
a couple of mouthfuls and enjoyed the sensation it produced.

"We have much to thank Captain Pukh for, my
friend." The admiral had dropped his voice to his conspiratorial whisper.

Filek leaned forward to listen carefully.

"Geppugo tried to move the fleet south, abandoning
us."

Filek swallowed. Such treachery was hard to fathom.
"The priests will rip his heart out of his chest."

"Only after they have questioned him for days. It will
not be an easy death for Geppugo."

They sipped wine, thinking quietly.

"And what of ourselves. What are we going to do?"
Filek wondered.

"Isn't it obvious?"

Filek shook his head. "No. This was a terrible defeat."

"My friend, how many times was Aeswiren defeated
before he won the throne?"

"Thrice, of course."

"Well, our men are soldiers of Shasht. They will fight
much better next time."

"Next time?"

"We will regain our strength and make another landing. This time we will choose a place that is farther away
from a monkey town. We underestimated them. I will
not allow us to do that again."

"General Raltt did his best."

"Perhaps." Heuze did not tell Filek what Raltt's fate
was to be. "It was Uisbank's fault mostly. The early attack had no subtlety to it. He simply assumed the Blitzers

could smash their way in. They killed an ungodly number of monkeys, but they could not break their lines."

"What do you think became of General Uisbank?"

Heuze shrugged and drank off the last of his wine.

"Frankly, I hope they roasted him alive. He was unforgivably stupid."

Heuze made no mention of his own mistake, riding in showily in his barge in full view of the enemy. They had struck at him just as they'd struck at Uisbank, and but for Captain Pukh they might have taken him, too. He had already decided that he would never step foot on this accursed land again until it was pacified and the monkeys were no more.

Filek was secretly appalled at the thought of another battle. They had lost more than a thousand dead and many more would die of their wounds in the next few days. He sipped the wine, but now he scarcely tasted it.

There came a knock, and they heard excited voices on deck. Feet were thundering in the corridors. The door shot open.

"Sir, we have sighting of another fireship. Sir."

"What?" Heuze bolted up out of his chair, sending his mug clattering across the floor.

They ran on deck. Heuze jumped up to the rigging.

"Off the starboard side, coming from the harbor. Same kind as chased out the fleet before."

Heuze stared at the dirty little cog, dimly visible in the moonlight as it came around the end of the mole.

Orders rang out across the three ships, and crews hurried to raise the anchors and set sails. Within ten minutes *Perch* was under way and began to tack out of the inner bay. The cog was slower than the elegant frigate and would never catch them.

The fleet's boats, filled with exhausted men, pulled after them.

Shark came around quickly, her captain wasting no time, and left the boats in her wake.

Grampus threw down lines for the nearest boats to

take up, then turned and set sail. But she was not a good ship in light winds and was slow in getting under way.

By the time *Grampus* was moving seaward at more than a crawl, the evil little cog with her black-daubed sails was astride the route out of the bay. Captain Fulz ordered *Grampus*'s catapults readied, and men with oars stood by to repulse the cog if she came alongside.

On the next tack *Grampus* turned, ahead of the cog, but she was approaching on an intersecting course. Fulz trimmed sail, slowed, turned back. The cog matched his maneuver and, with the wind in her favor, came on quickly.

At the last moment Fulz tacked again, the terrified sailors racing through the changes of sail.

For a long moment it looked as if they had succeeded, but then a puff of wind picked the small ship up and thrust her forward. The sharp ram drove home directly into *Grampus*'s bow and the bigger ship shuddered all the way down to her beam ends.

Men hurled themselves down into the cog to fight the mots, but it was already too late. Flames were licking up from the hold, the fumes of paraffin caught with a dull boom, and a blue ball of fire rose and ignited *Grampus*'s main foresail. Flames engulfed the cog, and the men were forced to dive overboard and abandon her, still held fast to *Grampus*'s side by the ram.

Ropes and yards were alight above, and tackle fell with a crash as the sails burned. *Grampus* became a scene out of hell, as hundreds hurled themselves into the sea to avoid the spreading conflagration.

Shark and *Perch* returned, and every boat was summoned from the fleet hovering outside the bay. But nothing could save *Grampus* herself, and she burned to the waterline, while the boats continued plying to and from the shore bringing off the army.

Unfortunately the process was slowed by the long trips back and forth to the fleet, waiting outside the bay. By the early light of dawn there were still two hundred men trapped on the beach.

The enemy moved forward immediately, and a hail of

rrows and stones fell on the doomed rear guard. Then
or a moment it stopped, and a voice called clearly and
oudly for their surrender, in perfect Shashti.

But the warriors of Shasht did not surrender.

There was a long moment of hesitation, and then the
nemy moved forward with a rush. The fight was short
nd horrid and ended with the mots overwhelming the
ing of men, pulling them down while dozens of spears
hrust home.

They already had sullen, uncooperative prisoners.
'hey had decided to take no more of them.

Out on the fleet the disaster was still being tallied up.

"I have a list of sixteen hundred dead and eighteen
undred with wounds."

"Does that count the women from *Grampus*?"

"No. Nor the women from *Growler*."

Heuze stared across his stateroom at the eerily beauti-
ul rug on the wall. The bright ocher birds chased the
vil-looking beetles in such a merry manner. He felt a
trong urge to scream and smash things.

Two yellow tops had summoned him to visit Nebbeg-
ebben aboard *Hammer,* the royal heir's flagship. The
Iand were waiting for him over there.

Chapter 53

Simona was shocked by how many bodies there wer
laid out in neat rows along the top of the beach. Most
they were men, stripped of armor, weapons, even the
boots and sandals, but among them were the women wh
had drowned. Many had a strangely peaceful look abo
them, as if they'd died in their sleep and not drowne
in the cold waters of an alien land. The men, on th
other hand, were often open-eyed, faces still imprinte
with the final agony, exhibiting every kind of woun
Simona had often thought about the things her fathe
dealt with in his work; here she confronted it. It wa
simply horrifying.

She was violently ill on the sand after the first disen
boweled corpse, but after that she just paused an
squeezed her eyes shut when she saw something particu
larly awful. Thru Gillo helped her with a steadying han
at the worst times.

It was the strangest day in her life, she thought, an
she'd seen some strange ones indeed, since that fishin
boat had plucked her from the sea.

All her life had been lived inside a bubble of safet
until Filek Biswas had been cast into the expeditionar
force. Aboard the *Growler* she'd learned a lot of awf
lessons. And then when she'd tried to kill herself a whol
new set of lessons had been laid before her.

It was the first daytime she'd been outside since tha
rescue. The sky felt huge, the land enormous and gree
The city was both familiar and yet alien, with tall house

of stone and slate roofs, but all so strangely designed compared to classical Shasht.

"How do you keep the streets so clean?" she'd said to Thru, as they went through the city. There were eyes everywhere, but in her hooded cloak, she drew little interest from the passing throngs.

"In the city, I don't know, it's probably someone's job. I don't know if a Guild controls it or not. In the villages everybody helps clean up all the time. A few lazybones are always a problem, but mors are quick to let them know about their bad ways."

"Where are the slaves?" she said next.

He stared at her blankly. She had to explain what a "slave" was.

"We have no slaves."

She was stunned into silence the rest of the way. Thru asked her several times if she was all right, because it wasn't like her to be so quiet.

And now, standing on the top of the beach, she understood that the battle had been a disaster for the colony expedition. She had never imagined that the men of Shasht could be defeated like this.

She looked at every face, searching for Filek or Rukkh, pointing out the handful of men wearing purple or red tunics, signs of high rank.

"I'm sorry that you had to see this," said Thru, as they came to the end of the ordeal. Neither Rukkh nor Filek was among the dead, for which she was endlessly thankful.

"My father was not there, nor was the admiral, so either they are still in the water or they got away."

"There are some bodies still afloat, but not many now. Later, if you like, we can look at them."

"Thank you. I would like to. Not knowing is terrible. And thank you for being so kind to me, Thru Gillo. You have helped me enormously in this ordeal."

She took his hand and pressed it between hers. It was like a man's hand, virtually identical except for the smooth fur that covered the back of hand and fingers.

"You are not responsible for any of this," he said. "You deserve our help."

She turned back to the dead and muttered a prayer for their souls. *Take care of your worshipers Great God! Keep their souls warm by your fire, Orbazt Subuus!*

"Maybe the fleet will go home now," she said, convinced the colony was utterly defeated.

"Would you like that? To go home?"

"I don't know. My father told me that if we went home the entire colony would be sold into slavery. The Emperor would have no mercy on failures.

"It's horrible," she said through clenched teeth. "So many dead; why did there have to be war?"

"I don't know. Why did your people's ships come here?"

Simona gave a sad shrug. "The Emperor decreed that we should send out colony missions into the world. Our land is worn-out. It is not like this in Shasht." She gestured to the trees that covered the headland, recalling the sun-baked rocky hills of home.

"How many dead are there of my people?" she said after a moment.

"Two thousand, one hundred thirty-three, so far."

It was like a physical blow. More than two thousand dead. On top of the plague, it would have reduced them by more than a third.

"And, how many of your own folk?"

"Seventeen hundred eighty dead, and more who will die of their wounds."

She grimaced. What a slaughter for such a narrow, stony beach. "It is all so stupid, so horrible. Why did they send us here to destroy you?"

He looked away for a moment.

"We thought that was what Man would always do. In our memory, Man the Cruel looms large."

"What do you mean by Man-the-Cruel?"

He looked away again, remembering the piled-up heads at Bilauk.

"It is difficult to talk about. I will show you the Great Book. It tells the story as we understand it."

"The Assenzi said you were raised up by the ancient men of Highnoth. Long, long ago, before the ice. The priests teach us that the Great God took over the world and vomited up the first men. The men then vomited up the first woman, and they took turns with her and she brought forth many children and they are the ancestors of the Shashti people."

Thru's eyebrows lofted as he listened to her.

"We have never heard of the Great God. We listen to the Spirit, but that message is a gentle one."

Simona gave a somber little laugh.

"That is not the way of Orbazt Subuus, He Who Eats!"

Thru's eyebrows bobbed up and down.

"This god of yours is filled with rage. So are your people. We wonder what they have done that has made them so angry. If this god is such a great god, why does he need to kill anyone who forsakes him? Why does he need anyone to kill anyone for that matter? Why should such a great god demand to be worshiped? If he is the great god, then he will be worshiped anyway, surely?"

She laughed. "You should be allowed to put those questions to the priests yourself. I, for one, would love to witness that encounter!"

But she knew that the only encounter the priests would accept would involve tying poor Thru over an altar and ripping his beating heart from his chest as an offering for He Who Eats.

"Come," said Thru, "the Assenzi wish to speak with you."

They made their way back to the south gate. The mots and brilbies who held the allotments were all at work repairing the damage done during the fighting. Simona was unused to being outdoors in ordinary society, and seeing this army of mots and mors at work she was struck again by the enormous difference with Shasht society. At home this work would have been done by slaves.

"What will you do with all of us?" she asked Thru at one point.

"Who do you mean?"

"The prisoners." Earlier she had examined the men

taken prisoner. There were almost a hundred of them, and they'd been herded briefly into a courtyard so she could look down at them from a window above without being seen. The experience with Uisbank had convinced her captors that it was not wise to allow her to be seen by any of the men.

"I don't know," said Thru, honestly. "I expect the Assenzi will have an idea. Maybe they will take you to Highnoth."

"Where is that? You mentioned this place before."

"It is many days' march north of here, hundreds of miles."

"And that is where the Assenzi live?"

"Yes."

"What would they do to us there?"

"I don't know exactly. But the men are not cooperative and we cannot send them back, because they would only be given new weapons, so we may have to kill them."

That shook her for a moment. He sounded so calm about the impending slaughter.

"I suppose," she said quietly. And she asked herself, what other choice did they have, than to keep the men chained up for the rest of their lives? "What about imprisoning them?"

"That is being considered. Some grumble that your people have already cost ours too much. Easier to kill them and bury them and make some field fertile."

"And what do you think, Thru Gillo?"

"I would send you all to Highnoth."

On the way back through the city streets Simona observed the city up close for the first time. Shutters painted in bright red or brown were serried up and down the streets.

The squares and plazas were all small by Shashti standards, but the buildings were graceful and rarely overbearing. The Guild Hall was a large place, with turrets and towers of a most antique appearance to her eyes.

There were a lot of trees and shrubs in the gardens at intersections. It was very unlike Shasht in that way.

The royal palace was almost invisible from within the city, since it was a fortified extension of the city wall. She knew that it was a palace because she'd been told, but the corridors and rooms she'd seen had been small and plainly furnished. But she had also seen works of art hanging on the walls of important rooms. Incredible pieces, often strong in color, that she knew would fetch a fortune at auction in Shasht City.

She was ushered into the room where she had met the Assenzi. All three were present. Utnapishtim held out a tiny scroll.

"Simona, we have decided that you must go back to your people."

For the second time that day she was stunned. This really was the strangest day of her life!

"But why? They will kill me."

"There is a risk of that, we agree." Utnapishtim looked over to the other two Assenzi; the one that always wore a blue cap nodded thoughtfully.

"But you will bear a message from us, and we think the message will protect you."

"Who will I give this message to?"

"Take this scroll. It is addressed to Karnemin."

"I have never heard this name."

"Understandably, but we believe the message will reach him nonetheless."

"And this message will protect me?"

"We think so."

"Will it stop this war?"

"Perhaps. It is worth trying. We think they will send you back to Shasht with the message."

"Oh that would be good. If they don't kill me back there."

"I'm afraid we cannot be sure about that. But we must make every effort to try and stop this killing."

She nodded slowly. There was no choice.

Chapter 54

The meeting place was on a spit of land about six miles south of Dronned. Stunted pine forest competed with incredibly gnarled oak trees for the available ground. The woods were alive with wildlife. Simona was startled by the number of deer and elk she saw. Once they came out of a thicket onto a meadow and counted eleven whitetails bounding away toward the far side. Another time they surprised an immense flock of ducks, which took to the air above a quite unremarkable pond. Wild ducks had been hunted close to extinction in Shasht.

Thru walked just ahead of her. They were alone, as requested by the message from the admiral of the fleet. Watching his back, Simona realized she was going to miss her daily lessons in the language of the Land, which were also Thru's lessons in Shashti. She had become used to life among the mots.

At the next turn of the trail the sea became visible in a wide, blue expanse. Her heart quailed for a moment at the thought of what lay ahead. She stopped and laid a hand on a tree and rested her head against her forearm. She just hoped she could find the strength to endure whatever was going to happen to her.

Oh God, her father! He was going to be so angry with her. And he had every right. She was a selfish girl who wanted what was best for her, not for him and his ambitions. A girl who had tried to kill herself.

Thru came back and put a hand on her shoulder. "You are strong enough, Simona. I know this."

"Thank you," she flashed him a small smile.

Strong enough? Truth to tell, she was terrified. The priests would want to rip her still-beating heart out of her chest and offer it to the Great God. But first they would question her, and she knew what that meant. By the time they were finished she would be begging for them to kill her.

She could tell that he sensed her fear. Mots had such keen senses. They seemed closer to the animals than men in that way.

"Are you all right?"

"Yes, thank you, it's all right. I can go on."

He continued to rest his hand on her shoulder, communicating support for her during this time of trial.

With an eloquent shrug, she confessed, "Part of me is afraid. You understand that, I'm sure."

"Yes. Your people have harsh ways."

She managed a brief smile.

"Let's just say that your folk live better lives than mine. Your buildings are not as grand as ours, and your emperors are quite unimportant, but your people are happy. Mine are not."

"Perhaps the message you carry will bring about change."

She seemed unconvinced. "How can a simple message do that? The empire of Shasht is enormous; it will not change very easily."

It was his turn to smile. "Perhaps you underestimate the Assenzi."

She smiled back more sincerely. Those strange little beings had a lot of secrets, that was for sure. "I hope so, I really do."

But inwardly she thought it was impossible. How could Thru, who meant no harm, ever really understand life in Shasht?

"You would go back to your own people sometime, I am sure of it."

"I don't know, Thru Gillo. I might prefer living out in the open, unconstrained by purdah, to going back."

Embarrassed, as he always was when the subject of

purdah came up, Thru looked down. The word conjured up a world of walls and veils and covered wagons and secrets and terrible punishments, almost unimaginable for someone like Thru.

"I think it would be better for you to live among your people. I would find it strange to be in your position."

"It is strange, my friend. But you have helped me so much to survive it. I couldn't have done it without you." Indeed, she thought, she literally owed Thru her life; the mots in the seacoast village would have killed her but for him.

"But among my own people, I must still accept the laws. I will be shut up indoors again, kept behind walls. It is a suffocating way to live."

"But you will live. The message will protect you. The Assenzi promised."

She nodded, wishing she could believe it as easily as he.

The meeting place had been determined by an exchange of messages with the fleet. Getting the first message out to the fleet had been difficult, but was eventually achieved by a cog, which drifted close enough to the flagship one night to allow a mot with a bow to shoot several arrows bearing copies of the message into the rigging of the bigger ship. The fleet had reacted to the presence of the cog with a panicky dispersal during which *Anvil* almost rammed *Sword*. But soon afterward the admiral in command of the fleet sent a response, as requested, written and sealed in a white-painted barrel that floated in on the tide to Dronned beach.

The admiral expressed interest in seeing Simona Biswas Gsekk returned unharmed to the fleet. Polite words, hiding a fervent desire to know what she knew.

There was a tall grey rock at the very end of the wooded landspit. Simona was to wait there for a boat to put in to pick her up. No ship would linger close to the shore, not after the fireships, so the boat would have to come in a long way.

When they came out onto the trail leading to the grey

rock, a couple of seals that were sleeping on the beach woke up, looked at them, and slid into the water.

Thru stopped when they were about a hundred paces from the rock. He did not trust the men in any degree, he had seen enough now of the face of Man to know that they felt no respect for such as he. They would as soon kill him as look at him.

He held her hands in his.

"Good-bye, Simona, I thank you for the gifts you brought us. You helped save all our lives."

There was a lump in her chest as she turned to him.

"And I thank you, Thru, for saving my life in return. If I can make it happen by going back now, then this war will end. My people must look elsewhere for a place to colonize."

And she put her arms out and held him close, as if he were a brother, and the soft fur of his neck rubbed against the pale skin of her own, and it felt quite natural. Then she went on down the track, and there were tears in her eyes, and she wondered at that. What had happened to her in these weeks among the strange little folk of the Land? She knew that she'd undergone an enormous change in certain attitudes. That she had thought of the mots and brilbies as "monkeys" when first she encountered them told her how far she had come.

And when she thought ahead of changing the minds of the colony fleet, she realized how great the task was that lay ahead of her. Even changing her father's mind might be difficult. If he was very angry at her for trying to take her own life, then he might shut his ears to her words.

But the imperative was firmly lodged in her heart. She had to stop the war; she had to go against the teaching of the priests. The mots were not animals, and the colony had no right to destroy them.

She came to the end of the trail and went on over the shingle of the beach to the very end of the spit, where she turned around the corner of the rock.

The heavy arm came up around her so quickly she

barely had time to register it, and then a hand clamped over her mouth while another huge arm grabbed her around the waist and lifted her cleanly off her feet. She was borne away down the track on the far side of the rock.

Men were waiting there, and a longboat.

She was bound, gagged, wrapped in a heavy cloak, and thrust into the boat.

Thru saw none of this, but he sensed something that troubled him. Some sixth sense was prickled into life. He looked back. His path back to the woods was clear. He looked to the rock again. There had been no sound, no indication of trouble except those seals that had moved into the water at their approach. Seals were only hunted occasionally in deep winter, for their meat and blubber. They had no reason to fear.

And there were fewer birds here than there might be. He took a cautious step toward the rock and heard a whistle in the air; he half turned his head and then the boomerang struck him on the back of the head and the lights went out.

When he came back to consciousness it was to a throbbing head. His hands were tied behind his back, and he was lying on a wooden surface. There were strong smells, salty smells.

The wood was in motion, tilting slightly one way and then the other.

He was on a ship!

His blood ran cold. The men had taken him captive. Unwelcome probabilities abounded.

His only bonds were on his wrists. He was able to move his legs and to sit up. His eyes grew accustomed to the dimness of the room. His head throbbed badly, and he felt something caked on his face and neck, his fur stretched uncomfortably beneath it as if it were dried mud. How had they got so close without him hearing a thing?

Suddenly there came heavy footsteps, the door opened, light streamed in, and tall figures loomed over him.

A deep-set voice said, "He's awake now" in Shashti.
Hands reached down and seized him under his arms and
lifted him from the floor. He glimpsed a dark, low ceiling,
then a door as he was half carried, half dragged out.
Men, larger and bulkier than he, were crowded into these
dark rooms. He saw a helmeted soldier holding a lantern
at shoulder height.

There was another door, a wider set of stairs, and a
corridor leading to another, much larger door. Inside was
a well-furnished room with chairs, rugs, and table. On
one wall hung a painting, a heroic landscape, on the
other wall hung a woven mat, a "Chooks and Beetles"
mat!

Thru had barely digested that amazing sight when he
was plunked onto his feet and steadied in place by
rough hands.

Sitting in a chair, observing him with intense concentration, was a large man wearing a splendid uniform in
blue-and-red cloth. Another man in a much plainer uniform stood nearby, also studying Thru very carefully.

Thru looked to his right and saw another couple of
men, one with a shaved head painted gold and beyond
him, swathed in dark cloth was another figure. He caught
a flash of the eyes behind the veil.

"Simona!"

"What have they done to you, Thru?"

"Knocked me down. Don't remember anything else."

"There is blood on your face."

"That explains why my head hurts so much."

The heavyset man in the fancy uniform sat up and
roared at them. "By the great purple ass of He Who
Eats, what is this talking in my presence without my
permission?"

Thru noticed that this loud-voiced man had a wooden
peg from the knee down on one leg and a big bandage
on one hand.

"And why should we need your permission to speak?"
said Thru coolly.

The man bolted up from his chair with an effort and

loomed dangerously over Thru. "Because I am ruler here, and you are nothing but a fornicating, sodomistic monkey! And if you don't do what I tell you, I'll have you whipped here and now."

The man calmed himself, shaking his head and looking to the ceiling for inspiration. "They told me this monkey could speak Shasht. I didn't believe it possible, but damn me if it ain't true!"

Suddenly the yellow top in the corner drew a knife and lunged at Thru. The admiral smashed his cane across the yellow top's arm while his huge young bodyguard sprang forward and punched the priest in the side of the head hard enough to drive him into the bulwark with a thud.

"That's it!" snarled Heuze. "Throw him out! Enough of these fornicating priests. They're nothing but trouble."

The yellow top was picked up and hustled outside, where the guards continued to beat him for a while longer. The sound of heavy blows kept up until someone finally shut the door.

"Thank you, Polok!" said Admiral Heuze.

The huge youth stood quietly in the corner again.

"So"—the admiral spun back to stare at Thru—"you can speak the language of men, can you?"

"I have learned some words of your language. We also taught Simona some words of our language."

"Ha! That'll be enough of that, my fine little monkey friend."

Heuze realized that it was the eyebrows that suggested the monkeyness of the slim figure more than anything else. Otherwise, the creature was a fur-covered man of slight stature.

Heuze had eaten them, but he'd never somehow imagined speaking to one.

He chuckled, turned to Biswas. "First time I've ever talked to my dinner . . ." Now he roared, slapped his knee with his good hand, and nudged Biswas in the ribs. Biswas, appalled, simply stared at the captured "monkey." His daughter was there in the corner, unrepentant, impossibly rude to her father and speaking to this mon-key creature as if it were her friend? Heuze's crude joke was not amusing either. To eat these creatures was far too close to cannibalism.

"Why will it be enough?" said Thru, confused.

"We aren't going to learn your language, that's why."

Thru was still puzzled.

"Why do you hate us?"

Heuze's laugh failed in his throat.

"I wouldn't dignify you by calling my feelings hate, little monkey."

Thru felt strangely unafraid. "You are angry now; why?"

"You impudent whelp!" Heuze slapped Thru into the wall with his bandaged hand and immediately let out a bellow of pain and clutched his wounded hand to his belly.

When he turned back to face the admiral, Thru was bleeding from his upper lip.

"And then you strike me while my hands are bound."

"Shut your mouth, until I ask you to speak." The ad-miral winced again, and the huge youth moved closer.

"Thru, listen to them," Simona spoke up suddenly. "They will hurt you. There's no point in giving them the excuse."

"Be silent, you little bitch! Or I will have you whipped 'til the blood runs down your back."

The admiral turned back to Thru.

"Normally in a situation like this, I would have you beaten for a while, to knock that cockiness right out of you, before I got down to asking you my questions. But I think you're bright enough to see there's no need to go down that road."

Thru stared at the man. That had been a heavy blow, indeed.

"What do you want from me?" he said.

"Answers, that's all. Just plain, simple answers; you don't have to try and get clever on me."

"Why should I answer you when you will kill me anyway?"

"Yes, and eat you, too. But not until I decide you won't tell me anything more that might be useful."

"You may as well kill me then; I'll tell you nothing."

The admiral had an unpleasant smile on his face.

"Well, well, such defiance. We'll see how defiant you are after the irons have been heated properly, eh?" He snapped his fingers. "Take it away."

Thru was seized and hustled out the door and back to the small cell he'd awoken in. There he sat in silence, listening to the sounds of the ship, the creak of timbers, the rattle of footsteps on an upper deck.

After some time had passed more men came in and took him to another room, with a sharp chemical smell. The man who'd stood beside the admiral was waiting.

"I am Simona's father. I believe you can understand my speech."

"I do."

"I am a medical man, and I wish to examine you, before, well . . ." He trailed of.

Thru had some idea of what might be in store.

"They kill me and eat my body."

"Urm, well, yes, I'm afraid so. But before then I wish to make a record of your physique."

Thru saw conflicting emotions warring behind the man's eyes, and noticed something of Simona's cast of features in the man's face. Certainly he did not bluster and threaten like the choleric admiral.

"If it will help your people to achieve understanding and peace, go ahead."

"I must thank you for saving my daughter's life. She has told me much concerning you. You are a weaver, she says."

"Yes."

"The weaving skills of your people are remarkable, far in advance of anything in our empire."

Thru made no reply, taken aback by this turn of

events. Then he recalled the "Chooks and Beetles" on the admiral's wall.

"Your admiral likes our work well enough to hang it up."

Filek licked his lips, embarrassed and humiliated by this plainspoken fellow from the strange New Land.

"Yes. It is beautiful work. Please take off your clothes for the examination."

Thru simply stared back. Filek remembered that Thru was bound at the wrists and took up a knife and cut Thru's clothes off him.

"You think I am an animal."

"Yes, of course. We are all animals. That much is obvious."

"But you think yourself superior to my kind."

"Well, of course. You are inventions of some sort. Who are these Assenzi that my daughter talks about? What is all this about a message?"

"Just let the message go to where it's supposed to go."

"That is not up to me. That is up to the admiral."

"The message is from the Assenzi. It is not wise to dabble in their business."

"Please breathe in deeply."

Thru hesitated, wondering whether to resist or not. Then with a sigh he relaxed and allowed the man to listen to his chest through the strange flexible tube he wore around his neck.

Later the man struck his knees with a small mallet and wrote things down in a notebook.

After palpating Thru's back, belly, and abdomen Filek wrote more notes. And all the while the thought that this creature had saved his daughter and brought her back to him safely weighed on him. He found it hard to concentrate on the notes. How could he let them kill this fellow, to whom he owed the life of Simona, his only child, his only link to the future?

When the examination was over, Filek looked carefully toward the door. He was about to do something that could threaten his own life, but he was impelled to do it anyway.

"You see this?" He held up a detachable scalpel blade a thin sliver of sharp steel.

Thru nodded.

"Open your mouth."

Thru's eyes widened, but he did as he was told. The man put the sharp metal onto his tongue.

"Keep it hidden," Filek whispered in his ear.

Then the door was opening, and the burly men were there to escort Thru back to his cell.

Chapter 55

They left him in the dark cell and slammed the door on their way out. Soon afterward the screaming began. Someone was being tortured, and Thru was sure he knew who it was. He gritted his teeth, his anger rising until it threatened to overwhelm his mind. Why were they torturing her? What purpose could it serve? It was easy to hate them.

The little blade glittered faintly in the dark where he'd spat it onto the floor. Now he maneuvered to get it into his hand. Unfortunately, it was only an inch or so long, and he was bound too tightly at the wrists to be able to flex his hand far enough to bring the blade to bear.

For a moment or two he was stumped. Then he felt a crack in the floor under his bare foot and immediately began to explore further. Soon he'd found a narrower crack and wedged the sharp blade onto it.

Then he was able to lower his wrists onto the blade's edge and after an initial jab or two into his own flesh began to saw into the tight thong that bound him. The blade was very sharp, and soon the thongs parted, and he was freed.

He pulled the little blade loose and put it back in his mouth, pressing it gingerly into his cheek to keep it from cutting him. He took a deep breath and stood up to explore the inside of the cell. It was tiny, as he'd expected. The hatch covering the window was fastened with simple wooden pegs. He undid them, and a waft of the night air spilled in. Immediately he felt refreshed, and told himself he could succeed, even if the odds against him were acute.

He lifted the hatch. Great Red Kemm was above the horizon, so the night was yet young. He pulled the hatch back and lifted himself out. The water splashed alongside the ship's hull down below, but the sea was relatively calm, and the ship's motion was slight. He discovered that he was looking out from a deck about halfway down the ship's side. He noted that the ship's timbers were lapped, but that there were regular cracks that he might take for handholds and toeholds. He studied them carefully. The tumblehome below curved inward, rising up to the rail of the sterncastle above.

The screaming he'd heard had come from somewhere up there. The admiral was somewhere up there, too.

He heard voices above, saw a hatch open and a bucket emptied over the side. The hatch doors were set in frames that offered the best footholds. He centered himself, took another breath, then got his other leg out of the hatch and stood on the hatch frame. The first step up, to the top of the hatch frame, was simple. After that he groped above for further holds. There was a seam two feet above the hatch, and another about three feet farther up. Then came the next hatch. His confidence grew. He might just be able to do this.

He got up onto the seam, found a smaller seam just below the next hatch, and heaved himself up. Now his weight was on the toes of one foot, jammed in that narrow crevice. He searched for a way to reach the top of the hatch, but it was just a fraction too high.

Then there was a noise, and he heard the pegs being pulled out inside the hatch. Desperately he shifted his weight, stabbed his other foot into the narrow seam, and clung to the ship's side out of view of the hatch.

A moment later the hatch popped open and a bucket of slops was hurled into the sea. Then the hatch slammed shut again, the pegs were rammed back into place, and he swung back and got a foot up on the side edge of the hatch and steadied himself while he found a handhold on his left. His other foot was aching from the strain, and there were trickles of sweat running down the sides of his head, but he hadn't fallen into the sea.

Fortunately he had a small stroke of luck and found a wider seam at shoulder level. He levered himself up until he could get his toes onto the top of the hatch frame, and a moment later he was clutching the ship's side while taking in another triumphant breath. His toes hurt, but he'd climbed one whole deck. Encouraged, he went on.

Eventually the tumblehome steepened to a vertical slope once more, but there were larger hatches and decorative woodwork that gave easy footholds. He climbed more quickly and eventually reached the rail.

On the deck in front of him stood a couple of men, one gripping a large steering wheel, the other standing by the far rail staring out to sea. Thru ducked back down below the level of the deck and began to move sideways toward the forward edge of the sterncastle. As he went he paused by the open windows and listened carefully.

A few windows along, inside his cabin, Admiral Heuze lay on his bunk cradling his wounded hand. The hand hurt. He felt a phantom twitch from his missing foot. By the wrath of He Who Eats, if this kept up, there wasn't going to be enough left of him to enjoy his final victory.

Hitting the fornicating little impudent monkey had been a stupid thing to do, but Heuze had been provoked. There were many elements in the situation that were provoking, and he'd just snapped there for a moment.

He felt the wounded hand with the good one. The stump of his little finger felt odd under the bandage. By the purple ass of the Great God, he'd never forget the humiliation. Having to kneel in front of Nebbeggebben and expiate for the disastrous battle by cutting off his own finger.

It was either that, as they'd explained, or they'd take something else off that he would miss far more. He was fortunate that great Nebbeggebben was so forgiving. His blunders had cost them thousands of casualties and two

ships. By rights, said some less-kindly souls, they should
be handing him over to the priests.

Heuze had wanted to scream in frustration. His blunders! When it had mostly been that fool Uisbank's fault.

He sobbed for a moment, then brightened.

At least Uisbank was in worse shape. He was in the
hands of the monkeys. God, Heuze hoped they were
doing something really unpleasant to the stupid bastard
right then.

Still, he reflected, as the pain in the hand ebbed again,
this had been a much better day. First had come the
news from the south, and then the recovery of the girl
and the capture of the little monkey fellow. Impudent
but interesting, that fellow. When they put it to the questions, they would hear some interesting information, he
was sure.

The girl had been questioned, lightly; Heuze had promised Filek that she would not be maimed. Nor would she
be given to the priests, despite their urgent appeals for
her heart to be thrown to He Who Eats.

She had painted a lively picture of the monkeys. They
had kings and a religion of sorts, apparently. Thought
themselves the image of men, and yet they feared men
deeply as a demonic "Man the Cruel."

Good, thought the admiral sleepily. That would make
it easier to terrorize them when the time came.

The girl had also pleaded with him to send the message
on to the Emperor. He hadn't made up his mind about
that. He thought he might even just burn the thing and
forget all about it. He didn't want to be sending messages
back to Shasht yet. There was nothing good to report,
so there could only come trouble from that direction.

The little scroll lay on the polished table at his side.
It had an odd, archaic look to it. Two small polished
wood handles, a strip of fine vellum bound with silk and
sealed with wax. It unnerved him for some reason that
he could not quite put a finger on. The girl had claimed
it was written in "words of wonder," whatever they were.

The priests had raged at him about the whole matter.

They'd demanded the girl and the monkey. Heuze chuckled to himself on the verge of sleep. Fuck the sodomistic priests. The girl would live. He Who Eats would have to wait. Perhaps he would even send the girl back to Shasht with his report, later, when the situation was worth reporting back about.

And then there was the good news from the south. That was in the other message on the table, a naval packet in Shasht style, in sober ink on plain squared paper. Not one of these weird, wizardly scrolls.

It was a damned interesting message, too. Captain Rukil of the frigate *Barracuda* had returned from a three-month-long scouting expedition to the southern waters. His most important news was that there was a large island, about a thousand miles to the south. It was a drier, rockier place than this, and it held only a sparse population of the monkeys. Their little towns had no walls, so they would be much easier to dispossess than the populations in the northern region.

Heuze had realized that this was the only good move open to him. The battle on the beach had produced unacceptable casualties. Their next fight had to be one they could win easily. So, he would take the fleet south, and from the southern island they could raid up the long fjords that ran deep into the continent. Then next spring, when they'd rebuilt their strength, they'd come back and resume the conquest.

Shasht wasn't built in a day, and Aeswiren was defeated three times before he took the throne. Heuze was no fool. All right, he'd made a mistake. They all had. Especially the sodomizing priests. They'd grievously underestimated the monkeys. But that would stop!

Actually, he was getting to the point of maybe letting the men put the priests to the sword. Nebbeggebben, too, while he was about it. The priests were nothing but an irritant, and life would be easier without them.

He slipped into slumber, and began to snore.

He awoke with something sharp and uncomfortable pricking the side of his neck.

"What?" he gasped. The prick deepened instantly. He froze still.

"Be quiet," hissed a voice in his ear, "or I cut your throat."

"Who? What?'

"Ssh!" The prick grew much sharper.

"Fine," Heuze whispered. "Please don't . . ."

"Have you read the message?"

Heuze was thunderstruck. It was the fornicating little monkey! How in all the names of hell had it managed to get free and get in here?

"Well?" the sharp metal stung the side of his throat.

"No."

"Why did you hurt Simona?"

"She was being questioned. The process is always uncomfortable."

"You are not to hurt her again."

"Well, of course not; her questioning is done with."

"I want you to read the message. Now!" There was a tug on his ear. The admiral moved to sit up, while the knife at his throat never budged. The little fellow was very strong for his size.

It was awkward in this position, but Heuze managed to light the lamp after a few scratchings in the dark with a match. The monkey was right beside him, holding Heuze's own dagger to his throat.

"Open it."

With shaking hands the admiral picked up the little scroll. The damned thing was like something out of the first dynasty. The paper had a heavy, creamy feel.

"Go on, read it."

Heuze broke the seal and pulled it open.

The words were written in a dense script, flowing evenly across the small page. The characters were unknown to him, but their shapes were intriguing, nonetheless. Sinuous loops and whorls of thick ink flowed past his gaze. There was something hypnotic about the shapes, and they seemed to move of their own accord. Heuze wriggled uncomfortably. What the hell was this?

"I can't read this. It's meaningless."

And then the script began to flicker with tiny gleams of color. A spark flowed through the symbols, tiny lights glimmered within the page. His eyes widened. What in the world?

And then with something that was almost a physical blow his mind was opened up like a hatch being lifted, and before him, as real as if he was actually there, hovering hundreds of feet in the air among them, stood a city of gigantic towers.

A swelling roar of noise rose up from the streets far below.

Then everything went black, and he seemed to float in nothingness. Admiral Heuze wanted to scream, but he didn't seem able to control any part of his body.

There was a weird little voice in his ears, a rustling, papery little voice.

"Karnemin," it said, "hear my thoughts."

What? He wanted to shout, but he could not make a sound.

"It has to end," whispered the little voice. "You cannot wreak destruction anymore upon the world."

The admiral found himself staring into a pool so pure it was transparent. The light shifted, and it became a mirror.

He saw himself and all his pathetic affectations and pretensions such as his wish to be considered part of the urban intellectual elite, when he was just a rustic sea captain. He was so inauthentic, it was laughable. To the men like Biswas, with their university learning, he must seem like a complete fool.

The mirror darkened, became a mouth centered on a web of tentacles. Something huge and hungry was trying to pull him into its mouth. Curiously serrated teeth champed expectantly ahead. He screamed and thrashed, and in a blink it was gone, and he stood on the ramparts of one of the enormous buildings. The place was sheathed in shining material and high above flew long pennons, ribbons of extraordinary color in the sky. He felt the wind rushing past his face, tears flowing down his cheeks. Then something like a giant bird flew past overhead with a great howl that shook the world.

Heuze finally dropped the scroll from nerveless fingers.

The vision cut off abruptly. He was back in his chamber, down on his hands and knees where he'd fallen. The monkey fellow was gone. A breeze came in the window and blew the message along the floor.

With shaking fingers he rolled the message up and sealed it again with fresh wax and his own seal.

By the purple ass of the Great God, he would send it on, oh yes. He wanted someone up the line to get that message. Oh yes. It would do them good.

Thru Gillo swam for the distant shore with a steady stroke. The Assenzi had said that once the leader of the men read the message, he would send it on. The Assenzi had great magic under their control, there was no doubt about that.

Far ahead was the line of cliffs. The sea was warm, and he felt like he could swim forever.

Coming Next Month From Roc

Ashley McConnell
Stargate SG-1:
The First Amendment

Oliver Johnson
The Forging of the Shadows
Book One of the Lightbringer Trilogy

Treachery and Treason
Ed. by Laura Anne Gilman and Jennifer Heddle